BLACKLIST

ALSO BY SARA PARETSKY

A V. I. WARSHAWSKI NOVEL

SARA PARETSKY

Doubleday Large Print Home Library Edition

G. P. Putnam's Sons   New York

This Large Print Edition, prepared especially for Doubleday Large Print Home Library, contains the complete, unabridged text of the original Publisher's Edition.

ıİP

G. P. Putnam's Sons
Publishers Since 1838
a member of
Penguin Group (USA) Inc.
375 Hudson Street
New York, NY 10014

ISBN 0-7394-3845-X

Printed in the United States of America

This Large Print Book carries the
Seal of Approval of N.A.V.H.

For Geraldine Courtney Wright, artist and writer—valiant, witty and formidable—a true grande dame:

I cannot rest from travel; I will drink life to the lees . . .

THANKS

Dr. Sarah Neely provided valuable medical advice. Jill Koniecsko made it possible for me to navigate Lexis-Nexis. Judi Phillips knew exactly how a robber baron would have constructed an ornamental pond in 1903. Jesus Mata helped V.I. with her neighborhood Mexican restaurant. Sandy Weiss was a demon on technology topics and Jolynn Parker's Fact Factory as always turned up amazing results. Eva Kuhn advised me on Catherine Bayard's music tastes. The senior C-Dog did his usual witty riff on chapter titles; chapter titles, as always, are provided in loving memory of Don Sandstrom, who cherished them.

Michael Flug, archivist at the Vivian Harsh Collection, was immensely helpful in directing me to documents about the Federal Negro Theater

Project. Margaret Kinsman introduced me to this great resource in my backyard.

The great forensic pathologist Dr. Robert Kirschner died in the summer of 2002. His presence in prisons and at mass graves from Nigeria to Bosnia, from El Salvador to Chicago's South Side, brought a measure of justice to victims of torture and mass murder, and his loss is a grievous one. Despite the nature and importance of his work, Dr. Kirschner also took pleasure in V.I.'s adventures. For the last sixteen years, he found time to advise me on the ways and means her adversaries used to murder. During his final illness, we talked about the unpleasant ends the characters in *Blacklist* were meeting. I miss him as an adviser, a friend, and a great humanitarian.

This is a work of fiction. I do mention historical events, such as the Federal Theater Project, the Dies Committee, HUAC, and some figures active in the arts in the nineteen-thirties, like Shirley Graham, as part of the background of the novel, All characters who actually play a role in the story, as well as events like the destruction of the Fourth Amendment, are solely the fabrication of a brain made frenzied by chronic insomnia. Any resemblance to any real person, institution, government or legislation is purely coincidental.

CHAPTERS

BLACKLIST

A Walk on the Wild Side

The clouds across the face of the moon made it hard for me to find my way. I'd been over the grounds yesterday morning, but in the dark everything is different. I kept stumbling on tree roots and chunks of brick from the crumbling walks.

I was trying not to make any noise, on the chance that someone really was lurking about, but I was more concerned about my safety: I didn't want to sprain an ankle and have to crawl all the way back to the road. At one point I tripped on a loose brick and landed smack on my tailbone. My eyes teared with pain; I sucked in air to keep from crying out. As I rubbed the sore spot, I wondered whether Geraldine Graham had s me fall. Her eyes weren't that good, but her binoculars held both image stabilizers and night-vision enablers.

Fatigue was making it hard for me to concentrate. It was midnight, usually not late on my clock, but I was sleeping badly these days—I was anxious, and feeling alone.

Right after the Trade Center, I'd been as numbed and fearful as everyone else in America. After a while, when we'd driven the Taliban into hiding and the anthrax looked like the work of some homegrown maniac, most people seemed to wrap themselves in red-white-and-blue and return to normal. I couldn't, though, while Morrell remained in Afghanistan—even though he seemed ecstatic to be sleeping in caves as he trailed after warlords-turned-diplomats-turned-warlords.

When the medical group Humane Medicine went to Kabul in the summer of ⁀01, Morrell tagged along with a contract book about daily life under the Taliban. ⁀vived so much worse, he would say ⁀orried that he might run afoul of ⁀'s notorious Bureau for the ⁀of Vice.

That was before September 11. Afterward, Morrell disappeared for ten days. I stopped sleeping then, although someone with Humane Medicine called me from Peshawar to say Morrell was simply in an area without access to phone hookups. Most of the team had fled to Pakistan immediately after the Trade Center attack, but Morrell had wangled a ride with an old friend heading to Uzbekistan so he could cover the refugees fleeing north. A chance of a lifetime, my caller told me Morrell had said—the same thing he'd said about Kosovo. Perhaps that had been the chance of a different lifetime.

When we started bombing in October, Morrell first stayed on in Afghanistan to cover the war up close and personal, and then to follow the new coalition government. *Margent.Online,* the Web version of the old Philadelphia monthly *Margent,* was paying him for field reports, which he was scrambling to turn into a book. The *Guardian* newspaper also occasionally bought his stories. I'd even watched him on CNN a few times. Strange to see your lover's face beamed from twelve thousa miles away, strange to know that a hund million people are listening to the voice that whispers endearments into your hair. That used to whisper endearments.

When he resurfaced in Kandahar, I first sobbed in relief, then shrieked at him across the satellites. "But, darling," he protested, "I'm in a war zone, I'm in a place without electricity or cell phone towers. Didn't Rudy call you from Peshawar?"

In the following months, he kept on the move, so I never really knew where he was. At least he stayed in better touch, mostly when he needed help: (V.I., can you check on why Ahmed Hazziz was put in isolation out at Coolis prison? V.I., can you find out whether the FBI told Hazziz's family where they'd sent him? I'm running now—hot interview with local chief's third wife's oldest son. Fill you in later.)

I was a little miffed at being treated like a free research station. I'd never thought of Morrell as an adrenaline junkie—one of se journalists who lives on the high of be- the middle of disaster—but I sent him ish e-mail asking him what he was rove.

ozen Western journalists have ered since the war began," I

wrote at one point. "Every time I turn on the television, I brace myself for the worst."

His e-response zipped back within minutes: "Victoria, my beloved detective, if I come home tomorrow, will you faithfully promise to withdraw from every investigation where I worry about your safety?"

A message which made me angrier because I knew he was right—I was being manipulative, not playing fair. I needed to see him, though, touch him, hear him—live, not in cyberspace.

I took to wearing myself out running. I certainly wore out the two dogs I share with my downstairs neighbor: they started retreating to Mr. Contreras's bedroom when they saw me arrive in my sweats.

Despite my long runs—I'd go ten miles most days, instead of my usual five or six— I couldn't wear myself out enough to sleep. I lost ten pounds in the six months after the Trade Center, which worried my downstairs neighbor: Mr. Contreras took to frying up French toast and bacon when I came in from my runs, and finally bullied me into going to Lotty Herschel for a complete physical. Lotty said I was fine physically, just s fering as so many were from exhaustion of the spirit.

Whatever name you gave it, I only had half a mind for my work these days. I specialize in financial and industrial crime. It used to be that I spent a lot of time on foot, going to government buildings to look at records, doing physical surveillance and so on. But in the days of the Internet, you traipse from website to website. You need to be able to concentrate in front of a computer for long hours, and concentration wasn't something I was good at right now.

Which is why I was wandering around Larchmont Hall in the dark. When my most important client asked me to look for intruders who might be breaking in there at night, I was so eager to do something physical that I would even have scrubbed the crumbling stone benches around the house's ornamental pond.

Darraugh Graham has been with me almost since the day I opened my agency. New York office of his company, ntal United, had lost three people in Center disaster. Darraugh had but he was flinty, chalklike in moving than the bluster we were hearing from too many mouths these days. He wouldn't dwell on his loss or the aftermath but took me to his conference room, where he unrolled a detail map of the western suburbs.

"I asked you here for personal reasons, not business." He snapped his middle finger onto a green splodge northwest of Naperville, in unincorporated New Solway. "All this is private land. Big mansions belonging to old families out here, you know, the Ebbersleys, Felittis, and so on. They've been able to keep the land intact—like a private forest preserve. This brown finger is where Taverner sold ten acres to a developer back in 'seventy-two. There was an uproar at the time, but he was within his rights. He had to meet his legal fees, I think." I followed Darraugh's long index finger as he traced a brown patch that cut into the green like a carrot.

"East is a golf course. South, the complex where my mother lives." At the best of times, Darraugh is a wintry, distant man. It was hard to picture him in normal situations, like being born.

"Mother's ninety-one. She manages on her own with help, and, anyway, I don't want—she doesn't want to live with me. She lives in a development here—Anodyne Park. Town houses, apartments, little shopping center, nursing home if she needs medical help. She seems to like it. She's gregarious. Like my son—sociability skips generations in my family." His bleak smile appeared briefly. "Ridiculous name for a development, Anodyne Park, offensive when you think about the Alzheimer's wing at the nursing home—Mother tells me the word means something like 'soothing' or 'healing.'

"Her condo overlooks the grounds of Larchmont Hall. One of the grand mansions, big grounds. It's been empty for a year—the original owners were the Drummond family. The heirs sold the place three years ago, but the new buyers went bankrupt. Felitti was talking about buying, so he could keep more developers out of the area, but so far that's fallen through."

He stopped. I waited for him to get to the point, which he is never shy about, but when a minute went by I said, "You want me to find a plutocrat to buy the place so it doesn't get divided up for the merely affluent?"

He scowled. "I didn't call you in for ridicule. Mother thinks she sees people going in and out of the place at night."

"She doesn't want to call the police?"

"The police came out a couple of times, but found no one. The agent that manages the place for the holding company has a security system in place. It hasn't been breached."

"Any of the neighbors seen anything?"

"Point of the area, Vic: neighbors don't see each other. Here are the houses, and all this is hundred years' worth of trees, gardens, so forth. You could talk to the neighbors, of course." He snapped his finger on the map again, showing me the distances, but his tone was uncertain—most unlike him.

"What's your interest in this, Darraugh? Are you thinking of buying the place yourself?"

"Good God, no."

He didn't say anything else, but walked to the windows to look down at the construction on Wacker Drive. I stared in bewilderment. Even when he'd asked me to help his son beat a drug rap several years ago, he hadn't danced around the floor like this.

"Mother's always been a law unto herself," he muttered to the window. "Of course people in her—in our—milieu always get better attention from the law than people like—well, than others. But she's affronted that the police aren't taking her seriously. Of course, it's possible that she might be imagining—she's over ninety, after all—but she's taken to calling me every day to complain about lack of police attention."

"I'll see if I can uncover something the police aren't seeing," I said gently.

His shoulders relaxed and he turned back to me. "Your usual fee, Vic. See Caroline about your contract. She'll give you Mother's details as well." He took me out to his personal assistant, who told him his conference call with Kuala Lumpur was waiting.

We'd talked on a Friday afternoon, the dreary first day of March. On Saturday morning, I made the first of what turned into many long treks to New Solway. Before driving out, I stopped in my office for my ordnance maps of the western suburbs. I looked at my computer and then resolutely turned my back to it: I'd already logged on three times since ten last night without word from Morrell. I felt like an alcoholic with the bottle in reach, but I locked my office without checking my e-mail and began the forty-five-mile haul to the land of the rich and powerful.

That westward drive always makes me feel like I'm following the ascent into heaven, at least into capitalist heaven. It starts along Chicago's smoky industrial corridor, passing old blue-collar neighborhoods that resemble the one where I grew up—tiny bungalows where women look old at forty and men work and eat themselves to early heart attacks. You move past them to the hardscrabble towns on the city's edge—Cicero, Berwyn, places where you can still get pretty well beat up for a dollar. Then the air begins to clear and the affluence rises. By the time I reached New Solway, I was practically hydroplaning on waves of stock certificates.

I pulled off at the tollway exit to examine my maps. Coverdale Lane was the main road that meandered through New Solway. It started at the northwest corner of the township and made a giant kind of quarter circle, opening on Dirksen Road at the southeast end. At Dirksen, you could go south to Powell

Road, which divided New Solway from Anodyne Park, where Geraldine Graham was living. I followed the route to the northwest entrance, since that looked like the main one on the map.

I hadn't traveled fifty feet down Coverdale Lane before getting Darraugh's point: neighbors couldn't spy on each other here. Horses grazed in paddocks; orchards held a few desiccated apples from last fall. With the trees bare, a few mansions were visible from the road, but most were set far behind imposing carriageways. Poorer folk might actually see each other's driveways from their side windows, but most of the houses sat on substantial property, perhaps ten or twelve acres. And most were old. No new money here. No McMansions, flashing their thirty thousand square feet on tiny lots.

After going south about a mile and a half, Coverdale Lane bent into a hook that pointed east. I followed the hook almost to its end before a discreet sign on a stone pillar announced Larchmont Hall.

I drove on past the gates to Dirksen Road at the east end of Coverdale and made a loop south and west so I could look at the complex where Darraugh's mother was living. I wanted to know if she really could see into the Larchmont estate. A hedge blocked any view into the New Solway mansions from street level, but Ms. Graham was on the fourth floor of a small apartment building. From that vantage, she might be able to see into the property.

I returned to Coverdale Lane and drove up a winding carriageway to Larchmont Hall. Leaving the car where anyone could see it if they came onto the land, I armed myself with that most perfect disguise: a hard hat and a clipboard. A hard hat makes people assume you're doing something with the air-conditioning or the foundations. They're used to service in places like this; they don't ask for credentials. I hoped.

As I got my bearings, I whistled under my breath: the original owners had done things on a grand scale. Besides the mansion itself, the property held a garage, stables, greenhouse, even a cottage, which I assumed was for the staff who tended the grounds—or would tend the grounds if someone could afford to have the work done. The estate agent wasn't putting much into maintenance—an ornamental pond, which lay between the mansion and the outbuildings, was clogged with leaves and dead lilies. I even saw a carp floating belly-up in the middle. A series of formal gardens was overgrown with weeds, while no one had mowed the meadows for some time.

The neglect, and the number of buildings, was oppressive. If you were grandiose enough to buy such a place, how could you possibly take care of it? Circling each building, trying to see if there were holes in foundations or windows, looked overwhelming. I squared my shoulders. Whining doubles the job, my mother used to say when I balked at washing dishes. I decided to work from smallest to largest, which meant inspecting the cottage first.

By the time I'd finished prying at windows, balancing on fence posts to see if any of the roof glass of the greenhouse was broken, and making sure that the doors to the stables and garage were not just secure, but showed no recent signs of tampering, it was past noon. I was hungry and thirsty, but dark still comes early the first week in March. I didn't want to waste daylight searching for food, so I grimly set about circling the house.

It was an enormous building. From a distance it looked graceful, vaguely Federal in design, with its slender columns and square façades, but all I cared about was four floors' worth of windows, doors at ground level on all four sides, doors leading off upper-level balconies—a burglar's paradise.

Still, all the windows on the two lower floors held the telltale markers of a security system. I checked some on the ground floor with a meter, but didn't see anyplace where the current was interrupted.

People did come onto the land: beer bottles, the silver foil from potato chip bags, crumpled cigarette packs, the inevitable condom, told their tales. Maybe Ms. Graham was only seeing local kids looking for privacy.

I was debating whether to shinny up the pillars to check the balcony doors when a squad car pulled up. A middle-aged cop came over to me at an unhurried gait.

"You got some reason to be out here?"

"Probably the same one you do." I waved my meter toward the house. "I'm with Florey and Kapper, the mechanical engineers. We heard some woman thinks little green men are hovering around here in the night. I'm just checking the circuits."

"You set something off in the garage," the cop said.

I smiled. "Oh, dear: I was trying brute force. They warned us against that at IIT, but I wanted to see if someone could actually lift those doors. Sorry to bring you out here for nothing."

"Not to worry: you saved me from our eighty-third call to look at suspicious mail."

"It's a hassle, isn't it," I said, hoping he wouldn't ask for my ID. "I've got friends in the Chicago PD who feel stretched to the limit these days."

"Same out here. We've got the reservoir and a bunch of power stations we have to keep an eye on. It's about time the FBI nailed this anthrax bastard—we waste an unbelievable amount of manpower, responding to hysterical calls about letters from old Aunt Madge who forgot to put her return address on the envelope."

We hashed over the current situation the way everyone did these days. Police forces were badly affected, because they had to gear up for incalculable terror attacks and couldn't keep up with their local crime loads. Drive-by shootings, which had dropped to their lowest level in decades, had jumped in the last six months.

The cop's cell phone rang. He grunted into it. "I'd better be going. You okay out here?"

"Yeah. I'm taking off, too. Place looks clean to me, except for the usual garbage—" I pointed a toe at an empty cigarette wrapper near the foundation. "I don't see how anyone could be using the place."

"You find Osama bin Laden in the attic, give me a call: I could use the extra credit." He waved good-bye and got back into his squad car.

I couldn't think of anything else to look for, and, anyway, it was getting too dark to see clearly. I walked to the edge of the gardens, where they faded into a substantial woods, and looked up at the house. From here I could see the attic windows, but they presented a blank face to the sky.

The Iron Dowager

I had to go through various security checkpoints to reach Geraldine Graham. Anodyne Park was a well-gated community, with a guard at the entrance who wrote down my license plate number and asked my business before phoning Ms. Graham for permission to let me enter. As I snaked along the curved road that suburban developers relish, I saw that the complex was bigger than it appeared from the outside. Besides the town houses, apartment buildings and a nursing home the size of a small hospital, it held a little row of shops. Several golfing quartets, undeterred by the dreary weather, were leaving their carts outside a bar at the edge of the shops. I ran into a grocery store designed like an Alpine chalet for a bottle of overpriced water and a banana. Getting my blood sugar up would help me interview my client's mother.

When she opened the door, I was disconcerted: Geraldine Graham looked so much like her son that I could almost believe it was Darraugh in the doorway dressed in rose silk. She had his long face and prominent nose and eyes of the same frosty blue, although hers were clouded now with age. The only real difference was her hair: over the years Darraugh's blond has bleached to white; hers was dark, a white-streaked nut-brown that owed nothing to a bottle. She held herself as ramrod straight as her son. I pictured her mother tying her to a Victorian backboard which she then passed on to Darraugh.

It was only when Geraldine Graham moved away from the doorway and the light caught her face that I saw how deeply lined it was. "You're the young woman my son sent out to see who is breaking into Larchmont Hall, eh?" She had the high fluting voice of deep age. "I wondered whether that policeman was going to arrest you, but you seemed to talk your way out of it. What made him arrive?"

"You were watching me, ma'am?"

"The hobbies of the elderly. Peeping through windows, prying into locks. Although I suppose my hobby is your livelihood. I'm making a cup of tea. I can offer you one. Or I have bourbon: I know detectives are used to stronger beverages than tea."

I laughed. "That's only Philip Marlowe. We modern detectives can't drink in the middle of the day: it puts us to sleep."

She moved down the short hallway to her kitchen. I followed and felt a stab of envy when I saw the double-door refrigerator and the porcelain cooktop. My own kitchen was last remodeled two tenants back. I wondered what it would cost to install an island cooktop like this one, with sleek electrical burners that looked painted into the surface. Probably two years of mortgage payments.

Ms. Graham saw me staring and said, "Those are designed to keep the old from burning down the house. They turn off automatically if there's no pan on them, or after some minutes if you haven't set a special timer. Although we're told the old should burn and rave at the end of day."

When she slowly pushed a small stepladder into position to reach her tea bags, I moved forward to help. She waved me off with a brusqueness like her son's.

"Just because I'm old and slow doesn't mean the young and swift need muscle me away. My son keeps wanting to install a housekeeper here so I can vegetate in front of the television or behind my binoculars. As you can see, we'd be tripping over each other all day in this tiny space. I was glad to give up all that nonsense when I moved out of the big house. Housekeepers, gardeners, you can't take a step without consulting someone else's feelings and timetables. One of my old maids comes every day to tidy and prepare meals—and to make sure I haven't died in the night. That's enough intrusion."

She poured hot water over tea bags into slender porcelain mugs. "My mother would be shocked to see me use tea bags, or to drink my tea out of a great mug. Even when she was ninety herself, we had to get down the Crown Derby every afternoon. Mugs and tea bags feel like freedom, but I'm never sure whether it's freedom or laxity."

These cups, with their gold-leaf rims and intricate stencils, weren't exactly Pacific Gardens Mission service. When Ms. Graham nodded at me to pick them up, I could hardly get my fingers into their slender handles. The tea scalded my fingers through the eggshell-thin china. Following her slow tread down the hall to her sitting room felt like some kind of biblical ordeal involving furnaces.

If Geraldine Graham had been living in a mansion like those across the street, the apartment might seem like tiny space, but the sitting room alone was about the size of my whole apartment in Chicago. Pale Chinese rugs floated on the polished wood floor. Armchairs covered in straw satin straddled a fireplace in the middle of the wall, but Ms. Graham led me to an alcove facing Larchmont Hall, where an upholstered chair stood next to a piecrust table. This seemed to be where she lived: books, reading glasses, her binoculars, a phone, covered most of the tabletop. An oil painting of a woman in Edwardian dress hung behind the chair. I studied the face for a resemblance to my hostess and her son, but it was the oval of a classic beauty. Only the coldness in the blue eyes made me think of Darraugh.

"My mother. It was a great disappointment to her that I inherited my father's looks: she was considered the most beautiful woman in Chicago when she was young." With her deliberate motions, Geraldine Graham moved the binoculars and glasses onto the books, then placed coasters for our mugs. Settling herself in her chair, she told me I might bring over one of those by the fireplace for myself. Her fluting voice started while I was still around the corner in the main part of the room.

"I probably shouldn't have bought a unit facing the house. My daughter warned me I would find it hard to see strangers in the place, but of course I haven't, except for the few months that they could afford the payments. A computer baron who melted like snow in last year's business upheavals. So humiliating for the children, I always think, when their horses are sold. But since they left, I haven't seen anyone until these last few days. Nights. I see nothing out of the ordinary during the day. Although my son hasn't said so, he seems to think I have Alzheimer's. At least, I assume he does, since he actually drove out to visit me Thursday evening, which is a rare occurrence. I am not demented, however: I know what I'm seeing. I saw you there this afternoon, after all."

I ignored the end of her statement. "Larchmont Hall was your home? Darraugh didn't tell me that."

"I was born in that house. I grew up in it. But neither of my children wanted the burden of looking after such a property, not even to hold in trust for their own children. Of course my daughter doesn't live here, she's in New York with her husband; they have his family's property in Rhinebeck, but I thought Darraugh might want his son to have the chance to live in Larchmont. He was adamant, however, and when Darraugh has made up his mind he is as hard as any diamond."

Why hadn't Darraugh told me he grew up here? Anger at feeling blindsided distracted me from what she was saying. What else had he concealed? Still, I could see that looking after Larchmont Hall would be a full-time job, not something a widower wedded to his business would take on willingly. I pictured Darraugh in a Daphne du Maurier childhood, learning to ride, to hunt, to play hide-and-seek in the stables. Perhaps it's only blue-collar kids like me who imagine that you'd feel nostalgia for such a childhood and find it hard to give up.

"So you watch the place to see how it's faring without you, and you've noticed someone hanging around there?"

"Not exactly." She swallowed noisily and set the mug down on her coaster with a jolt that sprayed drops onto the wood. "When you're old, you don't sleep long hours at a time. I wake in the night, I go to the bathroom, I read a little and doze in my chair here. Perhaps a week ago," she stopped to count backward on her fingers, "last Tuesday, it would be, I was up around one. I saw a light glow and go out. At first I assumed it was a car on Coverdale Lane. You can't see the lane from here, but you can see the reflection of the headlights along the façades."

Reflection along the façades. Her precise speech made her sound even more formidable than her commanding manner. I stood at the window and cupped my hands around my eyes to peer through the wintry twilight. Across Powell Road, I could just make out the hedge that shielded New Solway from the vulgar. Larchmont Hall lay on the far side, in a direct line from where I was standing. It was back far enough from the road that even in the dusk I could make out the whole house.

"Take the binoculars, young woman: they allow one to see in the dark, even an old woman like me."

The binoculars were a lovely set of Rigel compact optics, with a nightvision feature usually used by hunters. "Did you buy these so you could see in the dark, ma'am?"

"I didn't buy them originally to spy on my old home, if that's what you're asking: my grandson MacKenzie gave them to me when I still managed Larchmont. He thought they would be helpful to me since my vision was deteriorating, and he was correct."

The glasses brought the dormers of the attic into sharp relief. I couldn't make out great detail in the dark, but enough to see the skylight cut into the steep roof. The small windows underneath the eaves were uncurtained. The main entrance, where the local cop and I had both parked, was to the left, at right angles to the side facing Anodyne Park. Anyone coming onto the property from the road would be easy to spot from here, if you were looking, but if someone approached from the meadows at the rear, they would be shielded from view by the stable and greenhouse.

"I found empty bottles and so on when I was walking around," I said, still scanning the house for any signs of light or life. "People are clearly coming onto the property now that it's vacant. Do you think that's who you're seeing?"

"Oh, I suppose working people feel a certain triumph in having sex on the old Drummond grounds," she said dismissively, "but I have seen lights flicker in the attic late at night. The skylight is revealing of what's inside as well as what's out. It was the servants' common room when my mother managed Larchmont. As a child, I used to go up there and watch the maids play poker. She didn't know about their card games, but children and servants are natural allies.

"After Mother died, I shut up the attic and moved the remaining staff to the third floor.

I wasn't entertaining on a grand scale, I didn't use those bedrooms. Or all those servants Mother thought essential for running Larchmont as if it were Blenheim Palace.

"It's been most odd to see those lights, as if my mother's servants had returned to play poker up there. My son assured me you were a competent investigator. I do expect you to take my complaint seriously, unlike our local police force. After all, my son is paying you."

I turned back to her, laying the binoculars on the piecrust table. "Did you or Darraugh report this business to the titleholder, or the estate agents? They'd be the ones most concerned."

"Julius Arnoff. He's courteous, but he doesn't quite believe me. I realize that I no longer own the house," she said. "But I still feel a keen interest in its well-being. I told Darraugh when the police were so unhelpful that I would prefer my own investigator, who would owe me the necessity of reports. Which reminds me: I don't believe you told me your name, young woman. Darraugh did, but I've forgotten it."

"Warshawski. V. I. Warshawski."

"Oh, these Polish names. They're like eels sliding around the tongue. What did my son tell me he calls you? Vic? I will call you Victoria. Will you write your phone number on this pad? In large numbers; I don't want to have to use a magnifying glass if I need to summon you in a hurry."

Horrifying visions of Ms. Graham feeling free to call me at three in the morning when she had insomnia, or at odd moments during the day when loneliness overtook her, made me give her only my office number. My answering service would deflect her most of the time.

"I hope Darraugh hasn't exaggerated your abilities. I will watch for you tonight."

I shook my head. "I can't stay out here tonight. But I'll be back tomorrow."

That didn't please her at all: if her son was employing me it was my duty to work the hours that they set.

"And if someone else hires me tomorrow, should I drop my work for Darraugh to respond to that client's demands?" I said.

The heavy lines around her nose deepened. She tried to demand what obligation could possibly take precedence over her needs, but I wasn't about to tell her. To her credit, she didn't waste a long time on argument when she saw I wasn't giving in.

"But you will tell me personally what you find out. I don't want to have to get reports from Darraugh: there are times when I wish he was more like his father."

Her tone didn't make that sound like a compliment. When I stood to leave, she asked me—ordered, really—to take the cups back to the kitchen. I turned them over before putting them in the sink: Coalport bone china. Mugs, indeed.

I spent the drive to Chicago going over her surprising remarks. I wondered why Darraugh hated Larchmont so much. I found myself constructing Gothic scenarios. Darraugh was a widower. Perhaps his beloved wife had died there, while his wastrel father absconded with Darraugh's wife's diamonds and his own secretary. Or perhaps Darraugh suspected Geraldine of drowning his wife—or even his father—in the ornamental pond and had vowed never to set foot on Drummond land again.

As I returned to the small bungalows of Chicago's West Side, I realized the situation was probably something far less dramatic.

Darraugh and his mother no doubt merely had the the usual frictions of any family.

Whatever their history, Ms. Graham resented her son's failure to visit her as often as she wanted. I wondered if phantom lights in the upper windows were a way of forcing Darraugh to pay attention to her. I foresaw the possibility of getting squeezed between these two strong personalities. At least it beat fretting about Morrell.

3

Hands Across the Water

It was the thought of Geraldine Graham's binoculars that determined me to slide through the grounds around Larchmont Hall Sunday night without showing a light or making the kind of ruckus I'd set up if I tripped and broke an ankle. She had called once already during the day to make sure I was coming out. I asked if she'd seen her flickering lights the night before; she hadn't, she said, but she didn't spend the whole night looking for them as I would. Just as I was stiffening at being treated like a hired hand, she disarmed me, saying, "Even ten years ago, I was still strong enough to spend the night looking for intruders. I can't now."

I wore my night-prowler's costume: black jeans, dark windbreaker over a sweater, black cap pulling my hair flat against my head, charcoal on my cheeks to keep the moonlight from reflecting off my skin. Ms. Graham's eyes would have to be good to find me even with her Rigel optics.

For tonight's trip, I parked on one of the residential streets on the northeast corner of the New Solway township. I walked the two miles south along Dirksen, the road that divided New Solway from a golf course on its eastern boundary.

Dirksen Road didn't have any sidewalks, the idea of people on foot apparently being beyond New Solway's budget, or maybe their imagination. I kept having to duck into a ditch to get out of the way of traffic. When I finally reached the entrance to Coverdale Lane, I was out of breath, and peevish. I leaned against one of the pervasive stone pillars to pick burrs out of my jeans.

Once I left Dirksen Road, I was enveloped in night. The lights of the suburbs—the houses, the streetlamps, the relentless traffic—faded. Coverdale Lane was far enough from the hedge that guarded New Solway to block out both the streetlamps and the traffic beyond.

The dark silence made me feel untethered from the world. The moon provided some light, but clouds shrouded it, making it hard to stay on the asphalt. I kept veering into the weeds growing alongside the road. I'd measured the distance from Dirksen Road to the mansion in my car yesterday morning: two-thirds of a mile. About twelve hundred paces for me, but I lost count after six hundred something, and the dark distorted my sense of distance. The night creatures, moving about on their own errands, began to loom large in my mind.

I froze at a rustling in the underbrush. It stopped when I stopped, but started again after a few minutes. My palms grew wet on the flashlight as the rustling came closer. I gripped the stock so I could use it as a weapon and switched the beam on at its narrowest focus. A raccoon halted at the light, stared at me for a full minute, then sauntered back into the bushes with what seemed an insolent shrug of furry shoulders.

A few paces later, Larchmont Hall suddenly appeared, its pale brick making it loom like a ghostly galleon in the moonlight. I used my own night-vision binoculars now, but didn't see anyone in front of me. I circled the outbuildings cautiously, disturbing more raccoons and a fox, but didn't see any people.

I picked my way to the edge of the garden, where I could get a bit of a vantage point for the back of the house. The attic windows were dark. I perched on a bench to wait.

I'd been curious enough about Darraugh's family history to do a little research, spending the afternoon in the Chicago Historical Society's library, where I pored over old society columns and news stories. It felt soothing to be in a library, handling actual pieces of paper with people around me, instead of perching alone in front of a blinking cursor. I'd learned a lot of local history, but I wasn't sure how much of it illuminated Darraugh's life.

Geraldine Graham's grandfather had started a paper mill on the Illinois River in 1877, which he'd turned into a fortune before the century ended. The Drummond mills in Georgia and South Carolina once employed nine thousand people. They'd shut most of those plants in the downturn of the last decade, but still had one major mill going in Georgia. In fact, I had once done some work down there for Darraugh, but he hadn't mentioned its ties to his mother's family. Drummond Paper had merged with

Continental Industries in 1940; the Drummond name remained only on the paper division.

Geraldine's father had built Larchmont for his wife in 1903; Geraldine, her brother Stuart, and a sister who died young, had been born there. The *Chicago American* had reported on the gala around the housewarming, where the Taverners, the McCormicks, Armors and other Chicago luminaries had spent a festive evening. The whole story was like one of those period pieces on public television.

Your roving correspondent had to rove with a vengeance to get to the opening of Larchmont Hall, riding the tram to the train and the train to its farthest reaches, where a charabanc obligingly scooped her up along with the men delivering plants, lobsters and all manner else of delightful edibles to adorn the fête. She arrived perforce in advance of the more regal guests and had plenty of time to scope the grounds, where tables and chairs were set up for taking tea alfresco. Dinner, of course, was served in the grand dining room, whose carved walnut table seats thirty.

The tessellated entrance floor took the Italian workers eight months to complete, but it is worth the effort, the green and sienna and palest ecru of the tiles forming a rich yet unobtrusive foretaste of the splendors within. Your correspondent peeped into Mr. Drummond's study, a most masculine sanctum, redolent of leather, with deep red curtains drawn across the mullioned windows so that the great man isn't tempted by the beauties of nature to abandon his important tasks.

Of course, the greatest beauty of all is within. Mrs. Matthew Drummond, née Miss Laura Taverner, was the cynosure of all eyes when she appeared in her embroidered tulle over pale cornflower satin, the gold chiffon tunic edged with rhinestones (from Worth's own hands, my dears, as Mrs. Drummond's maid whispered, arrived last week from Paris), with a display of ostrich plumes and diamonds that were the envy of every other lady. Mrs. Michael Taverner, Mrs. Drummond's sister-in-law, seemed almost to faint with misery when she saw how com-

monplace her rose charmeuse ap-
peared. Of course, Mrs. Edwards
Bayard has a mind above dress, as
everyone who has seen that mauve
bombazine a thousand times or so
could testify—or perhaps her hus-
band's extra-domestic activities are
funded from her clothes budget!

The coy correspondent recounted with a wealth of description the thirteen bedrooms, the billiard room, the music room where Mrs. Drummond's spectacular performance on the piano held dinner guests spellbound, the ornamental pool lined with blue clay and the three motorcars which Mr. Drummond had installed in the new "garage, as we hear the English are calling the structure for housing these modern conveyances."

How very modern of old Matthew Drummond. The garage, which loomed to my right, could hold six modern motorcars with room for a machine shop to repair them. Then, as now, vast wealth needed flaunting. How else did others know you had it?

After reading about Larchmont's wonders, I'd searched various indices, looking for news of Geraldine. I wanted actually to see who Darraugh's father had been, or what had happened to engender the contempt in Geraldine's voice when she mentioned him. It was more than idle curiosity: I wanted to know what currents lay beneath my client's surface so I could avoid falling in them and getting swept away.

I found Geraldine's birth in 1912—a "happy event," as the language of a century ago put it, a baby sister to keep little Stuart Drummond company. The next report was of her coming-out party in 1929 with other girls from the Vina Fields Academy. Her Poiret tulle gown was described in detail, including the diamond chips bordering the front drapery. Apparently the crash in the market hadn't kept the family from pulling out all the stops. After all, some people did make money from the disaster—maybe Matthew Drummond had been among them.

The next family news was a clip welcoming Geraldine home from Switzerland in the spring of 1931, this time in a white Balenciaga suit, "looking interestingly thin after her recent illness." I raised my brows at this: was it TB, or had Laura Taverner Drummond hustled her daughter to Europe to deal with an unwelcome pregnancy?

There'd been a major depression on in the thirties, but you wouldn't know that from the society pages. Descriptions of gowns costing five or even ten thousand dollars dotted the gossip columns. Money like that would have supported my father's family in comfort for a year. He'd been nine in 1931, delivering coal in the mornings before school to help the family eke out a living after his father got laid off. I'd never met my grandfather, whose health deteriorated under the strain of not being able to support his family. He'd died in 1946, right after my parents were married.

No considerations like that marred Geraldine Drummond's 1940 wedding to MacKenzie Graham. The ceremony was a no-holds-barred affair at Fourth Presbyterian Church on North Michigan Avenue—eight attendants, two young ring bearers, followed by a reception at the Larchmont estate so lavish that I was surpised the mansion hadn't collapsed from the weight of the caviar. The happy couple left for two months in South America—the European war precluded a French destination.

Reading between the lines, it sounded as though Geraldine had been force-fed to the son of some business crony of her father's.

Her one brother, Stuart, had died in a car wreck without leaving any children, so Geraldine was presumably the heir to all the Drummond enterprises. Maybe Matthew and Laura Drummond chose a son-in-law they thought could manage the family holdings. Or maybe Laura had chosen someone she could control herself—in the wedding photos, the bridegroom looked hunted and unhappy.

MacKenzie Graham stayed at Larchmont Hall until his death in 1957. Tidy obituaries in all the papers, death at home of natural causes. Which could mean anything from cancer to bleeding to death from a shooting accident. Maybe that was what had turned Darraugh against Larchmont, seeing his father die here.

Cold was seeping through my layers of jacket and sweatshirt. Despite the unsettling mildness of the weather—here it was, early March, with no snow, and no hard freeze all winter—it was still too cold to sit for long. I got up from the bench and backed up to the meadow so I could see the upper windows. Nothing.

I made another circuit of the building, stubbing my toe on the same loose brick I'd hit the previous two times. Cursing, I sat on a step by the pool and listened to the night around me. For a time, I heard only the skittering of night creatures in the underbrush beyond Larchmont's perimeter. Every now and then, a car would drive down Coverdale Lane, but no one stopped. A deer tiptoed across the lawn. When it saw me move in the moonlight, it bolted back across the meadow.

Suddenly, over the wind, I heard a louder crashing in the undergrowth beyond the garage. That wasn't a fox or raccoon. Adrenaline rushed through my body. I jumped to my feet. The crashing stopped. Had the newcomer seen me? I tried to melt into the shrubbery lining the ornamental garden, tried not to breathe. After a moment, I heard the whicking of feet on brick: the newcomer had moved from dead leaves to walkway. Two feet, not four. A person who knew his way, coming purposefully forward.

I dropped to my belly and slithered around the pool toward the house, sticking to the paths so I wouldn't announce myself on dead leaves. When I reached the shelter of a great beech, I cautiously lifted my head, straining at the shadows of the trees and bushes. All at once, a darker shadow appeared, ectoplasmic limbs floating and wavering in the moonlight. A slight figure, with a backpack making a hump in the silhouette, moving with the ease of youth.

I put my face back down in the turf so that moonlight wouldn't glint from the white of my nose. The figure passed a couple of yards from my head, but didn't pause. When I heard him at the north wall of the house, I got up and tiptoed after him. He must have seen the movement reflected in the French doors, because he whirled on his heel. Before he could bolt, I was running full tilt, tackling him around the knees. He cried out and fell underneath my weight.

It wasn't a youth at all but a girl, with a pale narrow face and dark hair pulled back into a long braid. Her skin gave off the sour sweat of fear. I rolled away from her, but kept a strong grip on her shoulder. When she tried to break away, I tightened my hold.

"What are you doing here?" I demanded.

"What are *you* doing here?" she hissed, terrified but fierce. Our breath made little white puffs in the night air.

"I'm a detective. I'm following up a report of housebreakers."

"Oh, I see: you work for the pigs." Fear muted her scorn.

"That insult was old when I was your age. Are you Patty Hearst, stealing from your fellow robber barons to give to the terrorists, or Joan of Arc, rescuing the nation?"

The moon was riding high in the sky now; its cold light shone on the girl, turning her soft young face to marble. She scowled at my mockery but didn't rise to the bait.

"I'm minding my own business. Why don't you mind yours?"

"Are you the person who's flashing a light in this house in the middle of the night?"

It's hard to read expressions in the moonlight, but I thought she looked startled, even afraid, and she said quickly, "I came here on a dare. The other kids thought I was too chicken to go through this big deserted place at night."

"And they're lurking on the perimeter to see you make good on your word. Try another story."

"You don't have any right to question me. I'm not breaking any law."

"That's true, not yet, anyway, although it looked as though breaking and entering was going to be your next step. Is this where you and your boyfriend come to make out?"

Her eyes squinched shut in disgust. "Are you with the sex police? If I want to fuck my boyfriend, I'll do it in comfort at home, not squirreling around in some abandoned attic."

"So you know that the light is coming from the attic. That's interesting."

She gasped but rallied. "*You* said it was the attic."

"No. I said the house. But you and I both know you know what's going on in here, so let's not dance that dance."

Her soft mouth puckered into a scowl. "I'm not breaking any laws, so let me go. Then I won't sue you for assaulting me."

"You're too young to sue me yourself, but I suppose your parents will do it for you. Since you came on foot, you're probably from one of these mansions. I suppose you're like all the other rich kids I've ever met, so overindulged you never have to take responsibility for anything you do."

That did rouse her. "I am responsible!" she shouted.

She wriggled out of my slackened grasp and rolled over. I grabbed at her arm, but only got her backpack. A furry wad came loose in my hands as she wrenched herself free. She sprinted through the opening to the gardens. I jumped up after her, stuffing the furry thing into my jeans as I ran.

As I crashed through the garden, she disappeared around the pond, heading for the woods behind the outbuildings. I charged up the path and tripped again on the loose brick. I was going too fast to catch my balance. I flapped my arms desperately, trying to keep upright, but tumbled sideways into the water.

Weeds and leaves clogged the surface. The water was only five feet deep, but I panicked, terrified that I wouldn't be able to push my head through the tangled roots. When I finally broke through the rotting mass, I was several yards from the edge. I was freezing, my clothes so heavy with the brackish water that they pinned me like an iron shroud. My feet slipped on the clay bottom and I grabbed at the plants to stay upright. Instead my numb fingers closed around clammy flesh. One of the dead carp. I backed away in disgust so fast I fell over again. As I righted myself, I realized it wasn't a fish I'd seized but a human hand.

Once More Unto the Pokey, Dear Friends

I worked my way around to the head. It was a man, weighted down by his clothes, kept on the surface only by the tangle of weeds underneath him. I thrust my arm under his armpits and started dragging him, holding his head out of the water in case he wasn't really dead. My feet kept slipping on the clay bottom. Pulling his waterlogged weight through that muck made my heart hammer. After some enormity of time, I managed to haul him to the pool's edge. The water was half a foot below the pool's perimeter. I took a deep breath, squatted in the rank plants, and did a dead lift to get him out.

My arm and leg muscles burned with fatigue. My own legs weighed about a ton each now. I lay my torso across the marble tiles surrounding the pool and managed to swing my legs over the side. My teeth were chattering so violently that my whole body shook. I lay on the sharp stone for a minute, but I couldn't afford to stay here. I was remote from help; I'd die of cold if I didn't move.

I got to my hands and knees and crawled to the man. I rolled him onto his back and cleaned the weeds out of his mouth and undid his tie and pushed on his chest and blew cold trembly gusts into his mouth, and, after five minutes, he was still as dead as he'd been when I'd clutched his hand in the water.

By now I was so cold I felt as though someone was slicing my skull with knives. I pried the zipper of my windbreaker open and dug my cell phone out of one of the pockets. I couldn't believe my luck: the little screen blinked its green lights at me and I was able to connect to the emergency network.

The dispatcher had trouble understanding me, my teeth were chattering so loudly. Larchmont Hall, could I identify that? The first house you came to off the Dirksen

Road entrance to Coverdale Lane? Could I turn on my car lights or the house lights so the emergency crew could find me? I'd come on foot? Just what was I doing there?

"Just tell the New Solway cops to come to Larchmont Hall," I croaked. "They'll find it."

I severed the connection and looked wistfully at the house behind me. Maybe the dot-com millionaires had forgotten a bathrobe, or even a kitchen towel, when they left. I was halfway to the house when I realized that this would be my one chance alone with the dead man. Larchmont Hall was sealed like Fortress America. Without tools, with my hands frozen, I'd be lucky to have a door open before the cops arrived, but I'd have enough time to look for some ID on the body.

I found my flashlight near the French doors where I'd wrestled with the girl. I took it back with me to the dead man.

Was this my teenager's boyfriend? Despite her smart remark about the sex police, were they meeting in the abandoned house—somehow bypassing the security system? Maybe he hadn't made tonight's rendezvous because he'd tripped over the same brick I'd stumbled on, fallen into the pond and hadn't been able to fight free of the weeds. He hadn't tried to take off his shoes or his clothes: I'd undone his tie and unbuttoned his shirt to give him CPR, but he had on a suit; belt, fly button and zipper were all tidily done up. The suit looked as though it had been a good one, a brown wool basket weave. He'd been wearing wing tips, not an outfit for the woods at night.

I moved my flashlight along the length of his body. He was about six feet tall, lean, not particularly athletic looking. His skin was a nut-brown, his hair African, which might explain the need for secret meetings in an abandoned house. Or maybe it was his age—he looked to be in his thirties. I could picture the girl attracted to an affair with an African-American: the need to do something dramatic, something daring, was clearly strong in her.

Who was he? Who would meet his end in such a remote and dreadful way? I dug gingerly into the pockets. Like my own, they had clammed shut from the weight of the water. I had a hard job of it, as cold as I was, and I wasn't rewarded with much when I finished. There was nothing in his jacket or his front trouser pockets but a handful of change. I gritted my teeth and stuck my hand under his buttocks. The back pockets were empty, too, except for a pencil and a matchbook.

No one in the modern age goes out in a suit and tie without a wallet, or at least a driver's license. But where was his car? Had he done like me? Parked two miles away and come on foot for a secret rendezvous?

My head was aching so with cold I couldn't think clearly, but I'd have been bewildered even if I were warm and dry. I know people drown in their baths in panic, and I myself had had a moment's terror when I couldn't get my head through those weeds, but why had he left all his papers at home? Had he come here on purpose to die? Was this some dramatic event planned for my teenager? Come out in the open about me or I'll kill myself? He looked in repose like a steady man, not the person for such dramatic actions. It was hard to picture him as Romeo to my young heroine's Juliet.

When the emergency crew arrived, I was still holding his matchbook and pencil. I stuck them into my own jacket pocket so I wouldn't be caught in the act of stripping the body.

Besides a fire department ambulance, the dispatcher had sent both the New Solway cops and the DuPage County sheriff's police. The body had turned up in unincorporated New Solway. That technically meant it belonged to the DuPage County sheriff, but the dispatcher had also notified the New Solway police. Even in my frozen state, I could understand why. The houses along Coverdale Lane were a who's who of greater Chicago Big Money: New Solway cops would want an inside track on who to blame if the local barons—or baronesses—got testy.

The two groups jockeyed for dominance in inspecting the body. They wanted to know who I was and what I was doing there. Through my chattering teeth I told them my name, but said I couldn't talk until I was some place warm.

The two forces bickered for another long minute while I shivered uncontrollably, then compromised by letting the New Solway police ride along while the sheriff's deputies took me to Wheaton.

"My God, you stink," the sheriff's deputy said when I climbed into his squad car.

"That's just the rotting vegetation," I muttered. "I'm clean inside."

He wanted to open the windows to air out the smell, but I told him if I ended up with pneumonia I'd see he footed the medical bills. "You have a blanket or an old jacket or something in the trunk?" I added. "I'm wet and freezing and your pals waiting for the shift change so they wouldn't have to take the call didn't help any: it's been over forty minutes since I phoned."

"Yeah, bastards," he said, then cut off the rest of the sentence, annoyed with me for voicing his grievance. He stomped around to the trunk and fished out an old towel. It couldn't be any dirtier than I was: I draped it around my head and was asleep before the car left the yard.

When we got to the sheriff's headquarters in Wheaton, I was so far gone I didn't wake up until some strong young deputy yanked me out of the backseat and braced me on my feet. I stumbled into the building, joints stiff in my clammy clothes.

"Wake up, Sleeping Beauty," the deputy snapped. "You need to tell us what you were doing on private property out here."

"Not until I'm clean and dry," I mumbled through cracked and swollen lips. "You must have some clothes out here I can borrow."

The deputy who'd brought me in said that was highly irregular, they didn't treat housebreakers like hotel guests in DuPage County. I sat on a bench and began undoing the zipper on my windbreaker. A chunk of some dead plant had worked its way around the pull. My fingers were thick with cold, and I worked slowly while the deputy stood over me wanting to know what in hell I thought I was doing. The zipper took all my attention. When I finally had the jacket undone, I pulled off the wet sweater underneath. I was starting to take off my bottom layer, a T-shirt, when he grabbed my shoulder and yanked me back to my feet.

"What are you doing?"

"What it looks like. Taking off my wet clothes."

"You can't do that out here. You produce some ID and some reason for being on private property in the middle of the night."

By now, a number of other officers, including a couple of women, had joined him. I looked past him and said to them,

"Darraugh Graham asked me to check on Larchmont Hall. You know, the old Drummond estate where his mother lived until the year before last. It's been standing empty and she thought she was seeing housebreakers. I found a dead man in the pool behind the house and got thoroughly soaked pulling him out. And that's all I can say until I get clean and dry."

"And how you planning on proving that story?" my deputy sneered.

One of the women gave him a sour look. "Be your age, Barney. You never heard of Darraugh Graham? Come along," she added to me.

My eyes were swelling with the onset of a head cold. I squinted at her badge. S. Protheroe.

Protheroe led me to the women's locker room, where I toweled myself dry. She even dug up an old set of uniform trousers and a sweatshirt, a size or two too big on me but clean. "We keep spares out here for officers who've been through the wringer. You can sign for 'em on your way out and get 'em back to us in the next week. You want to tell me your name and what you were really doing out here?"

I pulled on clean socks and looked with disgust at my shoes. The tiled floor was cold, but my shoes would have been worse. I sat on the locker room bench and told her my name, my relationship to Darraugh, his mother's belief that there were intruders in her old home, my fruitless surveillance— and the body I'd stumbled on. I don't know why I didn't feed her my young Juliet. Native caution, maybe, or maybe because I like ardent young women. I dug my wallet out of my windbreaker and showed her my PI license, fortunately walled in laminate.

Protheroe handed it back to me without comment, except to say the state's attorney would want some formal statement about finding the dead man. When she saw me rolling my foul clothes into a bundle, she even found a plastic bag in a supply cupboard.

Protheroe took me to a room on the second floor and called someone on her cell phone. "Lieutenant Schorr will be along in a minute. You do much work out here? No? Well, I know the Cook County sheriff's office is a cesspool of Democratic patronage and favors. Out here it's different. Out here it's a cesspool of Republican patronage. So don't mind the boys, they're not all real well trained."

Lieutenant Schorr arrived with a couple of male sidekicks and a woman who announced she was Vanna Landau, the assistant state's attorney. One of the New Solway police officers had stayed for the meeting, as well. A fifth man came hurrying in a minute later, straightening the knot in his tie. He was introduced as Larry Yosano, a member of the law firm that had handled Larchmont's sale—apparently a very junior member.

"Thanks, Stephanie," Schorr dismissed my guide. She gave me a discreet thumbs-up and left.

I was used to Chicago police interrogation rooms, with their scarred tables and peeling paint, and where strong disinfectants don't quite cover the traces of vomit. Stephanie Protheroe had brought me to something like a modern boardroom, with a television and camcorder ruling over blond furniture. Behind the modern façade, though, the smell of disinfectant and stale fear rose to greet me like an unwelcome neighbor.

Vanna Landau, the ASA, was a small woman who leaned across the table as if trying to make herself bigger by taking up as much room as possible. "Now just what were you doing on the land?"

In between coughs and sneezes, I explained in as mild a voice as I could summon.

"Spying on Larchmont Hall in the middle of the night?" Landau said. "That is trespassing, at a minimum."

I pinched the skin between my eyebrows in an effort to stay awake. "Would it have been better if I'd done it in daylight? Geraldine Graham was worried when she saw intruders around the house late at night. At her son's request, I went over to take a look."

Larry Yosano, the young lawyer, was trying to rub sleep out of his own eyes. "Technically, of course, it's trespass, but if you've ever dealt with Mrs. Graham, you'd know that she's never really acknowledged that she no longer owns Larchmont. She's a strong personality, difficult to say no to."

He turned to me. "Lyons Trust is the title-holder. They're the ones you should call if

Mrs. Graham sees a problem with the property."

I didn't say anything except to ask for a Kleenex. One of the deputies found some paper napkins in a drawer and tossed them across the table at me.

"Or the police," Lieutenant Schorr said. "Did that ever occur to you, Ms. Private Eye?"

"Ms. Graham called the New Solway police several times. They thought she was a crazy old woman making stuff up."

The New Solway cop, whose name I hadn't heard, bristled. "We went out there three times and saw nothing. Yesterday, when someone really was on the property, we responded to the alarm within fifteen minutes. Her own son even says she could be making stuff up because she wants attention."

I sat up at that. "I met with Ms. Graham yesterday afternoon. She didn't strike me as delusional at all. I know she's old, but if she says she's seeing lights in that house she is. What about the man in the pool? If nothing else, him being there proves someone was using that abandoned estate for something."

"I don't think Mrs. Graham makes things up," Yosano agreed, "but she doesn't listen to advice. We, for instance, advised her to move away from New Solway when she sold, but her ties to the community are very deep, of course."

I had a picture of the hapless dot-com millionaire, fending off Geraldine Graham's efforts to help him run Larchmont the way her mother had done.

The young state's attorney seemed to feel the interview was slipping away; she demanded to know my relationship to the dead man.

"We kissed once, very deeply . . ." I waited until one of the deputies had eagerly written this down before adding, ". . . when I was doing CPR on him. His mouth was full of the crud in the pool and I had to clean that out first . . . Did you get that? Need me to spell any of the words?"

"So you don't admit to knowing him?" Vanna Landau said.

"The verb 'admit' makes it sound like you think knowing him is a crime." I sneezed again. "Does that mean you know who he is? Some DuPage County career criminal whom it would be dangerous to admit knowing?"

"Black guy on the land, what else was he but a criminal?" one of the deputies snickered to his fellow.

I reached across the table and ripped a sheet from the state's attorney's legal pad. "Let me just write this last comment down word for word to make sure I have the quote exactly right when I call the *Herald-Star* tomorrow. 'Black guy on the land, what else was he but a criminal.' Right?"

"Barney, why don't you and Teddy go get us some coffee while we wrap this up," Schorr said to his deputies. When they had left, he pulled the paper away from me and balled it up. "It's late, we're all pretty tired and not using our best minds on this problem. Let's just go over a few last questions and let you get back to Chicago where you belong. Do you, or do you not, know who the dead man is?"

"I never saw him until tonight. I can't add anything to this discussion. You have any prelimary report from the ME?" I could feel a sore throat rising up my tonsils.

Schorr and the ASA exchanged looks. She pursed her lips but picked up the phone at her end of the table. She had a brisk conversation with one of the ME techs and shook her head. Even under the cold light of the DuPage County morgue, no one had found any clues I'd overlooked.

"You'll run a photo in the papers and on the news, right?" I said to the ASA. "And a full autopsy, including dental impressions?"

"We know our job out here," she said stiffly.

"Just asking. I wouldn't want to think that because he was a black man, you wouldn't put your best effort into cause of death and so on."

"You don't need to worry about that," Schorr said, the fake good humor in his voice not masking the anger in his face. "You go on home and leave this investigation to us."

When I told him where I'd left my car, he gave an exaggerated sigh and said he supposed one of the deputies could drive me, but I'd have to wait in the front hall.

My hamstrings had stiffened while we sat. I stumbled on my way out of the room. Larry Yosano, the young lawyer, caught my arm to keep me from falling. When I thanked him, I wondered why he'd joined our happy band tonight.

He yawned. "I'm the junior on call for difficult problems this week. We handle affairs for most of the estates in New Solway; we have keys, so if the lieutenant had wanted to get into the house I could have let him in. In fact, when they called me, I drove over to Larchmont, but your group had already left for here. I took some time to check the alarm; it hadn't been set off, and it's still functioning. I had a quick look around the ground floor, but there wasn't any sign of an intruder."

He yawned more widely. "I wish Lyons Trust—they're the titleholders—would find a buyer. It's not good to have a place like that standing empty. We advised hiring a caretaker, but the bank didn't want to spend the money."

Deputy Protheroe, the woman who'd given me my dry clothes, appeared: she'd been elected to drive me. Yosano walked out with us. Before climbing into his BMW, he gave me a card. I squinted at it through my swollen eyes: he was an associate with Lebold, Arnoff, offices in Oak Brook and LaSalle Street. I'd never heard of them, but I don't often have to deal with the property issues of the superrich.

"Give Geraldine Graham my number the next time she calls," Yosano said. "I'll try to talk her out of more private surveillance at Larchmont."

My cards were gummed together in my wallet. I wrote my office number on a scrap of paper for him.

"You awake enough to get that car of yours home?" Protheroe asked when we reached the Mustang. "I don't want to be called out in half an hour to scrape your body off the tollway. There's a Motel 6 up the road. Maybe you'd better check in for what's left of the night."

I knew I was tired enough to be at risk behind the wheel, but I was feeling so rotten that I wanted my own bed. I summoned a travesty of bravado, sketching a two-fingered salute and a smile. The dashboard clock read three-fifteen when I pointed my little Mustang toward the city.

Stochastic Excursion

I was in a cave, looking for Morrell. Someone had handed me a wailing infant; I was hunched over, trying to get out of the way of massive roots that pushed down through the rocks. The air was so bad I couldn't breathe; the rocks themselves were squeezing the air out of me. The infant howled more loudly. Next to me lay the body of a black man in a brown weave suit, dead from the bad air. A buzzing in the distance meant an air-raid warning. From far away I could hear planes whining overhead.

The howling of the planes, the wailing of the infant, finally forced me awake. The phone and downstairs doorbell were ringing simultaneously, but my head cold left me too groggy to bestir myself. I didn't even stick out a hand for the phone but rolled over onto my side, hoping to relieve the pressure in my sinuses.

I was startled to see the clock read two-forty: I'd slept the whole day away. I tried to raise a sense of urgency about the man I'd found last night, or about the girl I'd tackled, but I couldn't manage it.

I was just drifting back to sleep when someone pushed the buzzer right outside my third-floor door. Three insistent hoots, and then I heard a key in the lock. That meant one thing: Mr. Contreras, who has keys to my place, with strict orders to save them for emergencies—which he and I define very differently. I couldn't deal with him while flat on my back. By the time his heavy tread sounded in my hall, I'd pulled on a sweatshirt and the pants I'd borrowed from DuPage County last night.

He started talking before he got to the bedroom door. "Doll, you okay? Your car's out front and you ain't been out all day, but Mr. Graham, he just sent over a messenger with a letter for you. When you didn't even come to the door, I got kinda worried."

"Yeah, I'm okay." My voice sounded like Poe's raven after a night mainlining chloroform.

"You sick, doll? What happened to you? It was on the news, you being out in wherever diving into a pond after a dead guy. You have pneumonia or what?"

The dogs pelted down the hall and circled around me with delighted yips. All was forgiven in the three days since I'd last force-marched them down Lake Michigan to the Loop—they were ready for action. I fondled their ears.

"Just a cold. I didn't get home until four this morning—been sleeping. 'Scuse minute." I snuffled down to the bathroom, blenching at the sight of my face in the mirror. I looked worse than I sounded. My eyes were puffy. I had a bruise across my cheekbone and more on my arms and legs. I hadn't noticed banging myself up so badly when I was hefting bodies around the Larchmont estate last night.

I turned the hot water on in the shower and steamed myself for a few minutes. When I emerged, clean, and, thankfully, dressed in my own clothes, my neighbor had produced a large mug of tea with lemon and honey. Unlike Geraldine Graham's gilt eggshells, mine were real mugs, thick, clunky—and cheap.

"When I heard the news, them saying you'd been brought in to DuPage County for questioning about this dead man, I thought maybe you'd been arrested. You been fighting? You got some case that's gonna kill you and you ain't said nothing to me?" His brown eyes were bright with hurt.

"Nothing like that."

When I'd croaked out enough explanation to satisfy him, he suddenly remembered Darraugh's letter. The blistering prose raised welts on my fingers.

I have been trying to reach you all day to find out why you sent the police to my mother without informing me first. Since you aren't answering your phone or e-mail I am sending this by hand. Call *immediately* on receipt of this message.

How nice to be the man in charge and bulldoze your way through people as if they were construction sites. I checked in with my answering service. Christie Weddington, the operator I've known longest, answered.

"Is that really you, Vic? Just to be safe I'd better do our security check. What was your mother's maiden name?" When I'd spelled "Sestieri" she added severely, "When you're going to hole up, can you let us know? Now that Mary Louise has left your company, you don't have any backup person to call for emergencies. We got like eleven calls from Darraugh Graham's office, and five from Murray Ryerson."

Darraugh, or his PA, Caroline, had started in at ten and kept it up every half hour. Geraldine Graham had phoned four times herself, the first time at a quarter of ten. So the DuPage sheriff had been to see her by nine. At least they were taking it seriously. Murray had called early, before eight, presumably when he'd looked at the morning wires. I got back to him first, in case he knew something that would help me in my conversation with Darraugh. Murray was indignant that I hadn't called him when the blood was fresh enough to lick.

"Have they ID'd the guy yet?" I croaked into his barrage of questions.

"You sound like a frog in a cheese grater, Warshawski. So far the DuPage sheriff is clueless. I gather they're running your John

Doe's prints through AFIS. And they've put his picture on the wires."

"They have a cause of death?" I wheezed.

"He drowned. What were you doing, Warshawski, turning up so pat minutes after the guy plunged to his watery death?"

"You should write for the *Enquirer,* with prose like that. You drive out to Larchmont? No one could plunge to a watery death in five feet of water. Either he did like me, tripped and fell, or—" A coughing fit interrupted me. Mr. Contreras leaped up to pour me more tea, and to mutter that Murray was an inconsiderate jerk, keeping me talking when I was sick.

"—or he went in on purpose or he was put there," Murray finished for me. "What's your theory? Did it look as though he'd struggled?"

I shut my eyes, trying to remember the body as I'd found it. "I only had my flashlight to augment the moon, so I can't say whether he had unusual bruises or scratches. But his clothes were tidy—no undone buttons, and his tie was still neatly knotted. I undid it when I was trying CPR."

"Cross your heart, you never saw him before?" Murray demanded.

"Hope to die," I coughed.

"So you didn't go out there to meet him?"

"No!" I was getting impatient. "He's what Professor Wright used to call a 'stochastic excursion' in my physics class."

"Then what about the 'Warshawski excursion'?" Murray asked. "What were you doing in the land of hope and glory?"

"Catching the cold of a lifetime." I hung up as a cough started racking me again.

"You oughta go back to bed, cookie," Mr. Contreras fussed over me. "You can't talk, you won't have any voice at all you keep at it. That Ryerson, he just uses you."

"Street runs both ways," I choked. "I have to call Darraugh."

Darraugh interrupted a meeting on the fate of his Georgia paper division to take my call. "Mother had the police with her this morning."

"That must have pleased her," I said.

"Excuse me?" The frost in his voice turned the phone to dry ice against my ear.

"She likes people to attend to her. You don't visit her enough, the cops didn't respond when she told them about intruders in your boyhood home. Now she's gotten the attention she thinks is her due."

"You should have reported to me at once when you found a dead man at the house. I don't pay you to leave me in the dark."

"Darraugh, you're right." My words came out with annoying slowness, the way they do when you don't have a throat. "Hear how I sound? I got this way falling into your pool. After hauling out a dead man, futilely trying CPR, spending two hours with the sheriff's deputies in Wheaton, it was three-thirty. A.M. I could have called you at home then, but I went to bed instead. Where I regret that I slept through ringing phones, sirens, door-bells and atom bombs. I wish I weren't so human, but there you have it."

"Who was that man and what was he do-ing at the house?" Darraugh barked after a moment's silence—he wasn't going to agree that I had mitigating circumstances on my side, but he wasn't going to go for my jugular any more right now, either—from him a concession.

I repeated what little information Murray had given me, then said, "Why didn't you tell me Larchmont was your boyhood home?"

Darraugh paused another moment, before saying abruptly he was in an important meeting, but he wanted me to report to him at once if I learned who had died in the pool, and why he'd been there.

"You want me to investigate?" I asked.

"Give it a few hours. Not until your voice is better: no one's going to take you seriously when you sound like this."

"Thanks, Darraugh: chicken soup for the PI's soul," I said, but he'd already hung up. Just as well. He has plenty of options among the big security companies that handle most of his heavy-muscle jobs. He stays with me not because he likes to support small businesses, but because he knows there will be no leaks out of my tiny operation—I get the jobs that he wants total confidentiality for, but, if he got fed up enough, he'd take the work elsewhere.

When Mr. Contreras finally left with the dogs, I lay down on the couch. I didn't go back to sleep—I actually felt better after being on my feet for a bit. I put on an old LP of Leontyne Price singing Mozart and watched the shadows change on the ceiling.

I had one little bit of information that no one else did: the teenage girl. It wasn't only a wish to keep a hole card, although of course I wanted one, but that her spunk and ardor reminded me of my own youth; I felt protective of her the way you do of your childhood. I wanted to find her on my own before deciding whether the cops or reporters ought to have a crack at her.

I assumed she lived in one of the Coverdale Lane estates. I tried to imagine a strategy for going door-to-door looking for her. I was her scoutmaster coming to collect her Girl Scout cookie sales money. I was looking for my lost Borzoi. I'd found emerald earrings when I was jogging and wanted to restore them to the owner.

Perhaps I could check the area high school, although who knows where people in mansions like those in New Solway send their children. Not only that, I'd only seen the girl briefly, by moonlight. I wasn't sure I'd recognize her again, let alone be able to describe her.

I shut my eyes and tried to conjure her face, but all I remembered was her long braid and the soft cheeks of youth, the planes or lines that might show character not yet formed. Had she said anything that might lead me to her? I was a pig, she'd bet with some of the other kids, she knew someone was in the attic. What had I said that got her so mad she'd run away? Something about not taking responsibility for—

And then I remembered the little thing that had come loose in my hand when she jerked free. I had stuffed it into my jeans pocket. And my jeans were in the garbage bag the sheriff's deputy had given me.

I'd dumped the bag in the front hall when I came in this morning. With a ginger hand, I fished out the damp, mud-caked pants. Rotted leaves and threads of plant roots fell away when I shook them out. I had a feeling I was lucky be too congested to smell them. I had to pry the pocket flap open and pull the whole pocket inside out to get the thing I'd torn from my teenager's backpack. It was black with mud.

When I ran it under the kitchen tap for a few minutes, the mud washed off to show an ancient teddy bear. The last few years it's become kind of a fetish with kids, putting the toys of early childhood on their backpacks or binders. A high school senior had told me that the coolest kids use ratty crib toys; wannabes buy them new. So my girl was cool, or aspired to be: this little guy was missing both his eyes, and even without a night in my muddy pocket his fur had been pretty forlorn, worn down to the nub in places.

The distinguishing feature of the bear was a tiny green sweatshirt with gold letters on it. At first I thought it was a Green Bay Packers shirt, which would only narrow my search to the million Packer fans in the Chicago-Milwaukee corridor, but then I saw the tiny *V* and *F* monogrammed around a minuscule stick. The Vina Fields Academy.

Vina Fields Academy used to be a girls' school when Geraldine Graham had gone there, where they'd learned French, dancing and flirting. Since turning coed in the seventies, it's not only become the most expensive private school in the city but an important academic one. The stick on the teddy bear's little shirt was supposed to be the candle or lighthouse or whatever the school uses to illustrate that it's a beacon of light.

I only know all this because I see a life-sized version of the sweatshirt every time I go into La Llorona on Milwaukee Avenue. The owner, Mrs. Aguilar, wasn't noticeably proud of her daughter, Celine, getting a scholarship to attend Vina Fields: she only had one entire wall papered with her yearbook photos from sixth grade on, along with pictures of Celine with the school field hockey team, Celine accepting the top prize in mathematics for her class three years running, and the sweatshirt.

I hadn't eaten for almost twenty-four hours. I might as well drive down there for some of Mrs. Aguilar's chicken soup with tortillas.

Neighborhood Joint

Back when I signed a seven-year lease for my part of a warehouse at the south end of Bucktown, the surrounding neighborhood was chiefly Hispanic, with a handful of starving artists who needed cheap rent. Two taquerias within half a block of my front door served fresh tortillas past midnight and I had my choice of palm readers.

This evening as I drove south and west toward my office, all I could see was old six-flats like mine coming down and new town houses going up. Strip malls with identical arrays of Starbucks, wireless companies and home renovation chains were replacing factories and storefronts, as if the affluent were afraid to take chances on neighborhood places. The *taquerias* are a memory. Now I have to walk almost a mile farther south for the nearest good tostada. Of course, tenants like me are one reason the neighborhood is changing, but that doesn't make me any happier about it. Especially when I figure what my next round of lease negotiations will look like.

I drove past my office without stopping, although I could see lights in the tall windows on the north side; my lease partner, Tessa Reynolds, was working late on a sculpture.

A few blocks south of our building, Milwaukee Avenue narrows to Model T width, making for congestion at all hours of the day. I parked at the first meter I came to and walked the last two blocks to La Llorona, threading my way through the kinds of crowds that I knew from my South Side childhood. Worn-out women with litters of children straggling around them were stopping in the markets for dinner, or fingering clothes on the racks set out on the sidewalk. Boys darted in and out of the noisy narrow bars and I saw a girl of about eight slip a hair clip off a table and into her pocket.

When I got to La Llorona, some six or seven women were talking to Mrs. Aguilar while she packed up their families' dinner. Celine was at the cash register, her red-brown hair swept up in a ponytail. She was working math problems in between ringing up purchases.

"Buenos dias, Señora Aguilar," I croaked when Mrs. Aguilar glanced over at me.

"Buenos dias, Señora Victoria," she called back. "You're sick, no? What you need? A bowl of soup? Celine, *chica,* bring soup, okay?"

Celine sighed in the manner of all beleaguered teenagers, but she ducked smartly under the counter to fill a big bowl for me. While I waited, I glanced at her book: *Differential Equations for Math SAT Students.* A snappy title.

I sat at one of three high-topped tables that were stuck in the far corner of the storefront, drinking the soup slowly. When the shop was empty of other customers, I listened to Mrs. Aguilar's endless fret about her bad back and her rotten landlord, who was raising her rent but refused to fix the leaking pipe that had shut her store down for two days last week.

"He want to make it so I go away, then he take down the building and make condos or something."

She was probably right, so I didn't do anything but commiserate. I finally managed to steer the conversation to Mrs. Aguilar's third-favorite topic, Celine's education. I asked if she had a current yearbook for Vina Fields. Mrs. Aguilar came around in front of the counter and pulled it out from the drawer underneath the cash register.

"Field hockey, I don't understand this game, but at this school it is important, and Celine is the best." Celine squirmed and moved with her equations to one of the high tables. When another handful of customers came in I took the yearbook with me to my table, asking for a refill on the soup.

"Don't get no food on that, Victoria," Mrs. Aguilar admonished me, as she ducked underneath the countertop and returned to her skillets.

I started going through the class pictures, seniors first. So many fresh-faced, self-confident girls, so many with long dark hair and arrogant poise. I stopped at each such face, trying to match it to last night's phantom. I didn't think it had been Alex Dewhurst, favorite sport, showing horses, favorite singers, 'NSYNC, or Rebecca Caudwell, who loved figure skating and wanted to become an attorney, although both were possible.

"What are you looking for?"

I'd been so absorbed I didn't notice Celine shutting down the till and coming to stand next to me. Senora Aguilar was scrubbing down her counters. Time to pack up.

"I ran into one of your classmates when I was on a job last night. She dropped something valuable, but I don't know her name."

"What does she look like?"

"Long dark braid, kind of narrow face."

Celine offered to take the found item with her to school and post a notice on their in-house WebBoard, but I told her the girl probably wouldn't want the circumstances of her loss publicized. When I finished the seniors and moved on to the juniors, I saw my Juliet almost at once. Her eyes were serious despite the half smile the photographer had coaxed from her, and tendrils from her French braid were spiraling around her soft cheeks, as if she'd been too impatient to comb her hair just for a picture. Catherine

Bayard, who loved Sarah McLachlan's music, whose favorite sport was lacrosse and who hoped to be a journalist when she grew up. She probably would be: Bayard and publishing, the two words go together in Chicago like Capone and crime.

I didn't linger on Catherine's face—I didn't want Celine alerting her at school the next day. Instead, I shrugged as if giving up the search as a bad job. Celine eyed me narrowly. Girls who work advanced calculus problems find adults like me tiresomely easy to solve. She knew I'd spotted someone, but maybe she couldn't tell who it was.

Before giving the book back, I looked at the faculty section. The director was a woman named Wendy Milford, who had the strong expression principals put on to make you think their young charges don't terrify them. I asked Celine to point out her field hockey coach, and memorized the names of a math and history teacher. You never know.

I closed the book and handed it to her with money for my soup. Three dollars for two bowls—you wouldn't find that in 923 or Mauve, or whatever trendy name you'd see on whatever bistro ultimately muscled La Llorona out of business.

I stopped in my office on my way home. Tessa had left for the day and the building was dark. It was also dankly cold. Tessa mainly wrestles large pieces of steel into towering constructions, work which makes her sweat enough to keep the furnace at sixty. I turned up my thermostat and sat bundled in my coat while I brought my system up.

Calvin Bayard, one of the heroes of my youth. I'd developed a huge crush on him when he addressed my Con Law class at the University of Chicago. With his magnetic smile, his easy command of First Amendment issues, his ready wit in answering hostile questions, he'd seemed in a different world than my professors.

After his lecture, I'd gone to the library to read his testimony before the House Committee on Un-American Activities, which had made me glow with pride. Illinois's own Congressman Walker Bushnell, who'd been a leading member of the House Un-American Activities committee, had hounded Bayard for most of 1954 and 1955. But Bayard's testimony made Bushnell sound like a small-minded voyeur. He had walked away from the hearings without ratting out his friends, and without facing prison time. And despite the fact that many of his writers were blacklisted, Bayard Publishing had grown throughout the fifties and sixties.

My law school had been a conservative place. A number of students had written angry letters to the dean about being subjected to one more liberal, but I'd been so enthusiastic I'd even applied for an internship at the Bayard Foundation on South Dearborn. I only got to see the great man twice that summer—in company with a few dozen other people. I hadn't made the final cut for a permanent job, which hurt deeply at the time. I'd ended up with my third choice, the Public Defender's office.

After all this time, I didn't remember a lot of details about Bayard Publishing itself. I knew Calvin Bayard had been the person who moved it from a religious publishing house to doing secular books—the kind of books that got him in trouble with Congress. And there was some business about his supporting civil rights groups which HUAC perceived as Communist fronts.

I pulled up Lexis-Nexis and scanned the company's history. It had been founded by Calvin's great-grandparents—evangelical Congregationalists who'd come west in the 1840s from Andover, Massachusetts, to start a Bible-and-tract publishing house.

Calvin had taken over the company in 1936, a boy wonder, twenty- three years old. He'd published their first nonreligious novel in 1938, *Tale of Two Countries* by Armand Pelletier, who'd died in poverty in 1978, after years of blacklisting kept him out of print. That wasn't in the Nexis report—it was just one of those things I remembered.

I counted on my fingers: Calvin Bayard must be around ninety now. If Catherine Bayard was part of that family, she would likely be a granddaughter.

I turned to Nexis's personal search section. Calvin and Renee Genier Bayard had five addresses, including one on Coverdale Lane in New Solway. Of course. I'd read about Mrs. Edwards Bayard in the article about the gala opening of Larchmont Hall: she'd been the one with a mind above clothes. So last night Catherine had slipped through the woods between 17 Coverdale

Lane and Larchmont Hall, and had known exactly how to find her way back in the dark.

I copied down the address, and another one on Banks Street along Chicago's Gold Coast. The family also maintained residences in London, New York and Hong Kong. I wrote those down, too, although if Catherine had fled that far, I couldn't afford to go after her. The record included everyone who made their home at 17 Coverdale Lane. There seemed to be a staff of seven in residence. I added their names to my list and looked more closely at the Bayard family.

Renee was twenty-some years younger than Calvin. They'd married in 1957, right after his triumphal downing of Bushnell. They had one son, a man with three last names: Edwards Genier Bayard, born in fifty-eight, living in Washington.

I rubbed my sore eyes. Why was Edwards in D.C. while his daughter Catherine was here? And if Catherine had a mother, why wasn't she in the file? The screen offered no answers. I returned to the company reports.

Bayard Publishing was still closely held. It didn't approach the size of AOL Time

Warner or Random House in the book world, but it wasn't that far behind them either. Besides the publishing house that made up its core business, it held a thirty percent share in an online company, an audio label called "New Lion," a bunch of magazines and a part interest in Drummond Paper.

I leaned forward, as if I could dive into the files in front of me. Drummond Paper had been started by Geraldine Graham's grandfather. I guess it wasn't surprising that the Bayards owned part of it—the neighbors up and down Coverdale Lane probably did little deals together all the time. While Mrs. Edwards Bayard attended the opening of Larchmont in her mauve bombazine, her husband probably discussed business with Mr. Matthew Graham in his "masculine sanctum," as the 1903 society writer put it. It only made me uneasy because I kept finding places where the people from New Solway connected: Who knew whom? Who did what to or with whom?

I was closing the screen when I noticed *Margent* and *Margent.Online*—the magazine paying Morrell to hunt around Afghanistan for stories. I had a moment's fantasy of calling Calvin Bayard: look after Morrell—in fact, bring Morrell home, and I won't rat out your granddaughter. I shut my swollen eyes, the conversation and its after-maths rolling through my imagination. Morrell home, in my arms—then never speaking to me again after he found out what I'd done.

I sat up and left Nexis to check my mes-sages, including my log from the answering service. Among the litter of e-mails was one from Morrell. I put it aside to open last—dessert for doing my chores.

My phone message log took up two com-puter screens. I closed my eyes again, ready to turn my back on the whole caboo-dle, but, if I did that, the total would only be worse in the morning.

I squinted at the screen. Geraldine Graham had left two more messages this afternoon. She could wait until morning. Murray again. He could also wait. Inquiries from three clients whose projects were close to finished. I called them all, and ac-tually found one live person on the end of the line. I explained where I was on his problem and that he'd have a report in two days. One of the things Mary Louise started me doing was to keep a time sheet for each client, including due dates. I entered this one in big red letters so I wouldn't forget.

Stephanie Protheroe from the DuPage County sheriff's office had phoned at four-thirty. When I reached her, she said she thought I'd like to know that they'd identified the man I'd found.

"His name was Marcus Whitby. He was a reporter for some magazine." I could hear her rustling through pieces of paper. "Here it is: *T-Square.* Someone at the magazine called in an ID when they saw his face on the wire."

"T-Square," I echoed. "What was he doing out in Larchmont?"

"They either don't know or won't say. Lieutenant Schorr tried to talk to Whitby's boss, but didn't get anywhere. You know the magazine?"

"It's a kind of *Vanity Fair* for the African-American market—covers a mix of high-profile figures in black entertainment, politics and sports. They usually have a political section, too." Tessa, my lease partner, has a subscription; they'd profiled her last year in "Forty Under Forty: Brothers and Sisters to Watch."

"Did he live out there?" I asked.

"Uh, his address is somewhere in Chicago." She fumbled with her notes again. "A street called Giles. Also, we got an autopsy result. He hadn't been dead long when you found him, maybe an hour or two. And he died from drowning. They're saying he got himself drunk and went to a place to die where he thought he could be private."

"They're saying? That means they found blood alcohol levels of some alarming height?"

"I haven't seen the detailed report, so I can't tell you that. All I know is, Sheriff Salvi talked to the press this afternoon. I guess it will be on the news tonight. His secretary says he told reporters that Marcus Whitby came all the way out to DuPage County to commit suicide. I thought you'd like to know."

"Did they do a complete autopsy? Are they giving this a lick and a promise because he was a black man in white superpower country?" Hoarseness made it impossible for me to sound as forceful as I wished.

"I can only tell you what I'm told. I'm not very high up the chain of command here, but the summary makes it sound like they did check his blood alcohol level. And we'd have found him through AFIS, anyway—it turns out he had a sheet. The sheriff slid that into his remarks."

I frowned, trying to put a record together with the quiet-looking man I'd pulled from the pond. Although I guess we all look quiet in death; I probably will myself.

I tried to invest some enthusiasm in my thanks before hanging up—Protheroe hadn't had to call me, after all.

What had Whitby been doing at the Larchmont estate to begin with? Did the sheriff, or even the New Solway police, care about that question? If the magazine wasn't saying, did that mean they didn't know, or that they wouldn't tell? Maybe Marcus Whitby was thinking of buying Larchmont. Or writing a story about it for *T-Square* magazine. Or perhaps some wealthy black entrepreneurs had moved onto Coverdale Lane, and Whitby was doing a piece on what it was like to own the house that your mother could only enter as a housekeeper.

Catherine Bayard could shed light on all these speculations. I needed to talk to her as soon as possible. I wanted to do it right now, this minute, but it was an interview I'd need my best wits to handle; the only thing I was smart enough to know right now was that I couldn't corner a slippery teenager in my present condition.

Instead, I returned to Nexis and looked up Marcus Whitby. He owned—had owned—a house at Thirty-sixth and Giles, where he was the property's sole occupant. No spouse, no lover, no tenant to share the mortgage.

I looked up the address on my city map. Bronzeville. The part of Chicago where blacks had been confined when they first started migrating to the city in large numbers after the First World War. After decades of deterioration, the block where Whitby had bought was making a comeback. Black professionals were buying what are some of the most beautiful homes in Chicago and restoring the stained glass and ornate woodwork, returning them to the glory they had when Ida B. Wells lived there. Whitby had borrowed a hundred thousand from the Ft. Dearborn Trust to move into twenty-seven hundred square feet. Of course if he was thinking of buying Larchmont, he'd need about eighty times that.

I logged off and stared at the disarray that had built up on my desk and worktable in the short time since Mary Louise had quit. I hadn't needed Christie Weddington from my answering service to remind me that Mary Louise's resignation had left me with a pressing problem. Mary Louise had brought organizational gifts to my operation, along with eight years' experience—and contacts—from the Chicago police force. She'd only been working for me while she went to law school; now she'd taken a full-time job with a big downtown firm. I'd interviewed a number of people but hadn't found anyone yet who had both the street smarts and the organizational skills to take her place.

It hadn't been a problem the last few weeks, because I'd been so lethargic I wasn't generating a lot of business. On a day like today, when I was under the weather and clients were getting cranky, I realized I'd better put serious time into finding someone new. Papers on Mary Louise's old desk, on mine, filing so far in arrears I wasn't sure I could bring myself to start on it.

At least I'd better not just toss papers about this situation onto Mary Louise's work space—that's what I'd been doing with my other open investigations. I dug a hanging folder out of the supply closet and set it up the way she would have, labeled "Larchmont," subfolders for Darraugh and his mama, for Marcus Whitby, for Catherine Bayard. Stapled to the front, a time sheet. As long as Darraugh was paying me, I'd keep working.

7

No Rest for the Sick

Before shutting down my system for the day, I opened my message from Morrell. It wasn't as much of a treat as I'd hoped.

> Darling, I'm sorry it's been so long, but my phone isn't working. I'm borrowing a hookup through Giulio Carrera at Humane Medicine, so I don't know when I'll be able to get back to you again. I love you, I miss you, I wish you were here with me—it would be a help to have someone on my wavelength. I'm doing a tricky investigation, won't say more on an open line, but it's not physically dangerous, scout's honor. Giulio and I don't go anywhere alone—we've made friends with some

local toughs who seem to know their way
around both literally and metaphorically,
so don't worry, darling, although it may be
a week before I can get back to you.

His e-mail left me feeling hollow and
lonely—irrationally, I suppose—he wasn't
any further away now than he'd been ten
minutes ago. But a week before he could
write again . . . somehow the hopeful anxiety of thinking each day might be the one
with the message that he was coming home
was better than knowing there would be no
message at all.

"Okay, Penelope, time to start weaving
that tapestry," I muttered—and realized that
underneath my loneliness, I felt a spurt of
anger—toward Morrell, and also myself. I
was acting like the woman of tradition, home
alone and anxious, while my hero lover wandered the globe seeking adventure.

"That is *not* the story of my life," I croaked
loudly. "I do not sit around waiting, for you
or any person, Morrell."

I called up my phone log again, determined to work my way through the whole
backlog before I left my office. I returned a
dozen calls from reporters who had learned

I'd found Whitby's body, and even got back to Murray.

By then my cold and my sore legs made me long for bed, but in the end I decided to make one last call. A maid answered Geraldine Graham's phone. "Madam" was resting. I was Ms. Warshawski? "Madam" wanted to speak to me.

When Geraldine Graham's high flutey voice came on, I croaked out my name.

"Are you ill, young woman? Is that your excuse for not returning my phone calls sooner?"

"I return calls as I have time, Ms. Graham. I did speak to Darraugh this afternoon, since he's my client. Did he tell you what happened at Larchmont last night?"

"Young woman, I know what happened, since I had a visit from an extremely impertinent policeman this morning. He called himself Schorr; I should think it would be 'Boor.' I was seriously annoyed that you had not seen fit to advise me of what happened in my pool last evening."

"The Larchmont pool, ma'am. By the time I finished with the police myself and reached home, it was four in the morning. I doubt whether even someone of your restless sleep habits would have welcomed a call then—even if I'd had the stamina to make it. Which I didn't."

When that answer seemed to stop her, I asked what Schorr had wanted. I kept my eyes shut, massaging my sinuses.

"That a Negro man had drowned there. He wondered if it was someone who used to work on the estate, but we have had no Negro employees during the last twenty years. And I don't believe I ever saw one working there after I sold Larchmont. Mexicans, yes, but no Negroes. This Boor, or Schorr, showed me a photograph, but the man's own mother wouldn't have known him from it. Who was he?"

"A journalist named Marcus Whitby. I don't suppose he wanted to interview you?"

"About what, young woman? Journalists lost interest in me after my marriage. I haven't talked to one since then, not even during a time when I might have had something newsworthy to tell them. Was this man using the Larchmont attics for some purpose?"

"It's possible." I wondered what newsworthy events she'd concealed. "It's hard to know how he would have bypassed the security system."

"What's that? You have to speak up, young woman: you are not speaking clearly. My hearing is not sufficiently acute to understand mumbling."

I made a face at the phone. "This is as good as I can do tonight, Ms. Graham. We'll talk later in the week when I feel better."

She tried to bully me into coming out to New Solway to see her in person, but I deflected that as well. And what should she do if she still saw the lights in the attic?

"Call the cops, ma'am. Or that nice young lawyer who handles your affairs." I squinted, conjuring up his face, his name. "Larry Yosano."

"What? Who? I know no such person. Julius Arnoff handles my affairs, as he has done for decades."

Lebold, Arnoff, that was the firm on Larry Yosano's card. Naturally Geraldine Graham only dealt with principals. I said "Yes, ma'am" and took my aching head home. Mr. Contreras came out into the hall, scolding almost before he had his front door open: how come I went out in this weather as sick as I was, and without letting him know; he hoped I hadn't turned my cold into pneumonia.

Ordinarily his monitoring of my comings and goings sets up my hackles, but tonight I was weary down to my bones. His concern was a comfort, giving back an illusion of childhood with a mother whose scolding conceals affection and the promise of protection. I agreed to stay put for the rest of the night, agreed to wrap myself in a blanket—an afghan—on the couch while he brought supper up to my place.

We ate spaghetti and meatballs with the dogs at our feet and watched the nine o'clock news on Channel 13 to see how the DuPage sheriff would spin the Whitby story. We had to sit through a report on terrorism first, this time on some Egyptian immigrant who'd disappeared before the FBI could question him about his links to Al-Qaeda.

A reporter I didn't recognize explained that the man was a seventeen-year-old dishwasher whose visa had expired.

"Benjamin Sadawi came to Chicago from Cairo two years ago to learn English and to try to find a better job than he could at home. He lived with his uncle's family in Uptown, but, when his uncle died, his aunt moved back to Egypt with her children. Sadawi decided to stay here alone. The FBI says the job was a cover, that Sadawi was really here as a terrorist. Our Middle East correspondent spoke with his mother through an interpreter."

"My son is a good boy." A tired-looking woman sat cross-legged on a floor with a dozen people crowding around her. "Since my husband is dead, Benji works hard for me, for his sisters, washing dishes, sending money home to us. When would he have time for meeting terrorists? We only want to have him back safe with us. We worry all the time, but we cannot even come to America to look for him, we have only the money that he sends us to live on."

The anchor switched to an assistant U.S. attorney, who explained that every terrorist had a plausible cover story, and most of them had doting mothers. The anchor thanked him, then said, "Just ahead, a grisly death in one of Chicago's most exclusive suburbs."

I muted the set as a group of frantic beer drinkers began jumping and dancing across the screen.

Mr. Contreras grunted. "Kid is probably hand in glove with those Al-Qaeda thugs. That's why his ma won't come here in person to look for him: she knows as soon as Immigration looks at her passport the cat'll be out of the bag."

"You don't think she's just worried about her son? Morrell did a story last month about reaction in Pakistan to a guy who died out in Coolis prison. He'd been held for eleven weeks without anyone in our government telling his family where he was."

"All I'm saying, doll . . ." Mr. Contreras began. We'd had the same disagreement a few dozen times, ever since the FBI and INS started rounding up Middle Easterners on suspicion of terrorism back in September.

"I know, I know," I said hastily. "Let's hope he's not a terrorist and that he hasn't been kidnapped. Kids do funny things."

I turned the sound back on as a picture of Larchmont Hall filled the screen. Marcus Whitby's death was a made-for-TV story: the wealth and power of New Solway, the deserted mansion, the sinister weed-choked pond. The network had dug up file footage of a charity garden party at Larchmont some twenty years ago. We got to see the meadows when horses had roamed in them, and the formal gardens were in full flower. Well cared for, it had been a beautiful place. Channel 13 contrasted that with a view of the ornamental pool, shot at twilight, with a close-up on the dead carp.

"And here is where Chicago private investigator V. I. Warshawski found Whitby. Channel 13 has been unable to find out what brought Warshawski to Marcus Whitby's side; all we know is that she arrived too late to save him."

DuPage County sheriff Rick Salvi came on as Mr. Contreras was crowing at hearing me mentioned on television. Salvi took most of the juice out of the story by poohpoohing any suggestion that Marcus Whitby had been murdered. "There's no sign of foul play, no gunshot wounds or blows to the head that would have meant someone put him in that pond to die. We talked to the magazine that employed Whitby. They say he wasn't working on any stories that involved New Solway.

"For reasons we'll probably never know, he chose what he thought would be a secluded spot to end his life. If that Chicago investigator hadn't been out checking on the estate, we probably wouldn't have found the body until the next time a caretaker checked the pond, probably not for some months. We were lucky we got to see him while we could still identify the body."

"We heard he had been drinking," someone from Fox said.

"No one could face that water sober," the sheriff said, garnering a laugh.

Channel 13 moved from the press conference to reporter Beth Blacksin talking to Whitby's editor at *T-Square.* An austere-looking man in his fifties with a hatchet-shaped face, he said he wouldn't discuss an ongoing investigation, "even with our colleagues in the media," but none of Whitby's current assignments had a connection to New Solway.

"Marcus Whitby's family lives in Atlanta," Blacksin concluded. "His parents and his sister, Harriet, have come to Chicago to claim his body."

We watched a somber trio—the elder Whitbys and a young woman—arrive at O'Hare. They ducked into a cab as cameras and mikes were thrust at them.

"The Whitbys are utterly shocked by their son's death and insist he was not in any emotional turmoil that might have led him to take his own life. Reporting live from Wheaton, I'm Beth Blacksin, Channel 13."

"Thank you, Beth," the anchor said. "Next, Channel 13's own Len Jimpson is with the Cubs in Tucson. Do they have a prayer going into full workouts this week? Stay tuned."

I had been a Cubs fan for too many years to have any hope; I switched off the set.

"That the pond you was in, doll?" Mr. Contreras said. "Doesn't look like the kind of place a man would choose to drown in. Not if he lived in the city and had this whole great big lake right at his doorstep."

"None of it makes a lot of sense. Unless he was meeting someone out there." I told the old man about Catherine Bayard. "I don't know if she was a source he was meeting or a lover—"

"A lover? Sixteen-year-old kid and a black—" He caught my eye and hastily changed to "and a man that age?"

"Please," I coughed hoarsely. "You're the only person I've told about finding her there. I just learned her name this evening and I am counting the minutes until I can get my hands on her in person. But if Whitby didn't go out to New Solway to see her, what was he doing there? Maybe his magazine will talk to me. I know they've been stiffing reporters, but, after all, I'm the person who found their guy's body."

Mr. Contreras patted my arm reassuringly. "You'll have some bright idea in the morning, cookie: I know you. Right now you need to go back to bed, nurse that cold."

The phone rang as I got up to help him stack the dishes. I looked at the clock: nine-forty. I almost let it go, figuring it was either Beth Blacksin or Murray Ryerson, wanting to talk about the sheriff's report on Marcus Whitby, or, even worse, Geraldine Graham wanting more attention. But what if Morrell—I jumped on the phone before my answering service could pick it up.

"Is this V. I. Warshawski? It is? You sound different. This is Amy Blount."

"Ms. Blount?" I was surprised. Our paths had crossed last summer: she had a Ph.D. in economic history and had written a book on an insurance company I was investigating. We'd achieved some degree of mutual respect during the course of my investigation, but we weren't friends.

"I'm sorry to call so late, but—Harriet Whitby is with me. We were roommates at Spelman. She wants to talk to you."

"Sure. Put her on." I tried to mask the dismay I felt: I didn't have the energy to talk to the dead man's sister. "Although I doubt I can tell her anything that she hasn't heard from the sheriff."

"She wants to talk in person. It's difficult to explain, and I shouldn't try to do it on her behalf, but, because I know you, it seemed easier for me than her to call you . . . I don't know if you remember, but you gave me your home number last summer."

Of course Marcus Whitby's sister would want to talk face-to-face to the person who found her brother's body. My morning was free; I told Amy I'd be glad to drive down to her Hyde Park apartment if she and Ms. Whitby didn't feel like coming to my office.

"Can we do it now? I know it's late, and I can tell you've got a cold, but she'd like to see you tonight. Before all the funeral arrangements get so far under way that they can't be undone."

I thought longingly of my bed, but I infused what brightness I could into my hoarse bark and said I'd be on my way in short order. Mr. Contreras frowned at me and deliberately rattled the stack of dishes.

Amy Blount heard him. She apologized again for disturbing me so late, but only perfunctorily—she wanted me to see Harriet now. She did, however, offer to bring Whitby's sister to me: Harriet was staying with her parents at the Drake; Amy would drive her up to my place before taking her to the hotel.

When we'd hung up, I managed to shoo Mr. Contreras out of the apartment. He disapproved heatedly of my setting up an appointment this late in the day: I was sick, these weren't people he knew, nothing was so important it couldn't wait until morning.

"You're right," I said. "I'm sure you are, but this is the dead man's sister. She needs special consideration. If you take the dogs downstairs, I can rest for twenty minutes until she gets here."

He huffed and puffed, but when I pulled the blanket up to my chin and stretched out he rattled the dishes out to the kitchen and left.

8

Twinkle, Twinkle, Little Light
(Wonder If You're There Tonight)

A loud knock on my own door jerked me awake forty minutes later. I hadn't heard the bell for the simple reason that Mr. Contreras had been on the watch for my visitors: he let them in and brought them upstairs before they could announce themselves. It's a perennial source of conflict between us, his monitoring of my company. At least the pulse of anger I felt at his intrusion woke me up enough to greet the two women with some show of alertness.

Amy Blount looked much as she had when I last saw her, her long dreadlocks twisted in a bundle behind her head, her expression wary, solemn. She had an arm around the other woman, whose face had the drained, pinched look that follows on loss. We murmured introductions and condolences. While I got them settled on the couch, with herbal tea for Harriet Whitby and me, a glass of wine for Amy Blount, I managed to force Mr. Contreras to return to the first floor. He blurted out a final admonishment, directed at my guests, that I wasn't to stay up late: I was sick, remember?

As soon as he disappeared, Amy began. "When we heard your name on TV, I told Harriet I knew you. We'd been talking over what we could do, because it's outrageous to think Marc committed suicide. He was the most, oh, not optimistic, I wouldn't say that—"

"Hopeful. He was a hopeful man," Harriet Whitby said. "And he knew how much our parents not just loved him, but relied on him to make a difference with his life. You know, he was a Pulitzer Prize finalist for his piece on the Federal Negro Theater Project and he'd won several other awards. He wouldn't do something like this to Daddy and Mother."

I made noncommittal noises. It can be hard, when everyone relies on you, to let them know that you're feeling despair, but I didn't think it would be helpful to suggest that.

"How did you find him?" Harriet asked. "I don't know Chicago at all, but Amy says that mansion where he—he died—is forty or fifty miles away, in some kind of wealthy town most people never heard of."

"Your brother never mentioned New Solway or Larchmont Hall to you or your parents?"

She shook her head. "But he worked on a lot of different stories. If he was doing research, or even if he had a friend out there— we talked once a week or so, but he wouldn't go into those kinds of details, not unless it was something that was becoming, well, a regular part of his life. Did you think he was in danger? Is that why you went out there?"

I told them about Darraugh Graham and his mother, and the family connection to Larchmont. At Harriet's prodding, I told them about finding her brother, hefting him out of the water, trying to revive him. But I didn't mention Catherine Bayard.

I expected them to leave then, but they looked at each other with the kind of wordless communication that old friends or lovers develop. When Harriet nodded, Amy Bount said, "We want you to ask some questions about Marc's death. Mr. and Mrs. Whitby are too shattered to take any action, but we think, well, at a minimum, we want a better answer to what happened to him than the DuPage County sheriff is giving us."

Harriet Whitby nodded again. "It's not that Marc didn't drink, but he wasn't a drinker, if you understand me, and he didn't use alcohol to bolster his courage. What they said on TV was a cruder version of what they told us this afternoon when my parents and I met with them, that he'd been drinking and fallen in this pond and drowned. If he—oh, it's too hard to explain, but nothing about his death makes sense to me. Even if he had wanted to die, which I don't believe for one minute, he wouldn't do it like that. But they're saying that their examination showed he drowned and that he'd been drinking. Would they make that up?"

"No. But they don't do a complete autopsy on every body that comes to them. It's too expensive, and this—your brother—must have looked straightforward to them. They wouldn't do a complete screen for drugs or poison if they'd found traces of alcohol."

Harriet and Amy looked at each other again, and again it was Amy who spoke. "Do you think they could be making that up? The alcohol?"

I frowned, thinking it over. "It seems unlikely. You could get a lawyer to subpoena the medical examiner's report, I suppose. Do you have some reason to think they might make it up?"

"Their general indifference," Harriet said. "We didn't meet the sheriff, just some spokesman. He was polite enough to Mother, but not very interested. They don't seem at all curious about why Marcus was in that place to begin with. They want it to be that he got drunk and—stumbled onto a deserted mansion and drowned himself. Either by accident or on purpose, they don't care which."

"That's what we'd like to know," Amy said. "Why he was out there. And how he really died."

I was curious enough myself to want to take the job, but I had to explain that I couldn't work for free. I hate to talk about money to someone in the shock of bereavement, but I outlined my fee structure: if Harriet Whitby lived on graduate student earnings as Amy Blount did, she might find the bills mounting up faster than she expected.

"That's all right; I'm not like Amy—I was smart enough to get a real job when we left Spelman." She gave the glimmer of a smile. "I can tell you're sick, but if you're going to do this, I need you to start right now."

"Tonight, you mean?" I was startled. "There's very little I can do tonight. Anyone I might have questions for—people who knew him at the magazine, for instance, or his neighbors—wouldn't be available until morning."

"You don't understand," Amy said. "The Whitbys will be collecting Marc in the morning. They want to take him home to Atlanta for the funeral. So if there are any questions to be asked about—about his body—we thought you would know who to talk to even at this hour. I mean, just the idea that he was drunk is so odd it makes us wonder if they did an autopsy at all."

My eyes were swelling and tearing with a weariness that made it hard for me to think. But I suddenly heard the unspoken question in the room: had the DuPage ME given

Marcus Whitby's death a once-over-lightly because he was black, and out of place in wealthy New Solway?

I didn't know anyone in DuPage County, unless you counted the deputy who'd lent me the pants and sweatshirt, and she wasn't in a position to put pressure on the medical examiner to reopen the autopsy. If only he'd died in Cook County, where I know . . .

I got up abruptly and started tossing aside papers on the table I use as a home desk, trying to find my PalmPilot. When it didn't turn up there, I dumped out my brief-case. The Palm was buried in the bottom. I looked up Bryant Vishnikov, the deputy chief medical examiner for Cook County, but of course he wasn't in his office this late at night. It was after eleven now. I hesitated, but finally dialed his home number.

He wasn't happy at being awakened. "This had better be a real emergency, Vic. I'm on duty at six tomorrow morning."

"Nick, do you know the DuPage ME?"

"That is not an emergency question," he snapped.

"This is serious. They have Marcus Whitby's body out there. You know, the man who drowned at one of those big estates near Naperville Sunday night. I found him."

He grunted. "I can't keep up with every corpse you stumble on in the six counties, Warshawski. I have enough trouble with the ones right here in Cook."

I rode over his sarcasm. "I think DuPage only gave him a brief look-see and it's really important that they do a complete autopsy before they release him to the family tomorrow."

"On your say-so?" Vishnikov was sarcastic.

"No, Dr. Vishnikov, on *yours.* The sheriff is saying he was drunk, but it doesn't seem likely. They need to do a thorough exam, see if they've overlooked something."

"Like what?" he growled.

"I don't know. A blow to the head or sternum, or curare in the bloodstream, or—I'm not a pathologist. Anything. Anything that might have made him go into that pond. If he even drowned there. Maybe he died in Lake Michigan and someone carried him out to Larchmont."

"You've been watching too many *Law & Order* reruns. Give it a rest, and let me get back to sleep."

"Not until you tell me you'll talk to the DuPage County ME."

"Do you have any idea—no, apparently not. This is not like calling one of my own colleagues at Cook County. I only know Jerry Hastings very slightly, and if he called me to tell me to go back over a body I'd tell him to go to hell. So that's what I'd expect him to do to me."

"Can't you say you have a body that died in a similar way and you want to compare notes? Or get them to let you look at Marcus Whitby yourself for the same reason?" I started coughing again and had to stop to drink more tea.

"No. What I can do is a private autopsy if the family hires me. If DuPage is releasing the body to them, it's within their rights to make that decision."

I covered the mouthpiece and explained his advice to Amy and Harriet, who frowned in worry. "Mother—she won't agree to that. All she wants is to get Marc away from this place as fast as possible. Isn't there anything else you can do?"

When I relayed that back to Bryant, he said, "Then there's nothing I can do to help you. You want the autopsy, you've got to get the family to release the body to me or someone else who will perform a private exam. Or come up with some compelling reason for Jerry Hastings to revisit the body."

"I need to buy time for an investigation!" I exclaimed, frustrated.

"Look, Warshawski, if the family won't agree to a private autopsy, then you'll just have to let them take the body away in the morning. Speaking of which, the dawn is not far distant. I'm going back to sleep. And you, you start gargling, or your next stop will be one of my slabs—assuming you die in Cook County."

Vishnikov hung up, but just as I was explaining the problem to Harriet he called back. "In my morgue, I'm always having to battle with low-level clerks who lose the paperwork on bodies."

He hung up again before I could speak. I waved a hand at my visitors, urging them to silence, while I frowned over his advice. I only had one possibility. I combed through the papers I'd dumped from my briefcase until I found Stephanie Protheroe's cell phone number.

"I watched the television news tonight," I said when she answered. "The sheriff seemed pretty convinced that Mr. Whitby drowned on purpose."

"We didn't see anything to suggest foul play," she said.

"Deputy, I have Mr. Whitby's sister with me. They were pretty close; she finds it hard to believe her brother committed suicide."

"It's always a struggle for the family," Protheroe said.

"They find his car?" I asked. "Or discover how he got to Larchmont Hall? It's what, about five miles from the nearest train station. Do they have a cab service out there?"

A long pause told me Protheroe realized they had a biggish hole in their solution to Whitby's death. I didn't push on the point.

"Ms. Whitby's hired me to ask a few questions. Ordinarily, I advise the family to get a private autopsy when they're not satisfied with the medical examiner. But the mother only wants to get her son out of Chicago and interred; she won't consent to a tox screen or anything else."

"Then you have a problem, don't you?" Protheroe wasn't hostile, just cautious.

"Of course, if the paperwork for the body got misfiled for three or four days, I might come up with a different reason for why Mr. Whitby was in New Solway than just that he stumbled out there to die. I might find his car. I might find something that would make Dr. Hastings want to reopen the autopsy without anyone looking bad."

"And why should I risk my career on this?" Protheroe demanded.

"Oh, because I think you went into law enforcement for the same reason I did: you care more about justice than jelly dough-nuts."

"Don't knock jelly doughnuts. They've saved me more times than my Kevlar vest." She broke the connection.

"Will the person you just talked to help?" Harriet said anxiously.

"I think so. We won't know until your mother tries to claim your brother's body to-morrow."

Amy Blount looked at me with respect: I had a feeling she hadn't expected me to come through for her. "We should let you get to bed. Did you get sick from trying to rescue Marc?"

"It's just a cold," I said gruffly. "Who can I talk to tomorrow who might know what Mr. Whitby was working on, or what might have taken him out to New Solway? Did he have a girlfriend, or any close men friends here?"

Harriet rubbed the crease between her eyes. "If he was dating anyone in a serious way, it was still too recent for him to have told me or Mother. His editor is a man named Simon Hendricks; he would know what Marc was working on—if he was writing for *T-Square.* Marc did freelance stuff, too, you know. As for his friends, I can't think right now. I know his college friends, but not his Chicago ones."

"I'll start with the magazine in the morning," I said. "And maybe I can ask your mother about his friends?"

She gave another fleeting smile. "Better not—Mother would be terribly upset to find out I'd hired you."

I stifled a groan: this meant the second client in a week where I had to tread lightly between mother and child. "What about your brother's house? Can you get in there, do you think? We might find some notes or something. I looked in his pockets, hoping for some ID, and he didn't have any keys on him. It hadn't occurred to me until I was talking to the deputy just now, but there weren't any house keys or car keys, unless maybe those fell out of his pockets into the pond."

Harriet turned in bewilderment to Amy. "Then—but his car—I didn't think about that."

"What did he drive?" I pulled a notebook out of the heap on the table. "A Saturn SL1? We'll see if he left it at his house."

Amy volunteered to find a lawyer or someone else who might have a spare key to Marcus Whitby's house. I didn't say I could get past the lock myself if need be: I'd save that parlor trick for when I had to use it. Mentioning the search I'd made of his pockets made me remember the matchbook and pencil I'd found. I'd tossed them in a bowl by the front entrance when I took Catherine's teddy bear out of my pockets. I went back for them and showed them to Harriet and Amy.

Water had gummed the matchbook into a solid mass that wouldn't open. The cover had originally been some shade of green. Water had turned it blackish, and whatever the logo had been, it now looked like a child's amorphous picture of a star. The cover didn't have an address or phone number. I might be able to get a forensics lab to open it to see whether Whitby had written something on the inside. The pencil was an ordinary number 2 with no names stamped on it.

Harriet turned the matchbook over in her hands. Neither she nor Amy had any idea where it was from, but Harriet wanted to keep it, as the last thing her brother had touched. I looked closely at both the matchbook and the pencil again. They weren't going to tell me anything. I handed them over to Harriet Whitby.

When I'd ushered them out, I was utterly beat. I steamed myself for a few minutes in a hot pot of my mother's invention—herbal tea, lemon, ginger—and crawled into bed, where I fell at once down a hole of sleep. The phone dragged me out of it at one in the morning.

"Is this V. I. Warshawski?" the night operator from my answering service demanded. "We've gotten a phone call from a Mrs. MacKenzie Graham. She says it's an emergency and insisted that we wake you."

"Mrs. MacKenzie Graham?" I echoed, bewildered: I knew Darraugh's son, MacKenzie, and didn't think he'd gotten married. Then I remembered through the fog of sleep that MacKenzie had also been Darraugh's father's name. I switched on a light and fumbled around on the nightstand for a pen.

When I had Geraldine Graham's number, I was tempted to make her wait until morning. But—I'd found a dead man in her childhood pond Sunday night. Maybe someone was making a habit of tossing bodies there and she was watching them do it again. I dialed the number.

"I want you out here at once, young woman." She sounded as though she thought I was the night chambermaid.

"Why?"

"Because it's your job to discover who is breaking into Larchmont. You didn't find them last night, but they are here right now."

"What are you seeing?" I croaked hoarsely.

"What is that, young woman? Don't grumble at me."

I tried to clear my throat. "What are you seeing? People? Phantom lights? Cars?"

"I'm seeing the lights in the attic. Didn't I tell you that? If you come right now, you'll find whoever it is red-handed."

"You need to call the cops, Ms. Graham. I live more than forty miles from you."

She brushed the distance aside: the cops had proved how useless they were; she hoped I wasn't going to be similarly ineffectual.

"If someone is using Larchmont as a dump for dead bodies, you need to get the local cops there at once. Me arriving ninety minutes from now would serve very little purpose. If you'd like me to call them for you, I can."

She took my offer as a face-saving out. "And what is your direct number, young woman? I'm tired of relaying messages to you through your help. They're not cooperative."

"They're your best chance of reaching me, Ms. Graham. Good night."

I didn't want to call Stephanie Protheroe again: one favor a night is all I expect from anyone. I finally remembered the young lawyer on emergency duty for the rich and famous. I found his card with a pager number and beeped him. When he called me back ten minutes later, he was as groggy with sleep as I was, but he agreed to get someone from the New Solway police to drive over to Larchmont.

"Will you let me know what they find?" I asked. "I'm working for the Graham family, you know."

"It's a strange life, isn't it," he said, "responding to the demands of the very wealthy. I don't think I've ever heard a lawyer joke that covered that aspect of our work."

While I waited, I made myself another pot of herbal tea. My mother had brought me up to believe one drank coffee as a matter of course, but tea only in illness. I took it into the living room and drank two cups, idling away the early morning by watching Audrey Hepburn stare wistfully at Gregory Peck. All the time I looked at Hepburn's doelike eyes, I kept wondering whether the New Solway police would catch Catherine Bayard breaking into Larchmont Hall.

After an hour, Larry Yosano called me back. "Ms. Warshawski? I went over with the New Solway police, and we didn't see anyone. We made a circuit of the house and the outbuildings and didn't notice any breakage; the security company confirms that no one has tripped an alarm out here. We double-checked the pond: you'll be glad to know there aren't any new bodies there. Maybe Ms. Graham confused lights in the attic with the traffic going by on Coverdale Lane."

I felt absurd, breathing a sigh of relief. I saw nothing but shoals ahead in talking to young Catherine Bayard, but I was still happy that if she was the person Geraldine Graham had seen at Larchmont Hall, she'd finished whatever she was doing before the cops arrived.

Ice Cube Editor

When I woke again the sun was bright in the sky. I, on the other hand, was stiff and congested; when I tried my voice, I sounded more like Sam Ramey than Renee Fleming. I stumbled out of bed and into my clothes, but the late night with Harriet Whitby and Amy Blount—followed by Geraldine Graham's demands—had knocked out any reserves I had. I was too hoarse even to make phone calls. Finally I gave in to the luxury of a day off. I played tapes of my mother's old concerts, listened to Leontyne Price sing Mozart, and ate soup that Mr. Contreras brought in from the market.

On Wednesday, I was still snuffling, but finally had enough energy to get back to work.

I'd slept too late to catch young Catherine Bayard at home. So I could find out whether to waylay her at home or at school, I called the Vina Fields Academy, pretending I was part of the Bayard mansion's staff. The director's secretary answered.

"Did Catherine Bayard get to class on time this morning? We had to drop her at the train, and I don't think she caught the early one," I said in my basso profundo. "I promised her I would explain to the school if she was late."

They put me through a few hoops—protection for their students, since a school full of wealthy kids is a target for kidnappers. The sketchy data about the Bayard household I'd garnered from Nexis was enough to convince them to tell me she'd arrived late for algebra. I didn't push my luck by asking what time Catherine's school day ended: at least she was in Chicago, within relatively easy striking distance.

My day off left me fit enough to do a complete set of exercises, stretching my tight muscles, working up a modest sweat with my weights, and finishing by taking the dogs on a short jog around the neighborhood. ("You be sure you're bundled up, cookie, you get a chill on top of that cold, it could turn real serious," Mr. Contreras once again adjured me.)

When we got back, I did feel better. It's sometimes hard to believe that motion does you more good than bed; I hoped my looser muscles would get me through the day.

Lotty Herschel called to remind me we were having dinner together tonight: we have a standing date once a month to make sure we don't lose track of each other. "Yes, I can hear you're under the weather, my dear, but I see more germs in an hour than you could possibly shed on me, so unless you're too unwell to go out come and have some company to cheer you."

Her dry, wry concern was a good tonic. I dressed quickly, in a green-and-black-striped trouser suit that I liked: it was professional but had a bit of style in the jacket waist.

Down at my office, I started my calls with one to Darraugh, so I could report on his mother's early morning alarm. Darraugh was in New York, but his assistant said she would make sure he knew the sheriff's deputies hadn't found any signs of a break-in. She added that they'd already heard twice from Ms. Graham ("She wasn't sure you understood the urgency of the assignment, but I assured her that Mr. Graham has full confidence in your abilities.")

"I can't get a handle on what Marcus Whitby was doing out there," I told Caroline. "Jerry Hastings, the DuPage County ME, only did a superficial autopsy. It would be helpful if we could pin down the cause of death more exactly than drowning—if we could even make sure Marcus Whitby drowned in that water. Do you think Darraugh would be willing to call Dr. Hastings? Hastings won't respond to a Chicago PI, but—you know how the world goes. Darraugh's family has been prominent in DuPage for a long time."

"I'll mention it to him when we next talk," Caroline promised.

I next phoned Harriet Whitby at the Drake. I explained that besides trying a strategy to buy time on the release of Marc's body, I was also trying to get someone to push on the DuPage ME to do a more complete autopsy.

"In case neither of these ideas pan out, you should get your mother to agree to a private autopsy."

"I guess I can try," she said, without a lot of enthusiasm. "What else will you be doing?"

"I'm going over to Llewellyn Publishing, see if they'll tell me what your brother was working on when he died. They've been stonewalling the press, but they might tell me since I'm working for you. I'm going to be in motion all day; take my cell phone number so you can call me if you need to—especially if Amy finds someone to let us into your brother's house. How long will you be in town?"

"It all depends on Mother," she said. "If I can persuade her to slow down . . . but she'd like to hold the funeral on Friday or Saturday."

I offered to talk to her mother myself, but Harriet still didn't think that would be a good idea. "It's not as if there's any evidence of, well, that there was anything wrong, except for him being out there to begin with. Unless you find something concrete, she's not going to listen. She's determined to believe it was a tragic accident." She let out a harsh squawk of a laugh. "Maybe I'm just doing the opposite, pretending he didn't die for no reason at all."

"Let's not worry about your motives right now," I said gently. "The questions you're asking deserve answers."

Before going to Llewellyn Publishing, I wrapped up the work I needed to do on my three small jobs. I also looked up Marcus Whitby's previous work. His stories for *T-Square* had centered on African-American writers and artists: Shirley Graham, Ann Perry, Lois Mailou Jones, the Federal Negro Theater Project of the thirties. He had detailed the rise, fall and current resurgence of Bronzeville—the South Side neighborhood where he'd bought a house—as a way of showcasing Richard Wright's Chicago years. Whitby had occasionally written for *Rolling Stone,* and had done a recent piece on a young black writer whose first novel had made a big splash a year or so back. About ten years ago, Whitby wrote a biting essay on his arrest and imprisonment during an antiapartheid demonstration in Massachusetts. So that was how he'd picked up a sheet: he didn't have any other arrests on his record that I could see.

Before I could get out the door, Murray Ryerson phoned, hoping I knew something about Whitby that hadn't been in any of the official material.

"He had on an Oxxford suit," I said helpfully. "I think the shoes were Johnston & Murphy, but I'm not a hundred percent sure."

"So he was a conservative dresser. He wrote hip and dressed square. Anything else?"

I thought a long minute. Pros, cons. "The DuPage medical examiner seems to have given the body a lick and a promise. Some people are wondering if they would have been as cursory if Whitby had been white."

"What people?" Murray was on it like a flea on a dog.

"Unnamed sources," I said primly. "A client I won't reveal. Anyone been able to find out what he was working on at *T-Square*?"

"They've got a lockdown at Llewellyn. The editor, Simon Hendricks, he's the guy with a face like a tomahawk if you were watching last night's news, if you try to ask him anything he chops you off at the knees for violating editorial integrity."

I hoped that didn't apply to an ambassador from the dead man's family, but it definitely meant going in person with a note instead of facing the runaround of voice mail. I checked my e-mail one last time, even though I knew Morrell had said he'd be out of touch for a week. And of course the new messages in my in box were either spam or business related.

An old lover of Morrell's, an English journalist, was also in Afghanistan. Morrell traveling with Susan Horseley—I tried to put that thought out of my mind. What did Penelope really do those twenty years that Ulysses was sleeping with Calypso and fighting the Cyclops? Only a man would imagine she spent it all weaving and unweaving. She probably took lovers, went on long trips herself, was sorry when the hero came home.

I locked up and headed south to the trendy stretch of land developers like to call River North. Llewellyn's building was an eight-story cube, built when the streets west of the Magnificent Mile were a no-man's-land between the Cabrini Green housing project and the Gold Coast. Land was cheap then, and it was also spitting distance from both the river and the expressways—valuable for a publisher needing to bring in tons of paper every week.

Nowadays, the old warehouses hold chichi art galleries, while high-rise condos filling the vacant lots dwarf Llewellyn's cube. The boom has also made parking a supreme hassle. I finally found a meter several blocks west of the building.

Llewellyn's lobby was as spare as the exterior. All it held was a waiting area with beige-upholstered chairs, and a high horseshoe counter where a receptionist sat. No art, no glitz, only a photograph of Llewellyn himself hanging in the waiting area relieved the monotony. A uniformed guard lounged between the receptionist and modest elevator bank, although the receptionist was built on a massive enough scale to stop an intruder without help from the guard. She frowned majestically when I identified myself and said I was hoping to see Mr. Simon Hendricks.

"And do you have an appointment?"

"No, but—"

"He's not taking any unsolicited interviews."

"I have a note for him. Can you send that up, please?"

She took the envelope from me and opened it—even though it was sealed and addressed to Hendricks. I'd kept it simple:

Dear Mr. Hendricks,

I am the private investigator who found Marcus Whitby's body at Larchmont Hall on Sunday night; I got him out of the water and tried to give him CPR. His sister, Ms. Harriet Whitby, has hired me to investigate his death. I'd like to know if Mr. Whitby was working on something that took him to New Solway on Sunday.

V. I. Warshawski

When the receptionist had read it—taking her time, as if hoping to goad me into some display of impatience that would allow her to throw me out—she made a call on the house phone, speaking too softly for me to overhear. She mutely nodded me to a seat in the lobby. I sat on the scratchy beige upholstery, hoping my message was persuasive enough to open doors closed to Murray's aggressive style.

After a wait long enough to let me read most of the January issue of *T-Square,* which was on a small table with current copies of the other magazines in the Llewellyn Group, a woman got off the elevator and came over to me. She was about six feet tall, as lean as a whippet, wearing skintight turquoise leather and high-heeled boots that added another three inches to her height. The shiny turquoise made my striped suit look dowdy and conventional.

The woman didn't sit down, so I got up. It isn't often I feel like a shrimp, but my eyes just about connected with her breastbone. She ignored the hand I held out as I smiled and introduced myself.

"I'm Mr. Hendricks's assistant. What is it you're hoping to get out of a meeting with him?"

I let my hand drop, and spoke with a phony sincerity more grating than outright hostility. "I'm so sorry your receptionist didn't let you read my note. I'm a private investigator; Marcus Whitby's sister has hired me to find out how and why he died. It would be helpful to learn what he was working on these days that took him out to New Solway."

She curled her lip in disdain. "And for proof you offer—?"

I pulled the laminate of my investigator's license from my wallet. She looked at it, but told me she wanted proof that Harriet Whitby had really hired me.

I pulled out my cell phone and called the Drake. Harriet wasn't in her room, but when I rang the senior Whitbys I found the client with her mother. She answered cautiously, trying not to give herself away to her mother.

"I'm at the publishing company right now, Ms. Whitby. One of the secretaries wants to make sure you've really hired me, that I'm not using your name as a smoke screen for infiltrating Llewellyn Publishing. Can you talk to her?"

"I guess so, but I can't really, that is, well, let me see what I can do," Harriet stammered.

The assistant was frowning mightily, but she took the phone from me and had a terse conversation with my client. At the end of it, she gave me back my phone. "I'll talk to Mr. Hendricks about it."

She clicked over to the reception desk in her high heels and picked up the phone. I followed her over.

"She says she's his sister . . . No, I don't . . . all right, I'll tell her." She hung up and turned to me. "Mr. Hendricks wants some proof that we were really talking to Harriet Whitby."

By now we had drawn a small crowd—the guard and two people who had been on their way out of the building joined us at the reception counter. They weren't saying anything, but secret smiles and nudges showed Hendricks's assistant that she was putting on a good performance.

I leaned against the countertop, my eyes hot. "Are you seriously suggesting that this grieving woman leave her mother's side to produce a photo ID for you? Is there some scandal about Marcus Whitby that you're trying to hide? Did the magazine send him out to New Solway to die?"

The assistant's plucked eyebrows rose in great semicircles. "Of course not. We're only trying to protect our own privacy."

"Then take me up to Simon Hendricks now. If he knows anything about Marcus Whitby's death, the sooner he tells me the sooner I can help the Whitby family take their dead son back home for the funeral."

"That's right, Delaney," one of the onlookers said. "Stop horsing around and take the woman up to Simon."

Several others in the group echoed the sentiment. Delaney hesitated, but realized the group's mood had shifted against her. She stalked to the elevator, telling me over her shoulder to come with her. I followed her to the editorial offices on the sixth floor.

Trackless Desert

Hendricks himself was as bleak in person as he'd seemed on television Monday night. He didn't smile when his assistant introduced me, didn't change expression when I explained why Harriet Whitby had hired me, didn't as much as blink when I mentioned her concern that DuPage hadn't done a proper postmortem.

"I see, Ms."— he glanced at my card— "Warshawski. So the family believes you can tell them something the police can't? They have actually hired you to conduct this investigation?" He sounded as though it was about as likely as my being asked to pinch-hit for Sammy Sosa.

"Your guard dog here spoke with Harriet Whitby," I said. "And the family believes it, yes, or they wouldn't have asked me to do the job."

He and Delaney both stiffened at the "guard dog" title, but Hendricks merely said coldly, "And what do you expect to learn from Mr. Whitby's current assignments?"

I again went through my song and dance about trying to understand what had taken Whitby to New Solway.

"We'd all like to know that, Ms.—uh. I don't believe it was connected to his work. You spoke to Whitby's sister, Delaney? You're convinced it really *was* the sister?"

Delaney murmured a respectful assent.

Hendricks picked up a sheaf of papers: the busy man interrupted mid-decision. "Mr. Whitby was working on a story on the writers in the Federal Negro Theater Project. You know what that is?"

When I repeated the little knowledge I'd picked up from Whitby's articles, Hendricks curled his lip. "I see. I would have thought the family—but I suppose they know their own business best. Very well, Ms.—uh . . . You're welcome to look at the proposal he gave me, but he hadn't turned in the completed story. Nothing in the proposal would have taken him to the western suburbs. And I don't know of anything else he was working on that would have done so. He did freelance work, but he always cleared such projects with me, to make sure they didn't conflict with anything we were doing here. Delaney, take her out to talk to Aretha. And give her a copy of the proposal."

He returned to the printout in front of him before we'd left the room. When I asked Delaney who Aretha was, she said tersely, "Research assistant and fact checker who worked with Mr. Whitby."

The coldness I was meeting was riling me, and I braced myself for a confrontation with the fact checker. To my relief, Aretha Cummings turned out to be the opposite of Delaney in everything, from her height— about five feet tall in her pumps—through her plump, curvy body, and her warm energy.

"We're all devastated here," she said when Delaney had minced off in her three-inch heels. "Even Delaney, although she won't admit it. She has such a crush on Mr. Hendricks, so she thinks she has to act like him to get him to like her. I could give her a few tips, but she isn't the kind to invite them, and anyway she intimidates me. But I'm glad Marc's sister had the sense to bring someone in to investigate his death. He was a wonderful, wonderful man, a really inspired reporter. He'd had offers from *Esquire* and *Vanity Fair,* but he wanted to stay here. I think sometimes Mr. Hendricks sat on him because he was frightened that Marc would show him up. Not that Marc wanted an administrative job, he loved writing and tracking down sources."

All the time she was talking, she'd been motoring down the hall on her worn pumps, moving as fast as me, even though she took two steps for each one of mine. We passed cubicles and offices, all of them filled with paper. I spied production schedules pinned to different doors, shelves stacked with old issues of Llewellyn publications, reference books, a supply room where a woman and a man were arguing in fierce undertones.

We finally landed in a conference room, barren of everything but a scarred deal table and a couple of folding chairs. "This is where the writers get to meet," Aretha explained. "Nothing fancy for them or for us RAs. The editors have mahogany and a refrigerator and everything, but I can get you a soft drink or coffee from the vending machine."

My throat was dry; lemon soda sounded better than vending machine coffee. While Aretha was out of the room, I read through the proposal Delaney had handed me. The single page assumed the reader knew what the Federal Negro Theater Project was; Whitby was proposing to look at several Chicago contributors—". . . not the well-known Theodore Ward or Shirley Graham, but some who should be as well known, especially Kylie Ballantine. Their stories will be woven into the ongoing history of Bronzeville."

I read it through twice. When Aretha came back, I was studying an erasable board on the wall. It was covered with arrows and bullet points about Halle Berry and Denzel Washington and the upcoming Oscars.

She grinned. "Of course we're sending a couple of writers to the Oscars. I wish one of them was me, I adore Halle Berry. I suppose winning an Oscar is in line with the Talented Tenth, even if it's not the same as the Nobel Prize. We scooped everyone with our stories on Toni Morrison and Derek Walcott."

Oh. *T-Square.* W. E. B. DuBois's Talented Tenth of the Negro Race turned into a celebrity magazine.

"Were you helping Marcus Whitby with his story on the Federal Negro Theater Project? I don't really know much about it."

"It was part of the WPA, see, in the thirties, the federal theater project that FDR set up for out-of-work performers. They were trying to provide work for artists and playwrights, and they had this idea of people's theater. Can you imagine the government today doing something like that?" She grinned engagingly.

"So there was a Yiddish theater, experimental puppets, a lot of different things, including Negro theater, which existed in twenty-two cities, although they were only really productive in three, Chicago and New York, and, for some reason I don't understand, Seattle. So we had Richard Wright and Theodore Ward here in Chicago, they were playwrights, and Kylie Ballantine was a choreographer. Shirley Graham—she was DuBois's wife and a well-known stage director. They did some pretty amazing things—

the *Swing Mikado* was the most famous, but Ward wrote something called the *Big White Fog* about the real state of race relations in this country. Then the Republicans in Congress got freaked, almost like they were today's fossils screaming about the NEA: they claimed the Federal Theater Project was a Communist front and shut it down after only about two years."

"Was it, do you think?" I was curious.

She leaned forward, the brown check of her jacket sleeves straining against her plump forearms. "See, this was when *Gone With the Wind* was published, and everyone—well, a lot of white America—was buying Margaret Mitchell's idea that we were all contented little pickaninnies until the evil Yankees came and ended slavery. There were definitely some fellow travelers in the project, but mostly it was people for some brief time getting a chance to put real theater on real stages, instead of having to do minstrel shows or play mammies and Stepin Fetchit."

"So what was Mr. Whitby's interest? The ideological battles?"

She shook her head so vigorously her short curls danced. "No. Some folks think the NTP—the Negro Theater Project—was just a chance for the white bourgeoisie to exploit black artists, but Marc wasn't interested in the ideological angle. He wanted to follow the Chicago Writers Workshop that a lot of these artists belonged to, to see what happened to them. And he was especially interested in Kylie Ballantine. She was so complex, she danced, she did choreography, but she also was an anthropologist and wrote books on African dance and ritual. She had a studio in her home in Bronzeville. Marc tried to buy her house—he's been hoping to turn it into a museum—had been," she corrected herself mournfully, "but the new owner cut it up into a bunch of little apartments and refused to sell. So Marc bought a place close to hers, then he started a campaign to get her home in the national register of historic buildings. Maybe I'll try to take that over."

She gave a little hiccup and busied herself with her notebook for a minute. I waited until she regained her composure, then asked if she knew how much of Kylie Ballantine's story Marcus had finished.

"It was more like, how much he was cutting it back. He had so much material on

Kylie, he was turning it into a book. The piece for *T-Square* was almost finished. He's been doing occasional pieces on the history of Bronzeville, you see. You know Bronzeville, right?"

I made an apologetic grimace. "Not really. It was the corridor along Cottage Grove Avenue where African-Americans were restricted when they started moving to Chicago in large numbers after the First World War, I think."

"Not exactly," she said, with a friendly smile that made me glad it was she, not Delaney or Simon Hendricks who was educating me. "You're right that we were pushed into that narrow stretch along Cottage on the South Side. But Bronzeville—oh, in some ways it was a state of mind—it included the wonderful mansions on King Drive, you know, a bit west of Cottage—that's where Ida B. Wells lived, for instance, and Richard Wright when he was here, and Daniel Hale, he had a clinic there because even though he did the first open-heart surgery in the world none of the white hospitals would let him practice. But also, because the downtown stores were segregated there was a shopping district around Thirty-fifth Street. No one misses segregation, but it's really sad all those stores and little businesses disappeared."

We were both quiet for a minute, mourning the passing of the little shops, or perhaps the passing of Marcus Whitby.

Aretha gave her curls another shake. "Anyway, Marc was fascinated by Bronzeville. He came from Atlanta, so he had such a different experience—better in some ways, worse in others, but definitely different—and he felt like he had a mission to preserve and record Bronzeville. Then he fell in love with Kylie."

"She isn't still alive, is she?" I asked, startled.

"Oh, no. She died in 1979. But you know how you can be so fascinated by a dead person that they feel really present for you. I used to tease Marc about it, about how I could never—" She dissolved suddenly into tears.

I pulled some clean tissues from the stack I'd packed before starting out today, but didn't try to stop her crying. She'd loved him when he was alive, that much was clear, and now she was likely to have her own dead hero to keep alive.

"It isn't fair. He was so smart and so loving, he didn't deserve to die," she gulped out. "I don't believe he killed himself. I know people like Delaney laughed at me, just the way I laugh at her with her stupid crush on Simon Hendricks, but Marc was different, he was special, he never would have gotten drunk and jumped into a creepy old pond."

"That's what his sister thinks, too—that he wouldn't have done that, I mean," I said when Aretha's sobs had died down and she'd wiped her face. "No, don't apologize. Grief keeps hitting us at unexpected moments, knocking the wind out . . . But do you know why Marc—Mr. Whitby—went out there? Did Kylie have a house in New Solway?"

She swallowed the rest of her Coke. "No, she only ever lived in Bronzeville, except the years she spent in Africa. And she didn't have any family in those western suburbs: I did a search through Marc's notes, because I wondered the same thing."

"Did Mr. Whitby ever mention Calvin Bayard?" I asked.

"Is he in charge of Bayard Publishing? We're not supposed to go to them; Mr. Hendricks is afraid they'll scoop our stories because they own magazines with tons more reporters and money than we have. Marc would have known that." She stopped. "Oh. Does Mr. Bayard live in New Solway? Do you think Marc went out to see him without telling us because he knew it would annoy Mr. Hendricks?"

I shook my head. "At this point, I don't know enough to have theories. But it sounds like one possibility."

"I can look through his notes and see if Marc says anything about Bayard, but he never mentioned, well, either Mr. Bayard, or Bayard Publishing to me."

"Could I see Marc's notes?" I tried not to sound like Peppy with a rabbit in view.

She wrinkled her face up in doubt. "I don't think Mr. Hendricks would like it if I let his stuff leave the building. But I can see what Marc left at his desk if you'll read it here."

I followed her out of the conference room and on down the hall. Like most offices, the floor was laid out in a square around the elevators and bathrooms. We ended up at the corner near where we'd started, at a row of cubicles facing an interior wall. A few people were working at their desks, but most were leaning over the edges of the carrels talking to each other. They stared frankly at me, but didn't interrupt their conversations.

Marcus Whitby's name was on a black plaque two from the end. Unlike most of the other desks I'd seen, his was extraordinarily tidy—no stacks of paper on the floor, no leaning towers of files. I asked Aretha if she'd cleaned up after his death.

"No. Marc was just a neatness freak. Everybody teased him about it." Her voice wobbled but didn't break.

"That's right." A man in the adjacent carrel who'd been talking to his far neighbor leaned in our direction. "Whitby was Mr. Anal Compulsive. You couldn't borrow anything from him if you hadn't returned what you took last week. You his lawyer?"

"No—why? Did he need one?"

The man grinned. "Just a guess. Know you're not with the magazine. Jason Tompkin."

"V. I. Warshawski. I'm an investigator, hired by the family to see how he died. Did he ever mention going out to New Solway to you?"

Tompkin shook his head. "But Marc was a solo operator. Most people here share and share alike—you know, you're stuck, you want an opening, you bring your buddies up to speed on what you're doing. Not Marc. He *owned* his material."

"He was happy to help people," Aretha snapped. "You're just lazy, J.T., and you know it."

Tompkin grinned. "You ought to be a perch, Aretha, you rise faster to the bait than anyone I ever met. But you can't deny Whitby didn't let people in on what he was doing. Simon and he had a few words about it now and then."

"Is that why Mr. Hendricks was reluctant to let me know what Mr. Whitby was working on?" I asked.

Tompkin thought that was funny enough to laugh about, but, when Aretha glared at him, he subsided and returned to his other neighbor. Aretha rifled quickly through a plastic disk holder. "Here's Bronzeville, but I know Marc kept most of his Kyle Ballantine stuff at home. His notes, his notebook—he did stuff by hand—I don't see that. But he probably had that at home, too. A lot of the writers do most of their work at home. Can you imagine trying to work with Jason Tompkin blaring away all day?"

This last was said loud enough for Tompkin to hear, but all he did was laugh again and say, "Stimulation, darling. I was stimulating him, but Marc was too uptight to enjoy it."

I followed Aretha to her own desk. The research assistants and fact checkers were another peg down from the writers: her desk wasn't in a cubicle but one of four put together to make a square. She slipped the disk into her own computer, skimmed through the contents, but said there wasn't anything current on it.

I leaned over her shoulder to study what was on the screen. She brought up the file that showed Kylie Ballantine's history. It was annotated with his sources, mostly private papers labeled "VH"—"The Vivian Harsh Collection at the Chicago Library," Aretha explained. When she realized I was trying to scribble notes off the screen onto my own notepad, she printed out a copy.

"I can also give you the back issues of *T-Square* where he wrote about Bronzeville already. They'll tell you some of the history. There's nothing here about his new story. If his sister has his things, she'll have his notebooks and stuff. Do you think—could you ask his sister—I'd love to have one of his notebooks . . ."

I promised her that as soon as I'd sorted through what he'd left in his house I'd see she got some of his personal papers. I was disappointed, though: I'd hoped for some kind of breakthrough here, or insight. But maybe there wasn't anything to find. Maybe Marcus Whitby had gone to talk to Calvin Bayard—but about what? Blacklisted writers whom Bayard might have known? He hadn't mentioned it because you weren't supposed to go to Bayard about anything. And then he'd gotten lost on his way back to his car. He'd tripped on the loose bricks and fallen to his death. It could have happened.

"Why didn't Simon Hendricks want to let me know what Marc was working on if there isn't anything very secret about it?" I asked Aretha as she waited with me for the elevator.

She shifted uncomfortably. "Oh, corporate stuff, you know . . ."

"Oh." I grinned, suddenly making sense of Jason Tompkin's laughter. "He didn't want a white woman poking around?"

She blushed. "It's not personal. But Mr. Hendricks, well, he came up in the organization when Mr. Llewellyn was still fighting every inch of the way, to get funding, to get distributors, everything. I think he would have expected the Whitby family to hire a different investigator."

As I rode the elevator back down to the lobby, I hoped Hendricks was wrong.

A Child's Garden of Verses

BMWs and Mercedeses stood three abreast on Astor Street as parents and nannies waited to fetch their children from the Vina Fields Academy. Chicago taxpayers were helping out: city cops had blocked off the street and were directing outsiders like me away from the area. I found a sort of legal space on Burton Place and sprinted back, but the students hadn't yet started to emerge.

I was cutting it close because I'd hung around the entrance to Llewellyn Publishing hoping Jason Tompkin would come out for lunch—he hadn't seemed like the type to eat at his desk. After forty-five minutes, when I was about to give it up, he'd emerged with a couple of coworkers. One of them was Delaney, Simon Hendricks's assistant, who frowned when she saw me. The third was the woman Jason had been talking to when I was in Marc Whitby's cubicle.

Jason Tompkin came over to me, tipping the beret he was wearing. "Ah, the special investigator, looking for the X-Files. What can I do for you?"

His voice and smile were without malice; I had to smile in turn. "X-Files is right. I was hoping, since you worked right next to Marc Whitby, you might have heard something—anything—that would explain why he'd gone out to New Solway. Aretha said you all weren't supposed to talk to anyone at Bayard about work in progress, so I did wonder if he'd had a surreptitious appointment with Calvin Bayard."

Delaney said, "Marcus Whitby thought being a star reporter, he could write his own rules. It wouldn't surprise me if he thought he could bypass Mr. Hendricks's orders about this, too."

"And did he?" I asked Tompkin.

"I like to feed the rumor mill as much or more as the next man, but I unfortunately did not hear the ace reporter talking to or about the Bayard empire. He was working on something he thought was pretty hot, that much I can tell you, but he made sure I never heard him actually say anything."

"When did that start? His acting like he had something pretty hot?"

Jason shrugged one slim shoulder. "A week before he died, maybe. He'd started making a lot of calls, started hanging by his phone so he could jump on it when it rang. Being a finalist for the Pulitzer gave him a taste for glory. He kept hoping he'd got that big prizewinning story in his sights."

"Why aren't you supposed to talk to anyone at Bayard?" I asked, wondering if I'd hear the same reason Aretha had given.

"It's our policy with all our big competitors," Delaney said.

"Mr. Llewellyn is the proudest man on the planet," Jason added. "No, Delaney, that's not an insult. It's the truth. The Bayard policy dates from—"

"J.T., just stop it right there," Delaney said. "We don't need to tell every stranger on the street our business, and you know Mr. Llewellyn would say that louder than Mr. Hendricks. You hear?"

Tompkin rolled his eyes expressively, but a glance at his other coworker's frowning face shut him up. Delaney pushed him on the shoulder to start him up the street. I followed after long enough to give all three one of my cards. Delaney let hers flutter to the pavement, but Jason and the other woman tucked them away.

I sprinted back to my car—but not in time to avoid the meter reader. An orange envelope, my chance to give the city fifty dollars, was stuck to my windshield. I swore roundly and drove over to La Llorona for a quick bowl of soup.

So who was Marcus Whitby? The warm, loving hope of his family—and Aretha Cummings—who'd come close to a Pulitzer? The competitive, uncommunicative coworker? The star who thought he could make his own rules?

Huddled up against the restaurant window, away from the noise at the counter, I checked my messages. I had an urgent one from Harriet. When I reached her, I learned that Deputy Protheroe had come through for us: when Mrs. Whitby's funeral director in Atlanta tried to arrange the shipment of Marc Whitby's body, the DuPage ME's office gave them a runaround—they needed a little more time to process the paperwork.

"Mother got so angry I blurted out that you'd done it, to buy more time for the investigation, and then I had to confess that I'd hired you, which made her really furious. I was wishing the floor would open under me when Daddy suddenly said he thought it was a good idea. He never disagrees with Mother about—about, oh, domestic things—so she was completely surprised. And then he kind of put his arm around me and said thank goodness I'd had the gumption to take the bull by the horns, that he doesn't want a slur over Marc's reputation on account of how he died. But—he isn't ready to agree to an—well, to letting someone else look at Marc's body."

Getting her parents to agree to an investigation seemed like the most important first step: I could get going on more ideas, and keep pushing on the independent autopsy. Harriet said Amy Blount hadn't had any luck with locating a key to Marc's house. We agreed to meet there the next morning around nine, whether Amy had found a key or not.

I gulped down the rest of my chicken soup while I scribbled down my other messages, and then hightailed it to Vina Fields. Not that I often visit the Gold Coast, but I'd never really noticed the school before, so carefully was it tucked into its surroundings. It presented the same bland, inward-turning façade as the apartments and homes on the street, pushing outsiders away as firmly as a guard dog. Only a small plaque near the double doors identified the stone building—that and the waiting nest of mothers and nannies clustered at the bottom of the steps. Actually, two men stood in the group, one with a stroller and a toddler, the other with a copy of the *New York Times* tucked under his arm.

This late in the school season, those on foot seemed to know each other, at least by sight. They chatted about their children's triumphs and whether they could sell the tickets for the school play each family had been allotted, occasionally shooting a curious glance my way.

After about ten minutes, the doors opened and children began streaming out. The primary grades left first, in knots of giggling girls, of boys loudly haranguing each other, punching each other's arms, both sets ignoring the children alone, who hunched down in their coats as if already resigned at age eight to life as outsiders. A lot of the boys were in shirtsleeves, their coats slung over a shoulder: hey, we're men, we're too tough for sissy things like coats in winter.

The cars started to pull up, honking and jockeying for curb space, parents screaming invective at each other. A woman with a blond coiffure that spoke of weekly visits to the salon climbed out of her Lexus to yell abuse that would have made a truck driver squirm; the Jaguar in front of her replied with a finger.

The adults on foot were waiting on the young kids—older students living close enough to the school to walk could make their own way home. When the upper grades began to trickle out a little later, I was the lone grown-up still standing by the stairs.

I fingered the ratty teddy bear in my shoulder bag. As time passed, I began to fret that I'd missed my quarry, or that she had lacrosse practice or junior publishers' club. Just as I had decided to take my chances on getting into the Banks Street apartment, Catherine Bayard appeared.

Although she was paler than I'd thought from seeing her by moonlight, I knew her at once. Her mouth was wide and tremulous, her face so narrow the cheekbones almost seemed at oblique angles to her nose. Sleep deprivation had produced violet bruises around her eyes.

She was with two other girls who were expostulating loudly about someone's odd behavior, but Catherine herself didn't seem to be listening to them. Although one was blond and the other Indian, all three looked remarkably alike in their tight jeans and hip-length coats. Perhaps it was the healthiness and confidence they exuded. Or maybe the wealth that showed up in little details, like the diamond studs ringing the blonde's ears and the Indian girl's cashmere cap and scarf.

"Earth to Catherine," the Indian girl said. "Aren't you listening?"

Catherine blinked. "Sorry, Alix. I didn't sleep much last night."

"Jerry?" the blonde grinned suggestively.

Catherine forced a smile. "Yeah. Like Gran wouldn't lose it completely if he came around on a school night."

Just as the trio turned south on Astor I stepped in front of them. "Hello, Catherine. V. I. Warshawski."

The three girls froze, alarm bells of what happens when strangers accost you ringing in their heads loudly enough for me to hear. The one who'd mentioned Jerry looked over her shoulder for help.

"We met Sunday night," I said heartily. "When we both decided to go for a late-night run. You left something of yours with me, remember?" .

"I'll get Ridgeley," the blonde turned back to the stairs.

"No, Marissa, it's okay." Catherine produced another unconvincing smile. "I forgot. I was jogging at midnight and I ran into this woman."

"Jogging? At midnight? You've always said runners were the biggest losers on the planet," Marissa exclaimed.

"Yeah. It's just, you know, the SATs, my grandfather's health, all that stuff, I thought I might work some of it off and I couldn't exactly go out riding in the middle of the night. Anyway, let me find out what this person wants. She seems to think she's in charge of the universe."

"Just a small stretch of Chicagoland," I said, smiling affably. "Where can we talk privately? Banks Street? Or would you like to come to my office?"

"There's a coffee bar on the corner," Catherine said.

"Not quiet enough. My office is just a couple of miles west along North Avenue. Or—maybe you'd like to visit the old Graham estate. You choose."

She shot an unhappy look at her friends, at me, at the school, and finally decided we could go to her apartment. Her friends stood uneasily by, clearly wondering whether it was safe to leave her alone with me. Finally, Alix said forcefully that Catherine had her pager number; she should just beep if she needed help.

"We'll be at Grounds for Delight, like, reading until six or so," the other girl said. "You can catch us there."

We walked down the street together, an awkward foursome, until Catherine's friends turned west at the first cross street. Alix reminded Catherine to beep if she wanted them to call 911.

"I worked for the Bayard Foundation one summer when I was in law school," I said when we were alone. "Before I joined the sex police, I mean. I am one of your grandfather's many admirers; I'm sorry if he's ill."

She turned her head away from me: she was not going to help me.

"I fell into the pond when I was running after you Sunday night," I said. "That's how I caught this cold. But it's also how I found Marcus Whitby."

"Whoever that is. You made your point, you saw me Sunday. Do you really have something of mine, or was that just blackmail to make me come with you?" She kept her head turned away, so that all I saw of her was her left ear. It exposed her youth, that pale shell, and made her seem vulnerable, breakable.

"I really have something of yours. It's how I found you so easily. What I don't understand is why you went back to Larchmont last night."

That startled her into facing me again. "How did you—I wasn't—I was here in town last night."

"Your grandmother will no doubt back you up on that. We'll ask her when we get to your place."

After a pause she said, "You can ask the housekeeper. My grandmother is still at the office. I was in bed before she got home last night."

I nodded. "Is the housekeeper Ms. Lantner? She moves between the New Solway mansion and Banks Street?"

"How do you know all this about my family?" she said. "Where I live and everything? How do I know who you are?"

"You don't. You haven't asked. I'm exactly what I said I was on Sunday: a private investigator. I used to be a lawyer, a public defender. I don't know whose account of me you would trust, but I can refer you to a reporter at the *Herald-Star,* or someone on the Chicago police force. Or better still, Darraugh Graham. I do a lot of work for him. You do know him, right, hanging around his boyhood home the way you do?"

She bit her lip but didn't say anything.

"It would be an excellent plan for you to call one of these people and ask if they know me. You shouldn't trust a stranger who comes up to you on the street. But we're still going to talk, because if we don't, I'm giving your name and phone number to the DuPage County sheriff. Right now I'm the only person who knows you were at the crime scene Sunday night, but as soon as the sheriff learns about you, he will be here with as much force as he can use on the granddaughter of a powerful taxpayer." Of course he'd also be on my butt like a horse-fly for concealing her presence, but I hoped she was too inexperienced to think of that.

"What are you talking about? You think Rick Salvi is going to care that I was tres-passing?"

"It's nice, you knowing the sheriff by his first name and all, but we're not talking about trespassing here. And even if he dan-dled you on his knee when you were a baby, he's going to want to know what you're up to at Larchmont."

"I can't help being born into a rich family, but that doesn't mean I think I have a right to special treatment," she burst out, her eyes bright. "I know if you have a special position you have special obligations."

I nodded. "You don't look much like your grandfather, but you sure sound like him. Your yearbook statement said you hoped to go into the publishing company. Do you do much around there now?"

"I was an intern last summer. I got to work with Haile Talbot, I mean I just brought him coffee—" She broke off, remembering we were enemies, and refused to speak again until we turned the corner onto Banks Street.

I was glad I hadn't tried to talk my way in: her family's town home was in a five-story building, hidden from the street by a high stone wall and a wrought-iron door with opaque safety glass filling the curlicues. A microphone was set into a recess beside the door, where I could have bent over and tried to persuade someone inside to buzz me in.

Catherine unlocked the door and led me across a flagged courtyard. A little garden with a couple of fruit trees and an old stone bench lay on the east side of the building, continuing, as far as I could tell, around to the back. We walked up gray flagstones to the front entrance, also locked, and took an elevator to the fourth floor. No doorman. Catherine could come and go with no one seeing her.

The elevator opened onto what was essentially the apartment's entryway, an area so big I could have set up my office there and no one would have tripped over me for at least a month. We went on through an arched doorway into the body of the apartment.

A middle-aged woman in a maid's uniform came out from some back room. "Oh, it is you, Miss Katerina. And your friend?"

"A business acquaintance, Elsbetta. We'll be in my room."

"You want me to bring tea? Coffee? Juice?" Her English was precise, but her voice was soft and heavily accented, the "esses" slurred the way my father's mother's used to.

"We're fine without anything," Catherine said firmly: I was not a guest, I didn't get refreshments.

"Were you here last night?" I asked Elsbetta.

"Here? Yes, I sleep here."

Catherine looked daggers at me, but she said, "This woman wants to know if I was here also."

"What do you mean, was you—were you—here? Yes, of course you were here. You ate with friends, you came home, at ten-thirty you went to bed, so I also, I then went to bed." Elsbetta turned to me. "When

Mrs. Renee is not here, I stay awake until Miss Katerina is in bed."

Catherine gave a tight, triumphant smile and led me to her room. It was decorated in bold colors, and furnished in a way that would remind you every time you came in that you had been born to special obligations—the Bang & Olufsen TV-stereo for starters, and then the antique armoire and desk, Navajo rugs worn enough to show they dated to the pre–Machine Epoch of Indian work. These lay on a hardwood floor so polished it reflected our legs as we walked across it. Another few were draped across a pair of ottomans in front of the working fireplace.

The room overlooked the back garden. I opened the French doors and looked out on a small balcony. You wouldn't have to be a great athlete, only reasonably confident, to move from the balcony to a fire escape screwed into the brickwork about a yard away.

"So you went to bed at ten-thirty, you waited until Elsbetta's light went out, then you climbed down, went out the back gate and headed for the western suburbs. You have a driver's license, or anyway access to a car. You did your business out at the Larchmont estate, and retraced your steps. Only you were so worn out that you over-slept and missed your algebra class this morning."

She scowled ferociously. "What are you trying to prove, that you can stalk me? You know that's against the law in Illinois."

"Lots of things are against the law here. I'm not stalking you—I'm just a reasonably competent investigator. If I wanted to go to the trouble, I could probably find traces of your clothes on that fire escape: rough metal like that always snags some fibers."

While she tried to think of a response, I went over to inspect the photographs on the mantelpiece. Calvin Bayard and an eight- or nine-year-old Catherine fly-fishing, he with his easy smile, she with her face furrowed in intensity. Calvin with a short dark woman; Catherine with the same woman. Various other family groupings. It wasn't immediately clear which ones were her parents.

"What do you have that's mine?" she de-manded of my back.

"Your little teddy bear. It came off your backpack in my hand when you broke away from me Sunday night."

"Oh. That. You can keep it."

I could see her in a mirror over the mantel. Her little face was pinched with anxiety. She wasn't as unconcerned as she was trying to sound.

"Did you not know Marcus Whitby was dead when you went back last night?" I spoke to the trophies, keeping an eye on her in the mirror.

"What are you talking about?"

"You must have been worried when he missed your rendezvous on Sunday. Or did you just assume I had frightened him off?"

"I don't know any Marcus Whitby, so stop trying to pretend you're, like, Jack McCoy."

I swung around to look at her. "You don't know Marcus Whitby? The man I fished out of the Larchmont pool? You don't know he's dead?"

Her eyes and jaw opened in what looked like genuine bewilderment. "You found a dead man out there? What happened to him?"

"Don't you look at the paper or the news? When you log onto your fancy computer there, doesn't CNN or NBC or something come up to tell you what's happening outside the Gold Coast?"

She stiffened. "For your information, I'm very involved in current events. But that doesn't mean I read about every dead person in the world. Is that why you were at Larchmont? To look for him? Who was he?"

I sat down on one of the ottomans in front of the fireplace and gestured to her to take the other. "Marcus Whitby worked for *T-Square* magazine."

She gave the elaborate shrug of adolescent indifference.

"Black arts and entertainment, middle class." When she continued to mime ignorance, I added, "He wrote a piece on Haile Talbot. I thought maybe that was how you met."

"I don't know him. Marcus whoever, I mean. And I hardly know Haile Talbot. Just because I did PA stuff for him doesn't mean I hung out with him when he did media. He had a publicist who took care of that."

"Then who were you meeting out at Larchmont?"

She bit her lips. "No one. I was there on a dare. You caught me fair and square. Now you can give me my teddy back and go home."

I shook my head. "No. I know you were there again last night, so even if I was gullible enough to believe—"

"And you say you're not a stalker?"

I ignored the interruption. "I told you at the get-go that it was me or the cops. Since you won't talk to me, it's the cops. You were at the scene of a mysterious death, a crime scene, you fled, they will be incredibly interested in you. The good news is they'll only talk to you with your parent or guardian present. So—your dad, your mom, your grandparents—which one of them should I explain this to?"

Her eyes darkened with dismay, but, before she could say anything, someone tapped on her door, and immediately opened it. The short dark woman from the photographs swept in, moving across the room to Catherine like the Wabash Cannonball.

The Wabash Cannonball

Gran!" Catherine jumped and looked from her grandmother to me in alarm. "What are you doing home so early?"

Renee Bayard leaned over to kiss Catherine. She was older than in the mantel photos. Her dark hair was now well streaked with gray, but her skin was remarkably smooth and clear under its light foundation. Her red dress, made from a wool so soft I had an impulse to stroke it, looked as though it had been cut to fit her short, square body. A bracelet of ivory mahjongg tiles clacked when she put her arms around her granddaughter.

"I felt tired of the same meetings churning over the same stale material. I want to get to your school tonight for the parents' meeting on what we can do with all these Justice Department efforts to look at student files, so I thought I'd come home first, have a family supper if you're not already engaged."

Catherine bounced up from her ottoman. "I hope you make all those wusses take action. So many of them are like Marissa's dad, yacking on and on about how it's our duty to cooperate fully, we're in a war situation, ordinary privacy doesn't apply. Like it's never dawned on him what they might find out about his own kid if the school gives them total access to our files. Marissa has—well, never mind. The Feds have been ruthless talking to Leila, since she's from Pakistan. They figure since she's Muslim she must have known Benji, but she's such a snob she's like totally offended they think she'd even talk to a dishwasher. And Marissa's dad, well, how would he like to have the FBI in his files? I bet they'd find stuff like Enron if they only started looking."

"Yes, darling, I know you're ready to get on your horse and raise the siege of Orleans." Renee smiled fondly at her granddaughter. "We can talk about it over dinner. Unless your friend is staying?"

"Oh. Oh. This isn't a friend. It's—" She floundered, unable to remember my name.

I stood. "I'm V. I. Warshawski, Ms. Bayard. I'm a private investigator, although I originally trained as a lawyer."

Catherine made a fast recovery. "I'm doing a story on her. On her work, I mean, for *Vineleaves,* you know, the school newspaper. A lot of kids meet private eyes who've been working on their parents' divorces, but I figure not too many know anything about murder investigations."

If Renee Bayard found her granddaughter's restless manner odd, she didn't comment on it: she was more concerned with me, saying in a voice heavy with censure, "Murder investigations? Why did you seek out my granddaughter?"

Catherine once more leapt into evasive action. "She didn't, Gran. I mean, I called her. I had the idea, and I knew Mr. Graham worked with a lot of investigators, so I called and asked if he could suggest someone."

"Mr. Graham needs a murder investigator?" Renee Bayard persisted, watching me sharply.

"Most of my work involves financial and industrial crime," I said. "But some of my cases have included murders, and that's always sexier to young people than someone shredding company papers to keep their financial fiddles secret."

Renee Bayard gave a little nod, as if to acknowledge that I'd scored a point. "And are you working on something now for Mr. Graham?"

"Just think, Gran, she found a dead man in the pool out at Mr. Graham's old home," Catherine intervened.

"So it was you who found that unfortunate young man," Renee Bayard said to me. "What made you look for him to begin with? Was that what Mr. Graham hired you to do?"

I smiled. "My clients appreciate having their private affairs kept private, ma'am. But I will tell you I found Marcus Whitby completely by accident. I was looking for—something else—and tumbled on him. Literally."

"And you're regaling my granddaughter with this tale?"

"We hadn't got that far. Catherine was more interested in the techniques investigators use for getting information. She shows a remarkable capacity for imagining ways to circumvent the law."

Renee Bayard frowned at me, perhaps because she found my words unacceptably frivolous, or maybe because she didn't want me to encourage her granddaughter's lawlessness: a girl enterprising enough to climb out through her bedroom window and drive off in the middle of the night probably had plenty of other escapades under her belt.

"Do you have any idea how the young man—Whitney, is it?—came to die out at Larchmont? Is there any thought of whether it was an accident or intentional?" Renee Bayard asked.

"Whit*by.* I don't know what the DuPage sheriff is thinking, but Catherine has just been explaining to me that Rick Salvi is an old friend of your family. Salvi might say more to you than he would tell the press."

Renee Bayard cocked her head at Catherine. "Trina, you shouldn't call Sheriff Salvi a family friend. He's a political acquaintance."

She turned back to me. "I know you don't want to reveal client secrets, but are you looking into young Whitney's—no, Whit*by*'s—death? If he was murdered—my husband spends the whole year out in New Solway now."

"We should call the Lantners," Catherine said. "If there's a murderer roaming around New Solway, they need to be on the look-out."

I shook my head. "If Mr. Whitby was murdered, it was more likely by some homeowner out there who resented his presence on their land. I assumed when I found him it was an accident: I assumed he was meeting someone by appointment, and that he tripped on a loose brick by the pool and fell in—because that's how I happened to find him." I broke off to look at Catherine, fidgeting on her ottoman. "Wouldn't it be helpful to take some notes, in case you actually decide to write up our interview?"

"Yes, darling," Renee Bayard agreed. "You should never assume that you will have an accurate memory of what someone has said."

Catherine glowered at me, but went to the work counter built into the far corner of the room and fished a spiral notebook from her backpack.

Her grandmother frowned over what I'd said. "But if he was meeting someone out there, why haven't they come forward?"

"He could have been having an affair with someone who lived out there and was taking advantage of the old Graham house standing empty, although he'd have to have a key to bypass the security system."

Catherine jabbed her pencil through the holes in her notebook and started pulling apart the ends of the paper.

"Is that what you think?" her grandmother asked.

"I did at first, but he didn't have any keys on him, not even his car keys. It's possible they fell into the pond when he went in, but his car wasn't anywhere on the grounds. I suppose the sheriff's police will be finding out how he got there—he could have gone by train." I wasn't hopeful about that—Salvi seemed to want to wrap the story up in a package and be done with it. "After I met with Mr. Whitby's associates at *T-Square* this morning, I did wonder if he'd gone out there to consult your husband."

Ms. Bayard's hand went to her throat in a reflexive gesture of self-protection. "Why would—what made you think that?"

"It was a leap. Mr. Whitby was doing a story on someone in the Federal Negro Theater of the thirties. You probably know they were pilloried in Congress for being Communists. I just thought—if some of Bayard Publishing's writers had been blacklisted, Mr. Whitby might have wanted your husband's inside view on how that affected them."

"Mr. Bayard doesn't grant interviews these days. If a journalist tried to call—well, our staff are very protective. They would have turned him away."

"Then maybe Mr. Whitby tried to pay a visit without an invitation," I said, wondering whether it was Calvin or Renee's decision that he didn't grant interviews. "The *T-Square* staff don't seem to know why Mr. Whitby went to New Solway—unless his editor, Simon Hendricks, does and won't say. Hendricks says they have a policy against talking to anyone at Bayard Publishing."

Renee Bayard smiled faintly. "Augustus Llewellyn muscled his way into becoming a

journalism giant against a great deal of opposition—he was launching *T-Square* about
the time my husband acquired *Margent*
magazine. None of the big banks would
fund a venture by a black publisher. My
guess is that Augustus is simply unwilling to
make the white journalism establishment a
present of one of his reporters' work."

"Didn't Grample help him out?" Catherine
said, continuing to twist the edges of her
notepaper. "I thought he put together the
consortium—"

"Yes, darling, but we're not talking about
your grandfather right now. Why don't you
finish your interview with Ms.—"

I fished a card out of my briefcase.
"Warshawski. If you know Mr. Llewellyn,
do you think he'd be willing to talk to you
about what Marcus Whitby was working
on?"

She gave a grim smile. "The fact that my
husband helped him get financing doesn't
make him an automatic ally of mine, but if I
have time I'll try to call him."

Elsbetta appeared in the doorway. "Mrs.
Renee, excuse me, a man is calling from a
television station. Are you wanting to talk to
him?"

Ms. Bayard cocked her head to one side. "You don't know what it's about, Elsbetta? No?" She brushed Catherine's forehead with her fingertips and steamed out of the room as quickly as she had entered it.

"Your grandmother has a lot of energy," I remarked. "Running a publishing house and looking after you—I couldn't do it."

"No one wants you to," Catherine said. "You can stop bugging me now and go home."

"I think I should give you a tip first. For *Vineleaves.*" I sat down again, facing her. "You told your grandmother a lie about Darraugh Graham and—no, don't interrupt—it's one she can easily check. The two of them know each other; when she asks him if he referred you to me, Darraugh will be astonished and he won't bother to hide it."

She flushed. "You could ask him to say I had called."

"Why would I want to do that for a girl who's been lying to me and stiffing me? I admit I terrified you by tackling you Sunday night, but I still don't know why you were at Larchmont Hall the same night that Marcus Whitby died there."

"It was a coincidence," she muttered. "Can't you believe that?"

"Not really. You're a pretty accomplished liar—your grandmother, who's known you your whole life, believes what you're saying." In the background behind us the phone kept ringing, and then the doorbell.

Catherine's mouth set in a mutinous line. "I did not know this man was out there dead. And I never heard of Marcus Whitby, just because he was on the local news, which I don't watch. And I am not the person he was meeting out there."

"So who were you meeting at Larchmont?"

"That isn't any of your business. Believe what you want, be with the sex police if you want, I'm not going to tell you." Panic was rising in her voice.

"There is someone in the old Graham house. And you know a way in that doesn't trigger the alarms. What is it, I wonder?"

"You're wrong, there's no one in the house. If old Mrs. Graham thinks there is— she's almost a hundred and she can hardly see."

"She's not blind, she's just nearsighted, and she's by no means deranged. And after talking to her, and talking to you, well, if she said your hair was green, I'd believe her before I believed you telling me it was brown."

I paused, hoping she'd blurt out something—her flushed, turbulent face showed she wasn't used to being called a liar. After a moment, I went on.

"You wouldn't have to meet a boyfriend there. As clever as you are about jumping out of fire escapes, if you wanted to see someone your grandmother didn't like you'd find an easier way to do it, unless there was a thrill attached . . . Is that how you get into Larchmont? You shinny up a drainpipe or something to reach a third-floor window that doesn't have the alarm system wired to it?"

"No. Is that what you would do?" She had her arms crossed, the very portrait of a hostile teenager, but it felt to me more like a pose than a real act.

"Whoever you're meeting, you don't want your grandmother to know, because you tap-danced your way mighty fast past anyplace where she'd ask a question. She's obviously proud of you and your strong beliefs. I guess I'd have to find out what would hit her the wrong way. I can't imagine drugs, since even if you were a user you'd have an easier place to score than that." I got to my feet. "It's a puzzle, and puzzles make me curious, even when they aren't my business. When they may be—and I don't have any way of knowing this one isn't—well, then I keep digging."

Catherine scrunched up her face. "One night last summer when I couldn't sleep, I saw my grandfather going through the woods. I followed him and he was going over to Larchmont—that was after the nounous moved out. I don't know why he had a key, I guess from when the Grahams lived there and they were all good friends, but he was letting himself in. And—and I went in after him. So Sunday when I couldn't sleep I went in to his room to see if he was sleeping—Gran had gone back to Chicago because she had an early meeting Monday, but my first class wasn't until ten. Anyway, Grample, my grandfather, wasn't in his room, so I just thought I'd go see if he was over at Larchmont. It's a private place to talk. Out at our house, you know, someone on the staff is always around and it's hard to be private."

"Right." I smiled affably. "And last night when you couldn't sleep, you drove out to Larchmont to find your grandfather and talk to him. Privately, I mean."

Her flush deepened, but before she could say anything, Renee Bayard sailed back into the room. "Trina, something unexpected happened: Olin Taverner has died and the local television stations want to talk to me. I don't know how long it will take, so we won't be able to have dinner together. Elsbetta will lay something out for you in the kitchen."

"No, I want to hear you do your stuff, Gran. I hope he was writhing in agony."

Oh. Olin Taverner. He'd been senior counsel to Walker Bushnell, the Illinois congressman who'd been HUAC's point man in going after Calvin Bayard all those years ago. Catherine had presumably grown up on tales of him as the family villain.

Renee put her hands on her granddaughter's shoulders. "Darling, you absolutely must not say that in public. And in public includes in front of strangers. We rise—"

"Above these things so that no one can tell from our public face that they matter to us," Catherine finished in chorus with her.

"It's okay," I said. "I admired your husband's work so much that after he spoke to my Constitutional Law class, I got a job as an intern at the Bayard Foundation."

Renee ignored me, telling her granddaughter that she was going over to Channel 13 to do a segment for their post–news discussion show, *Chicago Talks.* "You can sit in, but you cannot butt in. Do you understand, Trina? It's very important."

"Don't worry, Gran. Even if you start saying that Olin Taverner was a well-respected member of the bar, I won't barf or anything on camera."

"You need to show your guest out: I have to leave for the studio in ten minutes. I told them it was now or never, because I'm determined to get to the parents' meeting at Vina Fields."

"We were done anyway, Gran." Catherine hopped up from her ottoman.

"That's right," I smiled again, holding out my card. "You need my address, though, as well as my name and phone number, so that you can follow up on your

interview. And send me a copy of the finished piece."

"Yeah, sure," Catherine mumbled, shoo-
ing me down the hall before I could say anything else in front of her grandmother.

Quicksand?

I left the Bayard apartment feeling confused and annoyed. My mood wasn't improved by the bright orange envelope on my car—another fifty dollars, this time for leaving the front end across a yellow line. A hundred and one dollars so far today in parking fees. I could have screamed in frustration. My eyes and joints ached from my cold, which made it hard for me to think clearly. I pulled the lever to recline the driver's seat as far as it would go and leaned back with my eyes shut.

Strictly speaking, whether Catherine was lying or not about her grandfather was none of my business. The only thing about her that could remotely justify my scrutiny was whether she had known Marcus Whitby. And I thought she hadn't. She wasn't yet a sophisticated liar—her breathless manner when she was twirling away from the truth would disappear with practice.

That farrago she'd spun about her grandfather and Larchmont was truly infuriating, but I thought she was merely oblivious to Marcus Whitby. Hers was an adolescent absorption in her own affairs; it was so intense that she brushed off the dreadful notion of Whitby lying dead in the pool while she went about her own separate business. I don't usually believe in coincidences, but Whitby and Catherine—and me—all being there on the same night could actually be one.

She was frustrating enough for me to want to find out what she was doing at Larchmont Hall. But I couldn't ask Harriet Whitby to pay me to pursue a teenager for no reason except that she'd made me feel foolish.

I switched on the radio to see if they had anything on Olin Taverner's death. More bombing runs outside Kandahar, dissension among the Afghan warlords, Illinois cutting funds for schools and health care to balance the state budget. Since September 11, just about every public figure in America has been declaiming that we're a Christian nation; I guess that's why widows and orphans carry the load for fiscal responsibility here.

During the interminable commercial breaks, I began to doze, but I jerked back awake at Taverner's name.

One of Chicago's most prominent figures, and one of its most controversial, is gone. Olin Taverner gained notoriety in the fifties when he served as counsel to Illinois congressman Walker Bushnell on the House Un-American Activities Committee. For two decades, Taverner was one of the most important voices of American conservatism. Of late years, he had been living quietly, almost reclusively, in a retirement home near Naperville. His personal attendant found Taverner in his armchair this morning, dead of an apparent heart attack. He has left no immediate survivors. Again, Olin Taverner, dead at ninety-one.

Are you sick of turning to your ten-year-old every time you want to cruise the Web? Well, here's a perfect solution—

I switched off the sound. Dead in a retirement home near Naperville? Could that have been Anodyne Park? Maybe Taverner had been Geraldine Graham's neighbor in that exclusive little retirement resort. Maybe I could talk to her about him. And find out whether by some remote chance Catherine Bayard was telling the truth when she said her grandfather had a key to Larchmont Hall.

A Chicago cop started purposefully down the street, ready to give me a second ticket. I put the car in gear and drove to my office. I should check a few things, anyway, before seeing Ms. Graham again. Come to think of it, I could get a detailed report on Taverner from the Web.

As I let myself into the building, Tessa was locking her studio door. She backed away from me when she saw I had a cold: she's a bit of a nut about germs. I made a show of covering my mouth with my scarf. She laughed, but still edged quickly out the front door.

I went down the hall to the back of the building, switching on the tiny cooktop we put back there. We share a shower room and a refrigerator, too, but we meter our gas and electricity separately because Tessa's metal sculpting is so power-demanding. I scrounged one of Tessa's tea bags, conscientiously leaving an IOU: one ginger-lemongrass tea bag, and took it into my office.

On an impulse, while my system came up, I phoned Morrell's editor in New York. Don Strzepek and Morrell had known each other for years, since their Peace Corps days in Jordan, and I hoped Don might know what Morrell was up to. When I only reached his voice mail, I didn't bother to leave a message.

I wanted a human voice. I wanted Morrell. E-mail is too remote. A traditional letter has more intimacy—you can hold the paper that someone else touched, but with e-mail, you type and send but never touch or hear. Morrell himself was beginning to seem so distant it was hard for me to feel that he was real. I studied the photo I had on my desk, his wiry curly hair, his thin face, the mouth that had kissed me, but I couldn't summon his voice or the touch of his long fingers.

Ulysses chose his path, Penelope: don't let that control you, I adjured myself sternly. "Don't weep over yourself," my mother had told me—I was eight or nine, and wrapped in misery because the girls I usually played with had gone to a birthday party I wasn't invited to—"Do something." That afternoon she'd abandoned dinner preparations and let me play dress-up in her concert gown, weaving an improbable story for me as Signora Vittoria della Cielo e Terra. Today I began searching the Web for stories about Calvin Bayard. Maybe I could find out why no one was allowed to talk to him. Or had Renee been spinning me a line?

When my Web search brought me the Bayard phone number, I called out to the New Solway estate, and my heart beat a little faster: What if I did get through to him? What would I say to my hero?

When a woman answered, I said I was one of Calvin's old interns. "I'm in town this week; it would mean a lot to get to see him."

"He isn't scheduling that kind of appointment now," the woman said in a deep rough voice.

"I'd settle for a chance to say hello on the phone," I wheedled.

He couldn't come to the phone. There wasn't a good time to call back. I should try Mrs. Bayard at the company number if I had business with the Bayards. Her good-bye was truncated by the clicking of the handset.

So what was going on? If he was sick, why didn't they just say so? Something about New Solway made me imagine Gothic scenarios: Calvin was dead, and to keep control of the company, Renee had organized a massive conspiracy to make the world think her husband was still alive. Calvin's embalmed body lay in a giant freezer in the estate's old icehouse. Marc had found it there, and Renee had murdered him.

Making things up was more fun than research, but research gets the job done. I started reading news stories on Nexis, hoping to find out when Calvin had last been seen in public. Five years ago, he'd stepped down from formal leadership of Bayard Publishing and Renee had assumed the CEO spot. The *Herald-Star* and the *New York Times* both did big stories on it. Industry scuttlebutt said she'd been in charge for a good four years already.

That was all the Web could tell me. Calvin hadn't been at charity balls or any other public event, at least not any reported in the

press, since his retirement. To find out anything more, I needed to do old-fashioned
legwork, talk to friends and neighbors. For
which Darraugh would definitely not pay
me. Although come to think of it, he probably knew—that would be an easy question
to slip in when we next spoke.

When I switched my search to Olin
Taverner, I picked up a slew of hits. I chose
the National Public Radio report, which had
the advantage of being something I could
absorb with my eyes shut. I logged onto a
real-time player and leaned back to listen to
the report.

Taverner had died in Anodyne Park—but
he had grown up in New Solway. So not
only were he and Calvin Bayard old enemies, they must have been old playmates;
they were roughly the same age, after all.
They used to gallop around New Solway on
their ponies together or knout the servants,
or whatever it is that very rich children do to
amuse themselves.

Perhaps Marcus Whitby had been on his
way to see Taverner when death stopped for
him. I was getting up to find my detail map
of the area, to see if there was a way for a
man going on foot to Anodyne Park to end

up in Larchmont's pool, when the Bayard name arrested my attention again.

> *In recent years, publications like the* Washington Times *and the* Wall Street Journal *have tried to change public perception of Taverner, Bushnell and other leading McCarthy era figures. Many on today's right say that the left damaged the reputations of true patriots, and they have sought to revisit that history. One of the greatest oddities of this attempt at rehabilitation is provided by Edwards Bayard, son of Renee and Calvin Bayard, who jousted with Taverner in front of the House committee. Some years ago, Edwards Genier Bayard joined the ranks of liberal-turned-conservative pundits. He now works for the influential Spadona Foundation, the right-wing think tank that has set the agenda for much contemporary political discourse. Our political affairs correspondent Jolynn Parker spoke with Mr. Bayard in his Washington office.*

Jolynn's throaty voice came on, explaining the highlights of Bayard's career: Ph.D.

in economics from the University of Chicago, a stint at the International Monetary Fund running the program to sell Bolivia's water supply to U.S. and French engineering firms, and now heading the Spadona Foundation's economic policy division.

"Your father is a legend in liberal political circles. How did he feel about your taking a position with Spadona, which has opposed so many of his policies and politics?"

"We had a number of interesting Christmas dinners," Bayard said, "but both my parents are great respecters of free speech, as I am, and we all believe there is room in America for many different public opinions."

"How did your views come to differ so greatly from your father's?" Jolynn asked.

"It was my work at the University of Chicago, which coincided with the end of the Allende government in Chile; I became convinced that supporting a Communist like Allende—as my parents did—was damaging for U.S. interests there, and not fair to the Chilean people, either."

"Some people would say that the United States intervening to overturn another country's election was unfair, especially in light of the many thousands of people the Pinochet government imprisoned and killed during the eighties."

Bayard gave a dry laugh. "I've heard those complaints many times, Jolynn, but the Chilean economy is stronger today than ever."

I clicked the stop icon. I wondered what form those interesting Christmas conversations had taken, and why Catherine had adopted her grandparents' values instead of her father's, and where her mother was. None of my Web researches gave any private gossip about Edwards's marriage. I left Nexis and switched to my phone messages.

To my surprise, Geraldine Graham hadn't called again. However, Amy Blount had phoned to say that Whitby's housekeeper would come to his house in the morning to let us in.

Darraugh had phoned from New York, just to say he had heard from his mother as well as his PA, Caroline; he had full confidence in my abilities, but he thought we'd put enough energy into his mother's problems for now.

My answering service has a neat little program that identifies the phone number of

incoming calls; they include that in the report they e-mail me. Darraugh was staying
at the Yale Club in New York, which tracked
him down in the bar.

"What is it? Didn't you get my message?"
he demanded.

"Yes, two minutes ago, and I'll wrap up
my report in the morning. Two things,
though: the first is that the dead man's family has hired me to look into his death, so I
will be continuing my inquiries out in New
Solway."

"I would rather you didn't—"

"I'm telling you as a courtesy, Darraugh,
because you're one of my most valued
clients. You know I normally never reveal
one client's business to another." I paused
to let him digest that before adding, "The
second thing is that I talked to Calvin
Bayard's granddaughter this afternoon. She
says Mr. Bayard has a key to Larchmont. Is
that possible?"

"Possible? Possible that he has a key to
my family's house? You had damn well not
be spreading that story around town." His
anger made the receiver vibrate.

"Darraugh—take it easy. The kid told me
he had a key."

"She's wrong. She's lying for whatever reason teenagers lie." His voice retreated from fury to mere wintriness.

"I see." I pinched the bridge of my nose, wishing I did see. "I tried to talk to Mr. Bayard, but was soundly rebuffed. Do you know why?"

"Not for any nefarious reason. He's in poor health; Renee protects him with her usual energy. Send in your bill for the hours you've put in on my mother's complaint. I hope you will remember as you look for this dead man's murderer that I've paid your bills for many years now. I expect you to keep that in mind if you feel your inquiries must take you out to New Solway for any reason. You should realize you could fall into quicksand faster than anyone could get to you to pull you out."

He hung up before I could say anything. I had known Darraugh Graham for fifteen years, but I had never heard him threaten me before.

Gaps in the Newsreel

Many people saw Olin Taverner as your husband's greatest enemy, Renee. Can you explain to us why Calvin Bayard continued to see Olin Taverner socially?" Dennis Logan cocked his head at Renee Bayard with an intense sincerity that made her withdraw deeper into her studio chair.

Lotty and I were sitting with Max Loewenthal, watching the interview in the back room where Lotty keeps her television. Max, who's known Lotty practically her whole life, is the executive director of Beth Israel, where Lotty has her surgical privileges. The two have been lovers for many years, but since last fall they've become much closer. In a way, I resented not having

Lotty to myself as much as I used to, but I like and respect Max.

Over roast chicken and a bottle from Max's impressive cellar—which I was still too congested to appreciate—we talked idly about a number of things, including Max's perennial struggle to find a way to bring more paying patients into the hospital. One of his board members had suggested getting designer hospital gowns for affluent patients.

"Great idea," I applauded. "How can we really tell we've got a two-tier health care system if we don't have outfits that demonstrate it? Armani in a soft gold silk for the privately insured, gray overwashed nylon for the wretched poor."

Max laughed, but Lotty wasn't willing to joke about the matter. She uses her substantial surgical fees to fund a number of health programs for the un- or underinsured, but she's acutely aware of how small a drop that is in the health care bucket.

I changed the subject hastily, describing my encounters with young Catherine Bayard. Lotty and Max had immigrated to America from Britain in the late fifties. By the time they'd arrived here, the HUAC hearings had pretty well died down, so she and Max didn't know the names or histories of the key players, but they were interested enough to follow me to the television after dinner. We turned on the nine o'clock news on Channel 13.

To my surprise, the show started not with Olin Taverner's death, but with the parents' meeting at Vina Fields that Catherine had mentioned. I wouldn't have thought that was newsworthy, but I guess angry rich people shouting at each other makes good theater.

The segment opened with Beth Blacksin standing in front of Vina Fields. "This discreet stone façade hides the entrance to a Chicago power institution. It's here that Grahams, Bayards, Felittis and other Chicagoans whose names spell clout send their children. It's a mile from the Cabrini Green housing projects, but a light-year from the turmoil of an inner-city school. No gangs, no guns here. But lately this calm building has itself been caught up in turmoil over whether they've been harboring not street gangs, but an inter-national terrorist. Parents and administrators have been anguishing over whether student records, including what books students check out of the library, should be open to law enforcement agencies. At the center of this upheaval is an Egyptian dishwasher, Benjamin Sadawi, who disappeared three weeks ago."

The station showed a photo of the youth in the white shirt and tie Mr. Contreras and I had seen last night. "The Justice Department claims he fled to his terrorist cell's hideout. They want to examine all school records to see if these might shed some light on his disappearance. The First Freedoms Forum is trying to intervene to keep the Justice Department out of school files. We spoke to lawyer Judith Ohana before the meeting. Judith, what's at stake here?"

A tall, slim woman took the mike with practiced ease. "This is basically a witch-hunt, Beth. If one of the children from this school was in Cairo, and the army came in to confiscate books and papers and computers because of a rumor about a missing dishwasher, everyone in America would be outraged. That's what's happening here: a few parents are fanning the flames of mob hysteria. Do they really want their children's private thoughts to be the bedtime reading of FBI or INS agents?"

Beth then took us inside the school so we could watch the parents discuss what they wanted school administrators to do. People were screaming at each other with the hearty venom of a hockey game. An angry man came to the center mike to say his daughter was a student at Vina Fields. "My child's safety is paramount. I won't have the school sheltering terrorists because of some First Amendment gobbledygook that puts my child's life at risk."

Other parents jumped into the fray, then Renee Bayard came to the mike. She was still wearing the red dress, which stood out vividly against the gray suits and ties around her.

"We all want our children to be safe in school, at home, on the streets, in the air. When our children are at risk, we don't care about law, or justice, or abstractions, we only care about their safety. I'm the same way. And that's why I don't want police agents meddling in my granddaughter's school records. I don't want some private opinion my daughter put in an essay scruti- nized by the FBI to see whether she's a security risk. Adolescents think in extremes. It's their nature. If they have to second-guess everything they write or read, then pretty soon we'll have a country of robots. We won't have the freethinking, creative young people who have the zest for experiment, even for risk, that makes American business lead the world."

The camera cut away during another angry salvo from the man who objected to First Amendment gobbledygook. "That was Renee Bayard, CEO of Bayard Publishing," Beth said. "Her husband Calvin, a leading First Amendment advocate, fought memorable battles with Chicago lawyer Olin Taverner, who died today at ninety-one. Stay with us after the news for *Chicago Talks,* when we'll be discussing Olin Taverner's life and career. Renee Bayard will describe her husband's clashes with Taverner in the House of Representatives. For now, I'm Beth Blacksin, live at Vina Fields Academy on Chicago's Gold Coast."

A battery of commercials came on; Lotty muted the sound. "Could the FBI really have put that kid in custody without telling his mother or anyone at the school?" Max was troubled.

I grimaced. "Morrell just did a story for *Margent* about a Pakistani immigrant who vanished from his Uptown apartment last October. His family searched frantically for him, but it was only after the guy died out in Coolis prison that the Feds told his sons they'd been holding the father for eleven weeks. I did the local legwork for Morrell on that—it seems a neighbor had reported seeing a suspicious-looking van pull up on September 15 with a large box: turned out to be a new toilet, but by then the FBI had moved on, and INS didn't think that bit of information was relevant."

"And this boy? They could do that to a child?" Lotty demanded.

"He's sixteen or seventeen. If he really is a terrorist, that's plenty old enough to be planning something."

"So you believe the FBI or whoever it is has a right to turn the school upside down looking for him?"

"I didn't say that. Just that in the context of terror, kids younger than he is are making and using bombs. As to whether the Feds have the right—I don't know what rights this Patriot Act gives them. If he's an undocumented immigrant, the kid doesn't have any rights under the new law—but whether that extends to the place where he worked, well, I guess that's why First Freedoms jumped in here. To test the act's limits."

Max and Lotty looked at each other. They'd met in London as child refugees from Nazi Europe, where they'd seen their own families and friends arrested and killed without being charged or tried. Neither of them spoke, until Lotty quietly said she'd make me a hot drink to help my cold. When I started to follow her, Max shook his head at me. By the time she came back, with a mug of something soothing and lemony, the interminable weather report and endless commercials were over.

Lotty returned as Dennis Logan gave his provocative introduction to his interview with Renee.

"I didn't realize this was a gossip show, Dennis," Renee responded. "It's been many years since my husband saw Olin Taverner except to say hello. Of course, they grew up in the same milieu and knew the same people; you don't walk out of a meeting with a senator or a governor just because you don't like one of his other guests."

"But your husband must have felt

strongly about seeing the man who tried to ruin him accepted at many of the same political and social gatherings you attended."

Renee leaned forward, her heavy brows meeting above her nose. "You know, Calvin and I were so busy building up Bayard Publishing, and then the foundation—looking after the First Amendment shouldn't have to be such a full-time job, but it is— that we didn't have time to think about Olin Taverner. Of course, we used to see him at the Symphony or the Chicago Club, but, once he moved into his retirement apartment, he stopped coming into the city. I hadn't thought about him for a long time."

"You didn't think about him even though some commentators—including your own son—have been urging us to revisit the McCarthy era and see people like Taverner, or Congressman Bushnell, as American heroes, trying to protect the country from internal enemies?"

Dennis looked as earnest as if he knew or cared what he was talking about: what he really wanted was to provoke Renee into some on-air reaction. But she had her advice to Catherine well in hand: rise above it.

"I think it's dangerous when we start to turn people who want to subvert the Constitution into heroes. We need to think especially carefully about that these days, where we're making it hard to hear any dissent from our current government's policies. But unlike some of our talk-show hosts and editorial writers, I don't believe those who disagree with me should be jailed, or hounded out of the country. All I want is for them to respect my right to hold differing views from theirs."

"Even though your own son has been among those leading the charge?"

Renee Bayard's smile grew wooden. "Edwards's essays in *Commentary* and the *National Review* haven't been leading a charge, Dennis. He takes a different tack on the issues than his father and I might—but at least I know that we raised a child who can think for himself. Child—of course, he's a grown man now, with a daughter Calvin and I are incredibly proud of. She insisted on joining me in the studio tonight."

Dennis looked a little sour as the camera moved away from him to a glowing Catherine seated at the corner of the studio. He started talking to force the camera back to his face. "Speaking of jailing people who disagree with us, Renee, people have often wondered how your husband walked away from those hearings without either a contempt citation or a sentence."

"There was no reason for Calvin to be in prison. He committed no crime and he was never charged with one. However much our son disagrees with our politics, I don't believe he would claim his father should be put in prison."

"But Calvin was a member of the Committee for Social Thought and Justice," Logan persisted. "And he refused to answer questions about it to Congress. That interview was shown on television; I found an old copy this afternoon when we were looking for footage on Olin Taverner."

Renee looked startled as the grainy black-and-white tape began to run. It took us back to the old House hearing rooms, with men in the double-breasted suits of the day. I recognized Calvin Bayard at once: his lean face, pale hair, even the good-humored smile with which he greeted someone behind him, were much as they'd been when he spoke to my law school class twenty years later. He sat alone at a table facing the committee, not even a lawyer at his side, his long legs stretched out in a pantomime of the man at ease. On a raised dais, six men faced him from behind a nest of microphones.

Channel 13 had written the men's names in white above their heads. Olin Taverner, austere, hair combed back from his fore- head, looked like the model for the upright public man. In contrast, Congressman Walker Bushnell, the committee chair, had a face as round as a lollipop; his buzz-cut hair turned him into the caricature of a thug.

Taverner spoke first. "You were at a meeting of the Committee for Social Thought and Justice on June 14, 1948, in Eagle River, Wisconsin, were you not, Mr. Bayard?"

Calvin Bayard chuckled. "I attend a great many meetings, Olin, just as you do. I don't remember all the names and dates. You must have an amazing calculating machine in your head if you can remember the exact date of meetings that far back."

Taverner leaned forward. "We have testi- mony from other witnesses whose memories are good that you were in Eagle River on June 14, 1948. Do you dispute this?"

Bayard answered impatiently, "I can't discuss the matter because I don't know whether you had testimony or not, and I don't know who did or didn't provide it."

Taverner slapped the tabletop. "We have reliable testimony that you were at this meeting. Who else was present with you?"

Bayard hooked his fingers in his belt loops and leaned back in his seat. "Mr. Chairman, when Mr. Taverner and I were boys in rural Illinois, we often found weasels and rats prowling around our henhouse. They like to slide through the cracks under cover of dark. The weasel doesn't come out in broad daylight and meet you face to face the way a dog will.

"Now, I wouldn't like to characterize any of my distinguished friends in the publishing or entertainment industry this way, or even those serving this committee, because every man at the end of the day has to face his own conscience in the privacy of his bedchamber, and my conscience may tell me something different than what yours, or those of my friends', do. But slithering around under cover of darkness, or under pretense of patriotism, why my dog would know what to do with a creature that acted like that."

A gasp went up among the spectators in the committee room. Taverner himself started to shout something, but Walker Bushnell silenced him by reaching across to put a hand over Taverner's microphone.

"So you refuse to tell this committee who was at the meeting with you on June 14, 1948," Bushnell said.

Bayard looked at him steadily. "Mr. Chairman, the greatest pleasure America's enemies have is seeing her leaders attack our cornerstone, the right to free speech, a free press, free association. I will not give succor to our enemies by violating those rights."

The tape ended there; the camera tonight flashed back on Renee Bayard. She was dabbing tears away from the corners of her eyes. I felt pretty sniffy myself.

Dennis Logan said, "That was a fine speech your husband gave, but people are still left wondering why it moved Olin Taverner and Walker Bushnell. After all, your husband was the only person who ever got Olin Taverner to let go once he'd dug his heels in. But Calvin didn't name names, he didn't go to prison, he wasn't even fined. What was his secret?"

"Poor Calvin, with all the work he did to allow people like you to say whatever you want whenever you want—and all you want is to put him behind bars."

"Renee, that isn't fair, is it? It's a legitimate question. Now that Olin Taverner is dead, is there any harm in letting us know how your husband persuaded him to leave him in peace?"

"Calvin always had a great deal of charm." This time her smile held genuine warmth—even a touch of mischief, which made her seem suddenly appealing. "He charmed me right out of Vassar when I was twenty. He might have been able to charm Walker Bushnell, too, although it would have been heavy work. You're too young to have known the congressman, weren't you, Dennis? But I typed up some of the—"

Logan could feel the interview slipping out of his control and hastily said, "We had hoped for a comment from Calvin on Taverner's passing, but he wouldn't come to the phone."

The heavy lines settled back in Renee Bayard's face. "On Olin's death, you mean?

Calvin hates euphemisms for the most common acts of our bodies, and nothing is more common to us all than death."

Logan conceded defeat. "When we come back, more on Olin Taverner and the House committee he served, this time with a team of constitutional scholars. Renee, thank you for coming in. I know this can't have been an easy evening for you."

The station shifted to a commercial before Renee's answer came on. Lotty switched off the set.

"I'd say game, set and match to the lady," Max said. "He wanted something that he couldn't get from her."

"It was very moving, that old piece they ran," Lotty added. "I'd never paid much attention to those hearings. But how extraordinary that their son is betraying them."

"Not *betraying* them," I objected. "They raised him to think for himself."

"He's not thinking for himself," Lotty said. "He's echoing what every other right-wing lunatic in America is saying."

"What I want to know is why he's living in Washington while his kid is in Chicago with her grandmother. And how he came to think so differently on politics from his parents.

And why Calvin Bayard has no comment on Taverner's death. And a lot of other stuff that's none of my business. I'm going to take my sore nose home to bed, although whatever you put in this drink, Lotty, I feel a whole lot better. Thanks—for everything."

She and Max saw me to the elevator, their arms around each other. Riding down the elevator I felt both the assurance one gets from seeing others in love, and the pang of feeling separate from the world of lovers.

House of the Dead

To me, the South Side has always meant the broken-down mills of South Chicago, where I grew up; when I got a scholarship to the University of Chicago four miles up the lake from my home, I used to scoff at Hyde Parkers, with their big yards and their kids in expensive schools and camps, for claiming to be South Siders—they might live below Madison Street, but they were more at home in the restaurants and theaters on the far side of the Loop.

Bronzeville, where Marcus Whitby had bought a house, was yet a different South Side, one I only knew secondhand. I got there early enough to do a little exploring. Whether because of Lotty's magic potion, or because Geraldine Graham let me sleep through the night, I'd woken early, with more energy than I'd had lately. I took the dogs for a brisk walk, went to my office to check messages and complete a report—and still reached Twenty-sixth and King, where Bronzeville starts, before eight-thirty. I paused in front of a statue commemorating the great wave of black immigration into the city. Driving on down King to Thirty-fifth Street, I passed the husks of the businesses that used to make up the so-called Black Metropolis. As Aretha Cummings, Whitby's assistant, said yesterday, no one wants those old segregation days back, but it was painful to see the wreck of buildings that once had been the heart of a vital community.

The same thing has happened in South Chicago; I can hardly bear to return to the scenes of my youth because of my old neighborhood's rotting buildings. But South Chicago has forty percent unemployment and the highest murder rate in the city, while Bronzeville is on its way back. True, many of the businesses around me were dilapidated, but an art deco building on the corner of Thirty-fifth and King had been turned into an insurance company, and the stately mansions that lined both sides of the boulevard looked well maintained.

Marcus Whitby had bought a town house on Giles, a short narrow street just west of King Drive. I found a parking space on the corner of Giles and Thirty-seventh, and walked back up the street to the address I'd found on Nexis. Some of the houses on Giles seemed to be teetering on their last beams, with broken windows and sagging roofs. Others had been restored even beyond their original beauty, with the addition of painted Victorian curlicues on the porches and window trim. Most, like Whitby's own, fell somewhere in between.

I stood on the pavement, staring at it, as if I could learn something about Whitby's life from studying his home. It had been built high and narrow to fit on a small lot. The dark red brick was old, cracked in many places, but freshly mortared, the modest porch and wood trim around the windows patched and painted. Louvered blinds were drawn on all three floors, making the house look forbidding, its empty eyes closed to the world.

Children straggled out of the nearby houses, backpack laden, on their way to school. They flowed around me like fish parting around a piece of piling—I was a grown-up, nonexistent. For the adults heading to work, it was a different story: I stood out as a stranger, and a white one to boot. Several people stopped to ask if I needed help. When I told them I was just waiting for someone, they eyed me narrowly: white suburbanites come into the black South Side to buy drugs, so they can keep their own little towns clean and crime-free. I'd dressed soberly, in my green-and-black-striped wool, to look both respectful of the dead and professionally competent—but that didn't prove I wasn't a crackhead.

If anyone probed further, I told them who I was, and asked what they knew of Marcus Whitby. People responded charily, not willing to discuss the dead man with a stranger, but I got the impression his neighbors hadn't known him well. Oh, yes, he got on with everyone, but he kept himself to himself. Not that he was mean in any way, not at all—if you needed your car jumped, or help installing a window, he pitched in. He just didn't sit out on the porch at night joining in the neighborhood chitchat.

None of the adults who stopped remembered seeing Whitby on Sunday night, but a ten-year-old, waiting impatiently while her father questioned me, said she'd seen Whitby come home.

"He was out all afternoon, then on his way home he stopped at the corner for milk. We saw him because me and Tanya went up there to get a Snickers bar. Then he went out again. About nine o'clock."

"How do you know?" I asked.

"Me and Tanya were jumping rope, we saw him walking up toward Thirty-fifth Street."

"What? In the middle of the night?" her father thundered. "How many times—"

"I know, I know," I cut in hastily. "It's dangerous, but you do it in the street because you can see under the lights—my girlfriends and I always used to, no matter how many times my mother yelled at us not to. So you saw Marcus Whitby leave?"

She nodded, a wary eye on her father. "He locked his door, called to us to be careful and headed on up the street."

"Was he in a hurry?" I asked.

She flung up her hands. "I don't know. Me and Tanya, we didn't pay special notice to him."

"Maybe he'd parked up the street and drove off," I suggested. "Do you know what his car looked like?"

When she pointed at a green Saturn SL1 across the street, I said, "That's what his looked like? A green four-door?"

"No," she said, annoyed with my stupidity. "That's his car."

"You're positive? Is that where it was Sunday night?"

"I dunno." She was tired of answering questions. "We didn't think nothin' of it. He took the bus to work most days. Then we saw he was dead. Daddy, I'm going to be late and Miss Stetson, she'll give me detention. *Please* drive me, please?"

"Yeah, okay, but you know I don't want you jumping rope in the street. And was Kansa part of your group Sunday night? Because if she was, you are definitely—"

They climbed into a car before I heard what she definitely was. I crossed the street to look at Whitby's Saturn. Underneath a film of dust, the body was in mint condition, no dings or scratches, except for a dent in the left front fender.

I peered into it, cupping my hands against the glare. If I could believe the girls, he'd left on foot. Where had he been going? And how had he gotten out to New Solway?

A cab pulled up in front of Whitby's house. Amy Blount hopped out of the front seat and opened the back door to help out a dimunitive woman in a severe black suit and hat. A man slowly climbed out of the other door, followed by Harriet. So the whole Whitby family had arrived. I sucked in a breath. This could make things more complicated.

The man bent over the driver's window to pay the fare. When I stepped forward, Mrs. Whitby turned to look at me. I couldn't see her face: even in high heels she only stood about five foot two, and the hat brim shielded everything but her chin. I made conventional noises of condolence and introduced myself.

"Yes, it's very difficult," she said in a dry, dead voice. "But since my daughter and my husband want you to pry open my son's life, I thought I should make the effort and come out to see you. Poor Marcus, I couldn't protect him in life, I don't know why I think I can protect him in death."

Harriet bit her lip; she'd obviously been hearing these sentiments for the last twenty-four hours. She introduced her father, a tall, thickset man. I guessed he was in his fifties, but he was walking with the stoop of someone older and frailer.

"So you're the woman who found Marc. I don't understand it, I don't understand it at all. And you think you can explain it? Find out why he was out there, how he came to die?"

Amy stepped forward with determined briskness and asked if I'd been inside yet.

"I was waiting for the family," I said. "When is Ms. Murchison getting here?"

She had already arrived. She must have stood inside the doorway watching while I talked to the neighbors, because before we had sorted out the protocol of who went first, and whether Mr. Whitby or Harriet would support her mother up the five steep stairs to the front door, Rita Murchison opened it.

Like me, like Mrs. Whitby and her daughter, Rita Murchison was wearing a dark suit, chosen to prove she wasn't a cleaning woman but a legitimate mourner. She didn't step back as our awkward group converged on the small concrete stoop. I was afraid she was going to demand IDs before she'd let us in.

I moved forward, forcing her to retreat. "Thanks for coming over here, Ms. Murchison. Was this your usual day to clean for Mr. Whitby?"

She scowled at me. "I'm a housekeeper."

"You look after the house?" I said. "Meaning you live here? What time did Mr. Whitby go out on Sunday?"

"I don't live here, but I do look after the house."

Mrs. Whitby pushed past me and Rita Murchison into the hall. The rest of the family followed her, leaving me alone with the housekeeper.

"So when you were looking after the house on Sunday," I persisted, causing her to say she was a Christian, she certainly didn't work on Sundays. "On Monday, then?" I asked.

After a stubborn minute, she finally admitted that she only came in on Fridays for four hours. "He was a bachelor. He lived a simple life. He didn't need a lot of help."

Behind us, Mrs. Whitby said, "I had no idea this neighborhood collected so much dust. Because I'm sure you must have gone over this last Friday, and yet here we are on Thursday knee-deep in dust."

Rita Murchison wheeled around. I peered over her shoulder down the narrow hallway to the staircase which rose halfway down its length. Mrs. Whitby had found the light switches. A spotlight was trained on a framed poster on the stairwell wall. It showed the silhouette of an African dancer, back arched, in the social realist style of the thirties; around the sleek figure was an intricate design of African prints and masks.

"The Federal Negro Theater Presents," proclaimed the header, and, underneath, "Kylie Ballantine's Ballet Noir of Chicago, April 15–16–17, the Ingleside Theater."

The light also revealed a thin film of dust along the edges of the stairs. Mrs. Whitby stood there, inspecting her finger. Rita Murchison surged forward, prepared for battle. Harriet put her arm around her mother, trying to persuade her not to worry about dust when Marc was dead. I slid away from the trio into the room on my right. Amy Blount followed me.

"I tried to persuade Mrs. W to stay at the hotel, but I could hardly blame her for wanting to see her son's house. She's been wanting to fight someone all week, anyone to distract her from her distress over Marc. When Harriet and I wouldn't play, I thought for sure she'd take you on."

I grinned. "I thought she would, too. Let's leave them to it and see if we can find any trace of his notes, or a diary, or anything that would tell us why he went out to New Solway."

Amy nodded. "It's not that big a place. It's got three floors, but only nine rooms and he didn't really use the third floor at all. His study was on the second floor, next to the bedroom. Want to start there? We can go up a back staircase from the kitchen."

"You spend a lot of time here?" I asked.

"We weren't lovers, if that's what you want to know," Amy said roughly. "We were friends—Harriet and I were close at Spelman, I used to spend Christmas with the family, so even though Marc was six years older than us, I knew him through the family. When he moved to Chicago three years ago to take the job at *T-Square,* I introduced him to people. He was quiet, not naturally outgoing, not like Harriet. Unless he was working on a story—then he would feel comfortable calling people and talking to them. Later he developed this interest in Ballantine, which began absorbing his spare time."

I followed her through a dining room to the kitchen and the back stairs, our feet echoing on the uncarpeted floors. Whitby had masks from one of Ballantine's productions on the living room wall, photographs from the *Swing Mikado* along the stairwell. He even had a pair of Ballantine's toe shoes under a glass bell on his dresser.

He'd also been rehabbing his house bit by bit. The kitchen walls were scraped and painted. He'd put in a new stove and refrigerator, but stacked all his pots and dishes on a trolley instead of buying cupboards.

The refrigerator held half a cooked, skinless chicken breast, skim milk, orange juice and a carton of eggs. No beer, no wine, was in sight; only a bottle of Maker's Mark, about a quarter empty, stood on a shelf with spices and pastas.

"His drink," Amy said when she saw the bottle. "Bourbon and branch."

He'd begun work on a bathroom, had finished two upstairs rooms, his bedroom and the study, but the rest of the house was still either half-built, or untouched. Books were housed neatly on board-and-brick shelves. Most dealt with black history and theater, or with African art and dance. He didn't seem to read much fiction. Next to his bed, though, he had a library copy of Armand Pelletier's *A Tale of Two Countries,* the first novel Calvin Bayard had published when he'd taken over the press—Bayard Publishing's first nonreligious novel.

Amy was right about the search. In this bare place, it took very little time. I pulled latex gloves from my bag and handed her a pair.

"We'll quarter the room," I said. "Everything you touch, you put back exactly as you found it."

"You think there's been a crime."

"He left on foot Sunday evening. How did he get to New Solway? If he went out there to die, surely he would have driven, instead of taking a train to a remote town, followed by a five-mile hike to that pond. No one goes to that much work to kill themselves."

"Then—the police?"

"If I can persuade one of my acquaintances there. But first let's check this out ourselves."

Amy was a scholar, a dogged researcher. She was willing to collect data before pushing me into further action. She was thorough, not as fast as me on her first search, but careful and tidy. We went through the drawers, shelves, looked in the books, looked behind pictures, under the neat stack of sweaters in his closet. Nothing. Nothing about Kylie, about the Federal Negro Theater, about New Solway. No datebook. No notebooks. We logged onto his laptop. The word-processing files had been wiped clean. Nothing anywhere.

Back in the kitchen, Harriet had somehow persuaded Rita Murchison and her mother to a cease-fire. Ms. Murchison was making coffee, her lips a thin angry line. Mrs. Whitby was in the living room, staring blankly at a photograph of her son in front of the old Ingleside Theater.

I had only seen Marc Whitby dead, by flashlight. In the picture, he was smiling, pointing at the theater doors, but his essential seriousness was still evident. Despite having his father's height, he looked very like his mother, with her slender bones and bronze skin.

"I took that," Amy said. "We went on a walking tour of Ballantine's haunts, and of FTP sites, and he liked this one particularly."

Mrs. Whitby clutched it to her breast, her face finally cracking into grief. "My baby, my baby," she crooned.

Harriet and Amy pulled her to a chair and knelt on either side of her. I went back to the kitchen to confront the angry housekeeper.

"Did anything in this house look different to you when you came in this morning?"

"Don't start in on me about the dust, I've had it. If it wasn't for Mr. Whitby being dead and me knowing him all this time, I wouldn't stay around here to be insulted."

"I don't care about dust or no dust," I said. "It's the house. I've been looking for his papers; they're gone."

"If you're accusing me of stealing—" She smacked the coffeepot down so hard the glass carafe broke. "Now see what you've done."

"Listen to me for a minute," I said, my voice rising a half register in exasperation. "I know you and Mrs. Whitby have been in each other's hair, but I'm not part of that fight. I want to know where he kept his papers. I want to know what you noticed when you came in. Maybe someone was here stealing them, or maybe he kept them someplace else."

She began to pick up the pieces of glass. "The door. It wasn't locked right. I thought, maybe he left in a hurry and forgot to put the deadbolt on, but he was a careful man, careful and saving, you know, because he didn't make a lot of money at that magazine, and what he made he spent on this house, this house and that dancer he was so crazy about. But I never came here once all the years I've been working for him and found only the one lock on."

I nodded. So someone had been in here. "Did you ever find anyone here with him when you came in? Or signs of a lover?"

"He was a man. He had a man's normal instincts."

I looked at her speculatively. She wasn't that old, and beneath her frown and ostentatious bustle she wasn't unattractive, but when I put out a tentative question she bristled. She'd been interested and he hadn't? It might explain her aggressive possessiveness when the Whitbys arrived this morning. Something to ask the neighbors, whether anyone had come and gone at odd hours. An angry lover could have keys. She—he—could have driven Marcus Whitby out to a remote place to die.

In the meantime, I went through the motions here, asking Rita Murchison to come with me to the second floor to see what was out of place. She opened the drawers and cupboards Amy Blount and I had already inspected, but all she could tell me was that the stack of notebooks he usually had on his desktop was gone.

16

Burke and Hare

I found Mr. Whitby in the basement, inspecting the furnace. "He got a good model, the one I told him to buy. Good fuel rating. I told him he needed that up north here. Of course he knew all about winter, going to the University of Michigan like he did. He wasn't good with his hands, I never wanted him to have to be a handyman, but I talked him through some of the work when he decided to do this house himself. He was methodical, he did things right. You see how he laid that tile in the bathroom? He called me, we talked it through, he did it right. 'Course, a furnace, I told him not to try installing that himself, get a plumber, spend the extra money, but he bought the model I recommended."

I looked respectfully at the furnace for a few minutes before taking Mr. Whitby upstairs to collect his family. I persuaded Rita Murchison to give me her keys—just a loan, I said, offering to pay her for the time she'd taken to come here. Money and keys changed hands while the family lingered in the living room.

While I drove the family back to the Drake, I tried to urge Mrs. Whitby to return to Atlanta. "There's something serious going on here, and I don't know how much time it will take before we can get it sorted out."

"I know something's serious," she said in her leaden voice. "My son is dead."

"But how he died—"

"I don't care how he died."

"Edwina," her husband said. "Edwina, we've had all this out before now. Listen to the lady. What do you mean, Miss—I'm sorry, I've forgotten your name."

"Warshawski," I said, "but people call me V.I. All of your son's papers are missing. I think someone came back to his house with his keys and scooped up all his notes and computer files. They even took time to wipe out his hard drive. This is a street where the kids at least notice who's coming and going; I might be able to canvass the neighbors and see if anyone noticed a stranger here Sunday night. In the meantime, getting a proper autopsy performed is the most urgent task. We need to know how Marc died."

In the seat next to me, Mrs. Whitby moaned but didn't interrupt again.

"I will be looking at everything your son was doing over the last few weeks," I continued. "I don't expect anything terrible to emerge about him, but—if it comes to that, I won't hide evidence of a crime. Within that constraint, I will be working for you and—"

"My boy never did a criminal deed in his life," Mr. Whitby growled. "If you're trying to imply that he did, we'll stop this business right now and take him home."

"No, sir, I'm not implying that. I just want you to be aware that an investigation like this doesn't follow a straight path."

"I am not having any investigation done that frames my baby as a criminal," Mrs. Whitby said. "That's why I never wanted you to start your digging around in the first place."

I glanced in the rearview mirror and saw Amy lean over to murmur something to Harriet. After a short dialogue, Harriet said, "V.I. isn't out to frame Marc. And if we don't let her finish the investigation, we'll always have that nagging worry about why he did die. And Mama, Daddy, you two should go home. We're spending a fortune on that hotel. I can stay with Amy until—until things are cleared up: the office urged me to take all the time I need."

"I just can't bear to go home with my baby lying in a drawer in the morgue," Mrs. Whitby fretted.

"Harry's right; we can't afford to stay in that hotel for God knows how long," Mr. Whitby said. "But if you want to stay on, we could move into Marc's house, I suppose."

"Not until a forensics team has been through it," I said.

They argued it over among themselves while I turned onto Lake Shore Drive. The lake, at its lowest level in a century, looked sullen, not the roiling of a usual stormy winter, but the dull surface of a creature in retreat. Mrs. Whitby, staring through the windshield, seemed just as remote.

When I pulled up in front of the Drake, they still hadn't decided who would stay and who would go, but Mr. Whitby had agreed that I could go ahead with "my business." Amy got out with them, but after she'd hugged Harriet and her parents she climbed into the front seat.

"I can drop you at the train," I said, "but I don't have time to take you home."

"I thought I'd ride with you, see what kind of help you need."

I opened my mouth to protest but shut it again. I did need help, and Amy Blount was a skilled researcher. I invited her to come with me to my office while I tried calling the cops. "We'll decide what to do next when I see what kind of reaction I get."

Amy lifted her brows at the unorganized stacks of files, but didn't say anything. She perched on Mary Louise's chair and watched me while I tried the police. I started with Terry Finchley, a detective in the First District's violent crimes unit. Terry had been Mary Louise's boss when she was with the police. He was also a close friend of a Chicago cop I'd loved and lost, and he's never quite forgiven me for how I treated Conrad. Still, we've sort of worked together several times, and he takes my opinion seriously.

After I'd laid out such facts as I had, Finchley said, "It's a jurisdictional problem, Vic. He died out in DuPage County. He's their puppy."

"But, Finch, he lived here on the South Side. His car's here, his house has been cleaned out."

"A car in front of an empty house isn't evidence of a crime, Vic. I can't send a forensics team down there, or ask the Twenty-first District to order one in. No crime has been committed there."

"Burglary—"

"On your say-so only. He could have burned his papers. He could have had a power surge and lost all his files. No sale, Vic. You can talk to the captain, of course, but I can't take it on."

The captain was Bobby Mallory, my father's oldest friend on the force. Like the Finch, he sort of respects my work without liking my doing it. In his case, it has nothing to do with my old lover and everything to do with my being his friend's daughter. He gave me less time than the Finch had, and finished by saying, "The last I heard, your intuition wasn't considered grounds for Chicago to demand jurisdiction of a body from DuPage County. We got five hundred unsolved homicides here in town. I'm not creating a political stink by trying to catch five-oh-one. Eileen wants to see you for dinner. Call her, set up a date. That nice boy of yours still being a hero in Afghanistan?"

"He's over there being something," I snapped.

"You watch your step until he comes home."

Meaning, don't sleep around, Penelope, even if Ulysses is lying in the arms of a British journalist. I hung up savagely on that thought.

"You're not seeing me at my most effective," I told Amy. "But at least I can find out if the Cook County ME will do the autopsy privately." I tried Bryant Vishnikov at the morgue, but he had the day off.

When I reached him at home, he snarled, "If I'd wanted live patients paging me day and night, I wouldn't have gone into pathology. I thought my home phone was unlisted, anyway."

"Is it? You didn't tell me that. Marc Whitby's father wants a second autopsy performed on his son. Would you be willing to do that?"

He waited a minute to answer. "It's something I do do, and can do, but it's not something Cook County can pay for, Vic. And you know, if I do a thorough autopsy and simply find that the guy drowned with alcohol in his system, the family may not accept those results."

"What would you charge?"

"For the tox screens, and the time and space, it could go as high as three thousand."

I had no idea what kind of resources the Whitbys had, but I told Vishnikov to proceed and asked how we should get the body to him.

"It would help to have a third party, like a funeral director, do it, so I don't have to step on Jerry Hastings's toes by going to him direct. So, Vic," he added, as I was preparing to hang up, "don't go babbling about this to the press. It could be very hard on me politically to look as though I'm taking a public position against DuPage's ME."

"Someone's going to have to know," I objected, "unless you're planning on stealing his body out of their morgue and doing this in your basement."

He burst out laughing. "You're outrageous, Warshawski, making me sound like Burke and Hare. But I still don't want this broadcast."

"Copy that, Houston," I said. "Your ass will be draped with the same discreet purple our government is using on the statues of Justice."

He laughed again and hung up.

While I'd been on the phone, Amy had been organizing papers. She'd cleared a space on Mary Louise's desktop and had spread out the contents of my Larchmont file to study.

"You're good," she said, looking up at me. "You don't bully unless it's the only way, do you? What are you doing next? Want me to hold Mrs. Whitby's hand while you move Marc's body?"

"No. I want you to find out everything you can about Kylie Ballantine."

She opened her eyes wide at me. "Whatever for—oh. You think that's why Marc went out to this mansion? Why?"

I grimaced. "I don't know, that's why. But I only have a couple of starting points. He's been thinking about her day and night for months, he's writing a book about her—and all his files have disappeared."

I pulled the printout on Ballantine that Aretha Cummings had given me yesterday from my briefcase and handed it to Amy Blount. I'd read it before I went to bed—I summarized the high points for Blount.

Kylie Ballantine had been both a dancer and an anthropologist. She'd been trained in classical ballet, but she'd gone to Africa to study tribal dance in French Equatorial Africa (modern-day Cameroon and Gabon, I was guessing). On her return she'd started the Ballet Noir, a deliberate pun on Diaghilev's Ballets Russes, incorporating African dance into classical ballet, using costumes and masks from Africa. With the Negro Theater Project money, she'd done an ambitious ballet called *Regeneration,* which depicted an African-American sense of awakening and self-respect as people reclaimed their African heritage.

"It'd be great to see that," Blount commented. "There probably aren't films of it, though. What did she do after the theater project lost its funding?"

"She went back to Africa, I think." I thumbed through the printout. "I know she wrote a couple of books on tribal dance, and taught briefly at the University of Chicago."

"That must have been something special," Blount said dryly. "Black woman at that school in the forties or fifties. No wonder she took early retirement." She took the printout from me to examine Whitby's brief paragraph on that part of Ballantine's life. "It looks like Marc was really only interested in her dance career. And then—I see. She ran a private dance studio from her home in Bronzeville until she died in 'seventy-nine. Okay. I'll see what else I can figure out. What are you going to do?"

"Go back to his house and canvass the neighbors. It occurred to me, private as he was, there might have been a lover in the picture you and Harriet never heard about. The kids on that block see everything. Someone had to notice something about him."

Amy looked at me speculatively from under her thick lashes. "You know, I'm second to none as a researcher, and I'd be glad to go on-line, or down to the Vivian Harsh

Collection. But I'm wondering if I wouldn't be more effective on that street than you."

I felt my cheeks grow hot, but I remembered the cautious response I'd already received this morning. The kids might talk to me as readily as to a black woman, but the adults were more likely to be open with Amy.

"Point taken. Do you have a cell phone?" We exchanged mobile numbers. "I'm not sure what I can pay you for this—I hadn't factored that into the estimate I gave Harriet for taking the case. But your help will make a big difference, and I don't expect you to donate it."

She shook her head. "It feels good to be doing something. Even after Marc moved here, I didn't know him all that well, but Harry—Harriet—is like my own sister. Doing something active to track down what happened to Marc, it's the one thing I can do for her. You don't need to be paying me."

Timmy's in the Well

We spent some time on-line, me looking for the Negro Theater Project, Amy checking the trains to the western suburbs. Marc could have caught a nine-thirty, which would have set him down in the station nearest to New Solway at ten-twenty. He still would have been miles from Larchmont Hall. One of us would have to fit in time to hunt down any suburban cabs or buses that might have picked him up. I ground my teeth at that prospect.

When the Web yielded only two meager references to the Negro Theater Project and none at all to Kylie Ballantine, I drove the fifteen miles south to look at real documents in the Vivian Harsh Collection.

Amy took off for Bronzeville when I left for the library. She'd described the Harsh Collection before we separated. Harsh, who'd been the first African-American to head a branch of the library, had been a private collector of material on black writers and artists. When she died, she donated everything—photos, documents, books—to the city. The Harsh Collection was the best of its kind in America, next to one in Harlem.

To my surprise, the papers were housed in a room off a major library branch—I'd pictured the collection in its own building. The library itself was doing a bustling business, mostly with women bringing their young children in to look at books, but also the usual collection of homeless and elderly that a library gathers. It's a respectable destination. It's warm, you can be with other people. All reasons why the Web cannot take the place of your branch library. Also it had books. And an archivist who knew and loved his collection.

At first, Gideon Reed frowned over my request. Yes, he knew those papers well, but why did I want to see them?

"I know Marcus Whitby's been looking at them for some time," I said. "That's why I'm here."

When I explained my role in Whitby's death—finding him, working for the family—and showed him my ID, the archivist unbent. Mr. Whitby had been a real scholar. They didn't get many here, mostly students working on term papers just wanting a few facts about Martin Luther King, not that he didn't love showing young people how to use books and documents, but there was something satisfying about seeing this collection in the hands of someone who truly appreciated it.

Reed set me up in a temperature-controlled room with photographs of black poets and artists on the walls. While Gwendolyn Brooks and Langston Hughes smiled down at me, I went through the same papers that Marcus Whitby had studied. The letters and other documents were encased in plastic sleeves. I tried to skim, looking for names or events that might mean something to me, but Ballantine had a fine, spiderlike handwriting and she'd often written in pencil, making deciphering a maddening task. She sometimes wrote on pages torn from school exercise books, sometimes on thin green paper, where her pale handwriting became even more undecipherable.

I read Ballantine's correspondence with Franz Boas at Columbia over her discoveries in Africa, her correspondence with Hallie Flanagan about the staging of *Regeneration,* her angry letter to W. E. B. DuBois's wife after Congress pulled the plug on the Federal Theater Project.

> We were doing good work, we were doing important work. The notion that a ballet like *Regeneration,* or your own *Swing Mikado,* are Communist-inspired because we try to tell the truth about Race in this country—is enough to make me look seriously at Communism. I don't know what I live on now—back to private dance classes for earnest little girls whose mothers tuck away a dime a week from washing white women's clothes so that their children can learn in my studio what would have been their birthright in Africa.

The archive was patchy, sometimes holding letters like Ballantine's to Shirley

Graham without Graham's response, sometimes letters or typed notes to her without
any way of telling what she'd written to the
correspondent. Several typed ones in the
late forties came from an anonymous committee ("...the Committee is grateful for
your involvement in the benefit. We were
able to raise $1700, which our patron
matched." "The next Committee meeting
will be on June 17 at the Ingleside church").

Right before the Second World War,
Ballantine somehow got a grant from the
University of Chicago to travel and study in
Africa. How she spent the war years, or
where, wasn't clear, but in 1949 she signed
a contract with University of Chicago Press
for her book on *Ritual Dance Among the
Bantu of West Equatorial Africa*. They paid
her five hundred dollars. Perhaps that was a
standard advance in 1949.

Her second book dealt explicitly with
slavery, and the dances she was able to
trace from America back to Africa. *The
Longest Leap: African Dance in American
Slavery* didn't come from an academic
press but from Bayard Publishing. That was
a bit of a surprise: maybe *Ritual Dance
Among the Bantu* had sold better than

you'd expect. Maybe Ballantine had lived on her royalties. Or perhaps Calvin Bayard had known her personally and wanted to support her.

I stared at the Bayard logo on the title page, the jagged outline of a lion, as if it could tell me something, but finally turned to the book itself. There were photographs of masks, photographs of shyly smiling African girls demonstrating dance steps, shyly smiling African-American girls demonstrating what were supposed to be similar steps—I couldn't tell from the pictures. I read paragraphs here and there about where Ballantine had been, what she had seen, how it compared with the dances she observed in the American South. She wrote fiercely about the patronizing attitude of white America to black dance.

They ignore the history of civilizations far older than theirs, African civilizations which each step and ritual encode. In their eyes, we Africans exist shamelessly in the body, and our dances are thought to be only a sign of our mindlessness, leaving the mind itself to the high civilizations that think up atom bombs and gas chambers.

A yellowed article from the *Daily Defender,* dated from 1977, gave a few biographical facts. Ballantine had been born in Lawrence, Kansas, in 1911, but her family had moved to Chicago when she was six. She had attended Howard University, where she studied anthropology and dance. She'd gone to Columbia when Franz Boas was welcoming black students there, and achieved a master's degree in anthropology before returning to Chicago, where she taught dance, performed dance, studied dance. In the *Defender*'s photograph, she was shown standing regally in front of a wall of African masks, wearing a dancer's leotard and an African-print skirt.

The reporter had been more interested in her dance than in her academic career. He burbled in print over her energy—there she was, sixty-six, still dancing four hours a day, still teaching children in her Bronzeville home. He hadn't asked how she'd spent the years from 1937 to 1977 except to discuss her trips to Africa—besides the two I'd already read about, she'd lived in Gabon for three years following its independence. The reporter did ask whether she felt any bitterness toward her treatment in the late fifties, and she had said that bitterness only wasted one's energy.

I skimmed the rest of the papers, hoping for a diary or something personal, but there wasn't much else here. A letter from the University of Chicago provost, dated October 1957, coldly stating that they would not need her services after the end of the fall quarter, but there was nothing from her to the university. Her contract with Bayard, a one-page document offering her seven hundred dollars. Not the advance of a commercially successful writer, after all.

Calvin Bayard's bold thick signature stood out against the faded paper, making him seem vividly present in the room. It seemed odd for a commercial press to publish a book with such an academic title. Had he and Kylie Ballantine been friends, or even lovers? Bayard had published her, they lived in the same town—if you thought the Gold Coast and Bronzeville were the same town. If Bayard had known Ballantine personally, that could easily explain why Marc had gone to New Solway on Sunday evening—to see what Calvin Bayard remembered of her.

I stacked everything in a tidy pile to return to the archivist. Gideon Reed was talking earnestly to a teenage boy, showing him something in a fat reference book.

When I handed him the stack of Ballantine documents, Reed gave me a kind smile. "Did you find anything useful?"

"Nothing that shed direct light on what might have taken Marcus Whitby out to New Solway. It's a bit of a stretch, but *The Longest Leap* was published by Calvin Bayard. He lives out there, so I'm going to drive out, see if Whitby tried to talk to him about Kylie Ballantine. Did Whitby ever mention Bayard?"

Reed shook his head. "It's not like I saw him that often. I'm sure he did a lot of research I never knew anything about—and of course he worked full time, he had a lot of other stories to cover."

"I read Ms. Ballantine's interview in the *Defender.* Do you know what happened to her in the fifties? The reporter asked if she were bitter—was that because of the U of C firing her?"

The archivist turned reflexively to the article, but didn't look at it. "Mr. Whitby was guessing she'd been blacklisted, but I don't think he'd found any evidence to confirm that. She was never called to testify before Congress, and except for that one letter, I'm sure you saw the one she wrote when she was so angry about Congress canceling the Theater Project, she never discussed Communism."

"What about something called 'the Committee'? You know the one I mean? Could that have been considered a subversive group?"

He flipped through the plastic sleeves until he found the references, but he couldn't shed any light on them. "I know Mr. Whitby wrote for her file under the Freedom of Information Act, but it's like so many of those files: most of what you want to know is inked out so you can't read it. Since September 11, they've made it harder to find out what records they're keeping on the citizens. It's kind of frustrating, our own government spying on us, then not letting us see what they claim we've been up to."

When I asked if there were other Ballantine papers anywhere—a diary, or financial records, Reed shook his head again. "If there are, they're not in a public archive. Her estate didn't amount to much, and even though she was highly respected in the black community, no one had the kind of money to do preservation or restoration in her home—it had to be sold to pay her debts. If there was some kind of trove of documents, I'm thinking they're in the CID landfill by now."

Reed paused to answer a question from a woman who'd been waiting for several minutes, then turned back to me. "Mr. Whitby did go through her old house. After she died, the bank or whoever bought it cut it into a bunch of little apartments, but Mr. Whitby hoped something might have been left in a basement or crawl space."

"Did he find anything?"

Reed slowly shook his head. "That may have been why he called me, maybe a week or ten days ago. I wasn't in and he left a message for me. I never did reach him when I tried calling back, but that could have been it—he knew I shared his interest in Kylie. If he'd found some papers, well, he would have wanted to show them to me."

Another patron was trying to get the archivist's attention. I turned to leave, feeling frustrated at how little information I was able to collect.

As I walked away from his desk, Reed called out to me, "Let me know what you find out about Mr. Whitby. If you get to the truth, it may not make the evening news, you know."

A sad commentary. Kylie Ballantine's life should have been seen on stage, under spotlights, but she'd died in the wings, and now Gideon Reed was afraid her lone champion was going to vanish into the same shadows.

I imagined melodramatic statements I might make, picturing myself as Annie Oakley riding to the rescue of both Ballantine and Marcus Whitby. Maybe I was just Lassie the dog, though, barking around frantically for help.

"Timmy's in the well," I said aloud as I unlocked my car. A woman with a couple of toddlers passed me just then, but she barely spared me a glance: people saying odd things to themselves are commonplace at the public library, after all.

# 18

Crocodile in the Moat

I'm going out to New Solway," I told Amy Blount when I reached her on her cell phone. "I didn't find anything definite in the Ballantine papers, but there's a possibility that Marc tried seeing Calvin Bayard, who published one of Ballantine's books. I want to talk to Mr. Bayard, if I can get in—his wife has a shark-filled moat dug around him. Did you find out anything?"

"Like you, nothing definite. The woman who lives on Marc's south side thinks she saw lights at three yesterday morning—she's got a newborn who woke her up around then, and she was rocking by the window, but she wasn't really paying attention. She couldn't be a hundred percent sure it was Sunday—she's up most nights and she's pretty sleep deprived. And anyway, she didn't look at the front walk, so she wouldn't know if it was Marc or an intruder. The old man across the street, he saw Marc bring a woman home with him once or twice, but no one had spent the night here for several months, as far as the local gossip columns know."

I was on Ninety-fifth Street, heading west to the tollway, doing the worst kind of driving: the steering wheel wedged between my knees, one hand on the cell phone, one on a raspberry smoothie I'd picked up in lieu of lunch. When I had to brake for a semi that suddenly changed lanes, I dropped the smoothie.

I swore and pulled over to the curb, where I daubed pink liquid from my green-striped trousers. I'd lost the connection by the time I finished with my clothes. When I redialed I asked how many people Amy had left to talk to. She hadn't reached the neighbor on his north, or the kids—school wouldn't get out for another hour.

"If you have the time, stay down there until you talk to some of the kids. What about the autopsy? Have the Whitbys come to a definite decision on that? They have? Then I'll find a funeral director who will get Marc's body from DuPage and deliver it to Bryant Vishnikov." That was the kind of detail Mary Louise Neely knew from her years of police work; I'd give her a quick call at her fancy new office.

"Finally," I said to Amy, "do you think Harriet is up to a trip to *T-Square*? I'm wondering if Simon Hendricks—Marc's editor—knows more than he would tell me about Marc's current project. Maybe he'd be more forthcoming with you and Harriet."

"What should I say?" Amy asked.

"Marc's assistant—Aretha Cummings—thinks Hendricks was jealous of Marc's abilities. Start with Aretha, see if you can get something specific to use as a lever. Usually, two emotions start people talking—resentment or sympathy. So try to get Hendricks feeling sorry for Harriet and the Whitbys. Talk about their need for closure. But if that doesn't work, see if anything Aretha tells you will goad him into revealing something. Augustus Llewellyn, he owns *T-Square* and all those other magazines, has a policy against talking to anyone at Bayard. I want to know if that's truly a pol-

icy about not going to any competing publisher, or if there's some specific issue between Llewellyn's enterprise and Bayard's.
The guy in the cubicle next to Marc, Jason
Tompkin, seems willing to talk."

"I can try," she said doubtfully, "but I'm
not very skillful sorting out office politics."

I was about to give her a hearty pep talk,
but her words triggered a memory from my
encounter with Renee Bayard. "I think
you're up to the job—but there is something
you might find on the Web or the SEC or
even from Aretha Cummings: Calvin Bayard
helped Llewellyn get his original financing.
There's some history there, something that
made Renee Bayard think Llewellyn
wouldn't respond to a call from her. See if
you can pick up anything on that. If I manage to see Calvin Bayard, I'll ask him, too.
Let's talk tonight, okay?"

While I finished my smoothie, I called
Mary Louise. We had a quick chat about her
new job, which she confided was more
work and less excitement than she'd hoped
for. As I'd thought, she knew a funeral director whose fees were reasonable and who
knew the ropes at the county morgues. First
I called Deputy Protheroe, and told her the

paperwork on Marc Whitby's body might be getting ready to show up. Then I called Mary Louise's funeral director, who set up the transfer for the next morning. Finally, I left a message on Vishnikov's voice mail to tell him to expect Marc Whitby's body. Only then did I reenter traffic.

With both hands on the wheel I was the model of the good driver, feeling superior to the people with books propped on steering wheels, cell phones in ears, hamburgers in mouths. As if to reward me, I had an easy run all the way from Kedzie to the tollway, and made it to the Warrenville Road exit well ahead of the afternoon rush.

When I reached the turnoff to Coverdale Lane, I pulled over to inspect my detail map. The woods behind Larchmont Hall belonged to a sort of common area in the middle of New Solway. The Bayard and Larchmont estates were about four miles apart if you followed the road, but only a mile if you went through the woods. I supposed that's what Catherine did Sunday night—skittered through the underbrush home. Even if I hadn't fallen in on top of Marc Whitby, I probably couldn't have kept up with her in the dark through woods she knew well.

All the way out to New Solway, I'd tried to think of a persuasive argument to get me into the Bayard house. Nothing came to me. Maybe I'd park at Larchmont and cut through the woods myself. But when I found 17 Coverdale Lane, the gates to the Bayard estate stood open. I turned through the stone gateposts onto the carriageway. After winding about half a mile through old trees, I came to a four-story mansion, its stone façade aged to a golden gray. Like Larchmont, the Bayard grounds also held a series of outbuildings: garage, stable, greenhouses, a barn. The surrounding gardens and meadows fed into the woods.

In front of the house, the drive split in three, one fork leading to the garage, one to the other outbuildings, and the third along the left side of the house itself, where a discreet sign pointed to a tradesman's entrance. The main entrance, where I pulled up, faced south; shallow steps led to a porticoed doorway.

I could hear voices from around the north side of the mansion, so I climbed out of the Mustang and followed the sign to the tradesman's entrance. A van and a small truck were parked there. Three men were unloading supplies while a woman in blue jeans and a black turtleneck and blazer supervised.

In the near distance, someone was doing something with hay and a wagon. How bucolic. Almost justifying calling this spread "rural Illinois," as Calvin Bayard had done in the testimony I'd watched last night. Out in his overalls at four in the morning like all the other Illinois farm boys who had forty-room palaces to protect from weasels.

"That'll see you through the weekend, Ruth." One of the men laughed loudly and handed a clipboard to the woman.

The woman in black signed, frowning at his familiarity, but he laughed again, clapping her on the shoulder, telling her he'd be back first thing Monday. He slammed the back panels of the van shut and jumped into the driver's seat, whistling "Danny Boy" in a cheerful tuneless way. The back panels proclaimed "Home Body—For All Your Home Care Needs" in green cursive.

The other two men were unloading groceries from the truck. Ruth checked each item before letting it into the house.

"Miss Catherine doesn't like this brand of yogurt. Why didn't you bring the Bulgarian? And we specified teriyaki tofu; she won't touch the Hawaiian." This was the woman who'd answered the phone when I called pretending to be one of Calvin Bayard's old interns; I hoped I'd been so much hoarser yesterday that she wouldn't recognize my voice today.

The man explained that the Bulgarian yogurt was past its shelf date. Ruth told him sharply to bring some when he came back on Friday, even if he had to go into Chicago for it.

If I'd thought about it, I would have guessed Catherine Bayard would be a vegetarian. She was rich; she could be a picky vegetarian.

Ruth scowled in my direction and told me she'd be with me in a minute. "You're not with the media, are you? If you are, you'd better leave now: we have nothing to say to you."

The media. People always say this as if it were some foul disease: you're not with the cholera pouring out of the sewer, are you? And yet we worship and bow down before the television's eye. I meekly denied connection to the sewage.

Ruth finished her work with the men, telling them they could have coffee in the kitchen, before turning back to me. "Yes?"

Trying to pitch my voice higher to disguise it from yesterday's croak, I explained that I was a detective investigating Marcus Whitby's death. "You know that Mr. Whitby died in the Larchmont pond Sunday night."

"I watch the news, yes, I saw that story, that he had come out here to end his life, and I fail to see why that means you can bother us."

"Oh, that's a story Sheriff Salvi put out to calm down the community," I said carelessly. "We know better than that. I can step you through the evidence that shows Mr. Whitby didn't go into that pond on his own, but you're probably more interested in his connection to the Bayard family."

She frowned more deeply but didn't say anything.

"We know Mr. Whitby came out here to see Mr. Bayard, because—"

"That is a lie. Mr. Bayard has seen no one this week."

"Because Mr. Whitby was writing about one of Mr. Bayard's authors," I continued as if she hadn't spoken. "Kylie Ballantine, who had such a difficult time in the fifties and sixties. Perhaps Mr. Bayard didn't talk to Mr. Whitby, but he did come out here, didn't he?"

She paused, as if deciding what she could reveal, then said, "The man telephoned, but we don't allow journalists to talk to Mr. Bayard."

"So you sent him to Ms. Renee Bayard in Chicago, but she wasn't helpful and he came out here hoping to gate-crash."

I held up a hand to forestall a further objection. "We know Catherine was at Larchmont both Sunday and Monday nights. She told me her grandfather—"

"You are full of lies," Ruth said scornfully. "Catherine was in the city Monday night, as she always is during the school year. And she certainly had no reason to be at Larchmont either of those nights."

"I talked to Catherine yesterday afternoon. She was certainly out here Monday night. We can call her." I looked at my watch. "School's out for the day. Unless she has lacrosse practice, she's probably with her friends, either at Banks Street or the coffee shop they go to—Grounds for Delight, it's called. I don't have her cell phone number, but you probably do."

It was a bit of a gamble—I had no idea what Catherine would say if the housekeeper called my bluff—so I only paused briefly before adding, "I'll be honest with you: Catherine would not tell me what she was doing at Larchmont. But she says that when her grandfather can't sleep, he goes over there, that he has a key, and she sometimes goes with him—they like the privacy at Larchmont Hall."

"A key to someone else's house? I never heard such a ridiculous suggestion." She sounded fierce, but her eyes were moving uneasily between me and the house.

I pulled out my cell phone. "I agree it sounds ridiculous, but that's what Catherine told me. Let's call her to check on that. All I really want to know was if Mr. Bayard did go to Larchmont, if he did see Mr. Whitby. I'm trying to find the person who last saw him alive."

Ruth looked again from me to the house. Hers wasn't really an indecisive nature: after a moment's further hesitation, she ordered me to come with her. I followed her through the side door to an areaway where people left coats and muddy boots. Beyond that, another door opened onto the kitchen, where the two deliverymen were drinking coffee and laughing with someone out of my field of sight. On our right, I could see the food cartons stacked in a pantry.

Ruth whisked me past a back staircase, whose narrow pine steps presaged perilous journeys for anyone carrying laundry or logs or whatever had to be hauled up and down. We passed through a swinging door into the body of the house, where the hall immediately widened. Something dark and highly polished, with thick blue runners down the middle, replaced the pine flooring. Our feet whispered in the blue pile.

Ruth moved so fast that I almost had to trot to keep up with her, so I got only a blurry sense of a dining room with a vast table loaded with silver, followed by a series of doors to smaller rooms, and pale walls hung with art of the kind people like me see only in museums.

When we reached the east end of the hall, Ruth opened the door into a small anteroom and commanded me to remain there. She continued down a right turn in the hall, heading to the front of the house.

The little room was primly furnished, with a couple of hard chairs standing in front of an empty grate. Mullioned windows gave a view of the back of the property. A series of gardens stair-stepped down to a small stream, beyond which lay New Solway's communal wood. I stared out the window at the bare trees.

A couple of deer stepped out of the woods into the gardens. A Border collie raced out to drive them back into the woods. A man appeared, whistling the collie to his side. The two disappeared toward the outbuildings.

With the live figures gone from the landscape, I turned away, looking for something to read or do as the minutes ticked past. The room held that sense of despair you feel in any waiting area. No one worked or lived here, they only waited for someone to make decisions about them. Like at the doctor.

I abruptly went down the hall in the direction Ruth had taken. This took me to the main entryway, where an ornately carved staircase rose from a marble floor. Life-sized portraits of bygone Bayards were hung on the walls.

I prefered Marcus Whitby's simple stair-case with its poster of Kylie Ballantine's "Ballet Noir," but I backed up to get a better look at a stern woman in mauve silk, wonder-ing if she was the Mrs. Edwards Bayard who had gone to the opening of Larchmont Hall in 1903; I could see a resemblance to young Catherine and to Calvin Bayard in the narrow planes of her face. Not the great beauty Geraldine Graham's mother had been.

I heard Ruth's voice above me and slid around behind the stairwell where the balustrade formed an alcove. "All you have to tell her is that he was asleep and in bed. But you know if this happens again, I will have to talk to Mrs. Renee about it."

A second woman mumbled something in-audible. I hurried back down the hall to the anteroom, the thick carpeting muffling my steps. I managed to be standing at the win-dow, gazing outside with supreme indiffer-ence, when Ruth reappeared. The mumbler was a woman in her thirties, with a bony, anxious face. Like Ruth, she wore jeans, not a uniform, and had on a heavy gray cardi-gan over a faded T-shirt.

"This is Theresa Jakes." Ruth fished my card out of her blazer pocket and did a creditable job in pronouncing my name. "Mr. Bayard has been ill and Theresa is helping Mrs. Bayard nurse him."

Theresa's hands were red from much scrubbing. She tucked them nunlike into the sleeves of her cardigan and looked at me nervously.

I repeated my little speech. "Did you take a phone call from Marcus Whitby? Did you try to arrange for Mr. Bayard to see him?"

Theresa shook her head. "I know better than to let journalists come here. It's Mrs. Bayard's strictest order. Anyone who wants an interview has to talk to her in town. No one can bother Mr. Bayard here at home."

"Could he have taken the call himself?" I asked.

Theresa looked helplessly at Ruth Lantner. "There is a phone in his room, but we've turned off the ringer so it won't bother him. Unless he—I guess I could check it."

"But he did go out Sunday and Monday night, right?" I said, plowing forward despite my growing uncertainty. "Was it you who brought him home?"

"He wasn't out," Theresa said. "He was sleeping, sleeping heavily."

"You were with him all night?" I asked.

"He doesn't need someone in the room with him," Theresa said. "He doesn't have that kind of illness. But if he leaves, an alarm goes off over my bed so that I can make sure he's all right."

"And that alarm never sounded?" I persisted, hoping to get some inkling about what she'd done that Ruth was going to report the next time it happened—since whatever it was explained why I'd been admitted to the house. "It's funny, because young Catherine emphasized that she'd used his key to get into Larchmont Hall."

Theresa made a little dismayed face at Ruth, who shook her head at the other woman and said, "Catherine wasn't here Monday night. Mr. Bayard did not leave the house on Monday. Or on Sunday. Whatever scheme you have in mind—"

"If something hadn't happened here, you wouldn't have let me into the house at all," I cut in ruthlessly. "I have the names of everyone who lives here; one of them will talk to me and tell me the truth."

"The men can tell you nothing that I don't already know," Ruth said with finality. "Theresa, you go back upstairs to Mr. Calvin so Tyrone can get on with the vacuuming."

Theresa put her chapped red hands into her pockets and scuttled down the hall toward the main staircase. I couldn't think of any way to press my point. If Ruth had seen Whitby, or any strangers, Sunday night she wasn't going to tell me. If Calvin Bayard had left the house, despite whatever illness he had, she wasn't going to tell me that, either.

I might be able to find a way to talk to the men working with the hay, but it wouldn't happen today under Ruth's stern eye. Theresa looked as though she'd be more likely to crack, but it would take me some time to find a way to talk to her alone.

I wryly conceded the field to Ruth, shaking her hand, thanking her for her help. I started down the hall toward the front door, but Ruth called to me to follow her back the way we'd come.

I smiled blandly. "My car is right outside the main entrance. It's ridiculous for me to use the side door."

Before she could order me out of the front hall, Calvin Bayard suddenly lurched around the edge of the great staircase and headed toward us, calling "Renee! Renee!"

Theresa walked next to him, a chapped hand on his arm. "Renee isn't here, Mr. Bayard. She's at work right now." With her patient, she was a different person: assured, gentle, her anxiety gone.

"Renee, this woman won't go away. I don't like her, make her go away." Calvin Bayard plucked at Theresa's hand, looking at Ruth, whose short dark hair and stocky build did give her a vague resemblance to Renee Bayard.

The voice that I'd loved as a student was still deep, but it had become tremulous and uncertain. His face with its long narrow hollows had shrunk and turned pinkish. Whatever illness I'd imagined hadn't come close to this. I dug my nails into my palms to keep from crying out in dismay.

He suddenly caught sight of me and stumbled to me, grabbing me in a rough hug. "Deenie, Deenie, Deenie. Olin. I saw Olin. Trouble, trouble. Olin is trouble."

He crushed me tightly against the rough fabric of his jacket. He smelled of talcum powder and stale urine, like an infant. I tried to move away from his embrace, but despite his age and his illness he was strong.

"It's all right," I said, as he continued to clutch me. "Olin is dead. Olin doesn't mean trouble now. Olin is gone."

"I saw him," he repeated. "*You* know, Deenie."

Between them, Theresa and Ruth managed to remove his arms from my back. "He saw the story about Olin Taverner on the news," Theresa panted. "He's been very agitated, thinking that this man is out to get him. He keeps claiming he's seeing him out the window."

"Why did you let him watch the news?" Ruth demanded.

"No one told me about the history, or I wouldn't have let him," Theresa snapped back. "Everyone in this house tiptoes around simple things and then blames me for not doing my job, because I'm supposed to use ESP to figure them out. Get a psychic off the TV hot line if that's what you need in a nurse."

To my surprise, instead of blistering Theresa for impertinence, Ruth said, "No one's trying to keep things from you, Theresa. It was before my time, too, but it was so important in the Bayard lives that people still talk about it—I just assumed someone had told you."

"Who's Deenie?" I asked, rubbing the place on my shoulders where Calvin Bayard had dug in his hands.

"It's a nickname for Mrs. Bayard," Theresa said. "He cries for her when he's really upset. Mr. Bayard, we're going to get you a nice hot drink and take a little walk. You come with me. You like to watch Sandy heat your milk, don't you? With Sandy and me to look out for you, no one can hurt you. Remember that."

Under the Dragon's Spell

I sat in my car, shaking. When I was a student I had daydreamed about being held in Calvin Bayard's arms. The nightmarish way my old fantasy had come true made me sick to my stomach. The man who'd stood up so valiantly to the Walker Bushnells and Olin Taverners of America now derived pleasure from watching the cook boil milk. It was too much. I couldn't bear it.

My eye caught a movement at one of the front windows. Ruth waiting for me to leave. I found a bottle of water in the backseat and drank it down. Not the pint of rye Philip Marlowe would have used, but it steadied me just the same.

I drove slowly down Coverdale Lane. At Larchmont Hall, I pulled in through the gates, trying to regain my composure. In the twilight, the whitewashed brick looked more than ever like the prop to a Gothic novel. But my Gothic ideas about why Renee Bayard had dug a moat around her husband were wrong: she merely didn't want people to know he had Alzheimer's.

Maybe Calvin really had somehow gotten hold of a key to Larchmont Hall. Maybe he did wander over there, and Catherine really did follow him—and was protecting him and the family secret. But why keep it a secret? Was it Renee's own pain—she couldn't bear her husband's diminishment and didn't want the world to know? Or were there majority publishers at Bayard who only let Renee hold the CEO spot because they thought Calvin was guiding the reins behind scenes? I couldn't make sense of it.

I got out of the car and walked up the drive to the pond. I couldn't see much in the growing dusk, but the sheriff's deputies hadn't treated this like a crime scene. No tape, no signs of any investigation. Only the scarring along the grass where I'd dragged

Marcus Whitby's body showed that anyone had been here.

I looked at the water in distaste. The dead carp was starting to bloat. I'd come back tomorrow with a wet suit and crawl along the bottom, in case Whitby's keys, or some other personal item, had fallen out of his pockets, but I wouldn't enjoy doing it.

I got in my car and continued down Coverdale to Dirksen. It wasn't until I found myself staring at the pink brick of Geraldine Graham's condo that I realized I'd headed away from the tollway. Darraugh had asked me to drop the investigation, so I was dropping it—but it would be rude not to pay a farewell visit to his mother.

The guard at Anodyne Park's entrance approved my admittance. This time, the maid Ms. Graham had imported from Larchmont Hall let me into the apartment. She took my jacket, then asked me to wait in the entryway while she checked with "Madam." A comedown from my wait at the Bayard mansion—not even a chair, let alone a view of the woods. There was a painting, a small piece, soft pinks and greens that resolved itself into a mountainscape as I examined it.

The maid returned and escorted me out to the sitting room, where Ms. Graham sat drinking coffee from an elaborate service. Perhaps when her maid was with her she couldn't escape her mother's rituals. I began to understand why she might relish living alone in her great age.

"That will be all, Lisa." Ms. Graham dismissed the maid and looked at me over the rim of her coffee cup. "So, young woman, you won't come when I send for you, but you do show up unannounced on your own whim?"

"Darraugh told me to stop the investigation into your old home. Did you know that?"

"He phoned this morning to tell me." She bit off the words.

"Did he explain why?" I walked over to the sideboard and poured myself a cup from the Crown Derby pot.

"He's always disliked Larchmont enough not to want to invest energy in its care. I think he suspects I made up lights in the attic as a way of forcing him to pay attention to the place. Or maybe to force him to attend to me."

The bitterness in her fluty voice made me ask, "Why didn't Darraugh want to keep it? Was it unpleasant for him, growing up there?"

She gave me what I was starting to think of as her Queen Victoria look: subjects will remember that they cannot interrogate the monarch. After a moment, she said stiffly, "Darraugh has never enjoyed country life."

My eyebrows went up. "He had to spend his boyhood getting up to slop the pigs, which gave him a lasting disgust for the sights and smells of the country?"

"You're impertinent, young woman."

"So I've been told." I pulled up a chair and faced her across the piecrust table. "I have this idea about people who live with enormous wealth and great position—that because they get exactly what they want when and how they want it, they believe they're entitled to privilege. And I imagine such people think the rest of us exist only at their pleasure. That means it's all right to summon us in the middle of the night, or lie to us, or do whatever else takes their fancy at the moment, because to them our lives have no existence away from their orbit."

I heard a gasp in the background and realized the maid was listening. Geraldine Graham herself produced a blistering look from her clouded eyes. "Do you truly imagine, young woman, that I have had exactly what I wanted when and how I wanted it? If so, you have shockingly little understanding of family life."

I was startled: I had braced myself for a diatribe that would end with her ordering Darraugh never to work with me again. Now I remembered the unhappy faces in the newspaper photos of her wedding.

"Your parents bullied you into marrying MacKenzie Graham," I said calmly. "You didn't feel able to stand up to them."

Her lips trembled with more than the uncertainty of old age. "My mother was not the kind of person one stood up to easily."

I looked at the frosty blue eyes in the portrait behind her head. They could have wilted ferns in the Amazon.

"You and your husband didn't want to start a life together in a house away from your mother? Was Larchmont that important to you?"

Geraldine Graham paused. When she spoke again, it was more to herself than to me. "My husband and I had so little in common that it was easier for us to stay with Mother than to try to live alone someplace else."

"Do you keep her portrait up there to remind yourself every day that she humiliated you?" I asked.

"You are impertinent, young woman," Geraldine Graham repeated, but this time with a touch of wry humor. "You may pour me more coffee before you leave. Rinse the cup with hot water first," she added, as I picked up the coffeepot.

I looked at her through narrowed eyes: what she wanted when she wanted it. Before I pushed my luck by uttering the thought aloud, Lisa bustled around the corner into the room and took the cup from me. She poured hot water from a small pot into the cup, swirled it, and emptied the slop into a bowl before refilling Geraldine's cup.

Ignoring Geraldine's implied command to leave, I refilled my own cup—without going through the rinse cycle—and leaned against the sideboard. "I'm still trying to figure out what brought Marcus Whitby to New Solway. I thought he might have gone to see

Calvin Bayard, not realizing how ill Mr. Bayard is."

Her hand stopped with the cup midway to her lips. "How ill is he? Renee has discouraged visitors."

"He seems to have Alzheimer's. He knows who he is, but not who he's talking to."

"Alzheimer's," Geraldine repeated slowly. "So the neighborhood gossip has been correct, for once."

"Why would Ms. Bayard keep his condition so secret?" I asked.

"With Renee Bayard, one never knows why she does what she does, but it is always safe to assume she is enjoying her power over all our lives—over Calvin's, in keeping him locked away—over his old friends, keeping us from visiting—probably over all the employees at the publishing company." She pressed her lips together in resentment.

"Calvin and I were friends from earliest childhood, and she has kept me from him most successfully all these years. So if your Negro writer was hoping to see Calvin, Renee would have made sure he wasn't able to do so. Why do you imagine your Negro wanted to talk to Calvin?"

I recited my piece on Whitby's interest in Kylie Ballantine and her contract with Bayard. To my surprise, Geraldine knew Ballantine.

"Calvin took an interest in her work. When he was enthusiastic, he wanted everyone to share his interests, so we all drove into the city to watch her dance. He bought art from her and we all had to follow his lead and buy one of her African masks. When she gave a recital, we all drove to the city to watch her dance. In 1957, I think it was, or perhaps 'fifty-eight. He had just brought Renee out here, I remember. I was prepared to feel sorry for her, a little patronizing toward her, twenty-year-old bride of an older, domineering man. What a mistake that was!"

She made a bitter face. "Ballantine was in her fifties the night I saw her, but she still moved like a young woman. I didn't care much for the dance. It was African, and I've never cared greatly for African art or music: it all sounds like boomlay, boom! to me. But heaven lent her enough grace for me to admire past the sound."

"It's a pity Mr. Whitby didn't have a chance to talk to you." I returned to my seat. "He might have found your recollections useful. Had Ballantine been blacklisted during the McCarthy hearings? Was that what brought her to Mr. Bayard's attention?"

Geraldine Graham slowly shook her head. "I don't know, young woman. It was about that time that my husband died, and Mother and Darraugh were—I remember the evening at the ballet because it was vivid, but much else that year is gray in my mind."

I would dearly have loved to know what Mother and Darraugh had done. Fought in a loud, unrefined way about MacKenzie Graham's death was my guess. After a decent pause to show respect for her unhappy memories, I pulled the picture of Whitby and his sister out of my bag.

"You notice a lot around you. Did you notice him?"

Geraldine Graham took the photograph from me and picked up her magnifying glass to study it. Her hands were misshapen by age and arthritis and they trembled. She laid the picture on her lap and held the glass with both hands.

"I've never seen him, but Lisa might have. She is always here in the evenings to help me with my meal and my night routine."

She picked up a bell on the table next to her, but Lisa had remained in earshot and came in before Geraldine could ring it. "This is the man who drowned in our pond, Lisa." She handed the picture to the other woman. "The detective is wondering if we saw him here on Sunday."

Lisa took the picture over to the window and looked at it closely. "Not on Sunday, madam. But I believe he was here, perhaps a week ago. I can't be sure, I see so few black men, but it looks like a man I noticed when I left you after lunch."

"When was that?" I asked.

She pursed up her lips, trying to remember. "It would have been the day I washed Madam's hair, because I realized I had brought the shampoo bottle with me. I was standing there by my car, wondering should I go back up, or could it wait until the morning, when he pulled in across the way from me. I felt foolish standing there looking at the shampoo, so I got into my car."

"So when was it?"

"I always wash Madam's hair on Monday, Thursday and Saturday." She seemed surprised that I wouldn't know that.

"So which was it?" I asked.

She paused again to think. "The Thursday, it would have been."

"A week ago! But why would he have come here, if it wasn't to see you, Ms. Graham?"

Geraldine Graham surprised me again. "If he was that interested in this dancer, and if she had been blacklisted, perhaps he went to see Olin. Olin Taverner, I mean. He lived here, after all."

Taverner, of course. He'd been one of HUAC's hatchet men, after all. And now he, too, was dead, so I couldn't ask him about Marcus Whitby. Or Kylie Ballantine.

"How well did you know Mr. Taverner?" I asked.

"Well enough. We grew up together. He was my cousin."

I vaguely remembered now, from that 1903 newspaper I'd read: Geraldine's mother had been somebody Taverner before she married whoever Drummond. "Mr. Taverner's death must be quite a loss, then.

Did you see much of him while he lived here?"

"Very little." Her voice frosted over again. "Consanguinity does not necessarily breed intimacy. I was sad to know he died only because it ended a chapter in my own life."

I tried to rearrange my ideas. If Whitby had come out here to see Taverner, instead of Calvin Bayard, it put him closer to Larchmont Hall. But I couldn't see why Taverner would have met him there, or sent him there. I asked Ms. Graham if Taverner had lived alone.

"I wasn't in close touch with him, but I assume he had someone to look after him. Lisa will know."

Lisa, when summoned again, knew the name of Taverner's attendant, how many hours a day the man had worked, and even what he'd said and done on finding the old lawyer's dead body.

"Did Mr. Taverner have a family? Children or other relatives?"

Geraldine Graham gave another involuntary glance over her shoulder at her mother's portrait. "He never married. His—tastes—ran in other directions than women. It was one of the things that made Calvin particularly angry during the fifties, Olin's hypocrisy."

I tried to add this to the bewildering array of information I was getting. Taverner had been gay, but in the closet. Maybe Whitby had uncovered Taverner's secret and— what? Taverner, afraid of disclosure, had murdered Whitby, rolled him over to the Larchmont pond, then come back here and died of a heart attack brought on by his exertions? The notion made me smile, which drew Geraldine's sharp attention and a demand for the "source of my amusement."

"Sorry, ma'am, I wasn't laughing at you, just my own absurd ideas. I went to the Bayard house before coming here, because my first thought had been that Marc Whitby wanted to talk to Mr. Bayard. The staff said he hadn't been around. Should I believe them?"

"Ruth Lantner," Geraldine Graham said. "She's what I had in mind when I said I didn't want a staff managing me. She and her husband run Calvin and Renee Bayard, oh, they do it well, they've been with Calvin since the boy was born. Edwards. One of those old family names people like to give their children. No odder, I daresay, than Darraugh calling his own boy MacKenzie, although Mother tried to change his mind at the time. I remember Mrs. Edwards Bayard—she and my mother had famous feuds. My mother thought she was a hypocrite, with her extraordinary causes and habits—she didn't allow any alcohol or tobacco in her house, although her husband's behavior was an open secret in our milieu. Mrs. Edwards thought Mother was an odalisque. Whereas Mother was something far more dangerous."

I was tempted to follow this historical byway: What had Mr. Edwards Bayard's behavior been? But I kept to the main topic. "Would Ruth Lantner lie about Whitby coming to the house?"

"Oh, don't ask me about servants' characters. I don't know her well. I daresay she would lie to protect Calvin, probably Renee as well."

So she expected Lisa to lie to protect her. Which meant if Geraldine Graham was hiding something about Whitby, or Bayard, Lisa would back her up. How nice and feudal.

"I met the Bayards' granddaughter the other day," I said.

"Catherine? That's a sad story, the mother dying when the baby wasn't a year old. The boy, Edwards, fell apart for a time under the blow. I will say in Renee's favor that she took on raising her granddaughter without a murmur. What kind of job has she made of it?"

I smiled. "Catherine's a lively, ardent young person—who so far has run rings around me. And she's extremely close to her grandmother. Catherine says Calvin wanders over to Larchmont at night."

"He does? How astonishing." She gave a dry laugh. "Perhaps in the secret recesses of his mind he is trying to escape Renee."

"Catherine says her grandfather has a key to Larchmont Hall, that he uses it to let himself in there at night. Is that possible? When I asked Darraugh, he became angry and hung up on me. Why?"

Ms. Graham put her down cup, her jaw working. "Do you have children, young woman? No? They are a mystery. You bear them in your body, you watch over them, but they grow up as strangers. Darraugh's anger is one of those mysteries to me."

Once again she danced away from talking about Darraugh and Larchmont. I reverted to the key: Would Calvin Bayard have one?

"I should be most surprised. But we live in a very odd world. Are they looking after him properly? How did he seem?"

"The nurse seems competent. He looks physically fit. He thought I was his wife. He clung to me and called me 'Deenie.' I always admired him—that was hard."

Ms. Graham's hands shook as she picked up her cup. Coffee slopped over the edge and onto her aqua silk skirt. "So clumsy," she murmured. "The thought of Calvin with his wits wandering is truly unsettling. Send Lisa to me on your way out, young woman."

My exit cue. I didn't need to summon Lisa: the maid continued to hover within earshot. As I let myself out, I could hear her clucking soothingly to Geraldine Graham, mother calming infant. The smell on Mr. Bayard's clothes, urine and talc, came back over me in a shuddering wave. That we all come to this, no matter how far or fast we run, we come to this, not away from it.

Lair of a Star Chamber Man

The emotions of the afternoon left me limp. I didn't go to my car, but walked aimlessly along the paths that wound through Anodyne Park. Night had fallen while I was in with Geraldine, but the paths were well dotted with fake gas lamps and I found my way easily. Not that I exactly knew what my way was, right now.

It was that time of evening when people were out with their dogs, or heading over to the bar on the shopping strip for a drink. I thought about following a dour couple into the bar, but I'd had too much company the last few hours. I kept walking.

I was too tired to try to make sense of everything I'd heard this afternoon, but the image of Geraldine and her mother kept floating in my mind, Geraldine's futile rebellions culminating in her unhappy marriage. Culminating, really, in her son Darraugh's wintry personality. I imagined scenes at the breakfast table, Laura Drummond giving her son-in-law his coffee with a barbed comment on his character, Geraldine slamming out of the house to do—what? I couldn't imagine her wasting time over bridge or shopping. I didn't know how she'd spent the years from 1937 until her mother died.

Beyond the bar, the path made a gentle descent. By and by, I found myself going under Powell Road and rising again onto the Anodyne Park golf course. The course itself was dark, but the occasional lamppost let me see the path. A late golfing foursome passed, going the other way in their cart. At the top of a rise, I came on the clubhouse, a well-lighted, sprawling building with a rack of golf carts at the far end and a couple of valets moving cars at the other. A wave of laughter rolled toward me. I shuddered away from the jollity.

I scrambled to the top of a hillock and lay on my back looking at the stars. The grass was velvety soft, but cold; it wasn't long before I started shivering and sneezing. I sat up again and pulled out my cell phone. Maybe I could reach Domingo Rivas, the man who had looked after Olin Taverner. He didn't have a listed number that I could find, but when I called the Anodyne Park management office and identified myself as a detective they were happy to give me his number: he lived with a married daughter in nearby Lyle.

"I hope there's not a problem, Detective. Domingo looked after Mr. Taverner as carefully as if he were his own father, and we have recommended him to another older gentleman in our assisted living compound."

I reassured her, explaining that I just wanted to talk to Mr. Rivas about Marc Whitby's visit to Olin Taverner. She put me on hold for a minute, then came back on to say that Rivas would be here in an hour to meet with the family of the "gentleman" who might be hiring him.

"We can ask him to stop by the office early to talk to you."

She gave me directions to the office. I found the underpass from the golf course back into the Anodyne Park community, but once inside the complex, the dark and the winding paths unsettled my sense of direction. I pulled a small flashlight from my bag, but couldn't make out any building that I recognized. I figured all the paths would end up either at the exit or the bar, and kept going. I was wrong—this particular walkway suddenly ended at a large shrub which caught on my trousers.

As I bent to untangle myself, I dropped my flashlight. Its beam picked out wheel marks going around the evergreen. Curious, I followed them and found myself at the entrance to a culvert. The ground was damp; I saw the tracks easily. It looked as though someone had driven a golf cart through here.

I was tempted to follow the trail to see whether this culvert ended up in New Solway on its far side, but I didn't want to muck up my good shoes in the damp soil. And I didn't want to miss Domingo Rivas.

I turned around. More by luck than skill, I found my way to the main part of the complex. A woman walking a toy poodle directed me to the management office.

The office took up a wing of the skilled nursing facility, a building tucked well away from the jolly parts of Anodyne Park so that no one had to think of disagreeable things like dementia or death. The woman on evening duty said, Oh, yes, they were expecting me. Domingo Rivas arrived soon after me, before it occurred to the woman to ask me for identification.

Rivas was a small man, perhaps my age, dressed like a waiter in black trousers and a white shirt. He watched me with worried eyes while the administrator explained that I was a detective with some questions to ask about "the black man" who'd died across the street last weekend.

After some urging, I got her to let us use a conference room where we could be private—she clearly wanted to be part of the conversation. With a little patient coaxing, I persuaded Rivas to sit down, and even to reveal his chief worry—that someone had complained that he didn't take good care of Olin Taverner.

"He has—had—very high standards, very high, but so do I. His apartment, it is always spotless when I leave him, his clothes also. His meals, I make them with my own hands, I am a good chef for the old who cannot eat strong food."

"No one has ever complained about your care of him," I assured Rivas. "I wanted to talk to you about something different."

I took out the photograph of Marc and Harriet Whitby. "This man came to see Mr. Taverner last week, didn't he?"

When he nodded and said, yes, the man had been there on Thursday, I continued, "You know he was killed on Sunday. I'm wondering if he came back to see Mr. Taverner Sunday evening."

Rivas slowly shook his head. "Sunday I do not work, I spend with my family. Maybe this man comes back again when I am not there, although Mr. Taverner, he says nothing on Monday, nothing about a visitor."

That was disappointing. "On Thursday, when Mr. Whitby did see Mr. Taverner, do you know what they talked about?"

"Papers. Old papers Mr. Taverner wants to show this man. He keeps them in a locked drawer in his desk. I never see them. I only help Mr. Taverner walk to the desk: with a visitor he does not like to use a wheelchair, he does not like to seem helpless. Many of my old people are like that, very proud. And he is the proudest of the proud, Mr. Taverner. I help him walk to his desk, I help him undo the lock, I help him walk back to the man, then I wait in the kitchen while they talk. In case he needs tea, water, whisky or suddenly needs help, you understand, with his private functions, sometimes they come—came—on him suddenly."

Rivas's solemn courtesy would be comforting to people whose strength was waning, but who prized their dignity. "Were the papers written or typed?"

"They were written by hand. That much I know. What they say, that I do not know."

"And did he give them to Marc Whitby?"

"No, Mr. Taverner shows them only. The other man, he writes things from the papers into a little notebook that he carries in his pocket, but when he goes away, Mr. Taverner, he locks the papers again in his desk."

"And did Mr. Taverner say anything to you about the papers?"

"He says what the old so often say, he says, 'I will die soon, the time to hold secrets is over.'"

I thanked him, but when I tried to offer him money for his time, he drew himself up to his full height and said quietly he did not take money for such things. I felt embarrassed, as one does in making a social mistake, and left the room ahead of him, stopping at the administrator's desk to get Taverner's address.

Rivas caught up with me at the exit. "I am thinking someone has been visiting Mr. Taverner on Monday night. Not Sunday, when this black man dies, but the next night. On Monday, I leave Mr. Taverner as always at nine-thirty, ready to go to bed but not in bed, that he likes to do by himself. He likes to sit in his chair with his whisky, to read or sometimes to write, and then move into his bed when he is ready for that. For the private functions in the night, he has a bottle on his chair and one on his bed.

"But Tuesday morning, when I find him, when he is still in his chair and I know he has never gone to bed, also his glass is clean. He never has washed a glass in his whole life, I think, and now that he is old and he walks so badly, he will not start now washing glasses. When I was finding him, then everything was too—too much drama, I didn't think about the glass, I didn't think until tonight, until now when you ask me did this black man come back on Sunday. But someone did visit Mr. Taverner on Monday."

My heart beat faster. "What did you do with the glass?"

"I put it in the cupboard, with the others. When someone comes for his things, they will find all of his glasses just so, everything just so."

"Do you still have a key to Mr. Taverner's apartment? I know you're meeting some people, but could you take five minutes to show me which glass? It's possible we might find something in it still, some fingerprint or something."

And then I could stay behind and break into the drawer where Taverner had locked the papers he'd shown Marc Whitby. The weariness that enveloped me an hour ago had vanished. Excitement made my fingers tingle.

Rivas led me solemnly from the nursing facility to a nearby apartment building. He said little, except that he was meeting his "new gentleman's" family in this same building, so he had enough time.

From the outside, the assisted living building looked like Geraldine Graham's, but inside it had been designed for people in wheelchairs and walkers, with handrails bolted into extrawide halls. Taverner had lived on the ground floor. Rivas took a key chain from his pocket and, with the compact motions that characterized him, opened the front door.

When he turned on the lights, I saw we were in an apartment similar again to Geraldine's, but again with wider halls and doorways to accommodate wheelchairs. The rooms as a consequence were smaller. Rivas led me past a sitting room to the kitchen, which was, as he had boasted, spotless, and opened a cupboard where the glasses stood at attention. It was only after he'd pointed out the relevant glass that he spoke.

"You think there is a problem with Mr. Taverner, with his life ending, because of this glass?"

"I'm like you: the washed glass makes me suspicious. Can you show me where you found Mr. Taverner?"

Rivas led me into the bedroom, a large room with heavy drapes covering a set of sliding doors. The bed was still as he'd left it on Monday night, the sheets turned down so that an old man could easily get under them. A leather easy chair was placed about five steps from the bed. A table stood next to it with two canes hanging from a rack; on the polished tabletop were a phone, Monday's newspapers and a bottle of Berghoff's fourteen-year-old bourbon.

"You've seen many people die, haven't you?" I asked. "Was there anything unusual about Mr. Taverner's body when you found him?"

He slowly shook his head. "He has gone in his sleep, I think, as we all hope will happen, without the hospital, the—the equipment, all of those things that hurt us."

"But something wasn't right," I suggested, seeing his troubled frown.

He looked around the room, again shaking his head. "You are right. It is something, not only this glass. Is it the pillow? I think it is, it has the"—he fumbled for a word, showing with his fist the way the head makes a hollow in the pillow after sleep—"yes, the hollow; the pillow looks like he sleeps on it, but he is in his chair. Now"—he crossed to the bed—"now it is normal, but—not quite right, not where I have been leaving it. And also, I think someone has moved this chair."

He pointed at a cane chair on the far side of the bed, next to the drapes covering the sliding doors. You could see four indentations in the pile where the legs had stood for months; whoever replaced the chair hadn't aligned it exactly.

I wanted to inspect the rest of the apartment, but Rivas was anxious not to be late for his meeting. I tried to get him to leave me his key, telling him the police would want to send in a forensic team, but Rivas didn't want to be part of a police inquiry. If someone had been here with Mr. Taverner the night he died, had moved furniture, moved pillows, it would seem as though Rivas hadn't looked after his gentleman carefully, even though Mr. Taverner always wanted to be left to go to bed alone. Besides, the new family would take it amiss to have Rivas involved in a police inquiry. The administrator would help with keys and entrance to the apartment, he said, if investigators needed to search Mr. Taverner's apartment in greater detail.

I nodded my understanding. Following him down the hall and out the door, I took advantage of his anxiety about the time to depress the lip of the dead bolt so it wouldn't fasten when we left. Rivas went to the elevators while I walked outside. As soon as he got into an elevator, I darted back down the hall, pushed Taverner's door open and flipped the lights back on.

A handsome old leather-topped desk stood in a corner on the far side of the sitting room. Nearer to me were the armchairs where Taverner and Whitby had presumably sat to have their conversation. I started toward the desk, then decided caution was the better part of valor. I returned to the kitchen, found some latex gloves under the sink, and put those on.

When I returned to the sitting room, I realized it was considerably colder than the kitchen and bedroom had been. I stopped on my way to the desk: a draft was seeping under the brocade drapes, which swayed with the air currents.

I crossed the room fast and flung the drapes open. Someone had broken the glass on the door to the patio and forced the lock from the inside. I pulled the heavy fabric away from the wall. A man was flattening himself into the corner. He swore and ran toward me bull-like, head lowered. I didn't let go of the drapes fast enough. The man butted me in the stomach, shoved open the broken patio door and took off.

I doubled over, gasping and gagging, and tripped in the drapes. I fought free of the heavy fabric and staggered after the intruder across the patio, through a small garden. I could hear his feet pounding away from me, but I was too winded to move fast. I lost him on the winding paths.

Damn and double damn. I hadn't gotten a good look at him, just a confused impression of a youngish white man with dark thick hair, in jeans and running shoes. A burglar who knew the place was standing empty, or someone after Taverner's secret papers?

I found my way back to the assisted nursing compound and returned to Taverner's apartment. It wasn't so hard to find the locked drawer. Except the lock was broken and the drawer was empty.

Like Domingo Rivas, I didn't want to spend a whole lot of time with the police, especially not the suburban forces. I thought of driving back to Chicago and leaving this mess for the Anodyne Park management to sort out when they got the apartment ready to sell. I thought of the hollow in the pillow disarranged on the bed, the glass rinsed out. What if Taverner's visitor Monday night had put something in his bourbon to make him drowsy, and then taken the pillow from the bed and held it against his face until—well, until, yes.

I couldn't think of one thing about Olin Taverner that I didn't despise. The careers he'd ruined through the blacklist, the homosexuals he'd hounded in public life while remaining deeply closeted himself, the list could go on for days. Did it really matter if someone had hastened the end of an old HUAC hatchet man?

On the other hand, he'd died soon after showing Marc Whitby some secret papers. And Marc Whitby had died soon after seeing them. Who had Whitby discussed those papers with? His young assistant? But then, why hadn't she mentioned them to me? Maybe she'd been more forthcoming with Harriet and Amy.

I rubbed my sore diaphragm. The man who'd butted me was either lucky or well trained. Maybe he'd murdered Whitby and Taverner and come back to search the premises. But that made no sense—he'd have had plenty of time to search when Taverner died. Unless he hadn't known until later that Whitby had seen the documents?

I pulled out my cell phone and called Stephanie Protheroe, the sheriff's deputy I'd been dealing with.

"Warshawski, isn't your boyfriend jealous of the amount of time you're spending with me? I've lent you clothes, I've lost and found documents for you. Now what?"

"You're right," I said. "I've been imposing. Maybe I should take this to the New Solway cops."

She sighed. "Okay, I'll bite. What is it?"

"I was visiting Geraldine Graham this afternoon. She lives in the same complex as Olin Taverner—the guy who died on Monday or Tuesday. As I was leaving her place, I discovered that someone had broken into Taverner's apartment."

"That someone wasn't you, was it, Ms. Warshawski?"

"No, ma'am. That someone was a man who knocked me to the ground when I went in to investigate. White, maybe forty, lots of hair—I didn't get much of a look."

"Okay," she sighed again. "We'll send someone over."

"And, Deputy—Marc Whitby visited Olin Taverner last Thursday night. I don't know if Whitby came back here on Sunday before he died—but it seems worth exploring. And Taverner had an anonymous visitor on Monday, someone who washed out Taverner's whisky glass. Just thought you'd like to know."

Jigsaw Puzzle

It wasn't until I was back in my own home that I remembered the wheel tracks going into the culvert. I was bone tired, too tired to think about it further, let alone try to decide whether I should do something about the tracks. I soaked in the tub for half an hour and ate a bowl of canned chicken soup. It wasn't anything like as good as Mrs. Aguilar's, but it was what I had.

I was drifting off to an early sleep when Deputy Protheroe called me back. I tried to rise to her level of energy as she explained what she'd done. The guard at the entrance to Anodyne Park couldn't possibly identify my intruder: too many people came in all day, either making deliveries or visiting families, for him to recognize anyone from my vague description.

She added, almost casually, "You didn't bust the lock on that desk, did you, during your look-around?"

"Deputy, if I'd gone into that desk, you wouldn't know about it. You got a crime scene team doing prints and so on?"

"The Anodyne management doesn't like a big police presence—it lowers morale and leads to lawsuits." She gave a dry laugh. "But just to keep you from calling six times an hour, I did take the glass into our lab."

"And you'll let me know what they tell you? Just to keep me from calling you six times an hour?"

"You never know: I might even do that."

When she'd hung up, I went back to bed, but I'd woken up too much and couldn't relax. It was still early, only nine. I phoned Amy Blount to see if she'd had any luck either at *T-Square,* or from Marc's other neighbors. Unfortunately, the nursing mother was the only person who'd been up in the middle of the night, or at least the only one who'd seen any sign of activity at Marc's house.

"When I asked who used to visit him, the kids thought I was some jealous girlfriend trying to stake him out—they could remember seeing me come out of Marc's house, but not anyone else. They began creating a scenario where I had murdered him. It made me laugh, and then it made me cry—I can't believe how lonely he must have felt, and I can't believe he's dead."

"Yeah. Investigation sometimes feels like a game, until you remember a person died who was important to their friends and family . . . What about Marc's editor—Simon Hendricks?"

"Umh. Cold fish. He had to talk to us, because Harriet was there. We started the way you suggested, with Marc's assistant Aretha, but she didn't think there was anything specific to the tension between him and Hendricks beyond professional insecurity. Marc had a contract for a book about Kylie Ballantine—we found that in his desk drawer at the office. Aretha said Hendricks was furious about that because he—Hendricks—had been trying for five years to sell a book about Martin Luther King's summer in Chicago."

"So why did Marc tell him about his own book contract?"

"Had to—terms of employment."

"Do you think Hendricks was bitter or jealous enough to kill Marc over it?"

She thought it over. "I'm no expert on why people kill each other. But—well, why would Hendricks lure Marc all the way out to that pond?"

"There is that," I admitted. "What about Marc's cellmate, Jason Tompkin? Did you get him to say anything about the company relations with Bayard?"

"He runs his mouth so much it's hard to know whether to trust anything he says. For what it's worth, the company policy is not to discuss work in progress with anyone outside Llewellyn Publishing. However, he says that Hendricks really stresses it in relation to Bayard Publishing. J.T. says that comes down from Llewellyn, that there's some kind of bad blood between Calvin Bayard and Augustus Llewellyn, nobody knows what, but he, J.T., thinks it's because Llewellyn took money from Bayard to start up *T-Square,* and Bayard acted patronizing—like Llewellyn was proof of what a good-hearted liberal Bayard was. But here's something really weird: according to J.T., Hendricks and Marc had a big blowup last week because Marc tried seeing Llewellyn in person."

I was astounded: you don't survive corporate life by trying to see the company owner behind your boss's back. "What was that about?"

"No one knows. Maybe Marc wanted to persuade Mr. Llewellyn to relax the company's policy on talking to Bayard because Bayard was part of the Kylie Ballantine story."

"So if Marc had wanted to talk to Bayard, he'd definitely have done it quietly," I said. "I found out today that Marc went out to New Solway at least twice, and the first time wasn't to see Bayard, but Olin Taverner."

I told her the odd things I'd learned about Olin Taverner's death, and the man who'd broken into Taverner's apartment. "I'd give a month's pay with chocolate sauce to know what was in Taverner's papers. Marc didn't say anything to Aretha Cummings, did he?"

"Not that she reported to us," Amy said. "And you know, that was a big story, an old man opening a locked drawer, showing off his secret papers. If Marc had mentioned it,

I think she would have said, even if he swore her to secrecy, although I can call her again in the morning to double-check."

"Right." I made a note. "We need the notes Marc took at Taverner's last Thursday night. Or we need the connection between Taverner and Kylie Ballantine—although I'm assuming it's something to do with the blacklist. Maybe she was hauled before HUAC, even though it isn't mentioned in any of her papers down at the Harsh Collection."

"I can go to the university library tomorrow," Amy offered. "All those hearings are on microfiche. I did try with Hendricks to see if he might have any of Marc's notes—I could sort of see him going to Marc's desk and helping himself when the news came in Marc had died—in case there was something he could either use, or needed to cover up. He definitely was jealous of Marc's success. So was Jason Tompkin. Tompkin thinks Marc flew solo too much because he wanted glory. His theory is Marc got hold of something dangerous, but all he saw was the prize he'd get for scooping the world, so he didn't tell anyone. I—don't like that idea. Someone like this J.T. would make Marc retreat into his shell, but not out of—of jealousy or ambition. More out of— he didn't like a lot of noise."

"It's hard when you have to investigate affairs of people you're close to," I sympathized. "I went through that when my cousin Boom-Boom died—it's almost like being the fly on the wall when people are talking about you, isn't it?"

I looked over the notes I'd been making. "Marc visited Taverner a week ago, on Thursday. When did he try to see Llewellyn? Or at least, when did he and Hendricks have their big dustup," I asked. "Before or after Marc met Taverner?"

"I don't know." Paper rustled as she went through her own notes. "You think Taverner told him something about Llewellyn? But what?"

"I don't think anything," I said impatiently. "I don't know enough to think."

"The fight was recent," she said slowly. "It could have been last Friday. I can call J.T. tomorrow and ask him."

"Do: it could be important," I said.

Before hanging up, we organized the next day's work. I told Amy that the archivist thought Marc might have found some original documents in Kylie Ballantine's old home.

"I'd like to make one last desperate effort to find those papers, or any papers of his. It just isn't natural, the way everything has vanished."

We agreed to meet at Marc's house in the morning. While I broke into his Saturn to see if any documents were there, Amy would start a fine-tooth-comb search of the house itself, in case we'd missed anything yesterday. Then Amy would go down to the university library while I tried to talk to Renee Bayard. After all, Renee had met Calvin doing volunteer clerical work for people who had been called before Congress; she might know if there had been a connection between Taverner and Ballantine.

While we'd been talking I'd had another idea about that secret file of Taverner's: young Larry Yosano, the lawyer doing odd jobs for Lebold, Arnoff. It was a little late for business calls, but he was on the emergency shift this week. I figured I'd get further faster by assuming Taverner had been another of Lebold, Arnoff's New Solway clients, and started by saying that Taverner's death must be generating a certain amount of work at the office.

He concurred, but added, "You know, Ms. Warshawski, nothing against you, but I do have a private life. It's hard enough when all those New Solway clients think I'm the Japanese houseman they can call in the middle of the night. Can't we have this conversation tomorrow in my office?"

I had to agree, although I didn't really want to add another trip to the western suburbs to my crowded Friday schedule. We settled on three in the afternoon—Yosano had wanted to do it earlier, but I wanted to get things clear at Whitby's house so that I knew whether I really had to clutch at straws by going into the Larchmont pond.

I was finally climbing back into bed when my phone rang. I was startled to hear Darraugh Graham's voice, bitingly angry.

"Didn't I make it clear that you were not to trouble my mother any further? You have thirty seconds to explain why you've so blatantly disregarded my orders."

I stiffened. "Darraugh, you are not a marine colonel and I am not one of your recruits. I owed your mother the courtesy of a visit to explain what I'd done and why I wouldn't be further involved in her problems. And I won't apologize for seeing her."

"It was unconscionable of you to upset her. That wasn't a courtesy visit, it was an interrogation."

"She called you to complain? Oh, no. Lisa called to complain. Your mother was upset by learning how ill Calvin Bayard was, not by anything I asked her. I think it's permissible for a woman to weep over the decay of an old friend."

"Talking to my mother can have nothing to do with your murder investigation. I warned you about that earlier. If you wish to continue in my employment, I am ordering you to stay away from my mother."

"I'll think about it, Darraugh. About my wishes, I mean. Good night." I hung up before my anger rode me into an outright declaration of quitting. His thousand-a-month retainer—one could pay too high a price for money sometimes.

But Where Are the Pieces
of the Jigsaw?

When I got to Lebold, Arnoff's offices in Oak Brook Tower, Larry Yosano took me in to meet Julius Arnoff: it was better that the senior partner know who was involving herself in the affairs of the firm's most important clients. Better for Yosano, anyway.

By the time I arrived—late—at the meeting, I had already had a long day. I'd woken early, from feverish dreams: I'd been hunting for Morrell through the caves of Kandahar, when the caves turned into the culvert under the road in Anodyne Park. It was miles long, the soil rank with rotted fish and rat droppings. I was no longer hunting Morrell, but fleeing from the man who'd butted me in the stomach. I ran as fast as I could, but my feet in my Bruno Magli pumps were sinking into the fetid ground, and the man was driving a golf cart. When I finally turned in a desperate effort to confront him, Marc Whitby was at the wheel.

I woke panting and sweating. It was only five o'clock. I tried to go back to sleep, but I was in that gritty state where it was impossible to slide away from my conscious brain. Finally, when the late winter sky was starting to streak red, I got up and took the dogs for a run.

I wanted to go as far as I could as fast as I could. I wanted to get away from myself and my tired gray mind, but at the end of three miles, Mitch and Peppy both balked: they planted themselves in the bike path and refused to move, despite both commands and bribes.

I finally turned around and took them home at a pace slow enough to please them, but one that left me prey to the uneasy images from my dreams. I couldn't shake the images, nor the feeling that something beyond mere unpleasantness lay in them.

Back home, I showered and made breakfast—eggs, in the hopes that protein would overcome my gray mood and give me the energy to organize my day. Work felt beyond me this morning, but I didn't have the income or the upbringing to indulge only myself.

Behind my bleak thoughts, I could see my mother at the kitchen table, mending socks. It was three in the morning; my dad hadn't returned from his shift and the West Side was an inferno of riots and looting. I had heard her, or felt her anxiety, I don't know which, and crept down from my bed under the attic dormer. She held me close for a time, then made me a cup of cambric tea, and showed me how to darn a heel.

"We don't give into our worries, *cara,*" she said. "That is for grand ladies, who can fancy themselves ill when their lover hasn't written or the new dress is commonplace. We aren't like that, self-indulgent. We do some job, like this, we do it well, we make the worries leave us alone."

My father had come in around five, to find us both asleep at the kitchen table, our faces in his socks. A cop's daughter, a reporter's lover, that gave you plenty of practice in showing you weren't a grand lady, or self-indulgent. I hadn't darned a sock since I was fifteen, but I had plenty of other chores I could be doing.

I started with a phone call to Luke Edwards, the lugubrious mechanic who's looked after my cars for years. Car locks are tricky; I didn't want to tackle Whitby's with my picklocks, where I might not only jam the lock, but get arrested if some cop saw me using a tool of questionable legality.

Whenever I talk to Luke, I have to endure a long lecture on everything I've done wrong to my current machine before he'll work on it, but he's kind of like the *Car Talk* brothers in what he knows about engines. When he heard I wanted to get into a locked Saturn, he made me sit through five minutes on the inadequate safety features of modern American cars, but at the end he agreed to send his own locksmith to meet me on Giles Street.

Next on my list was Renee Bayard. Naturally, I only reached a secretary; naturally, Ms. Bayard was in an important meeting, but I left a carefully rehearsed message: I was a detective Ms. Bayard had met Wednesday night, the one who had discovered Marcus Whitby's dead body. It was now clear that Whitby had met with Olin Taverner shortly before Taverner himself died, and I was assuming they had discussed Kylie Ballantine. I wanted to ask Ms. Bayard what she knew about Ballantine and Taverner. The secretary read the message back to me in a doubtful voice, but said she would pass it along.

After some internal debate, I also placed a call to Augustus Llewellyn's office. Once again I only reached a secretary, a polished woman with executive office manners, not the rough hostility of their lobby receptionist. Once again I explained my mission for the Whitby family.

"Mr. Marc Whitby tried to see Mr. Llewellyn last week. When he made the appointment, did he say why?"

"We have procedures for staff writers, for all staff, who want to see Mr. Llewellyn. I explained that to Marc when he came up to the eighth floor and told him he had to send me a memo stating the reason for the meeting." She put me on hold to answer another line.

"Did Marc send the memo?" I asked when she came back on the line.

"He didn't want to." Her tone hardened. "He said it was sensitive material that he didn't want to put in writing. He also didn't want to discuss it with his editor. I told him he couldn't be the only judge of what was worth intruding on Mr. Llewellyn. He was one of our best writers, but I really can't relax the rules for one person, just because he's a star."

"I understand," I said quickly, "but I'm also puzzled. It doesn't sound like him, to try to contravene company policy. I think he was troubled by something Olin Taverner told him, and that he might have wanted to consult Mr. Llewellyn about it."

"And what was that?"

"I don't know," I admitted. "If I could find out, it might explain who killed him. Mr. Whitby learned something unusual last week, something involving the old HUAC investigations. I can't find a living soul he talked to about it, so if that's why he tried to see Mr. Llewellyn, I'd really like to know. Could you check with Mr. Llewellyn, to see whether Marc actually talked to him? He might have waited for you to go to lunch, or even phoned Mr. Llewellyn at home."

She said stiffly that when she was away from her desk, her assistant sat in for her and logged in any callers. Still, she took my details before hanging up to answer another call.

I stared at the picture over my desk, as if I could see Marc Whitby in the blur of color. What had come up that made him risk his job at *T- Square* by going directly to the magazine's owner? Of course, it could have been anything—but no notes or papers remained in his desk or home. So I had to believe it involved the same story that took him to Olin Taverner last week. If I couldn't find any papers in his car, then I'd have to grasp at my last straw, and see whether he'd dropped something in the pond when he fell in. I called around to places that rented diving equipment just in case.

I found a shop on Diversey that could help me. I stopped there on my way to the South Side. They rented me a wet suit. I bought a headlamp, goggles and an underwater knife; at a hardware store near Marc's home I bought a roll of twine. That should get me through the pond if I had to go in.

I got to Marc's house after the morning rush to work and school had ended. A stay-at-home mom out with a baby buggy eyed me curiously, but no one else was on the street. When Amy arrived, we started a deeper search than we'd done before, going through the basement, looking under rugs and tapping wallboard in the unfinished rooms—all the labor of a truly thorough search.

Around noon, Luke's locksmith arrived. He had a box of keys and alarm codes. When he had opened the Saturn, he gave me the coded key that worked the ignition and alarm—for a hundred dollars.

While Amy continued doggedly inside the house, I made a similarly thorough, and equally futile, search of the car. I was lying under the chassis with a flashlight, while a couple of area winos offered helpful suggestions, when Renee Bayard returned my call.

I slid out from beneath the car and got into the driver's seat so I could talk to her privately. The Wabash Cannonball came over the ether at full speed.

"Ms. Warshawski, you were talking to my granddaughter on Wednesday without my permission. You were out in New Solway yesterday questioning my staff without talking to me first. And now, finally as an after-thought, you want to talk to me. You should have started with me."

My hand grew wet on my little phone. "I thought Catherine told you why we were talking."

"Give me some credit, Ms. Warshawski: I didn't just climb down from a tree and start walking erect. I've spoken to Darraugh Graham. Besides assuring me Catherine never asked him for the name of a detective, he says he told you to end the inquiry that took you to New Solway to begin with."

"He's not my only client, Ms. Bayard. I'm investigating Marcus Whitby's death. Mr. Whitby died in New Solway and—"

"And has no connection with my husband or granddaughter that I can discern."

"And has a definite connection with Olin Taverner, who also died this week in odd circumstances." Annoyance stiffened my attitude. "Mr. Whitby met with Taverner shortly before his death. Taverner showed him his secret files, which are now miss-ing. I'm assuming their mutual interest was Kylie Ballantine; I was hoping you knew what Taverner's involvement was with Bal-lantine."

"And I'm supposed to be your research file? Because we published one of Ballantine's books?"

"Because you met Mr. Bayard during the HUAC hearings and you might remember whether Kylie Ballantine was also a target of Olin Taverner's."

She paused for a moment, as if deciding whether I deserved an answer, before saying, "There used to be something called the Committee for Social Thought and Justice, a kind of left-wing think tank. Olin always wanted them to be a Communist front. Ballantine might have taken part in some of their meetings, I don't know. If she did, Olin might have questioned her privately, but I wouldn't know. What were the odd circumstances of Olin's death?"

"They're part of an ongoing police inquiry," I said primly. "I'm not at liberty to say."

"I'm amazed: you take so many other unauthorized liberties. One which you may not have again is access either to my granddaughter or my home."

She hung up without saying good-bye. I climbed out of the car, feeling shaky, the way one does after being run over by a high-speed train. I abandoned the car and the winos, who kept telling me they could get that engine going, no problem.

In the house, Amy and I finished our search, just going through the motions. We knew there wasn't anything under the floorboards or in a secret compartment—Marc might not have left documents under J.T. or Simon Hendricks's prying eyes at work, but he wouldn't have felt the need to hide papers inside his own home.

"I really hoped I'd find some of Kylie Ballantine's letters," I said. "I think I mentioned last night—Marc left a message with the archivist at the Harsh Collection, maybe ten days before he died. Gideon Reed knew Marc was going through her old home; he thought maybe Marc wanted to let him know he'd actually found something there."

"I could go over to her place," Amy volunteered, "talk to the owner or tenants or whoever, see whether they know if Marc turned up anything."

Ballantine's old home was just around the corner on King Drive. "Can't hurt if you have the time. But there's something else I was hoping you could do, as well."

I described my frustrating conversation with Renee Bayard. "While you're down at the University of Chicago library, see how much you can find out about the Committee on Social Thought and Justice. It's a slender thread, but it's the only one we've got right now. There are a couple of references to an unspecified committee in the Ballantine archives—it's a good assumption it's that one. And come to think of it, Taverner questioned Bayard about his involvement with the same committee . . . Let's leave: we're not going to find anything here."

I'd worn jeans and a sweatshirt for my search, but had brought a business suit to put on for my meeting with the New Solway lawyers. I changed in Marc Whitby's living room, picked up a homemade biscuit at a local diner to eat in the car and joined the early afternoon exodus from the city.

The Family Retainer

Even though I reached the Eisenhower at two-thirty, traffic was already heavy; by the time I'd found a place to park, found the right building in the massive shopping-office complex and used a ladies' room to brush biscuit crumbs from my blouse, I was fifteen minutes late for my meeting. Larry Yosano whisked me straight into the senior partner's office.

Julius Arnoff was a short, bony man, perhaps in his late seventies, with deep-sunk eyes under hooded lids. He didn't shake hands with me, just waved Yosano and me to a couple of straight-back chairs on the far side of his desk. "I understand from young Yosano here that you are a Chicago detective? A private detective, not with the Chicago police?"

"That's correct."

He produced a cold smile. "You are not the first Chicago detective to be curious about our clients' affairs."

"I expect not," I said. "From what Ms. Geraldine Graham's been telling me, your clients could have kept an entire bureau of detectives busy."

Larry Yosano sucked in his breath and looked from me to Arnoff in dismay, but the senior lawyer said, "If Mrs. Graham has been confiding in you, then Yosano here can hardly add anything to what you know."

"She's told me fragments, not anything like a whole, coherent story. She's told me about her battles with her mother, and that her mother . . . persuaded her to marry MacKenzie Graham. She's told me that Olin Taverner was a homosexual. I know that Calvin Bayard suffers from Alzheimer's and that Renee Bayard is at great pains to keep the world from knowing he's ill. But a lot of the connecting details are missing."

"And you hope we'll tell you what we wouldn't tell the detectives and reporters who sniffed around here fifty years ago?" His tone was supercilious.

"My concern isn't with New Solway's fifty-year-old riff on Peyton Place, but with a couple of contemporary murders. I'm investigating Marcus Whitby's death: he's the man who died—"

"I know all about the man who died at Larchmont. Even though the Grahams sold Larchmont Hall, we continue to be involved with the property. I know that Rick Salvi believes the man committed suicide, and that you are out to force us into a murder investigation."

"When murder has been committed, an investigation is usually a good idea," I said mildly.

"Not always, young woman, not always," he snapped.

"I've been wondering about that myself." I assumed a thoughtful expression. "I discovered evidence at Olin Taverner's apartment yesterday that makes me suspect he may also have been murdered. And yet, I have to ask whether that needs to be investigated. Does it matter that someone hustled an old man off the planet a few months before his time? Do I waste my energy on the death of a man who himself ruined many people's lives?"

"Olin Taverner began his legal training in Theodore Lebold's office," Arnoff said. "He went on to more important matters before I joined the firm, but we have always held him in esteem here."

"So you think his murder deserves investigation. But that Marc Whitby's doesn't."

"Don't twist my words, young woman." Arnoff turned his hooded gaze to Yosano. "What do we know about Mr. Taverner's death, Larry?"

Yosano sat up straight. "Only that Ms. Warshawski found something unusual in his apartment, sir. She was going to explain the situation to me in our meeting this afternoon."

"And that situation is—?" Arnoff turned back to me.

I leaned back in my chair, legs crossed, trying to establish that I wasn't a surbordinate. "Someone was in Taverner's apartment the night he died. That person took pains to cover up his, or maybe her, presence, but nonetheless left telltale traces. I know firsthand that someone broke into the place yesterday—I interrupted him.

Unfortunately, he knocked me over and got away. I know Marcus Whitby consulted Taverner last Thursday—a week ago yesterday. And I know Taverner let him see some documents that he kept in a locked drawer. Those documents have been stolen from the apartment. I'm hoping you know what was in them."

Arnoff slowly shook his head. "Our clients don't always confide in us. We are the executors, of course, of the Taverner estate."

"Who are the heirs, since he didn't leave a family?" I asked.

"Several foundations whose work he valued."

"Including the Spadona Foundation? I wonder how Renee Bayard will feel, seeing her son use money from his father's old enemy to set a policy agenda she and Calvin oppose."

Arnoff smiled primly. "If Calvin Bayard had kept better track of his own documents, Edwards Bayard might not be in such opposition to him today."

"Meaning?"

"Meaning all these great families have something they don't want anyone else to know. I'm sorry I can't help you with Olin's papers. I doubt I ever saw those."

I asked what Arnoff knew about Kylie Ballantine's connection to Taverner.

He gave his thin, supercilious smile again. "The African dancer? I don't think it was Olin who had a connection to her."

"Calvin Bayard, then?" I asked.

"Calvin supported a number of artists. I believe Ballantine was his protégée for a time. Before he married Renee, of course."

The brief pause he gave before the word "protégée" was supposed to let me know they had been lovers. Everything in this office—in New Solway—was done by innuendo. I wondered how long it would be before young Yosano picked up the same skin-crawling habit.

"Renee Bayard was telling me this morning that Taverner had a bee in his bonnet about the Committee for Social Thought and Justice. There's a rumor that Calvin Bayard gave them money." A rumor I myself was just starting, but he might have been the patron mentioned in the Ballantine archive.

"Oh, Calvin was generous with many left-wing groups in the thirties and forties.

There's never been any doubt where his politics lay. But just because he published known Communists like Armand Pelletier, I don't think anyone ever seriously believed Calvin was a Communist himself. Not even Olin, when he was hounding him back in the fifties. I think they were simply two men who didn't like each other. Calvin was the flamboyant young success, Olin had to climb his way slowly. And Olin was hampered by the homosexuality you alluded to. By the way, I understand Darraugh Graham hired you to find who his mother was seeing in the Larchmont attic. Did you ever discover who was there?"

I shook my head slowly. Somehow I'd forgotten the original inquiry that had taken me out to New Solway. "Catherine Bayard told me it was her grandfather, that he had a key to the old Graham house."

Arnoff made a sound like an engine starting in cold weather; I realized after a startled moment he was laughing. "So young Catherine has all the Bayard spirit. One never knows how the next generation will behave with so much wealth available to it."

"But when I asked Darraugh about it, he became furious."

"I'm afraid I'm not in Graham's confidence, young woman; he took his legal affairs elsewhere," Arnoff said. "He was much attached to his father, however, and Mrs. Drummond's attitude when MacKenzie Graham died did cause Darraugh to run away that summer. He was something like fourteen or fifteen. Eventually he returned to Exeter to finish his education but I don't believe he ever returned to Larchmont."

"Was there something especially difficult about MacKenzie Graham's death?" I asked.

"All deaths are difficult. But MacKenzie had hanged himself, as I understand it."

"But why?" Larry Yosano was startled into speaking.

"He was at that age," Arnoff said. "In my experience, the unhappy of the Earth either learn to live with it by the time they're forty-five, or they decide they no longer can make the effort. It was particularly unfortunate that Darraugh found his father's body. I believe his father didn't know Exeter had sent him home. MacKenzie was very attached to his son. I doubt he would have killed himself, at least not then, had he known Darraugh was there."

I tried to digest this. "By Ms. Graham's account, it was an unhappy household. Why did she and Mr. Graham marry in the first place? And why did they never move into a place of their own?"

"Had you known Mrs. Matthew Drummond, you would have understood the answer to both questions. Mr. and Mrs. MacKenzie Graham both caused their parents considerable anxiety when young, as Mr. Lebold explained the matter to me. Both Mrs. Drummond and Mr. Blair Graham—Mr. MacKenzie's father, that is—thought marriage would settle the two young people down. Of course, when I came into the firm, Mrs. Drummond was sixty-five, but she was still a formidable power. In fact, she refused at the outset to work with—" Arnoff broke off.

"She wouldn't work with a Jewish lawyer?" I suggested.

"She had old-fashioned prejudices," he said primly. "When Theodore Lebold made me a partner, a few took their business elsewhere, just as some did when we brought

Yosano here into the firm, but most of New Solway saw then, as they do now, that Lebold, Arnoff still has their interests very much at heart."

Scuba Diver

Twilight softened the pond's surface, blur-ring the tangled nest of weeds so that only the lily pads showed. Even the dead carp looked as if it might be merely floating near the surface waiting for a fly to land.

When I left Arnoff's office, I'd thought about returning to Chicago and leaving the pond until the morning, but that would have meant yet another drive out to the western suburbs. After all, it was going to be dark under all those weeds whether I went in at six in the morning or six at night.

All I had left in my thin arsenal was the dogged desire to find what Taverner had told Marc Whitby. Arnoff had dropped hints that I should be able to sort out. He clearly was proud of knowing the secrets swirling around New Solway. Like indiscretions that Calvin Bayard should never have committed to paper. Or at least made sure were far from his son's prying eyes.

I negotiated the turn onto the East-West Tollway, and joined the mile-long backup at the tollbooths. Arnoff had said no one, not even Taverner, ever seriously believed Calvin Bayard was a Communist. So what else had he done that had shocked his son into becoming ultraconservative? And done on paper?

I inched forward. That was what was so frustrating about this parade of prima donnas. All of their lives were intertwined, by history, by marriage, by shared lies. They were like a group playing three-card monte, and laughing as I kept diving for the court card. I was beginning to doubt a South Side street fighter could be a match for such smooth hustlers.

I oozed off the tollway at Warrenville Road. I could find my way from the tollway to Larchmont Hall on autopilot by now. At Larchmont, I pulled my Mustang around behind the barn, where it was hidden from both the road and the woods connecting to the Bayard estate. If someone—say, young Catherine, or even Ruth Lantner—were visiting Larchmont Hall, they wouldn't be able to see the car.

Before leaving Oak Brook, I'd stopped in the shopping center to change out of my business clothes and put on a swimsuit, sweatshirt and jeans. These last I took off now and left in the car. I squirmed my way into the wet suit. The rubber was hard to maneuver. I was sweating from exertion by the time I finished, but feeling clammy at the same time from the cold rubber against my skin.

I put on the diver's headlamp I'd bought this morning. Tucking the twine and small knife under my arm with fins and goggles, I padded around the barn, through the overgrown gardens to the pond.

I'd never done underwater work, but I'd learned to swim in Lake Michigan. In fact, my cousin Boom-Boom and I used to drive our mothers mad with worry by going into the foul waters of Lake Calumet, since that was closer to our homes. Funny how the stuff that's exciting when you're a kid with a scolding mother in the background seems horrifying when you're an adult on your own. If Boom-Boom were here, it would be an adventure. If Boom-Boom were still alive, I wouldn't feel so alone. Self-pitying tears spurted out. I dashed them away angrily. You're a woman saved by action, I mocked myself: get the damned fins on and get going.

The water was as nasty as I'd imagined. I made a face, then pulled the goggles over my eyes, stuck the breathing tube between my teeth, and did a handstand, trying to ignore the shock of cold water against my head. Almost at once, I became tangled in the nest of roots. Picking and kicking my way through them got my blood flowing enough to keep the cold at bay, although it also stirred up dirt from the bottom, making it harder to see anything—the headlamp couldn't penetrate more than a few feet of this murk. As I'd expected, it didn't matter that I'd gotten to the job late—daylight wouldn't have made it through the knotted vegetation on the surface.

I estimated I had about four hundred square feet to cover. I grimly set about working the lanes: headstand, paw my way through the roots, feel the bottom, surface for air, repeat. The breathing tube was useless, so I laid it along the pond ledge. Each time I reached one of the walls, I'd tie off a length of twine. I started at the west end, where I'd tumbled onto Marc's body on Sunday.

At the end of an hour, I'd covered about a hundred square feet. I'd found three rusty cans, a corroded watch, shards of china with edges worn smooth by the water and a crystal champagne goblet miraculously whole. I'd also found a number of pieces of wood so logged by water they'd sunk to the bottom.

It was seven o'clock and completely dark now in the upper world. My shoulders ached from pushing through the weeds, my nose was running and I was feeling sorrier for myself than ever. I put the goblet on the edge of the pond next to the china, tied off my line, and dove again.

At seven-thirty, I'd added more cans, some forks and spoons, more china shards and a woman's ring to my trove. The ring had been there for some time, judging by the amount of dirt on it, but it looked as though it might have impressive stones in it. I zipped it into a pocket of the wetsuit.

At eight, when I was so cold and discouraged I wanted to quit, I found a pocket organizer. I surfaced and stared at it. I was numb, unable to summon any excitement, but I knew it had to be either Marc's or his murderer's—beneath the muck of dirty water and plant detritus, the grain on the brown leather was still visible. My hands were too thick with cold to try to open it here. I hoisted myself out far enough to zip it into my pocket next to the ring.

I'd covered most of the pool by then. I was tempted to call it quits, but I only had one more section to do. If I didn't search it, I'd lie awake all night imagining the vital piece of evidence I'd overlooked. I sucked cold air into my damp lungs for a few minutes, then slid back into the water.

Nothing else was there except more wood. One piece felt as though it might actually be an artifact, not just a dead branch. I brought it to the surface with me. Pushing myself thankfully free of the murk, I walked around the pond undoing my lengths of twine, looping it around my shoulder. My legs were wobbly from two hours of diving and kicking.

Before I could start gathering up my trove of china and glass, I heard footsteps whicking across the lawn. I gripped the breathing tube between my teeth and slid into the pond, remembering at the last second to switch off my headlamp.

Water amplifies sound. The feet— Catherine Bayard's? Ruth Lantner's?— sounded as though they were pounding past in hobnailed boots. I waited a long minute, giving her time to clear the pond and head up the lawn to the house. As I was starting to climb out again, I heard another set of feet crunching along the brick walk next to me. I dropped back under water. The steps stopped. A light shone across the pond's surface.

My heart stood still. I held my breath while the light played through the tangle of reeds, lily pads, dead fish. Surely my breathing tube didn't stand out in that mess. After a moment, the light swept away; the steps moved on.

It was a windless night. If I scrambled out of the pond now, sound might carry to a suspicious ear. If I stayed where I was, someone might be attacking Catherine Bayard. I lifted my head out of the water, straining to see through the dark. In front of me, up near the house, a flashlight bobbed. I heard voices—an exclamation of surprise?—followed by murmurs. It didn't sound like an assault.

I'd been standing still in the cold water too long: my teeth were chattering so loudly I couldn't believe they couldn't hear me up at the house. The noise couldn't be louder than I'd make climbing out of the pond. For the third time, I hoisted myself out of the water, moving as carefully as I could. I slipped out of the fins and trotted to the far side of the pond where I'd left my shoes. Before I could put them on, the voices sounded more loudly. I was damned if I was going into that rank and chill water one more time. Grabbing my shoes, I rolled under one of the stone benches.

"Catherine, you're lying to me and I don't like it. Ruth told me the detective who was at Banks Street on Wednesday came out to see her yesterday with a tale of you coming over here in the night with a key belonging to your grandfather. So—"

"I told you, she made it up. I don't know why. Not Ruth, the detective—"

"No." Renee Bayard halted a yard from my nose. "I called Darraugh yesterday. I didn't like the idea that he would send a detective to you who dealt with murder. There's time, and to spare, for you to delve into human misery, but—at any rate, he said he hadn't heard from you recently, and nor had his staff. So either you found this woman on your own, or she found you. Why?"

"She found me, she stalked me!" Catherine cried.

Renee was silent for a few beats, apparently collecting her thoughts; when she spoke again, her voice was tired. "Darling, if she were stalking you, why did you support the stories she was telling yesterday afternoon? If she's blackmailing you, you need to tell me. If you think you need a detective for something, can't you tell me that, too?"

"I can't. If I could, I would, but I can't. Don't make me say any more because it will only be lies and you'll know and get angrier."

"Were you here Sunday night?" Renee said. "Did something frighten you?"

"You mean, if I was out here, did I interrupt whoever killed that journalist? No,

Granny: I wasn't here, I didn't have a clue a murderer was hanging around here."

Renee sucked in a breath, as if she was about to dispute Catherine's repeated claim of not being here, then paused, as if aware that this argument was futile. I clenched my jaws together to keep my teeth from rattling at her feet.

"But now you do know, Trina, you mustn't come back here. We don't know who killed that reporter. Someone is taking advantage of Larchmont standing empty to use the house: that's why your detective was here. Geraldine Graham has been seeing lights in the attic, and while Darraugh thinks she could be making it up to force him to spend more time with her, I don't agree: she's a shrewd woman, she doesn't use petty tricks. A deranged person could be hiding in this house. If you're coming here to meet a friend or a lover or to use drugs or anything you don't want me to know about, please—" She broke off, unable to complete the thought.

"No one can get into these buildings, they have a security system," Catherine said. "An alarm goes off in Julius Arnoff's office."

"Do you know that because you've triggered it?"

"It's not like it's a secret. I mean, we all
have alarms on our houses, and we all know
what to do when they go off, and everyone
knows they ring at the lawyer's office and at
the police."

Catherine was talking in the breathless
run-on sentences she'd used on me yesterday when she wanted to rush me past sensitive topics. What didn't she want her
grandmother to push on here? Renee
Bayard clearly was wondering the same
thing, because there was another long
pause before she spoke again.

"Do you have a key to the alarm system,
Catherine?"

"No, Gran—how could I have a key to
someone else's house?"

"By taking it if you found it lying around."
Renee Bayard's voice was casual, almost
as if she wasn't interested in the subject. "I
expect this house is like all the houses out
here. We're such special people in New
Solway, so unusually honest and moral by
virtue of our wealth and position, that newcomers don't have to bother with new alarm
systems: they know the old owners won't

come around breaking in. I daresay the— what was the name of the family that bought Larchmont?—I daresay they left the Grahams' alarm in place and keys to that system could have been drifting around out here for years. I'm not suggesting you stole anything, but that you couldn't resist using a key once you'd found it."

"Oh, please, Gran, I couldn't stand those Jablon kids long enough to get a key from them, they were such nou-nous with their—"

"Such what?" her grandmother demanded.

"Sorry," Catherine mumbled. "We use it at school. *Nouveaux-nouveaux riches,* you know."

"I do now," Renee said dryly. "Contempt for those born in different circumstances than your own is the easiest way to stop thinking."

"I know, I know, but if you'd—hey, Gran, someone has been here—look at all this stuff laid out, like they'd been having a picnic or something, except using all this old broken china."

Renee swept a circle of light outward toward the china shards Catherine had seen. These were from my first lot, at the end of the pond closest to us. I watched her feet march over. Catherine followed.

"Was the sheriff here, do you think? Was he dredging the pond for clues?"

"I don't know," Renee said. "Rick Salvi doesn't seem that interested in the situation. Maybe it was your detective, returning to the scene of the crime. These look like bits of Geraldine Graham's mother's Coalport. She had place settings for a hundred, all in this blue-and-gilt. They must have fallen into the water during alfresco evenings."

"People got drunk and threw china into the pond?"

"We weren't quite as wild as that, darling. I shall have to call Rick and see if he sent a crew to the pond. Recently it would be, too, there are still wet patches under these pieces. You didn't see anyone? I thought I heard—but I didn't see—" The flashlight swept around again.

"Here's something else." Catherine had moved to the far end of the pond, her own flashlight cutting a narrow cone along the pond's edge. If I'd left wet footprints on the walk she was obliterating them. "Oh, it's just more grubby old bits of something. Not more china from Mrs. Graham's drunken orgies, it's all dark and nasty—hey, if you look close, it looks like a mask, you know, like the one Grample has in his study. Didn't some friend in the arts or something give that to him? It looks like they gave one to the Grahams who didn't like it quite as much."

Renee's feet crunched on the broken brick as she strode over to her granddaughter's side. "I think you're right. We'll have to clean it up: most of it's here, it's just the top corner around the left eye that's broken off. I must say, this explains a lot."

"About what, Gran?"

"Life, Trina, although it is always an inexplicable mystery. Let's go home now." As their footsteps crunched out of the garden, she added, "What did you see here Sunday night?"

But Catherine wasn't to be tricked. Their voices were fading, but I heard her say, "Since I wasn't here, I couldn't possibly have seen anything."

Scaling the North Face

I slept three hours at the nearest motel. When the alarm went off at midnight, I lay blinking at the unfamiliar surroundings. Why had I set the alarm when what I really needed was eight—no, make that ten—hours in a warm bed? It was too cold, I was too old, for nighttime derring-do. But when I rolled over and wriggled back under the blankets, I couldn't get back to sleep.

Catherine had a key to Larchmont Hall. She was shielding someone inside the house. And Renee Bayard was too shrewd not to understand both these things. Renee would have the DuPage sheriff out there first thing in the morning and my chance of finding—Marcus Whitby's murderer, say, or a possible witness to the murder—would evaporate.

"As if it's your business." I could hear Catherine Bayard say that, her narrow face pinched up in scorn, but I got out of bed anyway.

I put my jeans back on, but my socks and sweatshirt were wet and stank of rotted vegetation. The silk blouse I'd worn to see Julius Arnoff was in my trunk. I didn't want to wear it for strenuous work, but one thing the suburbs have in abundance is all-night shopping. The motel itself was across the street from a twenty-four-hour behemoth. I put on my blouse and suit jacket and stuck the pocket organizer into my day pack before crossing the highway—I didn't want to leave my precious booty alone for a minute.

Before falling into the bed, I'd tried to pry the organizer open, but dirt and wet weeds clogged it shut. I didn't force it—if this was Marc Whitby's, I didn't want to destroy any notes or documents zipped inside. I'd get it to the forensic lab I use for this kind of problem.

The ring I rinsed off under the bathroom tap. A jeweler would have to clean it up properly, but as I'd thought, it was an expensive, garish piece of jewelry. A kind of beehive of stones was built up from a gold band—diamond and emerald chips banked around four good-sized rocks. A couple of the small chips were missing, but what remained could probably pay Mr. Contreras's and my taxes for a couple of years.

Had it been Geraldine Graham's? Her mother's? I pictured a teenage Darraugh throwing his grandmother's ring in the pond after they'd fought about his father—the father for whom he defiantly named his own son. Or perhaps Geraldine herself had thrown it away, out of disgust with her marriage. Or perhaps I was being melodramatic—maybe she or her mother, or even some guest, had lost it during one of those al fresco dinners Renee Bayard mentioned—the owner would be thrilled to see it again.

My fingers were swollen from the cold water, but at their normal shape the ring would have slid down over the knuckle. I held out my hand to study the ring in the bathroom mirror. Wedged against my knuckle, with my fingers showing a spider network of cuts, the piece looked even more grotesque. Definitely the possession of someone with more money than taste—although I guess a claim to superior taste is the weak comfort of the poor. I stuffed the ring into my jeans and went out to buy skulking clothes.

In the superstore across the road, I found aspirin, orange juice, socks, fresh batteries for the work lamp, work gloves with rubber palms and a hooded navy sweatshirt—all for twenty-three dollars. I had an uneasy feeling that slaves in China or Burma had made these items. They never say that on the label: made for Megatherium Superstores by slave labor so you can have it cheap, but a sweatshirt, gloves and so on for twenty-three dollars ought to tip you off. Ought to tip me off. I could have driven all the way home for gloves, sweatshirt, and so on, not to mention my gun, but I was an American—fast, cheap and easy, was my motto.

Back in the motel, I drank half the orange juice with two aspirins: that would do me as much good as another six hours in bed. The rest I put in my day pack along with the small knife and the headlamp. I left a "Do Not Disturb" sign on the door in case I wanted to use the room again, but I put all my stuff in the car: if my luck—and stamina—held, I wanted to drive straight home when I finished.

I was in one of the peaks of alertness that you sometimes reach when you're basically exhausted. At the entrance to Coverdale Lane, I pulled the Mustang behind a bush. I wanted to approach Larchmont on foot—I didn't want the noise of my car to alert anyone who might be hanging around.

Five nights ago the trip had spooked me; the road had seemed endless, the night animals major menaces. Now I knew the area well enough that I jogged along. I was wearing my diver's headlamp, but the moon outlined the road in enough ghostly light that I didn't have to switch it on.

Movement loosened my muscles, helping the aspirin kick in. I stretched my arms. Some muscle between my shoulder blades gave me a stab of pain sharp enough that I winced. I hoped it was a muscle I wasn't going to want again tonight.

Twice, cars went past and I ducked into the shrubbery. I thought about cutting across the fields, but I'd make less noise on the tarmac. I was betting Renee Bayard would wait until morning to call the sheriff, but I couldn't be sure of it—the Wabash Cannonball moved fast, and if she thought her granddaughter was sheltering a murderer, she'd act at once. I was also betting Catherine wouldn't try to slide out past her grandmother again tonight, but I couldn't be sure of that, either.

When I turned up the Larchmont carriageway, I slowed down, stopping periodically to listen to the night sounds. Jogging had warmed me up; now I could feel the late-winter air against my back. A wind had come up, rustling the leaves and dead grasses, making me stop more often—in my nervous state, every noise sounded like someone moving through the underbrush.

When I reached the house, I first made a tour of the outbuildings, looking for any signs of other people. I had uneasy visions of Renee Bayard or the DuPage sheriff leaping out at me, but I didn't see anyone. A loud crashing near the pond sent me to the ground, my heart hammering, but it was only a couple of white-tailed deer, startled into flight by my approach.

At last I crossed the yard to the big house, to the main entrance on the west side, where white columns supported a domed porch. Without giving myself time to think it over, I ran the last twenty feet, jumped and grabbed the crossbar between the column capitals. The sore muscle in my shoulder protested, but I moved fast, bending my arms, pulling my body up, hooking my legs around one of the columns so my thighs were bearing my weight. I stuck an arm up to the edge of the dome, found a stone knob that I could hang on to, and heaved myself up, landing like a dying fish on the curved surface.

When I'd caught my breath, I scooted backward until I was leaning against the wall. From my vantage point, I could see more of the grounds. The only movement I could make out, besides the wind rustling the dead grasses, was of the deer, returning to the pond. Through the bare tree branches I looked at the night sky. Wisps of clouds floated across the moon, but the stars were bright and crisp and close, the way they never are in the city. My burst of alert energy was fading; I started to doze off.

Get up and get your head in the game, Warshawski. I could hear my high school basketball coach's deep bark almost as if she'd been standing next to me. I forced myself to my feet and looked at the window behind me. It led into an upper hallway, but it held the telltale markers of the security system. Which meant going up another layer. There was no easy access to the third story, no columns to shinny up, but gaps in the old mortar left finger- and toeholds here and there. I started up.

I've always thought wall climbing was a stupid sport. Fumbling about for purchase, testing each hole where I stuck my fingers, pulling myself up half a foot at a time with throbbing muscles and trembling legs, going cheek to cheek with rough bricks, so that when I slipped I had a raw spot from forehead to chin—none of that made me change my mind.

I was very aware of how clear a target my dark clothes presented against the whitewashed brick. And that if I lost my grip and fell, I'd bounce off the domed roof underneath and break . . . well, a lot of bones. And that anyone lurking inside would have enough advance warning of my approach to be waiting for me with lead. A bullet or a pipe, or maybe molten in a pot, the way they did it in the Middle Ages. By now I was sweating freely, and not merely from exertion: imagination is not a gift for a detective.

The third-floor windows had narrow ledges, not wide enough to kneel on, barely wide enough for me to stand splay-legged like a graceless ballerina. I hung to the top of the frame, gasping for breath, soothing my raw face against the cool glass.

Before adding to my racket by breaking the glass, I tested whether the window was even locked. The sash was stiff, but it moved—the security system on the first two floors had made Julius Arnoff and the titleholder complacent. When I had a wide enough gap to stick my arm through, I pulled up on the inside sash to lift the bottom half. I had to move along the narrow ledge like an Egyptian figurine, but I managed to slide my right leg through the gap, to ease down to a sitting position, one leg inside, one dangling outside, and finally push the window far enough open to duck into the house.

I pulled the headlamp from my day pack and switched it on. I was in one of the thirteen bedrooms described in the 1903 newspaper. No one had thought it worth redecorating, or even cleaning, for years. Dust was thick on the floor. A water leak was sending brown fingers down the faded wallpaper.

I tiptoed through the dust and opened the door onto a long uncarpeted hall. I moved as quietly as I could, opening each door, looking in closets, in bathrooms, not seeing anything. Stairs rose from the lower floor halfway along the hall. I peered down. This was the top end of the main staircase—on the floor below me, the bannisters grew large and elaborate; presumably, by the time they reached the ground, they would be equal to what I'd seen at the Bayards' yesterday morning.

On the far side of the main staircase, tracks appeared in the dust. Catherine Bayard, I had to believe. I followed her steps to a door at the end of the hall. I opened it quickly, crouching low behind it in case someone started shooting. No lead came pouring down at me. Instead, a scared little voice called, "Catterine, it is you?"

The Jaws of a Giant Clam

I straightened up and turned on my head-lamp. I was looking up a flight of narrow stairs at a youth in sweatshirt and jeans. His dark eyes were wide with fear. Far from trying to attack me, he seemed too frightened to move.

I stood still and spoke in a calm, slow voice. "I'm sorry, but Catherine can't come tonight: her grandmother won't let her out of the house."

He didn't say anything. He looked very young and vulnerable, like a fawn frozen in a clearing. He was gripping the handrail so tightly his knuckles showed white through his dark skin.

"Can you tell me your name and why you are in this house?" I spoke in the same slow, gentle voice.

"Catterine, she say I stay here." His voice came out in a whisper.

"Why is she hiding you?"

He swallowed convulsively, but didn't speak.

"I'm not here to hurt you. But you can't stay in this place any longer. People know you're here."

"Who know? Catterine, she say she tell no body."

"The woman who used to own this house lives across the street. She has seen your light, your and Catherine's lights, through the attic windows. The woman has a son who is a—friend—of mine." The youth was so frightened I didn't want to tell him I was a detective. "Her son asked me to find out who is living in his mother's old house."

"And now what you are doing? You are telling police?"

"I'm not telling the police. Unless you killed someone."

"Kill? I not kill, you cannot say I kill, I am in house, not killing!" In his panic, his voice rose. We'd been speaking in whispers, so that the sudden shout was shocking.

Fatigue was making it hard for me to concentrate. Also I was getting a crick in my neck from staring up at him. "I want to come upstairs so we can talk properly."

As I started up, he began to retreat, his big eyes not wavering from my face. The staircase ended in a large open area with skylights overhead. So this was where light seeped out for Geraldine Graham to see. When Catherine came, she and the boy sat talking by flashlight or something. I switched off my headlamp—I hoped before Geraldine noticed it.

The roof was pitched steeply here. Odd corners stuck out into the room to accommodate the house's four chimneys. This had been the servants' common room during Geraldine Graham's childhood. I pictured a wistful girl with dark braids sneaking up the stairs to watch the maids play poker.

Old furniture was piled against one of the walls—I made out a couple of dressers, a jumble of chairs and a bed frame. The boy and Catherine must have dragged out the leather-topped desk that stood directly under the skylights. Some books were stacked neatly along one side next to a plate, cup and glass. I assumed the desk and the rest were Graham family discards—they looked too old to have been part of the nou-nou family's brief tenure.

The boy's eyes darted from me to the stairwell; he was trying to summon his courage to make a break for it.

"You can run down the stairs and out the doors." I kept my tone level, even friendly: good cop. "I won't try to stop you. But you won't get far, especially not without Catherine to guide you over the ground."

He slumped on the top step, his head on his knees, forearms pressed against his ears, so desolate that my heart was touched. Instead of Catherine, his one friend, whom he'd been longing for, he'd gotten me.

I walked over to the north wall, which overlooked the back gardens. The windows were small and set up high, but he had moved a chair over so he could stand and see out. I climbed up. From here, you could watch for someone to appear around the corner of the garage. You could spend long lonely nights on this chair hoping she had gotten away from Chicago to come see you. You could also see the pond.

I climbed down and explored the rest of the attic. The common room led to a short wide hall with six monastic bedrooms and a Spartan bathroom. I turned the taps; cold water came out. At least he could use the plumbing. A mattress with a sleeping bag on it was set up in one of the rooms; his few clothes were neatly folded on yet another chair. A couple of flashlights and a box of batteries stood next to the bed.

When I came back to the large room, he was still sitting on the top stair, head on his knees.

"Who are you? Why are you hiding here?" I asked.

He didn't answer me, didn't move his head.

"It's cold up here. You probably haven't had a proper meal in—however long it's been. Come on with me and tell me about it."

"I wait for Catterine. When she say 'going,' then is safe I going." His knees muffled his voice.

"She can't come. You can see the pond from your window here; you must have seen her grandmother arrive this evening. Her grandmother will not let her leave the house again tonight, and her grandmother may well call the police. We probably have until the sun comes up to get you out of here, but I need to know who you are and why you're hiding." I laughed suddenly. "You saw me, too, this evening, didn't you, jumping in and out of that wretched pond. Poor Sister Anne, with nothing to do but watch the horizon, did you see—"

"I am not girl!" His head jerked up and he glowered at me ferociously.

"Who said anything—oh, Sister Anne. A character in a children's story who has to keep watch from a tower. I know you're not a girl. But I know you saw me this afternoon. And you must have been watching for Catherine on Sunday. Sunday night, someone killed a man outside this house. They put his body in the pond. Did you see this?"

When he didn't answer, I moved so I was standing directly over him. "You were watching for Catherine; you knew she was coming that night, or, anyway, some night soon. You saw the killer put the man's body into the water. Who put him there?"

"Nothing, I seeing nothing."

"Did you help kill him? Is that why you're hiding?"

"No and no and no, and now—oh, where is Catterine? Only she—" He broke off and looked at his knees again. "I *am* a girl, crying, hiding behind another girl, I am a baby and a girl."

He lapsed into a mortified silence. I frowned, trying to force my tired brain into some useful line of questioning that would get him to tell me who he was—and what he had seen on Sunday. Finally, I went to the leather-topped desk to look at the books: one of them might be his, one of them might have his name in it. I needed more light than the moon provided. Hoping this wasn't one of Geraldine Graham's wakeful times, I switched on my headlamp and picked up the open book.

I had never seen anything as beautiful as the coral reef. It stretched away for miles and was soft to the touch, like velvet. Stupidly I forgot the dangers that lay all around as I watched the many bright-colored fishes swim through the red reef. Suddenly I felt a pain in my left leg so sharp I tried to scream, forgetting in my fear I was underwater. I took in a mouthful of water around my breathing tube. I looked down in terror. A giant clam had grabbed my leg!

I flipped to the title page. *Eric Nielsen on the Great Barrier Reef,* published in 1920. "Calvin Bayard, His Book," was printed underneath the title in a child's drunken hand. There were two other Eric Nielsen adventures, along with *Treasure Island* and an old Tom Swift. Catherine Bayard must have raided her grandfather's library for books she thought might appeal to a boy trying to learn English.

The other books were in Arabic, along with an English-Arabic dictionary. I looked again at the boy, light dawning.

"You're Benjamin Sadawi, aren't you? Catherine is hiding you from the FBI."

He jumped up in terror and started down the stairs, then came back and snatched up one of the Arabic books from the desk. I seized his arm, but he broke free and tore pell-mell down the stairs. I followed closely but didn't try to grab him—I didn't want to hurtle us both down on our heads.

We landed in the great front hall. Two wings led behind us and Benjamin darted down one, only to find himself in a closet. When he turned back, I wrapped my arms around his torso. His heart was beating wildly. I dragged him back to the stairs and sat him down. He was still clutching the book he'd snatched from the desk upstairs.

"Listen to me, you young fool. I am not giving you to the FBI or the police. But I am going to take you away from this house. It isn't safe here anymore, and it isn't healthy, anyway: cold house, no heat, no company."

He struggled in my arms. "You must not hold me, you woman."

"True enough, I'm a woman. With zero interest in your body: I'm old enough to be your mother."

A thought no less depressing for being true, but I took my arms from his shoulders. He edged away from me on the bottom step but didn't try to run again.

Glass panels framing the great oak doors let in just enough light that I didn't need my headlamp to see him, although I couldn't make out the details of his expression. I also couldn't see the different blocks in the tessellated marble floor, the one that had taken Italian workers eight months to install, but I knew the marble was there: it was bleeding cold through the soles of my running shoes.

"Come on." I stood up. "We have a bit of a hike to my car, and then we'll get you someplace where you can sleep and be warm and not worry about whether someone's coming into the house."

"You have the key for door?" he asked. "Alarm goes to police if you opening with no key."

I switched on my lamp and knelt to inspect the lock. Another depressing truth: the alarm was set on both sides of the door. I couldn't just open the door—I needed a key, and, of course, I didn't have my picklocks with me. We could go up to the third floor and climb down the way I'd come up, but I didn't want to do that if I didn't absolutely have to—the body of a woman old enough to have a teenage son was not happy after a night of pond diving, wall climbing and stair chasing.

The house had at least two other entrances—the one on the back terrace that Catherine had been using, and one out through the kitchen. There was probably also a basement exit that might be easier to use.

"I'm going to explore the other doors. You wait here for me, okay?"

When he didn't respond, I put my hands on his shoulders—woman though I was. "Okay?"

He stiffened but muttered, "Okay, okay," sounding like the universal teenager fed up with adult bossiness.

I switched on my lamp again to navigate the hall. With no furnishings or rugs to soften it, the high, wide space seemed not just barren but menacing. Shivering from more than cold, I opened doors on empty rooms, checking windows and locks, until I got to the back of the house, where the hall opened onto the terrace room. This was the area that led to the gardens and the pond, with the French doors that Catherine Bayard had used.

I switched off my lamp and peered into the night, wondering if she might be going to show up, after all. It was one-thirty in the morning; Catherine might try to slip out if she thought her house was sound asleep. It would be helpful if she arrived with her key.

If I couldn't get out any other way, I'd break one of the glass panels in the French door, but I moved on to my right, looking for the kitchen, moving past Geraldine's father's study, its floor-to-ceiling bookshelves empty, except for a CD by 'NSYNC, presumably left behind by the nou-nous. I came to the swinging door that I'd expected after my jaunt to the Bayards', and again found myself in servants' space: narrower hall, cheaper wood in the floors, lower ceilings.

The kitchen held an array of appliances, still shiny with newness—a six-burner, restaurant-weight stove; three ovens, including a stand-alone bread oven; a walk-in freezer, two refrigerators. The current vanity of wealthy homeowners, these monstrous toys—although maybe Mrs. Nou-Nou really was an accomplished chef. Maybe she'd been baking thousands of quiches to support the family since her husband's dot-com business went south.

I looked in the pantry, which was windowless. The computer for the house was there, too. Catherine had apparently switched off the motion detectors, but I'd need a code to turn off the current to the doors and windows.

Beyond the pantry I found a small bathroom. It did have a window, built high into the wall. Not only would it have been hard to climb out but it, too, had white security piping across it.

The back door had a heavy dead bolt, which I undid, but it was also keyed shut. I looked hastily through the cabinets, brushed stainless steel, covering one whole wall. A colander had been abandoned and a box of decorative toothpicks. I'd have to try to use the small knife in my day pack, but I needed a secondary tool. That meant the plastic toothpicks with their whimsical animal heads.

With the diver's light trained on the door, I began working the lock, using toothpicks to hold the tumblers in place as I found them. The first time I had two pressed back, the toothpicks broke. The second time, a soft footfall behind me made my blood run cold. I dropped the knife and jumped up to see Benjamin standing anxiously behind me.

"I think you are leaving me," he said simply.

"Just trying to open this lock. Look: kneel down here next to me, and hold this toothpick in place."

He was still carrying his book, but he laid it now on a counter and came to kneel next to me. I showed him how I was pushing the cylinders back, and how to hold them in place.

"There are three altogether. You'll have to hold two while I undo the third. No, don't push so hard." I spoke too late; the toothpick snapped in his nervous fingers. "Not to worry. Feel my fingers, feel the way I'm holding it."

His hands brushed mine nervously, as if contact would burn him, but the next time I had the roller pushed back he held the toothpick in place, and then a second. I was working the third and trickiest roller when we both heard the car.

"Don't move," I said sharply. "We're almost there."

His hand gave a convulsive jerk and the toothpicks clattered to the floor. "Is the police?"

"I don't know. Let's get this damned door open. Come on."

On the kitchen side of the house, we couldn't see the drive. We couldn't hear activity at the front door. We'd only heard the car because it had driven past the main entrance toward this side of the house.

Maybe Geraldine Graham had seen my

light and called the sheriff, in which case the deputies would make a brief survey and leave. But if fiddling with the lock had set off the alarm, or if Renee Bayard had summoned the law, then we were in trouble.

Benjamin Sadawi was shaking too hard to help me. I looked around the kitchen. He'd suffocate in the refrigerator. But he was a small, slim boy and the bread oven was big. I hustled him over to it.

"I'm not going to leave without you, unless I'm arrested and can't help it. But you stay in this oven until you hear from me."

He insisted on taking the book with him. I pulled the racks from their shelves, stacked them behind the refrigerator, and half-lifted, half-bent him into place. I took one of my work gloves and used it to keep the door open a crack, enough that he could breathe and hear, and then ran back to the outside door.

I was practically weeping with weariness, but I forced myself to work methodically. If the newcomers were outside the back door . . . I couldn't let my mind wander toward unknown terrors. Keep your head in the game, Vic.

One pick in place, now the second. The third tumbler rolled back just as I heard footsteps moving on the uncarpeted floor toward the kitchen. I opened the back door, pushed in the lock to keep it from closing on me again, and stuffed my makeshift tools into the nearest drawer.

"Who's there?" I shouted, pressing myself against the wall behind the swinging door.

Two uniformed deputies came in, holding flashlights so powerful I couldn't make out their faces; I could just see that a third figure loomed behind them.

A man's voice said sharply, "If it isn't the Chicago dick. I thought we told you to stay the hell away from DuPage County."

Well, Howdy, Lieutenant

It was Lieutenant Schorr, the sheriff's officer who'd been so aggressive Sunday night. Next to him, silent and ramrod stiff, stood Deputy Protheroe.

"Lieutenant!" I smiled an exuberant greeting. "You know how it is with us inner-city kids—we get one whiff of country air and we long for more. It's so clean and pure out here. Except when people drown remote from cars, trains and home, I mean."

Protheroe spoke quickly, before Schorr could react. "Warshawski, you are definitely the bad penny in this Larchmont soap opera. How did you get into the house?"

"The kitchen door was open, so I came in. Is that why you're here? The alarm get triggered?"

"Why we're here is none of *your* business, but why *you're* here is *our* business." Schorr walked to the door to check that it was, indeed, open.

I pulled myself up onto the counter floating in the middle of the kitchen—not as easily as I would have done if I hadn't been wall climbing, diving and the rest of it already this evening, but forcing Schorr to come between me and Benjamin's oven if he wanted to see me. Now that he was holding his flashlight away from my eyes, I could see that the third member of the party was the lawyer's dogsbody, Larry Yosano.

I gave Yosano a friendly hello before adding, "Lieutenant, Marcus Whitby's family doesn't share Sheriff Salvi's easy optimism about their son's death. They've hired me to investigate. I came out to look into the pond, which I did with interesting results."

"So you admit to trespass," Schorr said.

"We keep having problems with that verb, don't we?" I sounded as chipper as a cheerleader with a home-team victory. "I *agree* that I was on this land. I *assert* that Ms.

Geraldine Graham and her son Darraugh Graham, CEO of Continental United Group, asked me to come onto this land to see who was in this house. I *submit* that you, Lieutenant, dismissed Ms. Graham's claims that she saw lights in the attic. I *suggest* that you thought she was demented and failed to investigate. I *contend* that I did not share your view. So tonight, when I finished raking through the pond, I *decided* to take one last look at the house. The back door was open, and I *announce,* without hesitation, that I took the opportunity to come inside."

Schorr frowned heavily. He didn't speak, not because he'd been wowed by my delightful banter—which I thought impressive, given how tired I was—but because I'd reminded him that I had friends in high places. Before he had to say or do anything that might cost him face, two young men barged through the swinging door. They were breathless with excitement.

"No one's here now, Lieutenant, but someone's definitely been living up in the attic. Lookee what we found." The speaker held out the books that had been on the attic desk, with Benjamin's Arab-English dictionary on top.

"One of the windows was open on the third floor," the second deputy said. "We think he heard us coming and jumped down: you can get to the porch roof from the third floor and slide down the columns to the ground."

"Did anyone run past you when you were coming in?" Stephanie Protheroe asked me.

I shook my head. "He must have left when he heard me arrive, because no one was in the attic when I got up there. And I didn't see any open windows when I circled the house looking for a way in. I was just about to start exploring the basement when you guys showed up."

"There any place to hide in the cellar?" Schorr demanded of Yosano.

The lawyer gave a shrug. "I've never explored the house, but, as far as I know, only the usual stuff is down there, furnaces, laundry, no secret cupboards or anything like that."

"We'll search just in case," Schorr said, adding to the two young men, "Good work, you two. You start combing the grounds, see if this guy is hiding—these fields could conceal a lot of people. Arab, likely a terrorist on the run, he could have any kind of weapon, so you see him, don't hesitate. Just shoot."

The two young men saluted and departed, almost tripping over each other in their excitement. Puppies admitted to the hunt for the first time, so eager to get their fox they'd probably kill a unicorn if it crossed their trail.

Schorr shone his flashlight smartly in Protheroe's face. She winced and turned her head away. "You go through the cellar just in case, Steph. These Al-Qaeda guys, they're smart enough to make you think they've jumped out a window, when all the time they're hiding in the basement. Yosano, you get the power turned on. We need to see what the hell we're doing."

When Yosano said it would have to wait until the start of normal business hours— Com Ed wouldn't regard this as an emergency—the lieutenant slammed a hand against a stainless steel cabinet, and then swore as the hard metal bit his bone. "This fucking is an emergency, an Arab terrorist out here in New Solway. Get on it!"

Yosano kept his voice patient with an effort. "It will have to wait until morning, Lieutenant Schorr."

Schorr got half a swearword out, but bit it off to run to the door and call out to his two young deputies. When he didn't get a response, he turned back and shouted at Deputy Protheroe, who had found the stairwell leading to the basement.

"Before you go down there, call over to headquarters, see if they can send us out a generator, get something rigged up so we can see what we're doing. I don't want us shooting each other because we're crashing around in the dark."

So he wasn't totally stupid, only giving a good imitation. I slid off the counter and moved toward the cellar door, still trying to keep attention away from Benjamin's oven.

"Should we call Ms. Bayard first?" Stephanie Protheroe asked, her hand still on the doorknob. "Some camera crew is going to be scanning our calls, you know, and they'll get here. We might want to let her know we think there was a terrorist here before a TV outfit shows up trying to ask her questions."

So they were here because Renee Bayard had decided on a preemptive strike. I wondered how this would affect Catherine's relations with her grandmother.

The flashlights cast menacing shadows around the kitchen, turning Schorr's heavy frown into a gargoyle grimace. "Yeah, I'd better do that. Any place to sit and have a private conversation in this mausoleum?" he added to Yosano.

"All the furniture was taken out when the previous owners had to leave," the lawyer said.

"There are chairs and a desk in the attic," I said. "Ms. Graham probably forgot she had discards up there when she sold the house."

"You have a lot of slick answers, don't you?" Schorr said. "How do you know they're her things?"

"I don't. Really, I suppose Arab terrorists could have stolen them from some of the houses around here and carried them up to the attic. We can't be too careful about anything these days." I opened the basement door.

"Where the fuck you going?"

"You got your deputies searching the grounds and ordering generators; I thought I'd start on the cellar."

"You stay right here. Don't move from the kitchen until I get back from phoning. Yosano, you lock this back door so Princess Twinkle Toes here doesn't go dancing off into the night before I have a chance to check on her felony warrants."

So that was why he'd brought the lawyer: to unlock the doors for him.

"I still don't understand how a terrorist got in here without a key. The alarm has not been breached; despite what Ms. Warshawski is saying, we checked the house each time Mrs. Graham phoned in a complaint," Yosano said, but he obediently did up the lock I'd struggled so hard to open.

His remark made Schorr decide he ought to search me to see if I had a key to Larchmont or, heaven forbid, had used pick-locks to get in. Despite Protheroe's presence, Schorr patted me down himself, a little more roughly than necessary. I thought of Benjamin's cry of "You woman"—"You man," I wanted to say—"hands off," but I stood very still.

When Schorr found my house and car keys in my day pack, he made a big show of comparing them to the house alarm key.

He thought he was going to pocket them, but I took them from him.

Again, before her commanding officer could escalate hostilities, Deputy Protheroe intervened. "I'm going out to the car, sir, to order the emergency generator. Do you want to come with me to phone Ms. Bayard? It will probably be more comfortable in the car than the attic because we can run the heater."

"Yeah, okay. Stay here with her, Yosano. I don't have an extra deputy to keep an eye on this gal, and I don't trust her."

Yosano squirmed in embarrassment. "Really, Lieutenant. It's not as though Ms. Warshawski has a criminal record. She's working for the Graham family."

"Or says she is," Schorr snapped. "Every time something fishy has happened out here this week, this Chicago dickette has been in a front-row seat. I'd kinda like to know why."

"Is it all right if I use the bathroom?" I asked in a meek little voice. "There's one just off the pantry here and my cramps are starting to get the better of me. You don't have a tampon, do you? Mine are in my car."

Like many he-men, Schorr was disgusted by talk of real women's real bodies—he was out of the kitchen before I finished speaking. I went into the bathroom, switched on my diver's lamp and climbed up onto the toilet seat to undo the window locks. There was an extra bolt in the window for security, but that was to keep outsiders away: the key was on a hook next to the frame.

The bottom sash was stuck through years of disuse; flushing the toilet a couple of times covered the sound I made forcing it open. The alarm would definitely go off now, but since it rang in Lebold, Arnoff's office, and they already had their dogsbody on the scene, I hoped they'd think the deputies had tripped it looking around on the upper floors. I took a quick look out: the window faced south, toward the road. The deputies were searching the north.

Back in the kitchen, Yosano was fiddling with a handheld, trying to play some game by the computer's backlight. I didn't know how long Benjamin could keep quiet in that oven; I needed some strategy for getting the lawyer out of the kitchen.

"They interrupt your private life to bring you over here tonight?" I asked.

He nodded. "But I'm only on call one week a month. And usually we don't have such dramatic crises: usually it's just a client wanting to change a will, or being lonely in the night."

"Did Mr. Taverner call you in out of loneliness?"

He continued fiddling with the keys; the computer binged every time he made a score. "Oh, yes. And like many of the old ones, he thought of me as a servant. Oh, they all think the lawyers are their servants, but being a Japanese-American, I'm like a gardener in their eyes. They need to pee, I'm supposed to help them with their bottles and bedpans."

"Sounds horrible. Surely you could get a less demeaning job."

He shrugged. "The money is incredible. And some of it's interesting: we work for such powerful people, you're sort of part of history sometimes. Like these papers that Taverner had, it's been so long since Mr. Arnoff's done day-to-day work with the clients, he probably wouldn't know about them, but Taverner was a lonely old guy. He'd tap that locked drawer and say he knew people in New York who'd pay ten million bucks to get their hands on them."

I thought of Benjamin in the oven, but I couldn't miss this chance to ask Yosano what was in the papers.

"I never saw them." The computer made a derisive sound to let him know he'd bombed. "But he used to say they'd make the Hollywood Ten look like Goldilocks and the Three Bears, and it was a shame he was a man of honor who gave his word not to divulge them."

"Didn't you wish he'd show them to you?"

"Oh, sure," Yosano said. "But we're his executors, I knew I'd see them sooner or later. And then, you always wonder if it really is going to be such a big deal. It's human, when you get that old, to hope you've done something so big the rest of us will never forget you, but a lot of the time it's something no one cares about anymore."

I was about to argue that someone cared, or Marcus Whitby wouldn't have drowned outside the room we were standing in, when a gunshot ripped open the night.

When You Need a Ride—
Steal a Car

When you hear a .45, you never think it was a backfire or a firecracker. Yosano and I froze, and then he ran through the swinging door to the front of the house.

As soon as the door swung shut, I opened the oven.

"Come with me. Don't ask questions, and don't speak," I told Benjamin.

He was giving off the sweet sickly sweat of fear, and he couldn't stand, he'd been lying doubled up so long. I slung him over my shoulder, fireman-style, and humped to the bathroom double time. He was clutching his book still, and it dug into my sore shoulder. He was fifteen or sixteen, but such a skinny kid it wasn't as hard a ride as I'd feared.

Inside the bathroom, I set him down and worked on his legs. He was still shying away from my touch, but fear and cold had made him numb; he didn't resist. As soon as he could stand, I turned off my headlamp, opened the window and looked out. We could hear the excited yelling from the front of the house, but we were clear here in the back.

"I'm going to give you a boost up to this window." I spoke in the flat, tongueless speech you learn in prison because it doesn't carry far. "You slide through, you drop to the ground. You lie flat on your stomach and wait for me. Got it?"

I felt rather than saw him nod. I gave him a boost up to the sill and helped him wriggle his legs through. As he twisted, he dropped his book. He cried out.

I stuck up my hand and covered his mouth. "I'll hand it to you. Get through and get down."

When he seemed unwilling to leave without it, I pushed him. He clung briefly to the sill, and then fell. He didn't cry out again, so I assumed he'd landed without breaking anything. I climbed up on the toilet seat, dropped his book through the opening and hoisted myself onto the sill. The stab of pain between my shoulders was so intense I had to hold back my own cry.

I sat for a few seconds, gathering my breath, then began the hard job of wriggling through the window—a grown woman's hips are wider than a skinny adolescent's. When a second shot reechoed, it startled me so that I landed in a heap almost on top of Benjamin. The fall knocked the wind out of me and I lay gagging for air, trying not to make any noise.

We were at the southeast corner of the mansion. We could hear excited shouts as the puppies and Schorr tried to figure out where their prey had fallen. They had shot at . . . a raccoon or a deer. They had not shot—not—an ardent teenage girl running through the fields to protect her protégé.

I wanted to dash to the back, what are you morons doing, you macho-drunk fools, shooting at shadows and children? I grabbed the grass in front of me, tying myself to the ground here. If I joined the hunt, I'd leave the boy here where he would be found, arrested, if not shot. And Schorr was jumpy enough to arrest me or even shoot me if I showed my face.

"What they doing?" Benjamin cried in an undervoice.

"They shot at something. Probably a raccoon, an animal. As soon as they figure that out, they'll be looking for me, so let's move."

"Animal? You think not—" he thought better of finishing the sentence.

"Come on," I said roughly. "We're going. We are going to go straight across the lawn here. The house will keep the people in back from seeing us. When we get to that tall grass, we are going to go through it. You will stay right behind me, got it?"

He stumbled to his feet. We couldn't go fast. He could barely walk, and certainly not run. Cold, hunger, confusion, far from home in a country that wanted to put him in prison for being—what? If he was a terrorist, I'd deal with that down the road, but if he was just a kid in the wrong place at a time when fear was holding the horse's reins in America, I needed to deal with that, too.

We were halfway across the lawn when two more squad cars squealed up the drive, lights flashing. I turned to Benjamin and pulled him smartly to the ground, lying flat next to him until the cars were at the house.

Lifting my head, I watched the side of the house we were facing. They hadn't found the open bathroom window yet: all the action was in the fields and gardens at the back.

"Let's go. Hands and knees. You go forward, I'll keep an eye out."

The work gloves shielded my hands from the stickers growing in the untended lawn, but Benjamin didn't have any protection. When I saw him unable to put his hands down, I stripped the gloves off and forced them onto his hands. "Move. It's our only chance, while they're doing what they're doing."

We crawled through the unmown grass to the untended field beyond. I was light-headed with fatigue and hunger, my shoulders ached, I was scared. Only the snuffling from the boy in front of me, tears manfully suppressed, air sucked painfully in, kept me going.

The deputies had rigged up the searchlights while we were stumbling through shrubs. The sudden light arcing through the night sky behind us startled me. I tripped on a fallen branch and landed in rotting leaves.

At least if they sent dogs after us they wouldn't find us by our smell.

When we reached the ditch by the side of Coverdale Lane, I cautiously poked my head through the shrubbery to survey the road. A squad car blocked the intersection of Coverdale with Dirksen, where I had left my Mustang. I couldn't see clearly at this distance, but they had probably found the car, might be waiting next to it for me.

I sank back down into the ditch, close to screaming with fatigue and frustration. We were trapped. I fought back panic. Benji whispered, "How we are going to do?"

The only possibility was to cross Coverdale and fight our way through the hedge to Anodyne Park on the far side, taking a chance that they wouldn't see us in the road. If I had the wings of a dove or the shovel snout of a mole. A mole. If that culvert I'd stumbled on yesterday came this far . . .

Under cover of sirens and of a helicopter that had arrived on the scene, I explained to Benji as best I could what I was looking for. I would explore east, toward my car, he would crawl along the ditch to the west.

"Let it open up here, on this side of the road," I begged the whimsical ruler of the universe. "Let me find it, before they find me."

I crawled along slowly, patting the embankment, praying for it to give way. About fifty feet from where the squad car stood, Benji tapped my shoulder with a soft, timid hand. He had found the entrance.

I crawled back after him. The opening was a black hole on the road side of the ditch, not high enough for me to stand upright but just wide enough for us to move side by side. It smelled of mold and animal droppings, and it was as dark as the entrance to death. We couldn't afford to show a light. I grabbed Benji's left hand with my right. He didn't try to withdraw; indeed, he clung to me, trembling, as we squelched along the muddy floor.

It should have been a quarter mile, getting to the hedge, going under Powell Road, coming up in Anodyne Park, but the tunnel seemed to stretch endlessly in front of us. What if we weren't under Powell Road at all, but were shuffling into the Deep Tunnel? We could wander for hours until we collapsed and died of hunger and thirst. No one would find our bones for years, if they ever came on them at all. Morrell, Lotty, everyone I

loved who cared about me, they would forget me. Already they were so far away that
they didn't exist.

My breath rasped dry against my tonsils.
My back ached from walking in a stoop, red
darts flashed across my eyes. And then we
were suddenly breathing fresh air, smelling
the juniper berries, scrambling uphill, standing upright on asphalt.

I shuddered in relief. We stood trembling
for a few minutes, stretching sore muscles,
listening for pursuit. All was blissfully quiet.
Anodyne, the healing of pain. All we needed
was a car, and we'd be home free.

I led Benji up the winding path toward the
town houses, where cars were parked for
the night in the drives that lay behind them.
In this wealthy enclave I didn't expect to
find an old car, the kind where I could break
the steering column and pull out the ignition
rod. But the fifth house we came to, luck fa-
vored us: someone had left their keys in a
Jaguar XK-12. I'd always wanted to drive
one of these. I opened the door for Benji.

"You are stealing this car?"

"Borrowing," I grinned. "The owner will
get it back tomorrow."

Back to the Briar Patch

So it's you, my girl, is it? Been long enough since you showed your face around here. Come to serve early mass for me?" Father Lou stood at the rectory door in T-shirt and trousers, his face still red from shaving.

As I'd driven along Ogden Avenue into the city, I figured if I didn't get to the rectory before Father Lou started robing, I could slip into the church with the handful of neighborhood people who came for the six A.M. service. As it was, even taking the long slow route, I managed to pull around to the back of the building by five-thirty.

Benjamin had fallen asleep before we reached Warrenville Road. I kept my window open, needing cold air on my face to keep my own longing for sleep from over-powering me, but I ran the heater so that the vents pointed on the young man. His book fell from his slackened hand; I leaned over at a stoplight and put it in his lap so he wouldn't wake up distressed. He'd dropped it while we were in the ditch and revealed— in a defiant gasp, as if he expected me to strike him or abandon him on the spot—that it was the Koran, his father's own copy, he could not lose it.

"In that case, we'd better hang on to it," was all I said.

When I had us both strapped into the Jaguar, a wave of fatigue crested over me, pulling me under. I only woke a few minutes later because a helicopter thundered di-rectly over us, heading east. I blinked at it, hoping it was taking a teenager to a hospi-tal, not to a morgue.

I put the car in gear and drove slowly past the guard station. The man in the booth nodded at the car: he was there to keep the world out. It didn't matter who left the com-plex.

I bypassed the tollway, preferring to take Ogden Avenue. If Schorr decided to issue an APB on me, they'd stake out the expressways first. They wouldn't know what car I was driving, but they might guess I'd taken someone else's when I didn't show up at the Mustang.

Even forty miles out, Ogden is not a beautiful street. Every town along its route had decided this was the place for car dealerships, for fast-food joints, for gas stations and junkyards. Once the street crosses the city limits, it goes from tacky to grim, finishing its life near the Cabrini Green housing project. A number of Cabrini's towers have been torn down as the Gold Coast oozes west, but those that remain, with their broken windows and bullet-pocked playgrounds, still present an ominous face to the city.

As we drove in, a fair amount of traffic already filled the road—early commuters pulling into the endless strip malls for the day's first coffee, people coming off the night shift stopping for a burger. At one point I dozed off again at a traffic light. The hydraulic honk from the truck behind me scared me awake—I thought I'd heard another shot, I thought we were surrounded. The adrenaline from that kept me alert for the rest of the route.

The Jaguar engine was quiet as a feather dropping on a leaf, and the power inside made me itch to swoop in and out of lanes, or go sixty on roads posted for forty. On an impulse, waiting for a light at Austin, just before crossing the border into Chicago, I called Murray Ryerson on my cell phone. He was grumpy about being woken up, but became alert, even aggressive, when I told him I'd met sheriff's deputies out at Larchmont.

"They were going nuts, thinking they had some Arab terrorist in their sights. They shot someone. I didn't feel like hanging around— they were being mean to me—but I have a queasy feeling about the shooting."

"What about killing a terrorist makes you queasy?" he demanded.

"I don't think that's who they shot. I think they may have hit a member of the Bayard family. Perhaps even Calvin Bayard's granddaughter. And if that's the case, they will try to keep it very, very quiet."

"You actually see the body? Is that the basis of your feeling?" Murray was truculent—he's known me too many years.

"I was there in the early evening, looking for clues about Marcus Whitby in the

Larchmont mansion pond. I found his pocket organizer, by the way." That seemed like an unconnected time and place to where I was now. "Anyway, two of the Bayards came by then, and from their conversation I had a feeling they might be back. That's all."

"That's not enough. Not nearly enough. Tell me about Whitby's gizmo. Was there anything suggestive in it?"

"Yeah—four days of pond scum. I'm taking it to a forensic lab so they can dry it out and take it apart."

Another honk goosed me into remembering I was driving. I hung up hastily on Murray's indignant squawk. I turned off my phone—if Murray wanted to call back, the ringer would wake Benjamin. Besides, I didn't want to tell Murray anything else right now: I just wanted to make sure Lieutenant Schorr couldn't sit on it if he'd shot Catherine.

At Western Avenue, Ogden turns northeast, angling past the juvenile detention center. "You are not going there, my friend, if I can help it," I said to the sleeping boy. He muttered something guttural, probably in Arabic, and shifted in his seat.

I turned north onto Western and drove four miles through the drab hindquarters of the city's industrial zone. The lights from factories and trucks made it hard to tell whether the night sky was starting to lighten; the air was gray and gritty both day and night around here.

We were also close to the criminal courts and Cook County jail, so there was a heavy squad car presence. I tried to keep my mind on the traffic, not on the possibility that someone might be looking for a borrowed Jaguar's plates. I breathed easier when I'd moved out of the area.

At North Avenue, I was only two blocks from my office, but I turned west again, into Humboldt Park, where gentrification hasn't yet touched the Hispanic neighborhoods. If someone was hunting me, they'd have my office staked out, but I didn't think anyone would look for me in a Mexican church. I parked on a small side street behind.

It was a job to rouse Benjamin, and a bigger job to make him come with me to a Christian church. "I know what priests doing with boys in church. I know they hurting boys, doing bad things with boys."

"Not in this church," I said, pulling him up the walk like a recalcitrant mule. "This is the one building in Chicago that I know where you can be warm, where you can get something to eat and where you can be safe. This priest is a boxer—" I let go of him long enough to mime boxing—"this priest has harbored fugitives. He will look out for you."

"He will try to turn me from my believing, my—my—" he hunted for a word—"from the truth."

"No. He won't do that. He believes in his truth as much as you believe in yours, but he will not disrespect your belief. He doesn't disrespect my beliefs, which are different again from both yours and his."

"And Catterine, she cannot see me here, and how can I know she is not shotted? *Shot?*"

"Catherine will be able to see you here, if it's safe for both of you—it may not be. This really is the best place for you right now, Benjamin."

He didn't believe me, but he was old enough to know when he was out of options. And maybe, too, he figured I'd kept him safe this long, I might be trusted to keep him safe a bit longer. Or maybe he was just so tired he couldn't fight anything going on around him. Whatever the reason, when Father Lou answered my anxious pushing on the rectory bell, Benjamin stayed at my side.

Father Lou's T-shirt exposed the formidable muscles in his neck and forearms that he'd developed in his boxing years. His frown as he took in Benjamin's and my bedraggled appearance made him look like a menacing Popeye. I hoped he didn't frighten Benjamin into running.

"This someone Morrell sent you?" the priest growled.

My stomach felt queer at Morrell's name; the night's labors had kept me from thinking about him and now it came back to me in a rush, that he was missing, or missing anyway to me. "I've lost track of Morrell. Never mind that now: this young man has been hiding in an abandoned house out in the western suburbs. I found him moments before sheriff's deputies surrounded the place. He needs to be warm, he needs to eat and he needs to be in a place where the county cops and the city cops and John Ashcroft's cops aren't going to find him."

"They have a good reason to look for him?" Father Lou pulled back the heavy door far enough that we could come in.

"Yeah, they don't like his race, creed or place of national origin."

"That a fact. You got a name, kid?" His faded blue eyes looked directly at the boy, who didn't withdraw, as I'd feared—I'd forgotten the priest had dealt with generations of frightened boys.

"Benjamin," the youth whispered. "Benjamin Sadawi."

"Mass in seven minutes," Father Lou said. "Got to get to church. Ben, you go with Victoria to the kitchen, she'll make you tea and eggs, fix you up with a bed. Unless it's been so long since you've been here, my girl, you don't remember where anything is."

"I do not go to Christian church," Benjamin said.

"Not asking you to. Got other rules you have to follow if you stay here: no drugs, no weapons, no cigarettes. Say your prayers however you want. Special intention for Morrell," he added to me. "For the kid, too. Jesus doesn't care if he prays in Arabic."

He stumped off down a dark corridor connecting the rectory to St. Remigio's church. I took Benjamin down a different unlit hallway to the kitchen. Father Lou saves money in his financially strapped parish by not keeping lights in the halls. I had to switch on my headlamp again to guide us to the kitchen. The batteries were wearing out; the light was feeble, like my legs at this point.

In the kitchen, I found the matches to light a burner on the heavy old stove. I was surprised, in a way, that Father Lou even had spent the money on a gas stove instead of keeping a coal burner, or whatever had been in the rectory when the church was built in the 1880s.

In the refrigerator, I found the eggs that were the staple of the priest's diet. He had margarine and a big block of cheese, as well. I scrambled them all together in a cast-iron skillet. Father Lou ate a lot of bacon, but I remembered not to offer that to a Muslim youth.

While the margarine was melting, I switched on a transistor radio perched on top of the refrigerator. It was the wrong time for news highlights: I got ads and sports reports. The Bulls had lost again, along with the Blackhawks. It's no easier to be a

Chicago fan in the winter than in the summer.

Benjamin had removed his sweatshirt to fold it carefully on the cracked linoleum. He knelt down on it to recite his morning prayers, but when the radio came on, he looked up, his thin face anxious.

"No news," I said. "I'll turn it back on when you're done."

I cleared space on the enamel kitchen table. Budget figures, the sports pages from a week's worth of papers, school essays and advertising catalogs were all jumbled together. I swept them into a pile without trying to organize them—if he needed to find something, Father Lou would sort through the stack. I'd seen him do it a number of times, looking for old sermon notes. He's the only person I know more disorganized than I am.

I set down eggs, tortillas and cambric tea—a little tea and a lot of hot sweetened milk—for Benjamin and me. We both needed our blood sugar raised about now. I took a couple of aspirin from the bottle in my day pack and swallowed them with the tea. Maybe they would persuade my sore shoulder to calm down.

Benjamin finished his prayers with a defensive glance at me. His prayer schedule must have anchored him during his long days alone, given him something to rely on. His father's Koran, his father's prayer schedule, like my mother's vocal exercises: the routine of the beloved makes you feel that the beloved is with you.

"News now?" he said. "Please you are finding out of Catterine."

"About Catherine," I corrected him absently.

"About Cat-herine," he echoed.

I turned the radio back on. Finally, at half past the hour, we got the local news.

Responding to a complaint from neighbors, DuPage County Sheriff's deputies raided an abandoned house in unincorporated New Solway early this morning. According to Sheriff Rick Salvi, an Arab man wanted for questioning in connection with the September 11 attacks had been hiding in the house. The man made his escape through a third-story window as deputies were storming the house. As they combed the grounds, a local girl was injured by a gunshot. The sheriff's office refused to confirm reports that one of the deputies fired the gun, but the injured girl is Catherine Bayard, who was taking a late walk through the fields behind the home of her grandfather, Chicago publisher Calvin Bayard. Sheriff Salvi has said it's possible Ms. Bayard was shot by the wanted man; he will issue a full report after he has inspected his deputies' weapons. Ms. Bayard is in an area hospital in serious but stable condition.

The wanted man was in the same house where Chicago investigator V. I. Warshawski found a dead body on Sunday night. Warshawski was actually in the house when sheriff's deputies arrived on the scene, but left while they were still searching the grounds. Whether she has a connection to the missing man is unknown at this time, but Sheriff Salvi is anxious to talk to her.

"And I to you, Sheriff." I switched off the radio, turning to Benjamin. "How much of that did you understand?"

He shook his head. "Too quickly talking. Catterine, they talk of her, about her, they talk about September 11, about Arabs, but what they are saying?"

"Catherine was shot, but she will recover—she will get well. They didn't say where she was hit, but they did say 'serious but stable,' which means a bad injury, but not one that will kill her."

"That is true?" His eyes were painfully large in his thin face. "You—" His lips moved as he went through a vocabulary list in his head. "You swearing that is true?"

I swore to him that I was telling the truth about Catherine. I added that I would find out what hospital she was in and exactly how she'd been hurt, but that I needed to sleep first. I left out the rest of the story, the manhunt for him. He probably guessed it, but putting it into words would make it too stark; we both needed sleep, not anxiety, now.

I was too exhausted to think, or talk. When I got up to carry the plates to the sink, tears spurted down my face, involuntary, the body's protest against further effort. No heartening slogans from the basketball court, no remembered lectures of my mother's, could make me stop crying. Weeping, I led Benjamin to the second floor, where a series of narrow bedrooms stood, left over from the days when the Catholic Church was awash with priests and a parish like St. Remigio had five or six on its roster. Army blankets were folded at the foot of the beds, and thin down pillows, as ancient as the building, stood at the heads. The most elaborate furnishing was the wooden crucifix over each bed, carved so realistically that Benjamin looked at his in horror. I removed it from the wall over his bed and put it in the linen closet.

The rooms were cold, left unheated to save on fuel, but they held minute electric heaters for emergency guests like us. I turned them on, showed Benjamin where the bathroom was, put sheets on beds in two adjacent rooms and fell asleep, still weeping.

30

Warming Up

I awoke from my most familiar nightmare. My mother had disappeared. I was looking for her, panic-stricken, because the only reason she would leave was that she didn't love me any more. The search changes from dream to dream; this time I was in the dark culvert that connected New Solway with Anodyne Park. Behind me I could hear a hissing and knew, dream-wise, that it was the hissing of tires in the mud. I ran pell-mell until I crashed into the evergreen bush. The wheels came closer and I saw a giant golf cart about to run me over. I woke, my heart pounding, my arms and shoulders so stiff it was painful to move them.

When I pushed myself up on the narrow bed, my stomach muscles trembled. I sat blear-eyed, wanting just to lie back down and sleep for a hundred years. Until I felt well. Until Morrell came home. Until these times of fear and brutality passed. I thought of the horrors wrought in the hundred years now ending and didn't think waiting another century for peace would bring much solace.

I maneuvered myself to the head of the bed and found my watch. One o'clock—in the afternoon, given that the gray March light still seeped in through the dirty window. The single bar of the space heater did no more than take an edge from the cold room. I lay back down, pulling the army blanket up to my nose.

My mother died when I was in my teens. Like many people who lose a parent young, I believed it was my fault, some failing on my part, that had made her leave. All the times I'd upset her, racing into trouble with my cousin Boom-Boom . . . If I had come home on time, practiced my music as she so often begged me . . . and on mornings— afternoons—like this, awakening in pain brought on by one more headlong plunge into danger, my heart twisted again. My

mind told me differently, told me of the cancer that went unchecked, untreated, for too
many years—like many immigrant women,
she would not let a doctor, especially a
man, examine her in her private spaces; the
bleeding that went on and on after a mis-
carriage couldn't overcome her revulsion
against exposure.

I shut my eyes to keep from looking at the
crucifix. It was two feet high, with thorns
and blood no less vivid for being covered in
dust. I should have put it in the linen closet
with the one from Benjamin's room.

I knew I would feel better if I took a bath
and started stretching my muscles, but the
routine felt old and dreary to me—sore
joints, stretch, recover—in order to overtax
my body another time. It'd started as a
teenager when I'd gone cold into a basketball game, suffered the next day, and
followed Coach McFarlane's advice on
stretches and warm-ups. In the years since,
I'd had too many job-related injuries, too
many days when I'd woken up feeling as
sore as though I really had been run over by
a giant golf cart. The thought of beginning
again with heat and exercise only annoyed
me. What was I pushing myself for, any-

way? So I could keep racing around town looking for crooks and murderers that no one wanted me to find?

In the interview with Kylie Ballantine that I'd read at the library—was it only two days ago?—she'd said when she was twenty she could take a three-week vacation and be back in shape after one day's hard work, but that she'd reached an age where missing a single day took three weeks of conditioning to recover. And so she worked out every day. My heroine.

I pushed myself upright once more and stumbled into the bathroom. I began doing the things I knew I needed to do to recover—not easily, since the guest bathroom (to give the chipped, stained fittings and cracked walls a fancy name) had no heat. At least it made me move fast. I jogged back to the narrow bedroom, which felt downright cozy in contrast. I put the two army blankets on the floor and spent half an hour stretching out my legs and arms. I must have torn a muscle in my left trapezius, from the knife stabs it gave me when I extended my arms, but when I finished I thought my legs would carry me along.

I couldn't bear the thought of last night's torn and filthy clothes, but my suit was in the trunk of my own car out in New Solway. I put on the stained, rank sweatshirt and tried not to think about it.

On my way downstairs, I looked in on Benjamin. He was still asleep.

I found Father Lou in his study, working on his Sunday homily. He grunted when he heard me come in, but kept typing until he finished a passage. He used an old Royal electric, banging away with two fingers. I did leg lifts while I waited to keep the circulation going.

"Kid still sleeping?" Father Lou said, when he finally looked up. "Listened to the noon news. Guess he's the Arab they lost out in DuPage. You think he's a terrorist?"

I made a face. "I don't think so, but I can't say I know what signs to look for."

The priest wheezed hoarsely—his idea of laughter. "Neither does the FBI. Don't imagine a county sheriff is any smarter than the Bureau. What's the boy's story?"

"I don't know how or why, but Catherine Bayard—the young woman who got shot last night—scooped him up and took him out to this deserted mansion near her grandparents' country estate." I explained who the Bayards were, and how I'd come to be involved in the situation.

"Romeo and Juliet," Father Lou echoed my own image. "They in love? They making love?"

I shrugged. "Benjamin has pretty strong feelings for her, but she—I think with her it was quixotism—wanting to follow in her grandfather's footsteps. Catherine lives in a larger milieu than Benjamin, with school and horses and an important family; he had only her to think about for three weeks or however long it's been. But—she didn't tell her grandmother what she was doing, and I've seen her with her granny—they're pretty close. So I don't know what she feels for him personally. Maybe he's exotic, Egyptian, a blue-collar youth. For some rich kids, crossing so many boundaries of race and class can seem daring, even exalting."

"Teenagers. Everything too intense all the time. Probably gave her word not to tell a soul and felt that included the whole world. Girl's at Northwestern Hospital—they medevacked her into the city. Know the chaplain there. He says a bullet nicked the humerus, cracked it, not life-threatening. You going to see her?"

"Probably. But I don't think I should tell her Benjamin's here. When she was protecting him, she didn't have all the law enforcement agencies in the country breathing down her neck. I'll let her know he's safe, but I don't think she should have to worry about standing up to interrogation on his safety." I picked at a hole in the chair I was sitting in. "I don't know how serious the Feds and the rest of them are going to be about wanting to find Benjamin. They may talk to me and let me go after that, or they may try a trace on everything I do. To be on the safe side, I think I need to assume that all my phones—home, office, mobile—and possibly even my e-mail will be monitored."

"Think they'll charge you under this Patriot bill, whatever it is?" the priest asked.

I grimaced. "I hope not—the last few years I've already had more jail time than I can really use. Anyway, if the FBI gets involved, and if they really want Benjamin, they can put enough people on me that I may not be able to shake them. So once I show up at home, I won't be able to get back in touch with you. Or vice versa. If you can't keep Benjamin, let me know now so I can try to come up with some other safe house."

"Don't seem to be able to keep track of their own weapons these days, the Feds. Shouldn't think they'd have the manpower to follow one gal like you around town. Still, better safe than sorry. Baker Street Irregulars—I can send some of my toughs over to you on bikes—your office still over there near Milwaukee, right? Easy ride for these kids. If you want me—" He grinned, showing his yellow teeth. "Say a prayer, God'll let me know."

Meaning, I could come to church.

"As far as young Ben goes, I'll sort him out," Father Lou went on. "Think you're right, think he's a scared kid on the run. In which case, I'll keep him until we figure out where else to send him. If he's doing something he shouldn't be, give him to Uncle Sam. Let you know, either way."

"There's one other thing about him," I said. "I think he saw some part of what happened to Marcus Whitby Sunday night. He would stand at the attic window watching for Catherine, and you get a view from there of most of the pond. If he saw the person who put Whitby into the water—I want to know."

Father Lou thought it over, decided it wasn't an unreasonable request, and nodded agreement. "See what I can get him to say. What's happening with Morrell?"

My stomach tightened. "He's off on some hot lead that he didn't want to reveal online."

"And you're angry."

"I'm angry. I'm supposed to weave tapestries while he does God knows what, in God knows whose company."

The priest gave his wheezy laugh again. "You weave tapestries, my girl? You ain't the passive waiting type, so don't sit there feeling sorry for yourself. Get off your tail and get to work. I have to finish my sermon."

I blushed in embarrassment and stood up. Father Lou saw the flash of pain across my face from my shoulder. I tried to make light of it, but he led me through the church to the school on the far side. Even on a Saturday afternoon, the gym was filled with kids, some shooting baskets, but most working out on boxing dummies. St. Remigio's routinely won state boxing titles, and every boy in school dreamed of making the team.

Father Lou stopped to correct one boy's arm position, set another closer to the bag, and warned two others not to bring personal fights into his gym. They all nodded solemnly. Father Lou had the magic touch of believable authority in this world. He might chew out his kids, but he never let them down.

He took me into a small infirmary built off the gym. He handed me a towel to use as an improvised robe and told me to take off my sweatshirt. I sat on a stool with my back to him, draped modestly in the towel, while he ran his hands along my shoulders and upper back. When he found the spot that made me squawk loudest, he rubbed something into it.

"Used this on horses when I was a boy. Got them back between the traces in no time flat." He gave another of his sudden barks of laughter. "Put some in a jar for you, get someone to rub it in if you can't reach the spot. Best if you tape it up. Leave that stinking shirt here, take one of ours."

He handed me an orange and gray St. Remigio's sweatshirt, faded from much washing, but mercifully clean. When I pulled it on, my trapezius already moved a bit more smoothly.

He escorted me out the back door of the school to my borrowed wheels. "You get in trouble, girl, come back here. No one to look after you but those two dogs and an old man." He laughed again. "Probably only got six to seven years on Contreras, but I fight regularly and he don't: INS, city cops, they're around here all the time. FBI wants to join in, won't bother me."

When I put the Jaguar in gear and drove off, my shoulder moved only a little better, but my spirits were easier. The voice of believable authority—it worked on me, too.

Superhero

While I was still in the clear—I hoped—I went to a place called TechSurround to send Whitby's pocket organizer to the forensic lab I use. You can do everything at TechSurround, from photocopying to sending mail; I used their computer to type up a letter to the lab, explaining where the wallet had been, said that I wanted to see any papers Whitby might have kept in it, told them to make it a top priority job, and put the whole thing in a bubble-pack envelope.

I was about to stick the envelope into a FedEx packet, but today was Saturday; the lab wouldn't get it until Monday. I didn't want to use my cell phone, in case someone was actively tracing me, but the one thing TechSurround lacked was a pay phone. I risked turning on my mobile for a minute to phone the messenger service I use, arranging for a pickup at Tech-Surround—I planned to be here for a bit, checking messages.

I logged onto one of their computers and looked at both my phone log and my e-mails, which depressed me, since there was nothing from Morrell and a slew of messages from Murray Ryerson. Catherine Bayard had been shot, this was big news in Chicago, he had scooped the city because of me, so I got dinner at the Filigree—especially since DuPage had first tried to pretend she'd been shot by a fleeing Arab—but why the hell hadn't I mentioned terrorists? And did I know police from three jurisdictions wanted to talk to me? Make it four, if you counted New Solway's finest!

I sent him back a brief message saying it was nice to be wanted, I knew nothing about terrorists, I'd slept through the day in a motel, and I'd get back to him after all the fine men and women in blue had mauled me. I also typed a quick message to Morrell, shutting my eyes, trying to remember what he looked like, what he sounded like, but gray mist swirled behind my eyes when I said his name. "Morrell, where are you?" I whispered, but I exed that out. "I've had twenty-four unusual hours, upside down in a pond and squeezing out through mansion windows. Wherever you are, I hope you're warm, safe and well fed. I love you." Maybe.

Before leaving the machine, I pulled up my phone log, which only confirmed what Murray had said: DuPage sheriff Rick Salvi wanted me ASAP, in which he was joined by the Chicago police—which I couldn't figure out—and Derek Hatfield from the FBI, who would appreciate my calling at my earliest convenience. Behind the bureaucratic formula, I could hear Derek's baritone rumble with menace.

There were also two messages from Geraldine Graham. I hadn't expected to hear from her again after Darraugh's furious phone call, but I should have realized that his mother would want the inside story on what happened last night at her beloved Larchmont. She'd probably watched the helicopters and emergency vehicles from her living room. Darraugh had also called. I would get to the Grahams in due course, but I couldn't feel excited by yelps from the

rich and powerful right now. The only message I was really glad to get was one from
Lotty, asking if I was all right and to please
call.

As soon as the messenger service took
my packet for Cheviot Labs, I got ten dollars
in quarters from the cashier, and found a
pay phone in a Laundromat up the street.

I didn't think Benjamin Sadawi merited
massive surveillance. I didn't think I did. But
we were living in paranoid times. Everyone
in law enforcement was on edge, not
just the hormone-crazed youngsters who'd
fired at Catherine Bayard last night, but
everyone.

My first call was to my lawyer. Just
in case worst came to worst, I wanted
Freeman Carter to know what was going on
with me. To my amazement, I actually found
him at home.

"Freeman! I'm glad you're in—I thought
you'd be in Paris or Cancun or whatever
your usual weekend spot is these days."

"Believe me, Vic, when I heard your name
on the news, followed by the magic phrase
'Arab terrorist,' I tried to book a seat on
the first flight out. Why can't you get into
trouble during normal business hours?

And without pulling Homeland Security's chains?"

"Like a real criminal, you mean? I'm at a pay phone, but even so, I think I should keep this simple. I've been out of circulation all day, catching up on my sleep, so I don't know what DuPage or the *federales* will have in store for me when I go home. Under this Patriot Act, if they think I have something they want—whether it's a runaway kid or a library book—do I have a right to phone counsel before they hustle me away?"

"I'm not sure," Freeman said, after a pause. "I'll have to research that. But—just in case, leave word with Lotty or your tiresome neighbor to call me if you don't show up when you're expected. And for once in your own tiresome, ornery life, Victoria, check in with someone once a day until this blows over. Otherwise, Contreras will be on the phone with me and I'll be billing new hours to your outstanding balance. Which is not small as it is. Agreed?"

"Copy that, Houston." Nothing would bring Mr. Contreras more pleasure than to baby-sit me. Few things would bring me less, but Freeman was right. There are days when it's better to be pliant.

I tried Amy Blount next. When I got her voice mail, I phoned the client at the Drake. Harriet Whitby was in her room.

"When I saw the report on TV this morning, I wondered, well, were you out at Larchmont because of Marc or because of the terrorist?" she asked.

Every time someone referred to Benjamin Sadawi as a terrorist, he changed from a scared kid hiding in an attic to a bearded monster in a Yasser Arafat scarf. But if I started saying, no, he's not a terrorist, he's just terrified, then I'd have to explain that I'd seen him, and I couldn't do that.

"Your brother's affairs took me out to Larchmont; I was looking in the pond where he drowned to see if he might have dropped something. He did, in fact: his pocket organizer. I've sent it to a lab to dry it out and extract any documents."

A woman was waiting to use the phone, looking ostentiously at the clock above the dryers. I held up my thumb and forefinger to say, only a little longer.

"While I was out at Larchmont, I found the kitchen door open, I went in to see whether anyone was inside, and the sheriff's excitement kept me out there longer than I hoped.

I think I know who your brother was visiting in New Solway, but it doesn't bring me any closer to how he ended in that pond."

"Dr. Vishnikov called this morning," Harriet said. "Your funeral director delivered Marc's body to his—his place. But he wanted to warn me before he started what it would cost, and that I might find out, I don't know, things I wouldn't want to know. He terrified me, but, then, what could be more terrible than Marc's death?" Her voice was raggedy, the voice of someone who'd had to talk to too many people about too many difficult things lately.

"Dr. Vishnikov is just being cautious. I'll call him, tell him if he feels like being responsible to the client, do it through me, not you. And to get started—we've already lost a week on this. I can think of a lot of things one wouldn't want to know about a beloved family member, but, frankly, I can't picture your brother doing any of them—you know, running a prostitution ring or dealing drugs, that kind of activity doesn't fit with the man whose house I saw yesterday morning."

Harriet gave a shaky laugh. "Thank you, I needed to hear someone say that. All day

I've been thinking, my God, am I going to find out Marc was a drug addict?"

The woman waiting for the phone made a loud remark about how inconsiderate some people are. I smiled and nodded.

"Can you call Amy for me?" I said to Harriet. "I want to compare notes with her and I've got to surrender this phone. See if she can come to my office tomorrow morning."

"She's meeting me at the hotel tonight," Harriet said. "Why don't you join us?"

"If the police aren't holding me." I gave her Mr. Contreras's number in case she couldn't reach me on my cell phone. "And— just in case the law thinks I'm such a scintillating conversationalist that they want to listen in, keep your phone comments on the short and simple side."

The waiting woman grabbed the phone from me when I'd hung up. She snapped, "Short and simple? That's what you think is short and simple?"

The woman dragged out her conversation as long as she could, but I waited, since I still needed to talk to Vishnikov and to my neighbor, and I didn't want to scour the streets for another pay phone. When she finished, the woman gave a triumphant nod with the comment that now I knew what it felt like.

I blew her a kiss and dialed Vishnikov's home number. "Jeesh, Bryant, good thing you only deal with the dead: your bedside manner gets the living totally weirded out. You really think Whitby looks like a user?"

"I just don't want the family refusing to pay the bill if I find out what they don't want to know."

"Well, talk to me about it next time. I will guarantee the bill," I said grandly.

"In that case, we'll use the new spectrometer, Warshawski. Time on it's five hundred bucks an hour, but you'll be happy with the results."

He hung up, pleased with himself. I hoped he was joking. Or that the Whitbys could pay his bill.

I phoned Lotty next, but only got her answering machine. Where was everyone on Saturday afternoon? I needed a human voice right now. I left a message saying I was fine, just bruised a bit in body and mind, and I'd try her again over the weekend.

Finally, I put two more quarters into the phone and called my neighbor. Mr. Contreras was predictably upset and voluble. He, too, had heard the news, and not only had my name been on it as someone Sheriff Rick Salvi was eager to talk to—but deputies had come around the apartment twice already today, and where was I and what was I doing?

I fed quarters into the phone until my supply dried up, giving him the details of last night's excursion—except, of course, my escape with Benjamin. Mr. Contreras vigorously approved of my jumping out the bathroom window to get away from the sheriff, but wanted to know why I hadn't come home then.

"I was beat: I checked into a motel out there." I said. "I only woke up a little bit ago."

"So you didn't actually see the A-rab, huh, doll? What was that girl, that Catherine Bayard doing out there in the middle of the night? She mixed up with that terrorist, do you think?"

"Hard to picture," I said lightly. "Probably has some boyfriend in the area she doesn't want her folks to know about. I just put in my last quarter. Can you meet me at your back door in ten minutes? My clothes are a wreck and I want to change before I do anything else. Just in case DuPage has the place staked out, and just in case they haven't posted anyone in back."

The warning beeps sounded. We were disconnected before Mr. Contreras could finish his response. Waving a cheery farewell to the woman who'd wrestled me for the phone, I headed into the dank afternoon.

I switched on my cell phone—Earth to V.I. once more—and climbed back into the Jaguar. When the engine turned over, I found myself thinking that Luke could file off the serial number and repaint the car blue instead of red. I knew I had to return it, but driving the coolest car on the road brought me more cheer than Father Lou's horse liniment.

I drove up Western, past a new megamall that had driven away two little grocers, a small appliance rental and repair shop and Zoe's Homemade Pies and Cakes. Ah, progress. I crossed Racine, the street where I live, and parked a block to the east.

I walked in a square, south and west, away from the car, so I could saunter up

Racine looking for any unusual vehicles or loiterers. The overcast afternoon was bleeding into a gray dusk, cloaking my face from any watchers.

If I were a Clancy or Ludlum superhero, I'd have memorized all the license plates on the two-block stretch, and been able to tell you which ones hadn't been here when I left early yesterday morning. Since it's all I can do to remember my own plate number, I concentrated instead on vans that could hold listening devices, and cars where people were sitting with the motors running. One of these was a Chicago squad car across the street from my own building. Not too subtle.

After walking another block north, I turned east again and cut down through the alley behind my building. No squad cars were warming the night air behind my building. A woman I recognized was emptying her garbage, but no one else was in the alley.

Mr. Contreras was waiting for me inside the back gate, along with the dogs. The three greeted me with a heartwarming ecstasy. While we were still outside, I explained the possibility that the building might be under electronic surveillance. "I don't think that it is—I don't think my being in the house an Arab speaker fled from warrants huge attention—but I can't be sure. So—don't say anything to me you wouldn't want Clara to hear."

In the dark, I could sense rather than see the old man's embarrassment: Clara was his beloved wife, dead now for many years. I hastily changed the subject, explaining that I had borrowed a car and needed to drop it some place close to its owner. "I'm going upstairs to change, then I want to drive out to New Solway and collect the Mustang. Want to come along?"

He was delighted to take even a small part in my adventure. I left him in his own kitchen and went up to my apartment.

My living room overlooks Racine, so I moved through it in darkness, trying to remember where I'd left things like the piano bench. I only banged my shin once. Since no one seemed to be watching the back, I did turn on lights in my bedroom and kitchen, first making sure the blinds were pulled and the door leading from the back to the front of the hall was shut. After my night in Larchmont Hall, the apartment seemed tiny, but I was glad of my small space. It was like a cloak, protecting me.

I was ravenous, and badly wanted real food. In the last twenty-four hours, I'd had a smoothie, a plate of eggs and some toast and tea in the rectory kitchen. I put water on for pasta. In the freezer, I actually found part of a roast chicken. I stuck it in the microwave while I changed.

My shoulder muscles did not like it when I tried to fasten my bra, but I gritted my teeth and did up the hooks: it felt important not to be exposed, even beneath a sweater, when I finally got around to the law. I put some of Father Lou's embrocation on a bath brush so I could reach behind my head to rub it into my sore zone. It had an odd smell, not unpleasant, but conjuring up stables or locker rooms. Remembering Father Lou's advice to tape the area, I dug an Ace bandage out of the medicine chest. I managed to wrap it tightly enough to hold the sore muscle in place. With clean jeans and walking shoes, I felt strong enough to get by for a while. My running shoes were badly nicked from scaling Larchmont. I'd have to stretch the budget to cover a new pair.

I still had some decent-looking lettuce, a bag of carrots and fresh green beans in my refrigerator. I put these together into a salad, which I ate with the chicken and pasta, sitting down at the kitchen table. Too often I eat either in the car or walking around the apartment while I get ready to run out the door.

I wanted to keep things slow right now, not rush at whatever lay ahead. When I finished eating, I washed the dishes, including the ones I'd let build up in the sink while I was under the weather. Bringing a container of household cleaner and a sponge with me, I walked slowly down the stairs to collect Mr. Contreras and the dogs. We went out the back way, down the alley to the Jaguar.

Golf Cart Hearse

The roads west were clear; we made the forty-mile trip in forty-five minutes. To my relief, as well as my amazement, the Mustang still stood behind the shrubbery where I'd left it. Maybe Schorr's deputies hadn't spotted it: maybe they'd posted the squad car to intercept Benji, rather than to stake out my car. We drove on past the Mustang and parked the Jaguar in the Larchmont carriageway.

While the dogs tore through the under-brush, Mr. Contreras and I cleaned out the Jaguar. I was concerned about obliterating any trace of Benji, but he was happy to think he was getting dog hair and my fin-gerprints out of the car. We left it on the carriageway, keys in the ignition, for some New Solway cop to find.

We walked back along the ditch toward the Mustang. The route that had been so slow and fear-laden in the dark middle of night was an easy stroll now that I had Mr. Contreras and the dogs with me.

"I'm looking for the culvert where I got under the road," I told my neighbor. "It's got a muddy bottom; I'd like Mitch and Peppy to churn it up and hide my tracks."

The gray air had thickened into blue-black evening. Mr. Contreras used my flashlight while I turned on the headlamp I'd used yesterday. It was Mitch who found the entrance. I stooped to look at the culvert floor. Benji's and my footprints were clearly visible; they overlay the wheel marks I'd noticed at the other end on Thursday evening.

"Looks like some kind of little utility truck, forklift or something, come along." Mr. Contreras said. "Someone chasing after you?"

I stared from him to the wheel marks, suddenly making sense of what I was seeing. The golf cart that had been chasing me through my dreams. That was how Marc Whitby had been brought to the Larchmont

Pond. Someone had driven him there. It was so easy. You could get a cart from the Anodyne golf course, drive it into Anodyne Park along the path put up for members, and then, if you knew about this culvert, get to Larchmont Hall.

In disjoint phrases, I explained what I thought had happened. My neighbor nodded intently. "If you're right, doll, you better try to find that golf cart. Or you think your killer already disposed of it?"

"I don't know," I said unhappily. "Whoever it is—it's not they're so smart, but the law doesn't care enough to go after them. So it could still be lying around."

I looked at my watch. Six-thirty. The longer I put off confronting the law, the harder they would make it for me when I finally surfaced. Still, since we were out here, I'd take the extra time to talk to someone at the golf course.

I bumped the Mustang back onto the road and whipped down Dirksen to the golf course. Naturally there was a gate, an ornate affair with a picture, or maybe a logo, welded into the bars. A spotlight on the design highlighted a pond with cat's tails sprouting around it. "Anodyne Park Golf

Course" was emblazoned in gold and green across the top.

I told the guard in the gatehouse that I was working for Geraldine Graham and had some questions about a missing golf cart. He accepted this claim unblinkingly, but wouldn't let the car inside the course with dogs in it—"You never know, people say they'll keep their animals in the car, but then they let them out on the course."

I didn't waste time on argument, just got permission to leave the car at the entrance while we went in. I pulled my briefcase from the trunk, since it still had Marc Whitby's picture in it, and hurried up the drive to the clubhouse with my neighbor.

Saturday is such a busy golfing day that the head of the club was on duty in the clubhouse. A doorman pointed him out, a dapper fiftyish man laughing with a red-faced group of drinkers in front of the fireplace. When I said I was a detective, a hush fell over the group. The manager whisked us into his office, just in case I was going to breathe something ghastly over his members. But when he heard my story—I worked for Ms. Graham; her son had had a near miss with a golf cart on the road several days ago; she was concerned and wanted to know if one had been stolen—he quickly off-loaded me onto the equipment supervisor.

When Eli Janicek, the supervisor, trotted in, the club manager told him to get Mr. Contreras and me over to the equipment shed: we clearly lowered the tone of the place. We followed Janicek out the service entrance while the manager rejoined the drinkers at the fireplace.

Although Janicek's attention was divided between me and his crew, who were calling in with reports on abandoned carts and clubs on the fairways, he answered my questions pretty directly. None of his carts was missing. Yes, some had been picked up from Anodyne Park last Monday morning, but there was nothing strange in that— members were always driving them over to the Anodyne estate and leaving them for the equipment crew to retrieve.

I was turning away, disappointed, when Janicek added, "Now I think of it, one was caked with mud and when we come to clean it up, we found the front pretty well dented in. That didn't sit with me right. We clean up after the members, that's our job, but then they abuse equipment and don't even leave a note saying who was it that did it, that's not right. People need to act responsible."

The cart had been parked outside the bar, if he remembered right. When I asked if he could be sure of the date, he pulled out his log: yes, this was the one: the cart had been caked in mud up over the wheels. When they hosed it down, they found dents in the sides, deep scratches in the paint and the front axle bent. Some kid treating a golf cart like a dune buggy, and, even if they found out who, the parents more than likely would chew out the clubhouse manager, not the kid. On Wednesday, when Janicek had cleaned up the cart, he'd sent it on to the repair shop but he didn't think the mechanics had gotten to it yet, too big a backlog.

When Mr. Contreras started to chime in on modern-day manners, I cut both of them off.

"Can you hold off on the repairs? The Graham family may want to press charges, or at least get their insurance company to look at it. Nothing to do with the club, I promise you, but they're concerned about reckless endangerment and want to talk to Sheriff Salvi about the cart."

Janicek didn't like it, didn't like the thought of the club being involved in a serious legal problem, but he reluctantly agreed to talk to his mechanics in the morning and ask them to wait on the cart.

Before we left, I showed Janicek Marc Whitby's photograph. He called a couple of the valets over, but no one remembered seeing him, and they would have: the club's only black member was August Llewellyn and he hadn't been out for months. Black guests were rare.

Had Edwards Bayard been in the club last week? No, neither he, his mother nor anyone else from the Bayard household.

Mr. Contreras and I walked back to the Mustang while I thought this over. Anyone who knew about the culvert could have used it to get into Anodyne Park, and from there used the park's private path to the golf course to borrow a cart. They might even have parked it next to the culvert on the Coverdale Lane side. Whitby was in the pond, dead, by the time I got there. If I'd only gone to Larchmont an hour or two earlier last Sunday night!

It was frustrating, to come on one piece of the solution, and yet not be able to follow it. On the drive home, I mulled over the story of the cart with Mr. Contreras without coming to any satisfactory answer. When we got back to Lakeview, I dropped my neighbor in the alley with the dogs.

"I need to face the law—I've been putting it off for five hours. It's eight o'clock now. If I'm not home by eleven, call Freeman, okay? And also, until this business is cleared up, we'll talk every day between five-thirty and six-thirty. If you don't hear from me—call Freeman. Under this Patriot Act, if the law gets pissed off enough, they may be able to take me away without letting me talk to my lawyer."

I squared my shoulders and drove around to the front of our building.

Patriot Acts

I feigned surprise when the Chicago cops followed me into my building, but I didn't have to pretend anything when two other men jumped out of adjacent cars and hurried in after them. One was a federal agent who flashed a quick badge the way they're taught in G-man movies, the other a DuPage sheriff's deputy. I clearly was no superhero, since I hadn't noticed them earlier.

The four men weren't pals—there was a lot of pushing and shoving in the entryway as they all tried to speak to me. The DuPage deputy said he had orders to deliver me to Wheaton, and since I had "fled the jurisdiction where a crime was committed," he had first dibs. The Chicago cops said they had

told him already his orders had been super-
seded, that I was to go to Thirty-fifth and
Michigan with them as soon as the federal
agent had finished with me.

"I am operating under orders to search
your place of residence," the federal agent
announced.

That got my attention at once; I demanded to see his warrant.

"Ma'am, under the Patriot Act, if we believe there is an emergency situation affect-
ing national security, we are permitted to
bypass the warrant process." He had a flat
nasal twang that made him sound like the
quintessential bureaucrat.

"I'm not involved in any emergency situations. And nothing I do affects national security." I put my house keys into my back
jeans pocket and leaned against the inner
door.

"Ma'am, the United States attorney for
the Northern District of Illinois is the judge
of that, and he deems that the events of
yesterday evening are sufficiently alarming
to require us to examine your premises."

"The events of yesterday evening? Could
you stop talking like a damned manual and
tell me why you're here?"

The Chicago cops exchanged grins at that, but the agent continued in his flat way. "Ma'am, you vacated a house where a known terrorist was in hiding. We need to make sure you are not involved in shielding him in some way."

"Was there a known terrorist there?" I asked with polite interest. "I only knew that a DuPage County lieutenant thought he could lock me in an abandoned mansion all night."

"Irregardless, I have orders to search your place of residence; if you do not cooperate, the Chicago police are ordered to break down your door." He didn't speak with the aggressive glee that some law officers show when they can overwhelm you with force— he had a job to do; he was going to do it.

"What happened to 'the right of the people to be secure in their persons, houses, papers, and effects, against unreasonable searches and seizures'?" My voice was husky with fury.

"Ma'am, if you want to challenge my orders in federal court you will be able to do so at some later point in time, but these officers"—indicating the Chicago cops, who stood stolidly behind him, dissociating themselves from the proceedings—"are here to ensure that I examine your place of residence."

Before I could escalate the confrontation to a level where I'd spend the night as the taxpayers' guest, Mr. Contreras erupted from his apartment with the dogs. Mitch took exception to seeing men in uniform in the entryway and hurled himself at the hall door. Peppy barked in support.

I opened the hall door wide enough to slip through and grabbed the dogs by their collars, panting at Mr. Contreras to get their leashes. When I had the dogs under control, I wanted to stay on the far side of the entryway, hurling abuse at the law with the dogs, but I knew that would not just postpone the inevitable, it would make the inevitable more intolerable. I told my neighbor to let the men in.

"What in heck do they want?" he asked.

"To search my home. According to that walking manual in the tan overcoat, they can go to any home in America, claim the owner is concealing Osama bin Laden, and enter without a warrant. And if you object, they bust down the door."

We were collecting an audience. The medical resident who lives on the first floor across from Mr. Contreras stormed out, saying that if I didn't stop making all that racket she was calling the cops. When she saw the uniformed men, she blinked a few times, then demanded that they write me a ticket or impound the dogs.

The four lawmen were knocked off balance, but the federal agent recovered first and began intoning the fact that he was not here as part of a canine complaint unit. Before he could finish his first paragraph, a pair of guys from the second floor leaned over the stairwell and hollered down at the resident to shut up and get a life—they had an ongoing feud with her because she'd sicced the law on their late-night parties several times.

"Those dogs are well trained, they never bother anyone," they yelled.

The Chicago cops were now uncomfortable. When neighbors start to gather, simple situations turn complex in a hurry. The cops shushed the Fed and hustled our party up the stairs, sped along by the pair on the second floor who were singing "God Bless America" loudly enough to bring out the young Korean family from the facing apartment. As I undid the dead bolts on my door, I could hear their four-year-old ask, "Is it a parade?"

It didn't take the law long to hunt through my apartment for the obvious: you can't hide a body in four rooms without it coming to light pretty fast. Mitch and Peppy helped: every time someone opened a cupboard or looked under something, they were on his heels. I kept the dogs on short leashes, made sure they never actually touched one of the men, but a hundred-twenty-pound half Lab can make even a federal agent turn a few hairs. Mitch was also pulling on my sore shoulder hard enough to make me wince, but I pretended not to feel it.

During the search, Mr. Contreras kept up a running commentary on men who hid behind badges as an excuse for doing work no decent person would undertake: "Let me tell you, I saw plenty of that in Europe in 'forty-four, never thought I'd watch it in my own country. I risked my life on the beaches at Anzio, I know what real fire feels like coming at you out of real artillery, I saw my buddies cut up in pieces around me. If I'd known I was doing that so you could break into any house in America because you felt like it, they couldn't a got me on that landing boat."

That did sting the Fed: no manly man likes to be reminded that searching a woman's apartment for a runaway youth isn't as dangerous as facing real fire. He kept breaking off his search to try to rebut Mr. Contreras, but the beat cops told the Fed they were under orders to get me to Thirty-fifth and Michigan pronto, and to finish up.

Thirty-fifth and Michigan is the new Chicago police headquarters; I couldn't begin to guess what they wanted with me there. Whoever had set up the meeting was getting impatient: he—or she—kept calling the Chicago cops to move them along, and they kept complaining that the federal agent was taking his sweet time. When the Fed said he wanted to go through my papers, the Chicago cops dug in all four feet: they had orders to bring me in within the half hour.

"I don't require her or your presence to examine the documents," the Fed said in his flat voice.

"I'm not leaving you alone in my apartment," I said firmly. "You could plant evidence. You could steal something."

When he started to proclaim his essential honesty, I said brightly, "I know: Mr. Contreras and the dogs can stay with you. Make sure you get a detailed description of any document J. Edgar takes, Mr. Contreras. And for heaven's sake, don't let him walk off with the utility bills unless he promises to pay them—I can't afford to have my electricity turned off."

The thought of an evening alone with the dogs and my neighbor made the Fed decide my papers probably weren't worth going through. Perhaps the array of mail and books in the living and dining rooms also daunted him. At any event, he left my "place of residence" with the other lawmen. I locked up and followed them downstairs with the dogs.

At the front door, Mr. Contreras told me gruffly to keep my chin up; if I wasn't home by midnight he'd get Freeman to find me. I went out with the four lawmen, including the deputy from DuPage, who hadn't spoken since we'd gone inside. He went off to his own car without so much as a good-bye to his partners in crime prevention. At least the U.S. agent thanked the city cops for their "intergovernmental cooperation."

As I learned in the squad car, the DuPage deputy was sulking because the Chicago cops had overridden his orders. The two men thought this was such a good joke they shared it through the grill with me, but they wouldn't—or couldn't—tell me why we were going to Chicago police headquarters.

"You'll find out soon enough when you get there, ma'am," the driver said. At least they were calling me "ma'am" instead of "girlie," and I wasn't in handcuffs.

The driver covered the ten miles south in twelve minutes, blue lights flashing, occasionally hooting the siren to move cars out of the way. If I'd been president, I'd have felt important, but when we reached the underground garage behind the slick concrete building I only felt motion sick.

Police headquarters had been at Eleventh and State for my whole life. I used to go there with my dad when he had a meeting or needed to turn in special forms of some kind; the chief of the patrol division would ruffle my curls and give me a dime for the vending machine while he and my dad caught up on departmental gossip. I had a kind of nostalgia for the old headquarters' beat-up linoleum and its rabbit warren of offices. The new building felt cold and unfriendly—too big, too clean, too shiny.

My escort handed me over to a desk sergeant, who busied herself with the phone. I studied the wall notices. These, at least, hadn't changed in thirty years: armed and dangerous, last seen driving, workers' compensation, missing since January 9.

The desk sergeant summoned a uniformed officer, a heavyset woman whose equipment belt created a giant *M* between her breasts and hips.

"You got to cross that lonesome valley," I sang under my breath, following her down the hall to an elevator. "You got to cross it by yourself."

"Is it that bad?" she asked, as we rode up one floor. "What'd you do to get so many big men in a room together?"

I made a face. "Ran away from an ugly county lieutenant last night. But why that should get a lot of big men into a room, I don't know. In fact, I don't even know what big men have gathered on my account."

She held the elevator door open until I was in the hall in front of her: never leave a suspect alone in an elevator. "Well, honey, we've arrived, so I guess you'll know soon enough."

She opened a door, saluted, said, "Here she is, Captain," and left.

I couldn't sort out how many people were in the room, or which ones I knew, I was so astonished at seeing the man my guide had saluted. "Bobby?" I exclaimed. "What are you doing here?"

What Bill of Rights?

Bobby Mallory—Captain Mallory now—had been my dad's protégé on the force; my dad had been best man at his and Eileen's wedding. If my mother had believed in godparents, Bobby would have been my godfather. But that didn't bring a jolly twinkle to his pale eyes when he saw me. Nothing about my work makes him twinkle, but tonight he looked as grim as if I'd—well, helped a known terrorist escape.

I felt my knees weaken: Had he somehow learned that I'd taken Benjamin Sadawi to Father Lou's? I was smart enough at least to keep my mouth shut as I found an empty chair.

I had time now to take in the rest of the crowd at the table. I knew some of the people, at least by sight, but four were complete strangers. The lanky woman with bags under her eyes next to me was a Cook County state's attorney; we'd met in court several times. Of course I knew Bobby's own longtime subordinate, my sometime friend Terry Finchley. Lieutenant Schorr had made the long trip in from Wheaton; he was glowering at me like a man who wished his deputies had shot me instead of Catherine Bayard. Stephanie Protheroe, sitting next to him, didn't look at me. I also had occasionally worked with—or around—the FBI's Derek Hatfield.

"Vicki," Bobby said. "We've been waiting for you to surface. You have a lot of explaining to do, my girl. The superintendent asked me to head Chicago's task force on terrorism, and we seem to have a connection between a terrorist, suspected terrorist, who's been living in Chicago, and the man you flushed last night in DuPage. All these busy people have been waiting to ask you questions, so let's get going."

Lieutenant Schorr and a man I didn't recognize both started talking at once. "Just a minute," I protested. "You busy people all know who I am: V. I. Warshawski, Vicki only and solely to Captain Mallory. I'd like your names and affiliations."

A highly polished specimen next to Derek Hatfield was an assistant U.S. attorney for the Northern District. Along with Deputy Protheroe, Schorr had brought an assistant state's attorney from DuPage with him—a man who looked like the U.S. attorney's twin brother: young, white, thick brown hair perfectly combed. Everyone in the room had a sidekick but me. I wished I'd brought Peppy.

Mikes were set up on the table; a young woman in a Chicago PD uniform sat in a corner with sound equipment and earphones. The room and the sound system were as modern as anything I'd seen in the sheriff's office last Sunday night; I hoped Schorr was impressed.

After the pause for civilities, Schorr and the U.S. attorney both jumped in again, Schorr wanting to know why I had fled before he questioned me, the attorney angry because the Feds had been hunting Benjamin Sadawi for four weeks—I'd been within centimeters of him without telling them.

"Benjamin Sadawi? Is that the boy who's been a dishwasher at that fancy Gold Coast school?" I paused briefly, hoping they would stop picturing a big man in a head scarf and start seeing a skinny teenager. "I didn't know I was within centimeters of him. Larchmont Hall was empty when I got there. Lieutenant Schorr's men thought whoever was hiding in the attic jumped out a third-floor window when he—or she—heard me come in."

"It didn't make you suspicious when you found Arab-language books up in that attic?" Derek asked.

"The whole situation was so confusing that I didn't know how to make sense of it."

"You went upstairs, didn't you?" the U.S. attorney asked. He and the DuPage attorney had been introduced as Jack and Orville, but they looked so much alike that I couldn't remember which was which.

When I nodded, he said, "What did you think when you saw that some of the books were in Arabic?"

I wrinkled up my face, puzzled woman thinking. "There were a bunch of old kids' books with Calvin Bayard's name in the flyleaf. The house had belonged to the

Drummond family—Geraldine Graham's father—so I wondered why Mr. Bayard's books were there. Then I saw the Arab-English dictionary and thought maybe Mr. Bayard was coming over in the middle of the night to study Arabic. I thought he might be translating his childhood books or something."

"You couldn't possibly have thought that!" Orville or Jack slapped the tabletop.

"No, you couldn't have, Vicki," Bobby spoke quietly, but sternly. "Tonight isn't an occasion for joking. Since September 11, every law enforcement officer in this country has been stretched past the point of endurance. So give us straightforward answers to our questions."

Terry Finchley suggested I start by explaining what I'd been doing in Larchmont in the first place. For what seemed to be the thousandth time, I went through my litany about Marcus Whitby's death and his sister's hiring me to investigate.

We paused while the woman in the corner changed disks in the machine and checked that it was recording. When she nodded at Terry, he continued. "You didn't think that was police business? Dragging the pond?"

"I did. Completely. Just as I thought searching Marcus Whitby's house was police business. But I couldn't persuade your buddies in DuPage any more than I could persuade you. Since you all took a pass on the investigation, I went out to New Solway on behalf of the family."

"And searched the pool," the lanky woman from Cook County said.

"And searched the pool," I agreed.

"Find anything relevant?" Orville or Jack asked.

I spread my hands. "Hard to say. A lot of old china. Nothing that said who put Whitby into the pond. What I did find, though, was the golf cart that the murderer used to drive Mr. Whitby to the pond."

That got their attention in a hurry. Although Jack or Orville pooh-poohed the idea (we know he went there drunk to kill himself privately), Bobby spoke up, asking Lieutenant Schorr how Marc had gotten to the estate: Had they checked the trains, the taxis, and so on? Schorr and Jack or Orville blustered in a way that proved they hadn't done any digging into this problem. Bobby would have blasted a subordinate who'd been so slack; to Schorr, he only said quietly that he thought the question merited some research.

"What's this about the golf cart, Vicki?"

I told him about finding the culvert this evening, and talking to the equipment supervisor. The Finch nodded and made a note. I breathed a quiet sigh of relief. The police machinery was going to take over the labor-intensive part of the inquiry.

"But this doesn't make you a heroine," Bobby warned me. "What did you do after you searched the pond yesterday? Break into the house?"

"Bobby—Captain!" I protested, wounded.

Bobby glared at me and let Schorr take over the questions. We rehashed Geraldine Graham's interest in her old home. We rehashed the fact that the kitchen door was open.

"You say," Derek Hatfield put in. "I've worked with Warshawski before. She skirts the law; I've never proved it, but she's not above breaking and entering."

"This DuPage gorilla here—excuse me, this lieutenant—searched me. Thoroughly enough for a sexual misconduct claim. Ask him if he found any tools on me."

"You were there alone for God knows how long," Schorr shouted. "You had plenty of time to hide any picklocks."

I raised my brows in exaggerated disbelief. "You didn't search that mansion from top to bottom? And all the time thinking you had a terrorist cell hanging out there? On less evidence than an Arab-English dictionary, the government just took apart my home without a warrant."

"This isn't Comedy Central," the U.S. attorney said. "Those of us at this table are trying to protect our country."

"Well, I'll sleep easier at night knowing you've inspected my bras," I said bitterly. "What did Renee Bayard say about the books in the attic?"

"The Bayards and the Grahams are old friends. Ms. Bayard thinks her husband might have lent them to Mr. Darraugh Graham when Mr. Graham was a boy," the DuPage attorney said. "Of course, with her granddaughter in the hospital she was too distracted to give the matter serious attention."

"So the Bill of Rights still operates for wealthy voters," I said. "That's reassuring.

You do know why her granddaughter is in the hospital, right?"

"Because of an unfortunate accident." The DuPage attorney clipped off the words. "Why didn't you wait in the house to answer Lieutenant Schorr's questions last night? Jumping out the bathroom window—it makes us think you had some reason to run away to take such a risky exit."

"I would have preferred a door myself, but the lieutenant made the estate's lawyer lock me in."

"You could have waited until Schorr talked to you," Jack or Orville persisted.

"I was tired—I'd been dragging the pond—it was freezing in the house. I wanted to get some sleep. When Schorr's deputies shot Catherine Bayard, he was too busy to remember me. So I left."

"But you didn't go home." The Cook County attorney spoke up.

"No," I agreed. "I believe a safe driver is one who knows when she's too tired to control a vehicle. I checked into a motel."

The lanky woman nodded: they'd cared enough to find the place I'd stayed. They clearly didn't know I'd left my Mustang behind the shrubbery, or someone would have been all over me for that. The Cook County attorney pressed the attack. "You weren't in the motel when the maid went in to clean at noon. What were you doing today between noon and eight o'clock?"

"Is there reason you need to know that?" I asked. "If there is, I'll be happy to tell you, but I can't imagine why my movements are of interest to Cook County or DuPage, or, most especially, the Department of Justice."

"America is at war," the U.S. attorney reiterated. "If you aided a terrorist in escaping, you can be charged with aiding our enemies."

I suddenly felt very tired. I spread my hands on the table and studied my fingers while the silence grew.

"Well," the U.S. attorney prodded.

"It's not well," I said. "None of it is well. We're not at war, for one thing. Only Congress can declare war, which they haven't done—unless it happened while we've been sitting here."

"You know damn well what he means," Derek said. "Do you think it's a joke, what happened in New York, what our troops are doing in Afghanistan or the Persian Gulf?"

I looked up at him. "I think this is the most serious thing that has happened in my lifetime. Not just the Trade Center, but the fear we've unleashed on ourselves since, so we can say that the Bill of Rights doesn't matter any more. My lover is in Afghanistan. I don't know if he's dead or alive, I haven't heard from him in almost a week. If he's dead, my heart will break, but if the Bill of Rights is dead my life, my faith in America, will break. If I had found a terrorist in the Larchmont mansion, I would have done my best to deliver him to you, Derek—and hoped you'd pay more attention to me than your colleagues in Minnesota or Arizona did to similar warnings. But I didn't see any signs of a violent criminal. Did you? Were those Arabic books manuals on bombs, or did they contain diagrams of important U.S. targets? I assume you're finding that out."

I turned to the DuPage attorney. "Meanwhile, the net gain for the night was that Schorr's Arab-hunting tigers shot a local teenager. I had nothing to do with that, and I don't think my hanging around Larchmont while Schorr figured out what spin to put on that catastrophe would have been at all helpful."

No one said anything for a minute or two. I shifted in my chair, stretching my neck and shoulders.

"We need to reopen the investigation into Whitby's death. I don't believe in coincidences, a suspect hiding in a house, a man dead outside the house, those two have to be connected." Bobby spoke with the authority of his forty years on the force. He looked at the DuPage attorney. "Orville, can you get your pathologist to do a full autopsy, including a tox screen on Marcus Whitby?"

"We released the body to the family yesterday," Orville said. "I'll see if they've taken it back to Atlanta."

Bobby rubbed his balding temples. "I hope to Christ they haven't: I don't want to deal with an exhumation. Or with one more jurisdiction than the three already involved."

I didn't reveal that Bryant Vishnikov had already started a private autopsy: I was hoping Bryant could finish and give me the results before the law found out he had the body.

"We can expedite that if necessary," the U.S. attorney said. "Meanwhile, what about Warshawski here? We never got an account of how she spent those missing hours. Is she capable of hiding a wanted man?"

"You searched my home," I protested. "I'll be glad to take you to my office if we're done here. You can look in the trunk of my car."

"We had someone at your office this afternoon," Derek said. "And we're checking with your friends."

I tried to control the rising tide of fury in me. "Did you bastards help yourself to my Rolodex? Did you take files? Where the hell do you get off, harassing a citizen without probable cause."

"We don't need probable cause," the U.S. attorney snapped. "We have you and a suspect both missing from the same house on the same night. Like the captain said, no coincidences here. You might have thought he was an innocent kid and given him a boost out the window with you. But now that you know he's a wanted man, we expect you to cooperate."

"I am cooperating," I shouted, leaning across the table.

"Vicki, watch yourself," Bobby warned me.

I shut my eyes and took a breath, counting backward from ten in Italian as I exhaled. "I am cooperating," I said in a calmer voice. "Now you guys give some back. What's he done? How do we know he's a terrorist? Tell me that and I'll get more excited about your questions."

Derek and the U.S. attorney exchanged glances; the attorney spoke. "He stayed on in this country without a visa, and without a sponsor, after his uncle died. He goes to an Uptown mosque where they preach some pretty radical rhetoric. And he went underground when we tried to bring him in for questioning."

I asked him to expand on the radical rhetoric, or what they'd found in the room Benjamin had rented with a Pakistani family after his uncle died, but they refused to provide more detail: they knew what they knew.

"I see," I said. Really, though, I didn't see—anything. It didn't sound like a catalog of evil, but I didn't know what "radical rhetoric" covered. Death to Israel? Death to America? Death to abortion providers? Radical or patriotic, depending on your viewpoint. If Benji advocated all three, then I'd have to rethink covering up for him. But I'd wait for Father Lou to finish interrogating him before I turned him over to these guys.

My own judgment might be at fault, but I sure didn't trust any of the people at the table more.

Bobby said if I would just explain how I'd spent the afternoon, they'd wrap up the meeting.

"I returned phone calls. I ran errands. I ran my dogs. I ate dinner."

"No one saw you run your dogs," the Cook County attorney said.

"The fact that you staked out my building is sufficiently depressing without you boasting about it. You have a record of my phone calls, too?" The look that Derek and the U.S. attorney exchanged told me all I wanted to know about that. "I was at a TechSurround outlet on Fullerton. You can probably get a record of my transactions by raiding their cash register, or hacking into their computer, or whatever you feel you can do in the name of protecting the country."

Schorr wanted to bluster more about what I'd really done last night, but everyone else seemed as worn out as I was. Or maybe I'd embarrassed them into silence, just a little.

Bobby broke the silence, turning to look at the woman with the recording equipment. "Sissy, we're done for the night. You can collect your things and go."

Sissy? That didn't seem like a very imposing name for a police officer. Sissy said "Yessir," switched off the system and labeled her disks.

The DuPage attorney stood up, saying he had a long drive, but he'd call Bobby as soon as he knew the status of Marcus Whitby's body. That effectively broke up the meeting. Derek and the U.S. attorney left at once, along with the two county attorneys. Schorr threatened me with grievous bodily harm, or a month in prison, or maybe both if I crossed him again—I wasn't paying a lot of attention by that point.

"Can one of your team give me a ride home?" I said to Bobby when the room had cleared. "As you know, I didn't drive myself down."

Bobby nodded. "Finch, go find someone to give Princess Grace here a lift."

That was what Bobby called me when he thought I was being a nuisance. It wasn't exactly a term of endearment—but he would never have used it in front of the DuPage and federal officials.

When Terry had left to find me a driver, Bobby told me to join him at the head of the table so he wouldn't have to shout. "Jack Zeelander is a pain in the behind," he commented. "All the Feds these days are chasing shadows. They're so upset at missing the obvious last summer that they grab at every straw the wind blows by 'em, hoping it'll lead them someplace. I can understand that—we've had murder investigations here where the heat was so high we burned ourselves and never caught the perp. But Zeelander wants to be in Washington so bad you can smell the ambition on him and it doesn't make him a trustable colleague."

Bobby's remarks took me by surprise: he's never let his hair down in front of me before. "Do you think this is a straw blowing past? The missing kid, I mean?"

He grunted. "That's not my call, thank God. What is my call is you. I didn't lean on you in front of all those people, but don't lie to me now, Vicki. Do you know where that kid is?"

The hair-letting-down, that had been the tactic of a skilled interrogator. I felt the twist of guilt I was supposed to. Tony and Gabriella's good friend, I couldn't lie to him. I thought of Catherine Bayard crying out to her grandmother not to ask her anything else because she didn't want to lie to her. I thought of the vast expanses of St. Remigio's, the gym, the classrooms, the chapel, the kitchen and bedrooms. I had no idea which room Benjamin Sadawi was in right now.

I slowly shook my head. "I don't know, Bobby."

He narrowed his small gray eyes. "You better not be lying to me, Vicki."

I looked at him solemnly. "I know: Gabriella would hate it."

"Yeah, Tony wouldn't be crazy about it, either, but the two of them would protect you. Me, if I catch you in a whopper on this one, I'll hang you out to dry. What were you doing since checking out of that motel? After you went to that Tech-whatever place?"

I drew a circle in the tabletop with my finger. "Morrell has gone underground. I went to see a friend who knows him."

"For six hours? Don't try my patience."

"If I tell you my private business, you'll use it against me."

"What the— Oh. Unless you're about to reveal a criminal act, I'll keep it to myself."

I had played games with the truth about Sadawi; I'd level with him on this. "Your guys staked out the front of my building, but not the alley. I thought the Feds or that ape Schorr might be tailing me, so I went in through the back. I needed a decent meal, I wanted to run the dogs, I wanted some time with my neighbor. I did all those things, then changed my clothes, went out through the alley again and came up the street to the front door."

Bobby stared at me, then let out a hoarse sound somewhere between a laugh and a snarl. "No wonder we can't find a missing Egyptian boy. It's a wonder we can find our feet to put our shoes on in the morning, when we don't have the brains to cover both entrances to a building. Jesus, Mary and Joseph!"

Among Friends—for a Change

I slept in the squad car going home. It was only ten, but the two hours at Thirty-fifth and Michigan had worn me out almost more than last night's physical stresses. When the driver shook me awake, I blinked, momentarily disoriented: I had expected to see the little bungalow on Houston Street where I grew up. I had expected, or wanted, to find my mother waiting for me.

Instead, Mr. Contreras and the dogs came bustling down the walk to greet me, the old man voluble in relief that I hadn't been locked up. I lay on his living room floor with my arms around Peppy, running through the highlights, or maybe lowlights, of the evening. When he learned the FBI had also searched my office, and might well be tapping my phone, Mr. Contreras spoke his views on the law colorfully and at length. He might think any and all measures the government had taken in the name of protecting America were justified, no matter whose rights they violated—but when it came down to me, the Feds had crossed an inviolable line. I'd always miss my mother when times were hard, but having my neighbor as a partisan was a pretty good second.

"But going out the window of that mansion, doll, that musta shook you up bad. I see how you been favoring your shoulder."

"It wasn't the window, it was diving into the pond and then climbing up that wretched wall. I saw"—I stopped just before blurting out Father Lou's name—"a sports trainer on my way home this afternoon. He gave me some salve and told me to tape up the shoulder. I just haven't had time to stop at a drugstore for firm enough tape—I've been using an Ace bandage, which doesn't hold the muscle quite in place."

"Go see the doc tomorrow. Don't rely on no sports trainer's half-baked notions."

That was a good idea: Lotty dispensed more than medical comforts from her storefront clinic. I lay on the dog's shoulder, thinking I should get up and go to bed before I fell asleep on the floor, when my cell phone rang. To Peppy's indignation, I stopped petting her and got up to retrieve the phone from my handbag.

It was Harriet Whitby, apologizing for calling so late, but she and Amy were at the hotel waiting for me; did I still want to see them?

I was about to moan that I was too tired to move, but then I remembered that the DuPage state's attorney was going to ask the Whitbys to return Marcus's body. I needed to talk to Harriet tonight, so she didn't learn about it from some functionary. In case the Feds were really monitoring my calls, I didn't want them to learn that I had already organized a full autopsy. I told Harriet I'd be at the hotel in half an hour.

When Mr. Contreras realized I was going out again, he tried to argue me out of it: it was late, I was beat, I shouldn't be driving. I agreed with all of those things, but said I would take a cab. It's one of the few benefits of living in Chicago's most congested neighborhood, that taxis cruise the streets at all hours. Mr. Contreras and the dogs walked down to the corner with me and waited until a cab pulled up in front of a new hot spot at Belmont and Sheffield. He ushered me in with the assurance that he would wait up for me.

The usual Saturday-night eaters and drinkers filled Belmont. Cars honked, crowds spilled across sidewalks into the streets. As we crawled east, I kept looking out the back, wondering if the law was following me, but the SUV immediately behind us made it hard to see anything else. I finally decided it didn't really matter if the FBI knew I was going downtown and dozed off again until we reached the hotel.

The Drake's lobby is at the top of the kind of staircase Audrey Hepburn was always climbing in *Roman Holiday* or *How to Steal a Million.* A princess could negotiate those stairs in high heels with ease, but a tired detective had trouble lifting one leg after the other. "I could have slept all night," I sang to myself, "And still have begged for more."

Harriet and Amy were on a couch in the small lobby at the top of the stairs. When she spotted me, Harriet sprang up to greet me, clasping both my hands in her own, then exclaiming remorsefully when she saw the purple hollows under my eyes.

"This is the second time I've called you late after you'd been wearing yourself out on my family's account; I'm so sorry—this could have waited until morning."

I smiled in reassurance. "Something came up tonight that you should know about, anyway. Where can we talk quietly? Your room?"

"Mother keeps coming into my room if I'm there. She and Daddy are thinking of flying home Monday, regardless of what Dr. Vishnikov discovers, and she's fretting about the travel arrangements."

We found a corner table in the Palm Court, which was kept dark in the tradition of the old bars of the fifties. We sank into velvet plush and tried to see each other by the light of little tabletop fixtures. When a waitress materialized out of the gloom and Harriet ordered herbal tea, I started to follow suit, then realized I wanted whisky. Black Label might put me to sleep before we finished talking, but I wanted that glow of warmth to soften the knots between my shoulder blades.

We talked idly while we waited for our drinks. Amy had spent the afternoon hiking in the dunes southeast of the city; Harriet and her parents had met Aretha Cummings, Marc's research assistant. Aretha had brought them some of Marc's private things from the office. A nice young woman, clearly grief-stricken, Mother had wondered if Marc and she had been dating.

"And me, I spent the day dodging shots from three law enforcement agencies." The drinks arrived and I took a welcome swallow. "If you heard the news, you may know an Egyptian kid was hiding in the house on the estate where Marcus died. The police and the Feds now are imagining that the kid, his name is Benjamin, killed Marcus. And since that's the track their minds are running on, they will be looking for a connection between the two. They'll wonder if Marcus was writing about would-be terrorists in Chicago; they'll wonder if Marcus had a political involvement with a terrorist group."

Harriet let out a muffled cry. "Marc with terrorists? No and no and no. If you think that for even one minute—"

"I don't think that. But you need to be prepared for that kind of question from the police tomorrow, or whenever they try to talk to you. And another thing: now that the law has decided to take an interest in your brother's death, they want to reopen the autopsy. They agree they did a superficial job the first time round."

"But—you know Dr. Vishnikov is already doing that. Didn't you speak to him this afternoon?" Harriet said.

"Oh, yes. And maybe he's already done what he needs to do—barring results from the tox screens. But if he hasn't, it's up to you, whether you want to give your brother's body back to the DuPage County ME. If you don't, keep them away until Vishnikov is done: he's such an eminent pathologist, even the FBI will accept his findings. Also, since you're paying Vishnikov, he'll have to tell you what he discovers. If you send your brother back to DuPage, they'll do the work for free—free for you, I mean—but they may not share their results with you."

Couched in those terms, the decision to keep Vishnikov on the job seemed the only sensible way to go. Of course, I had an agenda, too: I wanted the autopsy results, and no one in DuPage was likely to tell me whether they'd drunk coffee for breakfast, let alone what Marcus Whitby had inside him. Harriet didn't think she would be very good at holding off the DuPage County sheriff's office; I told her she could refer them to me as her legal representative. "I'm used to them being annoyed with me. It won't bother me to have them add one more count to their list."

"I'll stay with you tomorrow, Harry," Amy promised. "Unless there's something Vic needs me to do?"

I slumped back against the thick upholstery, my eyes shut. It was hard for me to imagine the next day, but I guessed I'd be starting it at the hospital where Catherine Bayard was recovering from her surgery. With an effort, I remembered what Amy had been working on—was it only yesterday?—and asked if she'd found anything useful about the Committee for Social Thought and Justice.

She grinned. "I thought we'd never get around to that. That meeting in Eagle River, the one Olin Taverner was interrogating Bayard about, well, Kylie Ballantine was there—"

I sat up again. "What? You found it in the *Congressional Record*?"

She shook her head. "The University of Chicago archives."

She leaned over to pull a sheaf of papers from her briefcase and laid them on the table. Harriet and I bent over them, trying to read them by the flickering bar lights, but couldn't make out them out.

I signaled to the waitress for the check, but Harriet took it from me. "You've run yourself ragged for me and my family; the least I can do is buy you a glass of Scotch."

She signed the bill to her room and the three of us went out to the lobby, where we looked at the documents Amy had photo-copied. One was a photograph, blurry in re-production, that showed a group of African tribal dancers. You couldn't tell sex, let alone identity, because of the masks everyone was wearing. But stapled to the picture was a letter on Olin Taverner's sta-tionery, dated May 1957, to the president of the university.

This photograph was taken on June 14, 1948. It shows Kylie Ballantine and her Ballet Noir de Chicago performing at a benefit for the Legal Defense Fund of the Committee for Social Thought and Justice. This committee is a major supporter of known Communists in the arts and letters. A number of university trustees are my clients. They are deeply disturbed to find that Ballantine is actually teaching at the university. I don't know what students are learning in her classes, but if parents saw this photograph, and knew that their children were being taught by someone who not only supports Communism but engages in sexually explicit dancing, I doubt they would want them studying at the university—even one with the University of Chicago's leftist leanings.

Handwritten at the bottom of the letter was the phrase, "Get someone to deal with this."

"So Taverner got Kylie fired," Amy said. "That's probably why Marc went out to see him."

"Is there any evidence that Marc saw this letter?" I asked.

She grinned again. "Yes, because you have to sign into the rare books and archives room—not like the rest of the library, where you go in and out on your ID. Marc had been there about three days before he met Olin Taverner."

"But this doesn't prove anything," Harriet objected. "You can't tell where this was taken, or who was in it. How could they fire her just because of that?"

"America in 1956, baby," Amy said. "Communist? Black? You only needed to whisper it once."

Bedside Manner

Catherine, you're lucky to be alive. The sheriff's police may have been reckless— we agree they were way out of line, and we'll take appropriate action—but don't try to hide behind that with me. I know you're in pain, but I also know you're lying."

Whoever was speaking had a penetrating baritone; it carried easily through the hospital door, which wasn't quite shut. The volunteer looked dubiously from a vase of flowers in her hand to the door.

"I'll take those in for you," I offered.

She smiled gratefully and handed off the flowers. Before the private guard stationed outside the door could object, or ask me to identify myself, I was in the room.

I had spent the night at the Drake. It wasn't just that I was too tired to take another step, but the thought of going to bed at home under the watchful eyes of the law made my skin crawl. The hotel had toiletries for forgetful travelers like me; I took a toothbrush, toothpaste and comb from the front desk. I had just enough brain function left to call Mr. Contreras so he wouldn't rouse Freeman, and fell deeply and totally asleep.

When I woke the next morning in the pleasant, unfamiliar room, I felt a familiar unpleasant stiffness. I groaned my way out of bed to start stretching, and then lay back down, calling the concierge from bed to arrange for a massage. I'd worry about the bill when my American Express statement came next month.

Breakfast in bed. An hour in the hotel spa, followed by a massage and a makeup treatment. When I put my jeans and sweater back on, I almost looked as though I belonged on the Gold Coast. More to the point, I could move my arms without feeling like someone was sticking a knife into my back.

Before checking out, I went into the hotel florist and charged an attractive little bouquet to my room. I added a floppy-eared dog. Adorable. Only another sixty-five dollars on a bill long enough that I shoved it into my pocket without inspecting the total.

The Drake is only a few blocks from Northwestern Hospital, where Catherine Bayard had been sent. I walked south to the hospital along the lakeshore, the wind tearing at the paper around the flowers. Whitecaps danced up to the breakwater like daredevils, advancing, retreating. Fists of clouds tumbled across the horizon. The air was sharp. I was happy to be alive and walking.

At the hospital, I found that the Bayard family was guarding Catherine's privacy; the clerk at the information desk wouldn't give out her room number. I didn't argue, just nodded and handed over the flowers. The clerk put them on a shelf with a bunch of other offerings.

I retreated to a curtained alcove by the front entrance until a volunteer came by to load flowers onto a cart. After that, it was simply a matter of following the flop-eared dog up elevators and down corridors as the volunteer made deliveries. Catherine's room turned out to be the last one on the route, at the end of a long hall of private rooms. Most of those we passed had their doors firmly closed, but I could see into some, where the chintz curtains and couches made the rooms look more like the high-end hotel I'd just left, not a hospital.

The room I entered was charming, with armchairs upholstered in the same gold-flowered brocade as the curtains. Visitors could eat or read at the polished side table. The girl in the hospital bed, her shoulder swathed in bandages, her arm attached to an IV, struck a discordant note. So did the man shouting at her; in this setting, one expected visitors to behave with decorum.

"That Arab boy worked at your school. Don't expect me to believe it's a coincidence that he was hiding out in—" He broke off midsentence, as Catherine, who had looked dopily toward the opening door, recognized me and gave an involuntary gasp.

The shouter also turned to look. He was a lean, tanned man about my age, in a crewneck sweater and jeans, with a shock of thick dark hair. He ordered me to put the flowers down and leave, but I stood rooted to the floor, water slopping over the flop-eared dog onto my hand.

"Just who are you?" I demanded.

"Who am I?" he yelled. "Who the hell are you, barging in here?"

He strode over to me, grabbing my arm in an effort to propel me out. I leaned against him, a dead weight that made him stagger.

"We met in Olin Taverner's apartment Thursday night," I said. "Now, tell me who you are, and why you're in this hospital room."

He let go of me so fast that the rest of the water sloshed out of the vase. "I wasn't—who are—" he stammered.

"You may not have seen my face, but I saw yours," I said, my voice a nasty whisper. "My next call is to the cops. Your prints must be all over that desk drawer you jimmied. What was in it?"

"Father," Catherine Bayard said from the bed in the thread of a voice. "It's my father."

We both turned toward her, guilty that we'd forgotten her lying there. I should have realized he was Catherine's father from the snatch of diatribe I'd overheard, but I'd been too amazed at seeing Thursday's head-butter to think clearly.

I went over to her side. "How are you feeling?"

"Shitty. Like I fell off my horse and he danced on me."

I smiled. "That's a rich girl's image—when I'm injured, I feel like I've been hit by a dump truck. I'm sorry you got caught in the fire from those souped-up cowboys Friday night. I was in Larchmont Hall when they shot you."

Behind the morphine, her eyes flickered from me to her father. I smiled reassuringly. "The deputies were pretty pumped; I thought they'd been shooting at a raccoon or deer and when they went out to look, I hightailed it back to Chicago. I hope you weren't lying out in the grass too long before they got you to an ambulance."

Her father burst out, "You were in Larchmont? With that Arab terrorist? Are you responsible for—"

"No, Mr. Bayard, I'm not responsible for your daughter being shot, and I didn't see any terrorists Friday night. I was in New Solway on Friday for the same reason I was there on Thursday."

"And that was?"

"Investigating a homicide." I let the words die away.

"Homicide?" Edwards Bayard looked at me uncertainly. "Are you with the police?"

"I'm a detective. You may not have heard about the death of a journalist on the Larchmont grounds last week."

"Oh, that. When I heard about it, of course I was worried about whether it was safe for my daughter to be out in New Solway, but Rick Salvi says they think this Arab kid did it. The Arab can't have gone far, unless the gal who was in the house when they surrounded it—that was you, wasn't it? Did you help him escape?"

Catherine's eyes grew larger in her white face; I took her uninjured hand in a light clasp. "The sheriff and the Feds and even the Chicago police figure they can wrap Marcus Whitby's death up in a nice tidy package with Benjamin Sadawi's name on the gift card. But they're overlooking a lot of evidence in that convenient wrap-up, evidence that makes it clear that Sadawi had nothing to do with Whitby's death."

"Evidence? What kind of evidence?"

I let go of Catherine's hand to stand next to Edwards Bayard. I spoke to him in my prison yard undervoice so Catherine couldn't hear. "The law is starting to think Taverner was killed—instead of the popular theory that he died in his sleep. You showing up in his apartment like that, breaking in through the patio, skulking behind the curtains, well, it makes me wonder where you were last Monday night. And last Sunday night, when Marcus Whitby died, for that matter."

"Why, you—how dare you?" His eyes blazed with fury, but he also kept his voice low, glancing at his daughter to see how much of our talk she was following.

"What do you mean, how dare I? You knocked me down in your haste to flee the dead man's home. And your right-wing think tank is a major beneficiary of Taverner's estate. Give me one reason why I shouldn't hand you—not to the old family friend, Rick Salvi—but to the Chicago cops, who aren't going to be nearly so impressed with you."

"Get out of here right now," Bayard roared. "I will not have you slandering me in front of my daughter!"

"Daddy, please," Catherine cried from her bed. "Don't shout, I can't stand it. And let me talk to her, I want to talk to her."

"Not without me present, you don't. Don't you understand, Trina, you are in a lot of trouble right now?"

"Trina's in a lot of pain, and Sheriff Salvi is in a lot of trouble. Don't get hysterical, Eds." Renee Bayard swept into the room.

She moved me away from Catherine with an imperious glance and felt her granddaughter's pulse. Although Renee was dressed casually, in corduroy trousers and a sweater, she still wore her mah-jongg tile bracelet, which clacked as she felt Catherine's wrist. I couldn't help wondering how long she'd lingered outside the door, waiting for the perfect line for a dramatic entrance.

"It's not hysterical to be concerned when your daughter lets herself be sucked into involvement with a runaway terrorist—especially when you're twelve hundred miles away. What the hell were you doing, letting her roam about Larchmont like that in the middle of the night? I agreed to let her stay with you when I took the position in D.C., but if this is what's going to happen, then as soon as she's fit to travel she's moving out there where she can be properly supervised."

"Won't go." Catherine tried to speak with her usual fire, but her words came out slowly. "Stay with Grample and Granny. Won't listen to right-wing bullshit night after—"

"You see?" Edwards Bayard said to his mother. "She lives with you and she loses all respect for my work."

"Eds, she's terribly weak, she can't think straight right now. Let's let her rest and sort this out when she's stronger. And you," she turned to me. "I don't know what you're doing here, but it's time you left."

"Want her to stay," Catherine whispered. "Talk alone. Please, Granny." Tears trickled down the sides of Catherine's pale face.

Renee gave me a look that seemed to question what her granddaughter saw in me, but she moved with her usual decision. "You can have ten minutes. Eds, you and I will get a cup of coffee. And find out why the guard let this woman into the room."

When the two had left, I made sure the door was shut all the way, then pulled a chair up next to Catherine's head, leaning close to her so I could speak softly and keep any eavesdroppers from making out my words. "Benjamin is safe, but I'm not going to tell you where he is. You've been gallant and heroic, standing up for him, but the police will be coming through here in waves. You're Calvin and Renee Bayard's granddaughter—the cops won't abuse you—but they are going to question you. A lot. The less you know, the better for both you and Benjamin."

"I rescued him. I . . . have a right—"

"This situation isn't about rights; it's about keeping Benjamin safe until we find out whether he really does have any terrorist affiliations."

Her mouth set in a mulish line. "Benji is not a terrorist. I know him. He's scared. He's lonely. He needs me."

I shook my head. "You can't take him back to Larchmont. And even if you had some other place to hide him, you're wounded. You couldn't look after him. Besides which, the FBI is looking for him. Because they may be tailing me, I'm not trying to visit him. And as soon as you get out of this bed, they're going to be questioning you. He's safe where he is."

"On your say-so. I looked after him for three weeks and never breathed a word to anyone." She sat up in bed, her eyes fierce in her pale face. "You can't just barge in and take him away and not tell me where he is."

I shook my head, tired of the orders of the rich, even the young, ardent rich, but I said, "I will tell you if you promise not to try to see him until I let you know it's safe. And if you agree to answer my questions."

She thought it over for a minute, not wanting to give me anything, but finally agreed. When I told her he was at St. Remigio's, she objected to my putting a Muslim in a Catholic rectory, but, after I'd described Father Lou, she reluctantly agreed it might work. Mindful of Renee's timetable, I cut short Catherine's further questions to ask my own.

"How did you come to take charge of Benji?"

The ghost of a smile flitted across her face. "In the cafeteria one day. I'd left my books. Room was empty, 'cept for him. Saw him trying to read . . . out of one of the third-grade books . . . helped him. After, he'd stop sometimes during lunch . . . he bussed tables, you know . . . he'd ask what a word meant . . . never intruded . . . I liked him . . . didn't know his story . . . uncle died here . . . mom home in Cairo . . . three little sisters . . . a brother . . . sending them money . . . learned that . . . later."

She stopped, panting. I helped her drink some juice and looked at my watch.

"Yeah, Granny. Can't fight her . . . Day they came for him . . . Benji hid inside our sports equipment shed . . . Saw me . . . when I was putting away . . . field hockey sticks . . . begged for help. Hid him in the shed . . . took the padlock key home . . . Did like you guessed . . . down the fire escape . . . took Gran's car . . . picked up Benji at Vina Fields . . . drove him out to New Solway . . . He couldn't stay in the sports shed. I knew Larchmont was empty . . . only place I could think of . . . We found all that . . . old furniture in the attic. Turned off . . . motion sensors for alarm. Brought food . . . when I could get there."

"But how did you get into Larchmont?"

"Grample did go once . . . last year . . . I saw him leave, two in the morning . . . Theresa didn't wake up . . . I followed him through the wood and saw him . . . go into the house. Grample did have a key for the door, the alarm . . . that part was true . . . I don't know how . . . he got it . . . Got Grample home . . . He does come with me . . . even when he won't go . . . with Granny . . . Daddy was at home, so I didn't say . . . anything . . . but I kept . . . the key."

"I thought Theresa had an alarm over her bed so she'd wake up if your grandfather left his room in the night."

"She does . . . But sometimes she . . . has seizures and stuff . . . she sleeps through alarm . . . Granny mustn't know. It doesn't happen often . . . Grample likes her . . . she's good with him . . . don't tell Granny, please."

She was growing paler and shorter of breath. I assured her I wouldn't rat out Theresa to her grandmother, and told her to lie down and rest, that we'd talk more another time. Edwards and Renee came in as Catherine sank back against the mattress.

Edwards looked at his daughter, lying with her eyes half shut, her face white, and glared at me. "What have you been doing to her?" He bent over his daughter and added with surprising tenderness, "Trina, Trina, it's okay, baby, Daddy's here."

A nurse had followed the Bayards into the room. She pushed past Edwards and Renee and put her fingers on Catherine's wrist. "She's all right, just very fatigued. I'm going to give her something to help her rest better, and, for now, no more conversation with her."

Edwards turned to me. "What did you do to her?"

"I talked to her, Mr. Bayard. Just as I plan to talk to you." My glance swept from him to his mother. "We have a lot of catching up to do, you and I."

Renee's attention was arrested. "You and my son know each other?"

"Not well." I smiled tightly. "But I hope to change that. We've played soccer against each other. Or was it bullfighting? I get the sports confused."

Renee frowned: she didn't like the tone I was using, or she didn't like the secret relationship with her son I was implying. "It's time for you to leave Catherine's room, but you may wait outside. I want to talk to you about Friday's events."

More commands from the rich and powerful. I didn't snarl at her, because I wanted to find out some things myself, like whether Renee had been on the scene Friday night, and what kinds of questions the sheriff was asking. Above all, I wanted time alone with Edwards Bayard.

Out in the hall, I leaned against the wall next to the door, but the murmurs within didn't reach to me. The guard stared at me.

I hoped he was memorizing my face as someone with unquestioned access to Catherine's room.

I strolled to the window at the end of the corridor. As I'd expected, the private wing commanded a view of the lake, but directly below the window an apartment building was being deconstructed so the hospital could add yet another building to its gargantuan operation. They were taking the building apart slowly, instead of blowing it to bits—I suppose a blast would shock the cardiac pavilion. Where the outer wall had come down, I could see dangling pipe and a bed that someone had left behind.

After ten minutes or so, Renee Bayard came out of the room with her son. With a pointed look at me, she told the guard no one was to be allowed into the room except the private nurse, the two doctors whose names the guard had and herself and Edwards. No volunteers carrying flowers, no private investigators and absolutely no officers of the law. If any of the above tried to force their way past, the guard was to beep Renee at once: Was that clear?

When he agreed that that was clear, she beckoned to me to join them and sailed down the hall. Edwards and I were about the same height, a good four inches taller than Renee, but we almost had to jog to keep up with her.

In the elevator going down Renee kept the conversation casual: the doctor felt strongly that they should discontinue the morphine pump by the end of the day today; she hoped Edwards agreed? Catherine would be in the hospital a few more days; they should bring her laptop over so she could chat with her friends; they needed to decide when they could let her friends visit.

At the bottom, Renee led us out the front, into a waiting car. She told the driver to take us home. "The Banks Street house, Yoshi. Miss Catherine is very weak, but she is conscious and alert; we're pleased with the progress she's making."

I felt a reluctant sympathy for Edwards, who hadn't been able to edge in anything since saying, "Yes, I didn't want her on the morphine a second day, anyway." It would have been hard to grow up with such a strong personality rolling over you. Perhaps that's why he'd sought refuge in the right-wing causes anathema to his parents.

A Boy's Best Friend

At the Banks Street apartment, Renee stopped to tell Elsbetta she wanted coffee in her study, then swept down the hall without looking to see if her son and I were following. Edwards stalked after his mother, not wanting to talk to me—sulking because Renee had reduced him to eight-year-old status. I stared curiously into the rooms we passed, especially at a long sitting room with a baby grand, and walls hung with paintings. The hall was lined with curio cases. Edwards tapped his foot ostentatiously when I stopped to inspect a Greek-looking pot. I asked how old it was, but he only told me to come along and took me into a room overlooking the back garden.

This seemed to be Renee's private space in the apartment, where she had both office equipment and home comforts—books, family photos, worn rugs and chairs suitable for lounging. There was also an alcove with chairs less suitable for lounging, and it was there that she directed her son and me to sit.

"Edwards and I want to know how you came to be involved with Catherine. No more stories, please, about an interview with the school paper." Renee Bayard had the impersonal force of a hurricane—you couldn't take offense—you either held your ground or got flattened.

I smiled. "That was Catherine's story. Although I was feeling pretty frustrated with her at the time, I admired her resourcefulness in thinking it up on the spot."

"That doesn't answer the question—what is your name? It didn't seem important to remember it before."

"V. I. Warshawski." I handed her one of my cards.

"Yes, I see. Now. Why were you here on— Wednesday afternoon, wasn't it? How did you come to follow Catherine home? And why did you then go to New Solway on Thursday to bother my staff?"

"Ma'am, I have a great deal of respect for your husband, and am acquiring a fair amount for you as I watch you in action—but you mustn't jump over facts to get to the conclusion you want."

Edwards's eyebrows shot up; he apparently wasn't used to seeing people stand up to his mother. Renee studied me. "And what fact do you think I'm 'jumping over'?"

"You assume, or want to believe, that I followed Catherine home last week."

Elsbetta entered with a trolley holding another ornate china service. When she'd served us and left, Renee continued as if there had been no interruption.

"I know Catherine didn't get your name from Darraugh Graham. How did you meet her?"

I told her about finding Marcus Whitby, about my investigation into his death, and why I wanted to talk to Catherine in the first place—it seemed pointless to cover up Catherine's presence at Larchmont on Sunday night. I even told Renee about being in the pond on Friday, but not that I'd heard her and Catherine talking. And I stuck to my story about finding the kitchen door open at Larchmont Hall: I didn't want competing versions of my activities floating around.

"I was startled when the sheriff's police suddenly arrived," I said. "And I did wonder if it was you who'd alerted them to the notion that there really was someone in the house."

Renee's hand didn't pause as she lifted her eggshell cup to her lips. She drank and set it down. "And what made you wonder that?"

"You knew Catherine was wandering around Larchmont in the dark; she wouldn't tell you why. She's an ardent spirit, but she's very young—perhaps you thought she might not recognize as dangerous someone she'd agreed to help. Perhaps you thought she had some outlaw holed up, someone she'd romanticized into a Robin Hood. I don't know how you would have imagined this person, but you knew she valued her oath to protect him more even than the very strong bond between you and her. You wanted him found and moved off the Larchmont property."

"So you *did* know she was wandering around there," Edwards said to his mother. "And you did nothing to stop her!"

"I only learned on Friday." For once, Renee was on the defensive. "I called Rick Salvi to tell him someone was hiding in the house; of course I didn't tell him it was someone Catherine was meeting."

"Even so," Edwards burst out, "you should have—"

"I thought I had Catherine well under my eye," Renee said. "I looked in on her at midnight, right before I phoned Rick, and she was—she seemed to be—sleeping. I thought I'd have the problem solved before she woke up in the morning. Instead, she apparently waited for me to check on her, then went out her window onto the veranda roof and slid down a column to the ground. When I heard shots coming from the woods, I went back to her room—and found her gone. I don't think anyone ever covered that ground to Larchmont faster than I did that night. Which was fortunate, since when I got there they were staring down at Catherine as if she were a movie they were watching. They hadn't even sent for an ambulance."

Edwards's eyes flashed. "I'm sure your organizational skills saved her life. It's a pity you didn't apply them to keeping her from risking it."

"She's your daughter, Eds, she'll do what she wants to do no matter how much I try to engineer a different outcome." Renee spoke with the kind of saintly resignation that makes the hearer long to belt the speaker.

Edwards took a breath and turned to me. "How deep is her involvement with the kid, with Sadawi?"

"I've only met your daughter a few times, but I think she was in love with the romance of the situation, not with the young man himself. What did your buddies in Washington learn about him? Is he a serious security threat?"

"We don't know anything about him, per se, but he's connected to a suspect group. The mosque that he frequents puts out some pretty fiery rhetoric, and he's been renting a room from one of their members, a guy who's sent money to the Brothers in Harmony Foundation."

"I take it these Brothers aren't in harmony with American interests?" I pursued.

"Oh, they're murky, like all these groups. We know they've sent an X-ray machine to the Chechen rebels; they've bought food for Egyptian families, but we believe other funds get funneled through honey sales into Al-Qaeda hands."

The Spadona Foundation has a direct pipeline to the current administration. As I'd hoped, taking for granted that Edwards had spoken to the attorney general got him to answer without realizing he was being pumped. The fact that anger with his mother had knocked him off balance helped.

"An X-ray machine hardly sounds very dangerous, Eds," Renee remarked. "You're surely not imagining it can be used to make nuclear weapons."

He shifted uncomfortably in his chair. "Mother, don't let your hostility to the attorney general and his methods blind you to the reality of how dangerous our enemies are."

"You're right," she said. "His methods make it hard to remember who is more dangerous: the people who are attacking our liberties overseas, or those who are suppressing them at home."

"The most dangerous people at home are the ones refusing to cooperate with the government's efforts to root out terror, either out of real loyalty to Al-Qaeda, or ignorance, or through misguided ideas about the legal rights of America's sworn enemies." Edwards set his coffee cup down so hard that the delicate handle snapped off.

"Just because you express your anger more violently than I do doesn't mean you're right—it doesn't even mean you're angrier than I am," his mother said. "Don't you see that Catherine was shot because people like Rick Salvi believe they've been given a green light to use any means at their disposal if they think they have a terrorist in view? It was your daughter they had in view. And they acted literally on the old saw, 'Shoot first, ask questions later.'"

Edwards's eyes were angry slits in his face. "They knew they had a terrorist who'd fled the house; they didn't know my daughter was there. It was a shocking mistake, but if you'd been looking after her properly, it wouldn't have happened."

He turned to me. "As for you, if you were in Larchmont Hall Friday night, you fled the scene. You could have had Sadawi with you."

"Tucked under my arm like Anne Boleyn's head," I agreed.

When he exclaimed "What the—" I said, "You know, that old Bert Lee song—'The sentries shout is Army going to win/They think that it's Red Grange instead of poor old Anne Boleyn.' What did you tell the police when they asked about Mr. Bayard's books?"

"Mr. Bayard's books?" Edwards repeated uncertainly, looking from me to his mother.

"Your father's childhood books. Maybe the police don't ask people like you the same questions they ask people like me. They wanted to know why his book about the boy attacked by the giant clam was in the attic next to an Arab-English dictionary. I told them I thought Mr. Calvin Bayard was coming over in the middle of the night to translate the story into Arabic. At the time, I didn't know there was an Arab-speaking kid in the house." As soon as the words were out of my mouth I regretted them: it was a ghastly mockery of a man with Alzheimer's, to joke that he was studying a foreign language.

Renee frowned at me, her heavy brows almost meeting across her nose. "I think we all know why the books were there. And I can see that you are agile at dancing away from questions you don't want to answer. Did you see Benjamin Sadawi? Or talk to him? Or help him escape?"

"No, ma'am." The lie got easier every time I told it. "And I am most eager to talk to him."

"Why is that?" she asked.

"Because he had a chair set up in the attic where he stood looking out into the back garden. He was lonely; he probably stood up there watching, hoping Catherine would appear. So I think he saw what happened the night that Marcus Whitby died in that pond."

Edwards smacked his chair arm impatiently. "The FBI are confident that Sadawi killed Whitby."

"I told you in the hospital that their theory overlooks a number of important facts. Some of which you know better than I."

Edwards fell silent at that nasty reminder of his housebreaking.

"If you don't believe in the police version of this journalist's death, do you have any information yourself about why he went to Larchmont Hall?" Renee asked me.

"I know he visited Olin Taverner, I guess ten days ago. I know Taverner showed him some secret papers which he claimed would make the Hollywood Ten look like Goldilocks and the Three Bears. But I don't know what was in the papers, and, now that Mr. Taverner is dead, we may never know— since someone broke in and stole them."

"And neither the magazine nor his family had any inkling of what took Whitney to New Solway?" Renee persisted.

"Whitby," I corrected her. "I'm assuming it had to do with the dancer Kylie Ballantine— Whitby was interested in her."

"Oh, yes, the dancer," Edwards said, a spiteful undertone to his voice. "One of Father's special projects, wasn't she, Mother?"

"As you say, Eds," Renee spoke quietly, but her brows contracted again.

"It was good that he was in a financial position to help her out."

"I've always been happy we could support her," his mother said with more energy. "Like so many black artists of the thirties and forties, she suffered terribly. And she was a gifted researcher as well as an artist."

"Yes, by the fifties the press was in good shape financially. Father could give her a legitimate advance on a book instead of a handout. And now Whitby wanted to write a book about her."

"He did?" I said. "How did you know that?"

He looked uncomfortable for a moment, then said, "I thought that was what you said. I must have jumped to a conclusion."

Renee changed the subject. "You said you had dredged the pond where this unfortunate Mr. Whitney died. Did you find anything that was helpful?"

"Whitby," I corrected again. "Odds and ends. A lot of broken china—I wondered if Geraldine Graham threw a piece in whenever she was upset with her mother. And I found an old wooden mask, the kind of piece Kylie Ballantine collected when she was in Gabon. Oddly enough, the mask had vanished when I went back to collect my findings."

Renee looked absently at her empty cup. "Perhaps the sheriff's men seized it as evidence, or maybe it got kicked into the pond when they were racing around. Why didn't you take it with you to begin with?"

I smiled. "I was freezing. I caught cold Sunday night getting Mr. Whitby's body out of that wretched water and I didn't want to get sick all over again. I went to a motel to change into something warm and dry and then got sidetracked with all the excitement over young Benjamin Sadawi. When I finally remembered to return to the pond, that mask was gone."

"Was that one of the ones Dad bought from Kylie Ballantine?" Edwards asked.

"More than likely," his mother said. "It was part of how he helped Kylie. He insisted that everyone in New Solway have one. It was the year we were married; I remember the party where he brought the masks out of his study and persuaded even the Fellittis and Olin to buy one."

"So was that when Ms. Graham acquired hers?" I asked.

Renee paused. "Probably. It was over forty years ago and I still couldn't tell most of those people apart. I remember Calvin's glee at forcing Olin to buy one. Of course I knew Olin, because I had done volunteer

work for Calvin's defense in Washington—
that was how we met."

Her mouth twisted in a sad smile. "Eager
young women like me coming down to
Washington on the train, typing speeches
and press releases for the people under investigation. Congress could draw on an
open-ended budget, but Calvin—"

"Only had his private fortune to pay his
bills," Edwards interrupted. "Or was it a
fortune at that time? Or was it private?
Perhaps he had qualms about that, so he
used his charm on eager college girls like
you, Mother."

Renee Bayard gave her son a bone-shat-
tering look but didn't respond. This was the
second time Edwards had implied that his
father's fortune was shaky, perhaps illusory,
and the second time that his mother had cut
his comments short, but neither of them
spoke. I didn't know how to push the matter further, so I returned to the mask in the
pond.

"Even if Ms. Graham only bought African
art to please Mr. Bayard, I can't picture her
throwing it into the pond to be rid of it.
Would her mother have done that?"

Renee swallowed a smile. "Laura Drummond didn't like African art, and she was never shy with her opinions: she thought she spoke for Jehovah on everything from marriage to, well, masks. But I can't imagine her throwing anything, even African art, into her pond: she valued decorum more than anything else. Perhaps Geraldine did it to show Calvin how much she disapproved of his bringing his child bride home to New Solway."

I remembered Geraldine Graham's comment, that she had felt sorry for Renee Bayard, until she saw how well Renee could take care of herself.

As if echoing that thought, Edwards pushed himself to his feet. "I'm sure whatever happened, she was no match for you, Mother. I'm going back to the hospital. That guard doesn't seem reliable to me. I don't know where you found him, but I'm going to get Spadona to set us up with a better service tomorrow. I want to be in the room in case he lets in cops from some jurisdiction. You and Calvin may have persuaded Trina to reject my values, but she's still my daughter, not yours. And I still love her."

"Darling, we disagree about far too many things, but we agree about cherishing Catherine. I'll come along later, but you should have time alone with her, and I want a last word with Ms.—I'm sorry, I'm usually better with names."

I followed Edwards out of the room. When Renee called out sharply that she had more to say to me, I said, "In a minute," over my shoulder.

"You and I need to talk before the day is over."

Edwards tried to brush me off me off, but I forced him to face me. He scowled, started to protest, then realized he'd better make the best of the situation. He agreed to meet me in my office at four.

38

Conversation Between Hardheads

When I returned to her room, Renee had moved to the deep leather armchair behind her desk. I helped myself to water from a pitcher on the trolley and looked at the prints on the wall. Most were cover art from notable books published by Bayard Publishing. A Tale of Two Countries held pride of place above Renee's desk, with an inscription "To the Boy Genius" from "the weary old man, Armand Pelletier." I guess it was supposed to be a joke—Pelletier was only a dozen years older than Calvin Bayard himself when Calvin took on the press's first nonreligious novel.

"I'd rather speak to your face than your back," Renee said.

I pulled up a chair to face her. "When we first met last Wednesday, I mentioned to you that I worked for the Bayard Foundation during law school because of my admiration for your husband's work. When did your son start holding such very different views?"

"It was one of those things," she said. "It started as an adolescent rebellion that hardened into adult intransigence."

I made a sour face. "You are at least as agile as I at dancing away from questions you don't want to answer."

"I'm not subtle—I'd quell you when you asked intrusive questions, not dance around you, if I didn't want your cooperation. You wouldn't have betrayed a confidence with Edwards in the room, since it's obvious that he supports the attorney general's efforts to round up every Arab in the country for questioning. But now that we're alone, you can tell me where this Arab boy is. I feel certain that you know."

I was startled. "You're wrong, Ms. Bayard: I don't know where Benjamin Sadawi is. If he is in league with a terrorist group, I hope the law soon catches up with him, but if he's just a scared runaway kid—I hope he finds another friend as good as your grand-daughter."

She looked at me through narrowed eyes. "I don't know how to persuade you to tell me. Because I don't believe you don't know."

"Why does it matter so much to you? I should think you'd be glad to have him out of Catherine's life."

She stopped for a moment to choose her words. "I am. And the surest way for her to continue to be infatuated with him, or the romance of his situation, as you put it, is for her to think of him as being on the run. If she could see him for what he is—an immigrant dishwasher caught up in events out of his control—she'd stop imagining herself as a romantic heroine in his novel."

"She's impulsive and passionate," I said, "but I think she's fundamentally level-headed. Still, as I told you, I'm eager to question him myself, so if I find him I will let you know. You should realize, by the way, that my phones may be monitored by various law enforcement agencies."

She didn't want to be satisfied with my response, but she couldn't think of a lever to pry the information out of me. If all this had happened twenty years ago, she'd probably have made Calvin hire me as a personal assistant just to get what she wanted, but she couldn't come up with any good lever or bribe this afternoon. She was a smart woman—she didn't keep pushing when she saw she had nothing to push with.

"If Darraugh Graham hadn't hated Larchmont so much, it wouldn't be standing empty," I said idly. "Catherine might have brought young Sadawi to you in that case. I gather that Darraugh hates Larchmont because he was the person who found his father's dead body. Did you ever know what drove Mr. Graham to take his life?"

Renee looked at me steadily. "It happened around the time that I married Calvin, and I had a great deal else on my mind. I do remember that Mr. Graham's death was considered a scandal in the community, although old Mrs. Drummond made sure it didn't get into the papers.

"It was that kind of event that made me determined not to live in New Solway: the women spent their lives in the most backbiting gossip, while the men did deals with each other, and had affairs with their neighbors. The women married their sons to their neighbors' daughters and so the backbiting continued between mothers- and daughters-in-law. I insisted that we buy this apartment in town. I involved myself in the press. We spent weekends out on Coverdale Lane, riding and doing country things, but I didn't keep track of our neighbors' personal lives."

It was my turn to look at her distrustfully: I was sure she knew more about the Grahams and the other Coverdale Lane residents than she pretended, but, like her, I didn't have a crowbar for prying out more information. I changed the subject again.

"Kylie Ballantine's papers are in the Vivian Harsh Collection at the Chicago Public Library. I went down to read them and there were several references in them to an unnamed committee—and to the committee's patron. Would that have been your husband?"

She looked at me in hauteur. "Calvin's support of art and artists is legendary. But I must say I'm surprised you have time to visit libraries. Are you planning to follow in this dead journalist's steps in writing a book about Ballantine?"

"No, ma'am. Just trying to figure out why he went out to New Solway."

"Yes, well, I can't see that that concerns me. My only interest in your activities is how they affect my granddaughter's well-being." She got up to press a buzzer on her desk phone. After a moment, Elsbetta appeared and was told to show me out.

"When you decide to tell me about the Sadawi boy, call my office and set up an appointment. I'll make sure my secretary knows to fit you in immediately." She was right: she didn't dance, she slam-dunked.

I walked the four miles from Banks Street to my office. I'd heard a great deal today, and I was hoping I could remember enough of the nuances to let me sort lies from truth. I wished I had someone to talk it all over with. My old assistant, Mary Louise, with her astringent approach to the business side of detection, would have given me good feedback.

Or Morrell, whose thoughtful response to my own passionate ideas—Morrell—I was getting so I couldn't express his name without feeling something in my center disintegrate. I had a moment of despair so overwhelming that I collapsed onto a bench, head on my knees. I flung out a hand, as if I could touch him.

Something cold landed in my out-stretched fingers: a passerby had given me a quarter. I looked around, but I was at a crowded intersection on North Avenue. Any of the people leaving Walgreens or heading into Starbucks could have felt sorry for a woman so decrepit she couldn't hold up her head.

I sighed and stood up. Back to your loom, Penelope.

I continued west on North Avenue, doggedly thinking about the Bayards. Neither Renee nor Edwards would have said as much to me on their own as they had together. Edwards's anger with his mother over Catherine, and his mother's anger about his right-wing views, had let me learn that there was something fishy about Bayard Publishing's finances—either today, or sometime in the past. Edwards had also implied that his father had slept around—he'd called Kylie Ballantine one of his "special projects."

And Geraldine Graham? I had reached the bridge over the Chicago River, where I came to a halt, staring at a crane moving scrap metal in a plant at the river's edge. Had she also been one of Calvin Bayard's special projects? A lover, supplanted by the new young wife from Vassar? If that was the case, it was funny that MacKenzie Graham killed himself after Calvin arrived back in New Solway with Renee, instead of while Geraldine and Calvin were still lovers.

All those New Solway lives, they were like the twisted ribbons of steel dangling from the crane's magnet. You could turn them and see them in different combinations. I could see a version in which Geraldine Graham threw a mask into the pool so she wouldn't remember the lover who made her buy it. Or because she had found out that she shared the lover with the mask's provider. I could see, less clearly, her formidable mother throwing the mask away: No primitive art allowed? No primitive passions allowed? Or Darraugh throwing it in because he resented anything to do with Calvin Bayard—if Calvin had been Geraldine's lover.

Calvin had also forced Olin Taverner to buy a mask. And Edwards Bayard had grown up to give Olin any revenge against his neighbor and nemesis the old lawyer might crave. But why should Taverner want revenge—surely it was Calvin Bayard who was the wronged party here. And what did that have to do with Marcus Whitby—aside from his interest in Kylie Ballantine?

The crane dropped its load. The sound didn't reach me over the traffic noise along the bridge, but the end of the show galvanized me back into motion. At the corner of Damen, a drunk was panhandling. I gave him the quarter I'd gotten on Wells Street. He wasn't grateful—these days a quarter is a pathetic handout.

Tessa's truck was in the parking lot. When I passed the door to her studio, I stopped for a moment to watch. She was working weekends to finish a commissioned piece for a Cincinnati park, highly polished chunks of chrome that made you want to touch and slide on them. Despite the cool day, she had the heat turned off and was working in a tank top and shorts under her protective apron, her beaded hair pulled back under a hard hat.

I've learned not to interrupt her when she's got her blowtorch going full blast, but when she saw me in the doorway she turned off the flame and came over to me, removing her hard hat and flipping her protective eye shield up over her head. "Are you still full of germs? How far away do I have to stand from you?"

"Keep burning your blowtorch under your nose; it'll kill any viruses."

She laughed and came over to the door. "How many people have you given your office keys to lately, Warshawski?"

"Just one—a young economics Ph.D. who's doing a little work for me."

"Some men were here yesterday and again this morning who didn't seem to have any trouble with your front door. What's going on?"

So much for trying to operate without the fear that leads detectives to unacceptable levels of nerviness. "They think I'm hiding an Arab terrorist."

"If you are, keep him buried until these guys lay off—they're a thoroughly mean-spirited bunch. If I didn't have to finish 'Children at Play' this week, I'd take a hike, too—they make me nervous. These are what—federal agents? You know, my mother's family was from Cameron, Mississippi. My grandparents had to run away in the middle of the night when the local sheriff led a group in burning down their house because it was in a spot where some local white muckety-muck wanted to build. I am not crazy about citizens having to stand helplessly by while the law takes over their homes."

"Me, neither, but I don't know what to do about it at this point. They keep waving that damned Patriot bill in my face."

"Bastards!" She took me to a glassed-in cubicle at the back of her studio. She sat at a drawing board and began sketching rapidly with charcoal. In a minute, she had drawn four faces, two each on two separate sheets of newsprint. They were the same two men, dressed in service overalls in the first picture, in suits in the second. One of them was the man who'd insisted on searching my apartment last night.

"The one guy is a federal marshal, so I suppose his sidekick is, too." I took the sketches from her.

"Try not to do anything to get these boys in blue so mad they burn down our space here: I've got two hundred thousand dollars' worth of equipment that I don't want to try to replace. Insurance company never paid my granddaddy one thin dime for his house, you know." She stomped back to her blow-torch.

I moved slowly across the hall and undid the locks to my office. Why did I bother, when the FBI or whoever could come in with sophisticated lock busters and help themselves to my space?

At least they hadn't trashed my office, not like the horrible time I'd had a year or so back when I'd gotten on the wrong side of a malevolent city cop.

I booted up and checked my messages. I wrote Morrell a long e-letter, telling him everything I'd been doing since Friday morning, even about getting a quarter when I was reaching out a hand for him. I wanted to be able to discuss Benjamin with someone, or rehash how we'd run away from Larchmont, leaving Catherine Bayard bleeding in the fields behind us, and I poured it all into the letter. But when I read it through, I deleted that part. If they were tapping my phone line, they could pick up my e-mail as readily as my conversations.

Oh, darling, I wish I knew where you were. Surely you wouldn't have gone off with some set of extremists and not left word with someone from your team. Surely you're not with Susan Horseley or some other fascinating jet-setting journalist?

In the end, I deleted the whole letter and turned to my own phone logs.

Dirty Laundry

Edwards Bayard came late to our meeting. I figured that was to show me he was really in charge, despite agreeing to meet on my home ground. While I waited, I made my call to Mr. Contreras to let him know I hadn't been arrested, at least not so far today.

I still had a stack of unanswered messages from yesterday. Most that I returned just got me voice mail, since it was Sunday afternoon, but I reached Geraldine Graham. She was feeling cranky for being neglected, said she couldn't hear me when I mumbled into the phone, then lectured me for shouting at her. What she really wanted was for me to come out to New Solway. When I told her I'd try to make it tomorrow afternoon, if my schedule permitted, she got rather huffy and ordered me to remember who was paying me.

"Not you or Darraugh, ma'am. If you want to put me on your payroll, I bill my time at two hundred dollars an hour." On those occasions that I found clients who could afford it.

She paused. "I'll expect you at five tomorrow, then."

"If I can make it. If I can't—I'll let you know."

I felt honor-bound to call Darraugh, just to let him know I was visiting his mother, despite his orders to the contrary. He was home and slightly less arctic than the last time we'd spoken—although, naturally, he didn't apologize for threatening to fire me.

"So Mother actually saw someone in the attic. Maybe she's a heroine in the war on terrorism. She probably enjoyed herself at the social hour after church this morning."

He wanted a report on what had actually happened at Larchmont. Like Bobby Mallory and Renee Bayard, he didn't believe I didn't know where Benjamin Sadawi was, but, even if I'd been sure of my phones,

Darraugh sure hadn't earned the right to my secrets lately.

When we finished talking, I looked at Tessa's charcoal sketches of the men who'd broken into my office so efficiently. I wondered if they'd come in to bug my place. Even though I knew if the FBI wanted to tap my phones they'd do it from a remote location, I unscrewed the handsets and went out to the junction box but didn't find anything.

And if they wanted to bug the office . . . I looked around in dismay. Even though Tessa rents two-thirds of our warehouse, I still have a lot of room. I had it divided into human-sized work areas to make it look friendlier—there's a meeting space for clients with couches and a glass-topped table—my own work area with a long table for laying out big exhibits or maps—Mary Lou's old desk. And then the computers and the light fixtures and the pictures on the walls. The walled-off back area for supplies, a small room with a cot for when I needed to crash.

I supposed I could have someone come in and sweep the room, but, in the meantime, should I even let clients talk to me here? Should I take Edwards Bayard some-place else if he was going to spill his guts?

To amuse myself while I waited, I made headers for Tessa's sketches of the two federal agents: *Warning—Housebreakers. Pretend to be U.S. Marshals. Armed, Dangerous, Call 911 at once if you see them in the area.* I made twenty photocopies and did a circuit of the block, taping them to lampposts and getting the local shops and coffee bars to put them in their windows.

Elton, a homeless man who sells *StreetWise* on my stretch of Milwaukee Avenue, peered over my shoulder as I taped up my last copy. "They break into your place, V.I.? I see them on the street, you bet I'll let you know right away." He probably would, too, if he was sober: he struggles with his drinking, but it's not an easy habit to combat at the best of times, let alone while you're on the streets.

"Kind of looks like one of them right now," he added, jerking his thumb across the street at my building.

I whirled around. It was Edwards Bayard. He did look like one of the Feds, with the thick, side-parted hair that's become a kind of uniform among men in the corpo-political world. But no federal agent could have afforded his clothes, or his BMW convertible.

Bayard was looking from me and Elton to his car, not sure he and his valuable machine belonged near us. I crossed the street and greeted him cheerily.

"I don't have much time," he said sternly as I tapped in the code for the front-door lock.

"No, I know: you're a busy man," I soothed him. "I, of course, have nothing else to do, so I don't mind when you're forty-five minutes late."

He flushed and murmured something about his daughter and the hospital. Nyaa, I thought: the first person to apologize loses.

Edwards turned down offers of refreshment and aggressively moved my desk chair into the area where I meet with clients.

I sat on the arm of the couch. "So tell me why you broke into Olin Taverner's apartment on Thursday and then pretended to your family you'd been in Washington until Catherine was shot."

"I wasn't—"

"No, no, you're a busy man, let's not add to your burdens by sifting through lies. We both know you were there; you weren't wearing gloves."

"Yes, I was," he started, and then bit his lip midsentence.

He'd never been interrogated—he'd fallen for the easiest trick in the book. "We'll take that as a 'Yes, I was there.' Catherine will find it thrilling when she learns you're a housebreaker—it'll make you seem younger, more daring in her eyes. Not to mention your mom, who thinks you're on the stodgy side."

His jaw dropped. "I—my daughter is too young to understand why I might have to do something unorthodox."

I smiled sweetly. "And your mother is too old. So what was in those files Taverner kept in his locked drawer?"

"You know so damned much, you tell me."

"Bayard, for a smart guy, you're not so bright. Rick Salvi may be in your family's pocket, but Chicago's Captain Mallory is starting to pay serious attention to New Solway. He can call on some of the working cops out in DuPage to do a real criminal investigation out there. So stop stalling, because the next time you do, I'm on the phone to the captain."

He smacked his thigh with a balled-up fist. "I'm Olin's executor; I had a right to be there."

"Then why break in through the patio? Why not go over to Julius Arnoff's office and present your credentials and get him to let you in?" When he didn't say anything, I said, "Is it because Arnoff is really the executor and your Spadona Foundation is one of the heirs? Is it because you didn't want anyone to know you weren't really in Washington on Thursday? Had you flown out on Sunday and killed Marcus Whitby, without realizing the important papers were in Taverner's desk?"

Bayard turned pale. "That's an outrageous accusation. I did not kill Marcus Whitby or any other person."

"Including Olin Taverner?"

"Especially not Olin. He—was an important figure in my life."

"More important than your father," I suggested.

His lip curled in a scornful smile. "Certainly more important than Calvin, who barely registered my existence."

I looked at him curiously. "Olin Taverner paid active attention to you when you were a child? He was the one who took you to ball games and taught you to ride your first pony?"

He turned his head away, discomfited. "No, but Calvin sure as hell didn't—he was too busy being a hero to the whole damned world. Olin lived in Washington when I was growing up. He had an active law practice there, and, anyway, after the hearings, Calvin and Renee took over New Solway; they made Olin uncomfortable in his own home. Can you believe that? Calvin and Renee bore him such a grudge that they persuaded people he'd known his whole life to cut him!"

"He tried to destroy your father's life," I said. "It's not too surprising your parents weren't his biggest well-wishers."

"Well, they had their own dirty laundry to hide. Or at least Calvin did, and Renee, of course, trotted around after him in her busy efficient way helping him bury it."

"So when did Taverner show you what their laundry was?"

He cast me a sidelong glance, as if trying to decide what story I'd be most likely to believe.

I spoke before he chose a version. "This afternoon at your mother's, you were implying that your father's financial dealings were shaky. Did Taverner tell you that?"

"Not exactly."

"So what exactly?"

"I found a letter in Calvin's desk," he blurted out. "From old Mrs. Drummond—Mrs. Graham's mother."

"She knew about your father's financial situation?" I was incredulous.

"Apparently, Calvin was stealing from the Drummonds, or maybe the Grahams. I can still recite that damned letter by heart:

Dear Calvin,

I am aware of the theft you are committing against my household. A streak of hypocrisy seems to grow deep within your family's character; your mother had a similar tendency to parade the halls draped in righteousness while her conduct behind the scenes didn't bear close scrutiny.
I shall, of course, expect restitution, and you may be sure that I will take appropriate measures should your actions continue.

"She signed it with her full name, Laura Taverner Drummond, which is how I learned she was related to Olin. No one ever told me anything about all those people—I kept stumbling on bits of information like that and feeling goddamned blindsided."

The resentment from twenty-five years earlier still burned: his cheeks were red now, and his voice shaking with anger.

"So then did you take the letter to Taverner?"

"I was only sixteen, I went to Renee and demanded she tell me what the letter was about. She laughed—laughed, mind you, as if it were a joke, not a character flaw. She said Calvin had been 'a bit unscrupulous' in borrowing from the neighbors, but that when she married him she put a stop to all that. But you know, word always seeps out in a small town, and people gossip endlessly. It's one thing I owe Renee—growing up chiefly in Chicago instead of that dead-alive fishbowl on Coverdale Lane. Weekends there were bad enough."

"Yes, indeed." In any small community, including the urban neighborhood of my own childhood, people gossip mercilessly about Mrs. This's daughter's pregnancy and how poor Mrs. That felt when her husband lost all the rent money at craps. I felt momentary compunction for Darraugh and for the angry man in front of me—both of them poor little rich boys in their way.

"I wonder why your father kept the letter? Anyone on your family's staff might have found it and blackmailed him."

"Calvin is—was—an incurable pack rat. His study out in New Solway is crammed with papers. I can't imagine the Lantners being bothered to look through all that crap."

"And why were you looking at it? A congenital weakness for poking through other people's desks?" I spoke with deliberate roughness, hoping to goad a further response.

Deepening anger turned Bayard's blue eyes black. "All that damned talk. We'd had a big house party—the fortieth anniversary of Calvin taking over Bayard Publishing, his pals from the left's glory days came, even old Armand Pelletier—he stayed with us for three days, until he got into a huge shouting match with Calvin and stormed out. There was one of those daylong parties—people came to ride and have breakfast and stayed on all day until we had dinner for eighty—Renee loved showing off, not her possessions, her genius for organizing.

"All the neighbors from Coverdale Lane showed up, except Olin, of course. Old Mrs. Drummond creaked over in her diamonds. She was ninety-eight and forced everybody to drop anything they were doing if she had any kind of whim. Even Renee danced when Mrs. Drummond banged her drum. Geraldine Graham came, too, although she and Renee didn't get along. And she didn't get along that great with Mrs. Drummond, with her mother, come to think of it. And I heard some of the women talking in those delicious breathless voices, 'Does he even suspect, do you think? After all, he looks just like his mother, so why would he?'"

His chin jutted out as if he dared me to mock him. "I do look like Renee, so if Calvin isn't my father, I can't tell by looking in the mirror. When I was little, I kept believing I'd grow up as tall as he was, and then I was sixteen and stuck at five foot eight. I look like Renee's father, like his younger twin, there's not a trace of Bayard in me!

"So while they were having the time of their lives at that party, I went through Calvin's desk—I knew his study was the one room that people didn't go to fuck in. Sacred ground, not like even my own bedroom where I found Armand with Peter Felitti's wife! I was hoping there'd be one word in Calvin's old diaries about me, one thought that he'd paid attention to my conception or my birth!"

Bayard was panting as though he'd been running hard. "When Trina was born, I made a conscious effort to write it up. It was a big moment in my life, I should think in any father's life, his first child's birth, seeing that perfect little creature you made happen. But not Calvin. And I never knew whether it was because he wasn't my father, or because he was so damned wound up in his own importance that I didn't count for crap. Everyone worshiped him—you yourself do. Well, I wanted a father, not a god who expected to be on that pedestal."

My stomach tightened at the accusation, but I kept my voice steady. "Did your mother have affairs? It doesn't seem in character, although I didn't know her when she was twenty."

"That's what I would have thought, too," he said savagely. "And of course it's what she said when I put it to her."

"So what did you tell Taverner when you met? Did you ask him who your father really was, or just about the letter from Ms. Drummond?"

He began picking at the rubber edge to one of my legal pads. "It—I decided to explore other viewpoints than Calvin and Renee's and served as an intern in Senator Tower's office. That was when I really met Olin, got to know him. He was astonished, of course, to see a Bayard in that office, but he and Tower were good friends. Olin was a different kind of person than Calvin, not as easygoing, not expecting people to fall down and worship him. I liked him, and we got to be friends."

"And there was the added benefit that knowing him made your parents see red— so to speak."

"As if that isn't what they always saw." He ripped a length of rubber from the pad. Now the pages would all fall off, but that was a small price for the information I was getting.

"So you came to tell him about the letter from Ms. Drummond. Did he know about it?"

"He said he was surprised old Mrs. Drummond cared, that her views on Negroes were as antiquated as she was—she hung on until 1984, you know, running Larchmont like it had been when she moved into it, except she installed electricity, talking about the coloreds knowing their place and hiring four Japanese gardeners to keep the pond and gardens in order. Mrs. Drummond was Olin's aunt, but even though he made fun of her she intimidated him, too."

"What did her views on blacks have to do with your father?" I tried staying on the main point, but I had trouble figuring out what it was.

"Calvin had been stealing from Augustus Llewellyn, apparently. Olin never spelled it out, he said he wasn't there to stir up old wounds, but as I'd seen his aunt's letter, I should know that Calvin had been—"

"But that doesn't make sense," I interjected. "Your father lent Llewellyn the money to start *T-Square*."

He stared at me. "Did Renee tell you that?"

"Yes. And they confirmed it over at Llewellyn enterprises."

"Calvin did something with Llewellyn's finances," Bayard insisted. "Olin told me, and he wasn't a liar."

"So what else did he tell you?" I demanded. "Why did he hint around about your father's financial deals but never spell them out?"

"Because he'd made a promise, and he kept his word."

"Be your age, Bayard. Have you ever even read any of the transcripts of the hearings Taverner masterminded? He reveled in unveiling people's secrets. He kept quiet because—"

"I know you share Calvin's views," he shouted me down. "You can't believe Taverner had a sense of honor, because the Communists you admire so much didn't believe in the concept."

"You've said about twenty actionable things in the last five minutes, Bayard." My own temper was rising. "But let's keep to the real questions here. Isn't it more likely Taverner kept his secrets to himself because he didn't want his own secrets coming out?"

"If you mean his homosexuality, he didn't hide that from me. It didn't affect my respect for him," he said stiffly.

"It doesn't matter now the way it did in the fifties," I agreed. "So what secret of his own did Taverner care so much about that he kept one of your father's for four decades?"

"You are completely wrong about Olin's character because you only believe what you read in the liberal media."

"This line about the liberal media is the same kind of garbage as 'lies of the capitalist press' that the old fellow travelers reiterated," I snapped, exasperated. "Both of them are slogans to keep you from thinking about what you don't want to know. But have it your way: Taverner pledged his life, his fortune and his sacred honor not to tell people your father had been stealing from Augustus Llewellyn. Now, tell me: How did you know Taverner had this secret file in his desk, the one you broke into his place to find?"

He scowled. "It was a desk that had belonged to one of the early Supreme Court justices, William Johnson, and it was Olin's most prized possession. He had it in his Washington home, not his office, and he moved it back to Chicago with him. A couple of times when I was visiting him and we were talking about—about Calvin and Renee, he tapped the desktop and said, 'It's all in there, my boy, and when I'm gone you can learn the whole sorry story.'"

"So when you learned he was dead, you wanted to get to the whole sorry story before the lawyers did," I suggested, "just in case Julius Arnoff thought the papers ought to go to your mother or even be suppressed, instead of including them with what he turned over to the heirs."

"It would be like Julius," he said bitterly. "Damned little busybody, trotting around like Calvin's lapdog, wagging his tail anytime the big man threw him a biscuit."

"And when you got there, and went to all that trouble busting open the patio door, what did you think when you saw the papers were already gone?"

"I figured the Mexican who looked after him stole them to see what he could get for them."

I thought of Domingo Rivas, with his quiet dignity in looking after his "gentlemen," and felt another spurt of anger. "So did you talk to Mr. Rivas?"

"I told him I'd pay him a thousand dollars for anything he removed from Olin's desk, but he claimed he knew nothing about those papers."

"He has his own code of honor, and I doubt it includes stealing from his patients. You know, of course, that if he'd wanted to take something of Taverner's, he would have known where the keys were—he wouldn't have had to follow your sterling example and break any locks."

He flushed. "Who else could have them— unless that black reporter filched them. Because I sure as hell don't have them."

"Oh, it could be a black reporter or a Mexican orderly, but not a rich white guy?" I was thoroughly angry by now. "That's the question, isn't it: If you don't have them, and Marcus Whitby didn't take them, where are Olin Taverner's secret documents?"

Tangle, Tangle, Lives Entangled

The reporter must have taken them," Edwards insisted. "Not because he was black, because he was a reporter. Just because I'm against affirmative action doesn't mean I'm a racist, in fact, it's quite the opposite. Affirmative—"

"Yes, I've read all those position papers," I interrupted. "I understand how insulting it is for African-Americans if whites give up any privileges. Marcus Whitby didn't take Taverner's papers. When Whitby left, Taverner locked the documents back in his drawer: Mr. Rivas saw him do so."

"He could have come back for them later. Olin called me on Friday—he wanted me to know he was going to make his story public now, while he was still alive. I asked—begged him over the phone—to tell me what was in those papers, but he wouldn't, not on the phone. He was obsessed about phone taps, about the liberal media listening in on his conversations. So I said I'd fly out. I was going to Camp David with the president for the weekend, but I told him I'd fly out first thing Tuesday. But Tuesday Olin was dead."

"Camp David with the president. A rarefied life, augmented by a little housebreaking. But of course, there's a precedent for that, isn't there—didn't the Watergate burglars pal around at Camp David on the odd weekend? Maybe you got away early on Monday, though, and took an evening flight into O'Hare."

He narrowed his eyes at me. "Why do you say that?"

"Taverner had an unexpected visitor Monday night. It wouldn't have been you, would it, trying to argue him out of going public, or knocking him off prematurely so you could collect his—"

He got to his feet. "I've had as much as I can stand of your innuendos. I wasn't in Chicago on Monday, and it's your word against mine that I was here on Thursday."

"And the FBI's," I said lightly. "I think your pals in the Justice Department are listening in on my conversations. At least, they sent in a couple of agents who knew how to by-pass my alarm system and my locks. I don't know whether they installed voice-activated bugs, but they might have—you should ask them if they have a recording of our conversation today."

He turned white, then red. "You taped this conversation without telling me?"

"No, Bayard. Do listen to what people are really saying to you. I'm letting you know that the attorney general whose methods you applaud *may* be taping my conversations. On account of they think I know where Benjamin Sadawi is. Or because Marcus Whitby knew what was in Olin Taverner's files and they're hoping I'll find out. Or because they care passionately about what the average citizen is thinking and doing. Take your pick."

His eyes darted around the room, assessing where a bug could be placed. Like me, he seemed to find the possibilities both endless and daunting.

"And you're one of the people my mother has let into my daughter's life. By God,

Catherine is going back to Washington with me."

"That should be an interesting conversation," I said dryly. "Out of curiosity, why did you leave Catherine with her grandmother in the first place?"

"It was easier," he snapped. "When my wife died, I let Renee take over Catherine's care. I was too shattered to look after a toddler and then I was traveling a great deal. I thought—I assumed that Catherine would see through Renee and Calvin's political hypocrisy just as I had, and meanwhile she got the advantages of New Solway and that stable environment. But I should have known, easier is never better. And, by God, now I'll do it the hard way."

He stood so roughly that my desk chair rolled backward and cracked into the coffee table. "And the first change I'm making is that I forbid you to talk to my daughter again. I will not have you continuing to involve her with terrorists."

"I didn't involve her with terrorists—I met her the same way I met you—by interrupting her housebreaking. If I had a kid, I wouldn't let you hang out with her—I wouldn't want her thinking that it's okay to break the law if you're rich and powerful."

He glared at me, his square angry face looking very like Renee.

"You probably want to get back to the hospital." I got up. "When I visit Catherine, I won't mention our chat. I don't pledge my honor, because we both know I'm a liberal and don't have any, but I do care about disillusioning children's belief in their parents. For whatever reason, your daughter seems fond of you."

"I told you to stay away from my daughter, and I mean it." He stalked from office.

I followed him down the hall to the front door. "You might notice the strong resemblance between Catherine and the portrait of Calvin's mother that hangs over your big staircase in New Solway. Have you ever considered DNA testing? That could clear up your worries about your paternity."

He didn't thank me for my helpful advice, but walked around his BMW, looking for any damage. Elton crossed the street to offer him *StreetWise,* but Bayard ignored him and drove off with a great thrust of his afterburners.

I went back into my office. My anger had subsided, but Edwards Bayard's turbulent emotions hung heavy in the room.

I wished I did have a tape recording of the conversation. I tried to reconstruct it, especially the letter Laura Taverner Drummond had written Calvin. "Theft against her household," that could mean anything, from sexual to financial plundering.

I should have mastered my own temper better: I didn't get as much out of the interview as I would have if I'd kept my cool. Edwards interpreted the letter as proof that Calvin had been stealing from the Grahams, or at least from the Drummond-Graham household. And then Olin Taverner said he was surprised that Laura Drummond cared about Negroes. Had Calvin stolen from some black servant in the Drummond family?

Augustus Llewellyn was the only African-American whose name had cropped up in connection with Bayard's. Just in case . . . I logged on to Nexis and looked up Llewellyn.

Like Bayard Publishing, Llewellyn was a closely held corporation, so I couldn't find much on their finances. Besides *T-Square,* they published four other magazines, including one for teens, two for women and a general news magazine. Llewellyn also owned the license for an AM radio station that featured jazz and gospel, an FM station that played rap and hip-hop and a couple of cable channels. I couldn't see how they were financed or what their debt load was.

Personal data were easier to gather. Augustus Llewellyn was in his seventies, lived in a big home, some six thousand square feet, in Lake Forest. He had one get-away place in Jamaica, and an apartment in Paris on rue Georges V. He was married, had three children and seven grandchildren. His daughter Janice managed the two women's magazines, while a grandson worked at the AM radio station. Llewellyn himself still came to work every day. He was a big Republican Party donor, despite hav-ing been treated as a chauffeur by GOP op-eratives when he drove his Mercedes sedan to a recent fund-raiser at the opera house. He was a passionate sailor. A photograph showed a slender dapper man in tennis whites, carrying himself erect with no sign of aging except his grizzled hair.

From an old interview with him in *T-Square,* I learned that Llewellyn had gone to Northwestern University in the forties, where he'd majored in journalism. When he found it impossible to get the kind of job his white fellow graduates were finding, he'd started *T-Square* in his basement while he worked days as a mail clerk at the old *Daily News.* In the early days, he and his wife, June, carried magazines to stores on the black South Side, ran and repaired a hand-press and wrote all the copy for each issue.

In 1947, he was able to pay a photographer and a part-time staffer. In 1949, he found financing to set up a real publishing operation. By 1953, he was making enough money to start *Mero* for women and to buy his FM and AM licenses. The radio stations began to make real money; he started his other publications in the early sixties, about the time he built his cube on west Erie Street.

I whistled "If you miss me at the back of the bus" under my breath. The information was all interesting, but didn't tell me whether Llewellyn's family had ever worked for Laura Drummond in the dim past. I flipped back to the business reports and read them in more detail. And there, buried in the fine print on the third screen, was a fascinating little factoid. Registered agent for the Llewellyn Group: Lebold, Arnoff, attorneys with addresses in Oak Brook and on LaSalle Street.

"'Come on over to the front of the bus, I'll be riding right there,' yes, indeedy," I said aloud. "Why are you using New Solway's tame lawyers as your registered agent, Mr. Llewellyn?"

I didn't think Julius Arnoff would tell me anything, but the young associate might. I called Larry Yosano, both his home phone and his mobile, but only got voice mail at both places. I left a message with my own cell phone number.

Of course, Geraldine Graham would know. She'd also know what her mother was referring to when she talked about theft against her household. I called Anodyne Park. Ms. Graham was resting, Lisa told me, and couldn't be disturbed.

"I really just wanted to know if Augustus Llewellyn's family worked at Larchmont Hall before he became rich and famous."

"Who are you working for?" she hissed. "Does Mr. Darraugh know you're with the newspapers, trying to dig up that old dirt? We never knew the Llewellyns. Mrs. Graham met him socially through Mr. Bayard. And if you try to say something else, the lawyer will deal with you, or Mr. Darraugh will take care of you himself."

I hung up, more bewildered than ever. Had Geraldine been Llewellyn's lover? But what did that have to do with her mother's letter to Calvin Bayard?

Geraldine had met Llewellyn socially through Calvin Bayard. Which is also how she had met Kylie Ballantine. Who'd been fired from the University of Chicago because Olin Taverner demanded it of the university's president. Olin was Geraldine's cousin as well as a neighbor, even though he spent most of his time in Washington in those days.

Amy Blount had given me her photocopy of Taverner's letter to the university, along with the picture of Kylie Ballantine dancing for the Committee for Social Thought and Justice benefit. I still had the copies in my briefcase.

I took them out and studied them. Dancers in Western tights and toe shoes, faces obscured by African shields or masks—who had known one of them was Kylie Ballantine? Or, for that matter, where she was dancing? The shot was of the stage, not of the audience. All you could tell was that it was an outdoor venue, because evergreen branches appeared behind the wings.

Who had taken the picture? Who had sent it to Taverner? I dropped it on my desktop. The more bits and pieces about New Solway that I gathered, the more confused I became. And what about Edwards Bayard's conviction that Calvin wasn't his father? The gossip he'd overheard as a child—did that have anything to do with this story, or was it just gossip?

Amy had included a few notes on the Committee for Social Thought and Justice. She said not much had been written about it because it wasn't as well known as other left-leaning groups of the forties and fifties, "not like the Civil Rights Congress, where Dashiell Hammett sat on the board, and Decca Mitford and Bob Truehoft did ground-breaking legal and social work for African-Americans out in Oakland." She'd found one article in the *Journal of Labor History,* part of the oral history of black labor organizers of the forties, which included reminiscences about the beginnings of the group.

The article dealt mostly with the role that black members of the hotel workers union played in the struggle against the Mob and the hotel industry. One of the men inter-viewed had been a Communist who hung out at a West Side bar called Flora's, where left-leaning workers and intellectuals, both black and white, congregated.

Apparently, when Armand Pelletier returned from Spain, he started bringing some of his writer and painter friends to Flora's, where they had informal meetings, gave impromptu concerts and also helped the labor leaders write and print leaflets. Artists and writers from the Federal Negro Theater Project often showed up; ". . . the man in the interview definitely remembers Kylie Ballantine coming there," Amy had written. "Not very many other writers or artists were mentioned by name, except Pelletier, because he was the important organizer of the artists; the interview was focusing on black labor leaders."

One day Pelletier joked that the Dies Committee in Congress would shut down Flora's if they knew that the Federal Theater Project was still active there. "We'll call ourselves a committee, too, just like Dies does, one that keeps American values alive. But we're not here to investigate people's toilets and peer in their bedrooms; we'll have a committee for working people who believe in the real values of America." Someone came up with the cumbersome title,

Committee for Social Thought and Justice, which the members themselves shortened to "Com-Thought."

Com-Thought never had an active organization or board, but they did raise money to help fund some of the experimental arts programs Congress had cut out of the New Deal. And since many of the people at Flora's were Communists, and were arrested, Com-Thought began providing legal defense money for them in the late forties and early fifties. Pelletier himself served six months in prison, both for giving to the fund himself and for refusing to name any other donors.

I thought again of Geraldine and the pet charity of Calvin's she'd given money to. Her mother definitely would have hated any organization that she thought was a Communist front.

I looked at the clock. When I'd talked to Lotty yesterday, she had invited me to dinner with her tonight. It was five-thirty now— if the traffic gods were kind, I could make it out to Anodyne Park and back in two hours. I called to say I might be a bit late; she adjured me not to make it too late, since she had an early date in the OR, but if I could get to her by eight she'd still like to see me.

Charity Begins at Home

You're a determined young woman, aren't you, Ms. Warshawski?" Geraldine Graham was sitting in the chair under her mother's portrait, the remains of her supper on a tray on the piecrust table.

"It gets me places brains and brawn won't take me," I agreed.

When I'd reached Anodyne Park at six-thirty, Lisa had told the guard not to admit me. I didn't waste time on argument, but drove back around to Coverdale Lane. It was dark now, but I quickly found the entrance to the culvert under the road. I shone my flashlight around—it didn't look to me as though Bobby had organized an exploration of the area yet.

I was still in jeans and running shoes; hunched over, my back aching from the need to stoop, I stomped through Benji's and my footprints, trying not to obliterate the wheel tracks from the golf cart. When I got to the juniper bush on the Anodyne Park side, I stretched myself thankfully. I tried to clean the muck from my shoes, but when I got inside Geraldine's building, I took them off: no point adding mud to my other iniquities in Lisa's eyes.

Getting inside Geraldine's building didn't require any special skill, just the time-honored method of pressing apartment bells until someone buzzed me in. An old person in Chicago would have been more cautious, but they were a trusting bunch in Anodyne Park, at least trusting in their guard at the gate.

At Geraldine Graham's own front door, Lisa answered my insistent ring. She was so startled she didn't react at all for a second. By the time she decided to slam the door in my face, I had given her a genial "good evening," dropped my shoes outside the door, and moved past her into the hallway. I could hear Ms. Graham calling from the living room, demanding to know who was at the door.

I went in to greet her, and had the satisfaction of hearing her admonish Lisa for trying to keep me out: I was there at Geraldine's request, to tell her what had happened at Larchmont on Friday night. When I'd run through enough of the highlights—including my interrogation by the FBI—to satisfy her, I finally turned to my own agenda.

"I know we had an appointment for tomorrow afternoon," I said, "but I had Edwards Bayard with me this afternoon and he told me an odd tale."

"Edwards? I suppose he came out here because of the girl."

"Among other things. Do you know, I actually found him in Olin Taverner's apartment Thursday night? He had broken in, trying to find some secret papers that Taverner had promised him."

"How extraordinary. And did he find the papers?" She did a good job, keeping a tone of light interest in her flutey voice, but her hands had clenched at her sides.

"No." I waited for her hands to relax before adding, "but he did tell me about a letter he found from your mother to Calvin Bayard."

"And I suppose you drove out here to tell me about it?" Her hands tightened again, but she still managed to keep her voice steady.

"Your mother wrote Calvin about depredations he was committing against her household, and a demand for restitution— or she would take action."

The light bouncing from her heavy glasses made it impossible for me to see Geraldine's eyes. "Mother thought she was a law unto herself. She defined theft according to her own canons."

"And?" I prompted, when she fell silent again.

"I wrote a check for Calvin to one of his pet charities. It was a group Mother disapproved of, because it provided assistance to indigent Negroes who needed legal assistance." She gave one of her involuntary glances at the full-length portrait behind her. "I was forty-five years old, but she still thought it within her rights to examine my bank statement when it arrived each month. I didn't realize she was doing it until she confronted me over this check; for once I held my ground with her. I should have realized she would next turn to Calvin."

"She had such strong anti-black prejudices?" I was bewildered.

Geraldine Graham gave a tight little smile. "She had such strong feelings against her will being thwarted that I imagine she lost sight of the original issue."

"She threatened Mr. Bayard with reprisals. What would those have been?"

"Mother owned shares in Bayard Publishing. She was always threatening to sell them to Olin, who was her nephew, or to will them to him, whenever Calvin published something she thought was risqué. It was a hollow threat—she disapproved of Olin's sexual proclivities far more than she did of Calvin's daring authors. How odd it seems that Calvin's authors were once considered daring, now that every sexual act is described in such detail that they all become merely boring. Not to mention how they appear in films. Men like Armand Pelletier, who were glamorized for their bold language, have become passé."

"Why was Lisa so determined I shouldn't talk to you about this?" I refused to be diverted. "She accused me of working for the newspapers, trying to dig up old dirt."

"That's right, madam." Lisa popped into the room from her self-appointed listening post. "I remember well what Mrs. Drummond went through when Mr. MacKenzie passed, the work to keep—"

"That will do, Lisa. Miss Victoria is trying to find out who killed the Negro writer in our pond. She has no prurient interest in my affairs and we have nothing to hide from her."

The last phrase was uttered like a warning, like a way of saying, our hand is so much quicker than her eye, that you can speak of everything, except the elephant in the drawing room which she can't see. Lisa muttered something that might have been an apology. She retreated to the edge of the carpet, but she didn't leave the room.

"No one seemed to think I might mourn MacKenzie when he died, but his death marked the end of many things for me," Geraldine added for me. "To my mother, his death was one more inconvenience he had caused her: odd, when you consider that my marriage to him was her idea. Hers and MacKenzie's father's. Mr. Blair Graham was one of my father's business associates, and everyone thought that marriage would settle both MacKenzie and me down, turning him from the temptations of New York City and me from those of Chicago when we started our own nursery. Children are supposed to be a woman's greatest joy, after all. How strange that Mother would tell me that so often when I brought her no joy at all. Except perhaps the joy of exercising her will over mine."

"Your mother didn't think Darraugh should mourn his father's death, either?" As always happened in talking to Geraldine, I had to struggle to keep on the subject, or to remember what the subject was. "Was that why Darraugh ran away from school when your husband died?"

Geraldine's hands began to pleat the stiff fabric of her skirt. "My mother was still alive when Darraugh's son was born. She took his naming the boy 'MacKenzie' as a personal insult, rather than a tribute to a well-loved parent. She thought Darraugh ought to name the boy Matthew for my father. Or even call him after her own father. Virgil Fabian Taverner—he was named during the Victorian fashion for all things Roman. Be that as it may, Mother rewrote her will a few days after MacKenzie's baptism. None of the boy's charms, and my grandson has always had most winning ways, could persuade Mother not to punish Darraugh through his son."

"I know young MacKenzie; he does have a lot of charm. What was the charity your mother took such exception to?"

She didn't understand what I was talking about at first. When I reminded her that she had written a check to one of Calvin Bayard's charities, she again stiffened, but said, "How strange that I can't remember. At the time it seemed of consuming importance—my action, Mother's intrusiveness. And yet, the memory has vanished like some long-since plucked fruit."

"It wasn't the Committee for Social Thought and Justice? Renee Bayard said that was one that your cousin Olin was particularly determined to prove a Communist front."

She shook her head again. "Young woman, you must be now the age I was then. Everything seems fresh and clear in your mind's eye, but if you live to my great age, you will find that the past becomes such a broad landscape that many memo-

ries, even precious ones, get hidden under
leaves and hillocks. You will have to excuse
me now. Conversation fatigues me as it
didn't formerly."

I got up to leave; Lisa smiled in triumph.

"You're very kind to have taken the time.
How did Mr. Bayard come to be involved
with Mr. Llewellyn to the extent of providing
the money he needed to start his own publishing firm?" I asked.

"I was never involved in the business life
of New Solway's businessmen. When I was
a young woman, we were supposed to be
decorative, not to have heads for great affairs."

I shook off Lisa's arm as she tried to steer
me to the door. "Did Mr. Llewellyn support
the same charity that you did?"

She shook her head. "I wouldn't know,
young woman. It's possible. But it was all a
long time ago, in another country."

Ms. Graham often dotted her speech with
what sounded like quotations that I didn't
recognize. I knew this one. As I put my
shoes on in the building's foyer, I could even
supply the missing second part of it: besides, the wench is dead.

I didn't think Geraldine had forgotten anything: the name of the charity, why her mother had objected so strongly or even how Calvin Bayard came to support Llewellyn. But for whatever reason, Geraldine thought the person she'd been in those days was dead. Her mother had triumphed—her mother's portrait hung over her head day after day to remind her.

How had she spent her days back then, while Mrs. Drummond ran Larchmont? Maybe she'd thrown herself into motherhood and amateur dramatics, or county politics. Marriage had been supposed to settle both her and MacKenzie Graham. I remembered again the articles describing her return from Europe in the early thirties, looking "interestingly thin." She'd slept around, gotten pregnant, gone to Switzerland for an abortion? And MacKenzie? What form had his New York City peccadilloes taken?

Even with thirteen bedrooms to wander through, how had Geraldine endured all those years with her mother and a husband with whom she had nothing in common? What had she been mourning, when she said she mourned MacKenzie's death?

Silence Is—?

Lotty couldn't give me as much comfort as I wanted. Over a bowl of lentil soup, I recounted the details of my last several days, trying to puzzle out the complicated relations of New Solway.

When I finished, she asked, "Where does that Egyptian boy fit in?"

"He doesn't. Except I think he could tell me how Whitby got into the pond." I described the layout of the Larchmont attic to her and my imagined picture of Benjamin Sadawi standing on a chair, watching for Catherine.

Lotty pushed her reading glasses up into her hair. "So you do know where he is, Victoria."

I flushed, but nodded.

"And is that why you're concealing his whereabouts? Because you want to get information out of him? If he's a terrorist, you should turn him over to the authorities."

"If I knew he was a terrorist, I'd turn him over in a heartbeat."

"And you're the best judge of whether he is?"

I got up from the couch and walked over to the window, where I could see the lake glistening when car lights hit it. "It's the trouble with these times, Lotty. We don't know who to trust. But an attorney general who thinks that calico cats are a sign of the devil doesn't inspire me with greater confidence than I have in my own judgment."

"Your judgment on this isn't backed up by any experience or expertise. You've never worked with Arab militants, so you don't know how or what to look for to say whether he is one or not. You certainly don't speak Arabic, so you can't even talk to him."

I turned to look at her. "Lotty, do you think every Arab in this country should be interned?"

"Of course not. You know I loathe stereotyping of any kind. But this morning's paper ran a story about the mosque this youth attends. The anti-Jewish rhetoric there runs high." She sighed and looked down at her hands. "It seems to run high these days in London and Paris as well. Nothing has changed since my childhood. All over Europe and the Middle East, instead of blaming terrorists for our current woes, people are blaming the Jews. Even some poet in New Jersey is chanting that tired old litany. So I'd like to make sure this particular Arab boy doesn't want to see me dead before I applaud you for hiding him."

I pulled savagely on the cord for her blinds. "I understand: it's what makes everything so difficult these days. What if I cut Benjamin loose and he kills someone like you—someone beloved, who's saving lives, not a party to his quarrel with the universe? What if I turn him over to the authorities and they send him to a prison, remote from anyone he knows, where he can be gang-raped by the adult male population? If he's not already a terrorist, that seems guaranteed to turn him into one."

She nodded, her face pinched with worry. "So what are you doing to resolve this dilemma?"

"I've left him with Father Lou. He's sorted out a lot of gangbangers in his day, maybe he can sort this kid out, too."

"I hope for everyone's sake you're right about this, Victoria. I'm worried about, oh, everything, but also your own safety. You could get badly hurt yourself, you know. Not even necessarily by this boy, but by some gun-happy policeman like the ones who shot the Bayard child. Is this Egyptian boy's health and safety really worth the risk to your own life?" Her mouth twisted in an ironic smile. "Why am I even asking that question? You're like your own dogs—once you have a bone in your teeth, you won't let it go."

We talked of easier matters for a time, but at ten she told me she was due in the OR at six, and that I should go home. And try to be careful. She smiled at me, but her eyes were sad.

Lotty's somber words haunted my sleep, filling it with dreams where I caused disasters in which she died and Morrell stood in the entrance to a cave, shaking his head at me before turning his back and disappearing from sight. A little after four-thirty, I picked myself out of bed. It was better to stumble gritty-eyed through the day than get another hour of such tormented sleep.

I drove over to St. Remigio's for early Mass, taking a roundabout route through the early morning streets until I was sure that no one was on my tail. I slipped into the Lady Chapel about halfway through the lessons, read in Spanish by a stocky woman who was the school nurse. A handful of neighborhood women were there, and a sleepy boy, a student at the school, was serving.

After the service, Father Lou beckoned me into his study. Benji was doing all right, a bit nervous about being in Christian hands, but he'd loved going to the gym yesterday afternoon and had started a workout on the equipment. And still had nothing to say about what, if anything, he'd seen from his attic window the night Marcus Whitby was killed.

"Don't know how well this is going to work. I put him in the fourth grade, he can read enough English for that, he'll improve fast if he stays. Told the kids he was African—the truth, and keeps them from thinking he's an enemy. But they're teasing him for being in the kiddie class, so his pride is hurt. Explained to him and them what real strength is: not beating someone in the ring, beating your own devils at their game. Only weak people take part in mobs. Never know how much of a lecture like that gets through to them."

I nodded. "The mosque he goes to, yesterday's papers said they carry literature on how Zionism is responsible for the World Trade Center, and Jews make Purim cakes out of Muslim children's blood. I hate to think I'm protecting someone who wants to kill my friends."

He grunted. "Best I can tell you is, I grew up in the Catholic Church hearing same kinds of stories. Jews killed Jesus, made matzo out of Christian babies' blood. Grew up, learned different, learned better, hope this kid can do the same. How's the girl?"

"Healing nicely. She'll come home from the hospital today. To a showdown between her father and her grandmother. The father has the legal rights, but my money is on Granny . . . Can I talk to Benji for a minute?"

Father Lou looked at his clock. "Should be in the kitchen. Seems able to look after himself. I think he's a good boy. Shy, but eager to respond to people."

I walked down the unlit hallways to the kitchen, where Benji was washing dishes in the old zinc sink. He looked up nervously at my entrance, but relaxed when he recognized me.

I put a piece of bread in the toaster. "I saw Catherine yesterday. She's doing well: she got hit in the upper arm but not badly, and they're sending her home from the hospital today."

"That is very well, that news. You telling her where I am?"

I nodded. "She'll be in touch when she knows it won't put you in any danger for her to visit you. Benji—what do you want to do in the long run, if we can sort out your problems? Do you want to stay in Chicago, or go back to Cairo?"

He started drying the plates he'd washed, carefully, as if they were Sèvres china instead of industrial pottery. "Sort out my problems? You are saying what? End my problems?"

"Yes. Solve them."

"For my family, is good I am here. I send money and my sisters and my littlest brother, they go to school, they study. For me, always hiding is no good. Is unhealthy, is—" He made an expressive gesture, comprehending humiliation and anger. "And also when I hiding I cannot working. Cannot work. I cannot work when I am hiding always. This Christian priest is what you saying, he is good man, and he is helping with learning English, but still I cannot work, I cannot go mosque, I cannot see my people."

"So I need to figure out how to let you stay here but keep you out of the FBI's clutches." I spread butter on the toast. "Benji, last Sunday a man died in the pond behind Larchmont Hall—the house where Catherine hid you, you know its name is 'Larchmont Hall,' right? I think someone put this man in the pond; I think someone killed this man. When you were watching for Catherine, what did you see?"

"Nothing. I seeing nothing." He dropped the plate he was holding. It landed with a bang on the tiles, breaking into large jagged chunks.

I knelt to gather up the pieces, but squatted on my haunches to look up at him. "Why are you afraid to tell me what you saw? I got you away from the police. You saw how much trouble I took to keep you safe. Why do you think I would hurt you now?"

"I seeing nothing. I poor, I not a—a professor, but I know what be happening. I seeing someone, you telling police, they saying, ah, Egyptian boy, he terrorist, he killer. I seeing someone, and they killing me next. No, I seeing no person." He flung the dish towel onto the kitchen table and fled into the interior of the rectory.

43

Stiffed at the Morgue

I left the church feeling tense and jumpy. My conversation with Benji had confirmed my assumption that he'd seen Marc's killer. And he'd managed to explain why he was afraid to report what he'd seen. I couldn't exactly blame him; the law had shot Catherine Bayard in their eagerness to kill him. Why should he trust that I could keep them from executing him if he came forward to testify?

If I could figure out a way to get the Justice Department off his back, maybe Benji would give me the information in exchange, but I didn't have clever ideas about much of anything right now.

My day didn't unfold in a way that made me any happier. Back in my apartment, I found a message from Bryant Vishnikov. He'd phoned only a few minutes after I left. Hoping that meant he had hot information, I dropped my coat and purse on the floor and returned his call at once. He interrupted an autopsy to talk to me.

"Why didn't you tell me the city wanted an autopsy on your stiff?"

"Hi, Bryant. Have a nice weekend? Mine was good, too, thanks, just the usual two hours under bright lights with three law enforcement agencies. I don't know if you've ever noticed, but, despite my winsome manners, the police aren't my biggest admirers. They don't share their hopes and wishes with me. When did they order the autopsy?"

"The paperwork came over from Bobby Mallory's office yesterday afternoon. When I called to explain I'd already done it, as a private job, Captain Mallory not surprisingly wanted to know who for. He said you were at the meeting Sunday where they agreed to send Whitby here for a second opinion. And he was not happy that you hadn't told him that you'd hired me on behalf of the Whitby family."

"I was at that meeting," I agreed. "As a suspect in hiding an Egyptian boy from the Feds, not as a participant in discussions about crime fighting. What did you find when you did the autopsy?"

"Damn you, Warshawski, don't blindside me like this and then think I'll tell you what I know."

"And damn you, Vishnikov, for calling me up to yell at me instead of talking it through with me," I said, thoroughly angry. "I hired you in good faith, I followed the protocol you outlined for getting the body to you through a private funeral parlor. What did you find?"

"For nothing I'll tell you what I told Mallory: there weren't any external blows or wounds. Whitby wasn't shot or knifed or bludgeoned before he went into the pond. He drowned."

"And his blood alcohol?"

"The tox screen will come in tonight or to-morrow. That you can get from Mallory. I won't charge you for my work, since the county ordered the same job, but you also don't get a free look at the screen."

He severed the connection. *Whick,* like slicing off the top of a corpse's head. I

looked at my hands with a sense of defla-
tion. I had expected so much more from
Vishnikov. I'd been so sure there'd be some
kind of injury . . . and then, the golf cart that
had gone through the culvert—or maybe
those wheel tracks hadn't belonged to
a golf cart. Sherlock Holmes would have
measured a cart, taken a plaster cast of the
wheels, checked them against the tracks in
the culvert. Maybe I'd made up a whole lot
of connections that didn't exist, wanting to
create a murder where there'd only been an
inexplicable accident.

My father used to lecture me about being
too impulsive. "Don't ride your emotions so
much, Pepper Pot. Take the time to think it
through first. You can save yourself a lot of
grief, and me as well."

He'd said that more than once, but I
vividly remembered his voice from a day
he'd been called to meet me in the principal's office. I'd tried to stage a sit-in to
protest a schoolmate's expulsion. I thought
they'd done it because Joey lived in a
shanty and stank; it turned out to be because Joey was setting fires in the lockers.
I wondered now if riding my emotions was
leading me to shelter another Joey, whether

Benjamin Sadawi would prove to be a fire starter as well. I didn't seem to have learned much in twenty-five years.

I took the dogs for a short run, then went to the safe in my bedroom closet for my Smith & Wesson. I drove out to the range and fired a hundred rounds, venting my frustration with myself more than anything else. I was off the target more than I was on it, which didn't improve my mood; I went to my office feeling that I'd better be able to use finesse to solve my problems.

I didn't remember any finesse when Bobby called me a little after ten. It was his turn to chew me out, for not letting him know that Vishnikov was already working on Whitby. "You heard that whole discussion about where the body was and who would do the second autopsy, and you didn't let out one peep that you already had Vish working on it."

"I'd been the subject of a hostile interrogation for over two hours. If I said anything to that crew, I'd have been there another two hours."

"But later, when you were alone with me?"

"Bobby, you were focusing on the Egyptian kid, and I was tired—I forgot. Have you found him yet?"

"I'm telling you, Vicki, this isn't a joke. If you know where Benjamin Sadawi is and you're sitting on him, like you sat on the autopsy, I am personally going to tie you up in pink ribbon and deliver you to the federal marshals."

"Use some other color, okay?" I forgot I was going to think things through before speaking. "You know I hate sex stereotyping."

He slammed the phone in my ear. I sat staring at nothing for a long time. The front door bell finally roused me from my stupor.

It was a messenger with a large envelope from Cheviot Labs, which included the salvageable material from Whitby's pocket organizer, separated and placed in protective plastic, as well as several pages summarizing the work done on them and the results. Excitement at the contents made me forget my frustrations for a moment.

Kathryn Chang's cover letter explained that she'd had to come in on a different project yesterday and had found my packet.

You said your need for analysis was urgent, so I took care of it. Most of the paper had been destroyed, first by being wet too long, and then by drying out. For future reference, if you ever need this kind of work done again, keep the paper damp until we can work on it. As far as I can tell, a small notepad suffered the most damage.

Two documents had been folded and placed in a side compartment; these were relatively intact and I was able to restore them. Of course it's very difficult to judge paper and ink after they've been soaked as long as these pieces had. One was handwritten on school exercise paper that dated to the nineteen-thirties; the other typed on a 20-pound cream stock, around forty or fifty years old. I've placed the originals in protective casings; you should be very careful about touching them. Attached are photographed copies and transcriptions (photography preserves the original document better than photocopying).

I laid out the photoed pages. One was a typed letter to Kylie Ballantine, the other her own spidery handwritten response. So Marc *had* found some documents. The letters so precious that he'd kept them in his breast pocket, over his heart. My own heart beat faster as I read the typed letter.

Dear Kylie,

Despite the turns of Dame Fortune's wheel, which dictate when we mortals shall enjoy fame and money and when we shall live by writing bilge for women's magazines under pseudonyms (my own, in case you haven't been reading *Woman's Day* lately, is Rosemary Burke) I have a few friends remaining at the august institution you no longer grace. One of them tells me that Olin Taverner somehow came by a photograph of you dancing at the lodge for Com-Thought back in 'forty-eight. He sent it to the university president with a demand that they dismiss you. I don't know who was at the resort with a camera, and who would have supplied that prize Fascist with a picture, but you might ask Taverner.

What are you living on these days? Calvin is giving me fifty cents for *Bleak*

Land and being hoity-toity about it in the bargain—but at least it appears under my own name, not Rosemary Burke (and does she ever at the tripe she produces!), probably next April.

Ever yours, especially when I remember that night under the stars,

Armand

That didn't tell me anything I didn't already know from the material Amy had found in the university's archives. I pulled out my magnifying glass to help me read Kylie's response.

Dear Armand,

I am tired of the whole wretched business. I did write to Olin Taverner, and received back a reply expressing hauteur to the nth degree, as one would expect from someone who knows he is the sole right-thinking person on the planet—Walker Bushnell is only protecting the rest of America from the likes of you and me, and instead of inveighing against Rep. Bushnell and the rest of his feebleminded ilk I should talk to

"those of my own blood" to find out how
Taverner got the photograph, etc., etc. If
you want to pursue this with Calvin or try
to find a public forum for grievance, I won't
attempt to dissuade you—but I leave on
the 18th for Africa, where I shall celebrate
and renew myself as my mother celebrates
and renews herself. Let America chew on
itself, I no longer care. I can taste and
feel freedom's canopy over me already.

Her signature flowed from the *K,* indeci-
pherable as when I'd seen it at the Harsh
Collection.

I turned the two documents over and over
in my hands, as if somehow that would make
their meaning clearer. When Marcus Whitby
found these letters, he'd taken them to
Taverner. Surely even Sherlock Holmes
would assume that much. Or maybe not. But
something had taken Whitby to Taverner,
and what else could it be but these letters,
Whitby wanting to know about the photo
Taverner had sent to the University of
Chicago president all those years ago.

I wished Whitby's notepad had survived
the immersion, or that I'd known enough to
keep it wet until I got it to Cheviot Labs.

Marc had taken notes during his meeting with Taverner, that's what Taverner's attendant had said; the mess of gray pilling which Kathryn Chang had sealed into a protective wrapper was all that remained of those notes. Kathryn been able to pull some of it apart into fragments of pages, but only a few individual words survived: *inform, disgrace, and, tired, now, the, dead, sixty.* I doubt if even the Enigma machine could have put those into a meaningful sentence.

I glanced back at Kathryn Chang's letter to me. I hadn't read the last paragraph, in which she explained that Whitby's PalmPilot had also been in his pocket organizer. She could send it to the electronics division to see if they could recover the data, "but this is likely to be quite expensive, so I don't want to proceed unless you authorize the work."

Since her bill for doing the paper restoration was eighteen hundred dollars, I was afraid to find out what her idea of "quite expensive" might be. I entered the eighteen hundred into the expense sheet for the Whitby inquiry. The debit side was building nicely and I wasn't sure how much of it I could expect Harriet to pay—she hadn't authorized overtime costs at Cheviot Labs, for instance. I looked wistfully at my open file for Darraugh, but I couldn't push that expense over to him. I called Kathryn Chang and told her to wait on the PalmPilot.

The material she'd salvaged contained a lot of information, but I felt I needed some kind of key or clue to make sense of it. I hadn't learned enough from Ballantine's papers in the Harsh Collection, but maybe Pelletier's would be more revealing—if they were available.

I phoned Amy Blount and described the documents that Kathryn Chang had rescued. "Pelletier was more closely involved with Ballantine than I realized; maybe there's more information in his own papers. Do you know whether they're available to the public some place?"

The idea that Marc had found hidden documents brought real excitement to Amy's voice. She couldn't wait to see these letters; she'd locate Pelletier's papers at once.

While I waited for her to call back, I kept rereading the letters. Taverner had told Ballantine to talk to those of "her own blood." I winced at the phrase, with all its implications about race and heredity, but I also wondered who he had meant. It could have been Augustus Llewellyn, who certainly was involved in this drama. On the other hand, someone I didn't know about might have ratted out Ballantine. She'd been involved in the Federal Negro Theater Project, she'd known every important black writer and artist of the mid–twentieth century—Taverner could have been referring to Shirley Graham or Richard Wright or a host of other people. It seemed ludicrous to imagine one of them denouncing her to HUAC, but I couldn't imagine Augustus Llewellyn doing so either.

I stared at the photographed sheets until the words danced red in front of my eyes. I finally put them down to do work for a paying client, a tedious bit of tracking that I'd been putting off for a week. While I was deep in the background of an old insurance transaction, Larry Yosano, the legal dogsbody, called. I'd forgotten phoning him yesterday and had to look at my notes before I could remember why.

"Larry. You're on sensible hours this week?"

"Yep. That means I turn my phones off at ten P.M., so don't imagine you can call me if you're locked in or out of Larchmont Hall.

The junior who's covering this week is an aggressive young woman who is more likely to side with Sheriff Salvi than with you, so watch your step."

I laughed. "Larry, your firm is the registered agent for Llewellyn Publishing. How did that come about?"

To my relief he didn't interrogate me on why I wanted to know, just put me on hold while he looked at the back files. "Calvin Bayard secured Llewellyn's original loans back in the early fifties. He referred Mr. Llewellyn to us and we've been working for him ever since."

"Was there ever a time when Bayard's own finances were rocky? I met Edwards Bayard yesterday, and he was hinting that Bayard Publishing was on shaky ground during that same time."

"Mr. Edwards is bitter because of what Mr. Arnoff told you on Friday, that Mrs. Renee passed over him in distributing her shares."

"Who inherits them, then?"

He thought a minute. "I guess there's no real harm in your knowing. They go to Catherine Bayard, in trust until she's twenty-five."

Prodded further, he told me Darraugh was the trustee, jointly with the Lebold, Arnoff firm. And that the Drummonds, the Taverners and MacKenzie Graham's father, Blair, had all been among the original shareholders of Bayard. The Bayard family held a thirty-one percent stake, the Drummonds, Taverners and Grahams a thirty-five percent total, with the remainder divided among twenty-some smaller shareholders.

"So Geraldine Graham has a controlling interest in the firm now? She inherited from her mother, her father and her husband, right?"

Yosano hesitated again, but finally said, "Actually, she only holds her husband's five percent stake. Laura Drummond was angry both with Ms. Geraldine Graham and with Mr. Darraugh Graham when she made her will; she passed her shares on to Ms. Graham's daugher, Ms. van der Cleef, who lives in New York State."

"Laura Drummond really was a nasty woman, wasn't she! So was it financial need that made Ms. Graham sell Larchmont?"

"No, oh no, she had a large fortune, partly from her husband's estate, but her father also settled substantial monies on her when she married. No, I think—Mrs. Drummond could be very spiteful, especially where her daughter was concerned . . . Ms. Warshawski, I'd be grateful if you kept this information to yourself."

"Of course," I promised readily. I'd keep it to myself unless it had something to do with Marcus Whitby's death, that is.

Amy's return call came soon after I'd hung up. "Pelletier's papers are right here beside me in the University of Chicago library. Want me to go look at them?"

"I think I'll come down myself," I said. "It's a fishing trip and I don't know what I'm fishing for."

"From what I can tell on-line, it's a huge archive," she said. "Forty Hollinger boxes— what they call the special cartons made for documents, you know. I could help you sort through it if you're coming down now."

I looked at my calendar: nothing on it until four, when I had a meeting with a small corporation for which I ran background checks. I told Amy I'd be with her in twenty minutes.

Boy Wonder

Hey, Boy Wonder—

What meat doth Caesar feed on? Your child bride is an attractive little colt and your infatuation is understandable, but until she grows up and learns how to read don't fob my work off on her. If you don't like *Bleak Land,* say so yourself: getting a letter from the baby saying "it's not right for our list at this time" is such an outsized insult I'm even willing to believe— just barely, mind you, and only out of self-delusion—that you didn't know your infant had written to me. What I also will delude myself into believing is that you can't be as chickenshit as the rest of the industry,

afraid to touch me because the lesser
apes in Washington put me in the can for
six months and had my books yanked
from every embassy around the world. Me
and Dash. No undersecretary of protocol
in Canberra is going to have his morals
corrupted by the *Maltese Falcon,* or *A Tale
of Two Countries.* Dash, poor bastard, is
drinking himself into an early grave, but
I refuse to break so easily.

This was a carbon copy, and therefore
unsigned, but the smudgy type sizzled.

As Amy had said, the Pelletier archive
was enormous. She and I were facing each
other across a table in the University of
Chicago's rare books room, with boxes of
papers and books between us. When we'd
signed in, the librarian said Pelletier must
suddenly be a hot item—we were the
second people asking to see the papers in
the last month.

With the instincts of the born detective,
Amy said, yeah, her cousin Marcus always
had been a jump ahead of her, and the
archivist agreed that Marcus Whitby had
been looking at the boxes three weeks ago.
He'd only come once, the archivist said, so

whatever he wanted, he found on his first trip. We were lucky, she added, that Mike Goode, their premier processing archivist, had sorted and labeled the boxes.

Even so, we had a formidable hoard to inspect. The collection was probably a lit crit's dream come true, but made for a detective's nightmare. Pelletier had kept everything—bills, eviction notices, menus from memorable dinners. He thought highly enough of his historical importance that he'd made carbons of most of his own letters. Most were like this one to Calvin, long fulminations against someone or something. In the thirties and forties, the correspondence was energetic if caustic—astute observations on personalities or public events.

As time passed, though, Pelletier became more embittered and more embattled. He wrote angrily to the *New York Times* over the review they gave *Bleak Land,* to the University of Chicago for not keeping him on as a lecturer in the sixties, to his landlord for raising his rent, to the laundry for losing a shirt. Amy and I looked at each other in dismay: What had Marc found in this mass on his first pass through it?

The *Herald-Star* had given Pelletier a two-column obituary. I read it for biographical information. He'd been born in Lawndale on Chicago's West Side in 1899, gone to the University of Chicago for a year, volunteered to fight in France in 1917 and had come back to join the radical labor movements sweeping Chicago and the country.

Pelletier made no secret of having been a Communist during the thirties and forties. *A Tale of Two Countries* was based on his fifteen months in Spain during 1936 and '37, where he fought with the Abraham Lincoln Brigade during the Spanish civil war. Supposedly it was filled with thinly disguised references to historical figures, including scathing portraits of Picasso and Hemingway, and it revealed the arguments about the war that took place in a Communist Party cell, each member possibly a real person Pelletier had known in his own Chicago cell.

When called to testify in front of Representative Walker Bushnell and the House Un-American Activities Committee, the committee pressed Pelletier hard to identify the characters in the book, but he refused, claiming that it was a work of fiction, and spent six months in prison for contempt of Congress. Afterward, as a blacklisted writer, he found it difficult to get his work published and wrote romances under the pen name "Rosemary Burke." He died Thursday of pneumonia exacerbated by malnutrition at the age of seventy-eight.

Pelletier wrote one novel before *A Tale of Two Countries* and two in the decade after. All four were published to critical and commercial acclaim, although the reviewers all agreed *Two Countries* was his masterwork. After that, there'd been a gap of over ten years before he finished *Bleak Land,* which he apparently had shamed Calvin into buying, since Bayard published it in 1960.

We found a 1962 carbon of another letter to Calvin, saying it wasn't surprising Bayard had sold only eight hundred copies of *Bleak Land,* since they'd refused to spend a nickel on promotion.

Eight hundred people must have been stumbling around in the dark inner recesses of their local bookstores, trying to avoid hangovers or tax collectors, when they fell down and found themselves clutching a copy of *Bleak Land* on the way up. What did Olin do to you in that hearing room? Tell you he'd lay off if you'd forever foreswear the friends of your youth?

I rubbed my eyes. "This is more than a day's work. I almost wish Pelletier had ratted to Bushnell and Taverner—I'd love to know who his Communist cellmates were in the thirties."

"Does that have anything to do with Marc's murder?" Amy asked.

"I don't know," I said, petulant. "But scanning the reviews, I see *Two Countries* has an earnest young black photographer who's a homosexual male—maybe that was meant to be Llewellyn. There's a crowd of intellectuals, and worker wanna-bes from the university—kind of like the kids in SDS back in the sixties. It would be nice if he'd provided a key."

Amy grinned. "That's someone's doctoral dissertation, not the job of the great writer himself. I read *A Tale of Two Countries* for a lit class. It's beautifully written, and more substantial than *For Whom the Bell Tolls,* but *Bleak Land,* I think it didn't sell because it wasn't a good book. Maybe Pelletier was too angry when he wrote it, or maybe he was out of practice. Even before the blacklist, he'd stopped writing fiction and was doing a lot of work for Hollywood."

"Did *Bleak Land* deal with things as autobiographically as *Two Countries*? I mean, would I learn anything about Calvin and that group from reading it? Because Pelletier only got to be friends with Calvin after Bayard Publishing brought out *Two Countries* in such a big way."

"You mean was it another roman à clef? If *Bleak Land* is, I wouldn't have known when I read it, because I didn't know who any of the players were. I guess I could check it out of the library and try to see now if I recognize any of them."

The librarian looked at us warningly: other people were trying to read in the reading room. We continued in silence for a time, only stopping briefly to eat some odd-looking sandwiches out of a vending machine. While we ate, I told Amy that the police were starting their own investigation into Marc's death.

"The bad news is, they think he was killed by Benjamin Sadawi, the kid in the Larchmont attic, so they're not interested in following up on the ideas we've been generating. But at least they say they'll do some digging on how Marc got out to Larchmont. And they've ordered a full autopsy from Dr. Vishnikov. Vishnikov has ruled out any external blow or wound to Marc before he went into that pond, but he's mad at me— he thinks I blindsided him with the cops, so he says he won't give me the tox screen results when those come in. Can you get Harriet to request them as next of kin? I'd be glad to supply my lawyer to run interference for her."

Amy scribbled a note in her pocket diary and took Freeman Carter's information from me. "Harriet's moving into my place tonight. Her folks are flying back to Atlanta this afternoon—thank the goddess!"

We dusted the crumbs from our fingers and went back to the rare books room. At two, knowing I had to leave soon, I stopped reading letters in detail and began flipping through the contents of the remaining cartons. In the middle of a set of manuscripts, I found a manila folder labeled "Total

Eclipse: Unfinished, unpublished ms., 122 pp." It was typed on yellowing paper, with Pelletier's handwritten notes in the margins. The writing itself was shaky; this must have been written at the end of his life, when he was often drunk or ill or both.

They want us to think that when Lazarus rose from the dead, his friends and sisters were beside themselves with joy. But inside the grief when he was buried were the secret thoughts: thank God we got him safely underground, revolting drunkard, couldn't keep his hands to himself. Thank God he won't live to tell a soul about that night in Jericho when he caught me with my mother's maid behind the sheepfold. No more scurrying when we hear him coming in late from tavern or tussle, demanding hot food and wanting it now.

And then he rose again, and behind the joy saw his loved ones' thoughts writ large: we were just settling down with the new shape to our lives, minus his sharp words and demands, and here he is, raised from the dead.

I know. I was dead, and now that I've slunk out of the grave into a corner of the basement, trailing my winding sheets, I can smell the stink of fear rising from my dear ones. Although maybe it's just the stink of my own rotting flesh.

Gene, who is the most terrified, predictably wept loudest at my grave. The baby, the darling, he used to tag after me when he was five, let me play, Herman, show me how, Herman, following me from sandlot ball to taverns [crossed out; "bar" written in by hand] and then to girls. I should have known from the way he watched me, but that was when he was still my eager golden brother, the one I teased and gave a little careless attention to.

I was the hero back from the war, a hero in some places anyway, with my arm in an interesting sling and my eyes dazed from too much blood, so much blood that I couldn't drink it away. A hero to my golden brother, who'd spent my war years getting rich. I was fighting, he was taking over the family firm.

No George Bailey role for Gene, nossir. No, Gene had a truly wonderful life. Big brother risking his life on the Ebro, little brother minting the stuff in buckets, turning a sleepy family business into an international power. So that when I came back, although the girls clustered round to hear my battle stories, they slipped out the side door with Gene. He was renting the apartment on Elm Street in those days, just the place to take the girls, where Mother couldn't see, and then come home for church on Sunday, hair slicked back, bending solicitously over her, butter not melting in his mouth.

We hung out at Goldie's. It was just one of those west Loop bars. Guys heading home for work stopped for a quick one, listened to the racing results or a late ball game. We used to go after a meeting, Toffee Noble all excited about his basement magazine. He sometimes came with Lulu, who painted outsized canvases of African ritual dances. He also hung out with Edna Deerpath, the tiny black whirlwind who represented the hotel laundry workers in their bloody battles against the Mob.

Toffee never joined in anyone's battles, just smirked from the sidelines, Mr. Cool, then went home and wrote us all up in stories he cranked out on his basement press. We never knew whether he held one of those pasteboard squares, the pass to the inner circle, or not. Some said he was too chicken to join, others that he was too chicken to admit he traveled all the way.

We were all brothers then, or brothers and sisters, even Gene, my blood brother, although everyone knew he only came to meet girls. We used to tease him, you think you're the good capitalist? The one who won't be hanged from the lamppost just because you like Red nookie?

I was the grand old man, being five or six years older than everyone but Lulu, and the only one who'd ever been shot at for being Red—although Edna and Lulu had ducked their share of stones for being black. Goldie herself didn't care if you were black or white or red as long as your folding paper was green, and she set the tone; everyone at Goldie's took you as you were, so of course it was a place where rich girls came, because rich girls gravitate to poor men when they want a little kick on the side.

And one of those was Rhona. I'd met plenty of Rhonas before, or thought I had, rich girls with too much money and too little to do. When they've tried dope and skiing and race cars, then they dabble a little in politics, a little in Communism because it's daring and exciting. In the powder room at the Drake the next day, "Oh, darling, I went to this hovel on the West Side, can you believe people live in two rooms, there wasn't even a closet, I had to hang my Balenciaga on a nail, and a shared bathroom halfway down the hall, and they're all so earnest, comrade this and that, but Herman fixes me with those black eyes and I feel actually pinned to my chair, a wet puddle, I can't get up or everyone will know, and it's all so exciting because the government could raid us at any second. I brought him to Oakdale and Mother never guessed, she would have turned fifteen shades of red herself."

Oakdale. Larchmont Hall, Coverdale Lane. The name seemed deliberate. I looked at my watch and tried to read faster. Rhona, with her silk teddy and painted nails, became enthusiastic about Communism, but was terrified of being discovered by her family. She would type fliers in Herman's Kedvale Avenue apartment—wearing nothing but her rose teddy, to Herman's intense satisfaction, then put on overalls and a blond wig to march on picket lines or to leaflet commuters. She and Herman made love in the afternoons on his unwashed sheets.

The sheets were gray from too little soap. A girl like Rhona, she might type or run a mimeograph machine, but she stood baffled in front of the washing machine in the basement, teased by thirteen-year-old girls who'd been turning a mangle since they were five. I didn't get to the laundry more than once a month, so the sheets came to smell like Rhona, and like sex, a little Joy by Patou, a little joy by Herman.

"Cute," I muttered, showing the paragraph to Amy. "Couldn't he operate a mangle himself?"

"Don't get so exercised. It's only a novel, and anyway, the guy is dead. And for heaven's sake, don't mark on it!"

Shamefaced, I put my pencil down and turned back to Pelletier's words.

I loved leaving my own scent on her. She was too fastidious to wash in the communal bathroom, rich little Communist girl, and when I'd licked her nipples into red cherries against her whipped cream body,

I'd ask what Ken would think when she raced home to undress and bathe. "Won't he lean over you and wonder who or what he's smelling over the bath salts." At first she would laugh it away, but one day she explained the sad truth, that Ken was impotent, that he'd long since stopped leaning over her in the bath or bed or any other place.

It was Dryden who said that pity melts the mind to love, and maybe that's when I started to love her, when I started to pity her. Maybe if she'd whined about it the first time she unbuttoned her white silk blouse, "I only fuck strange men because my husband's impotent," I would have despised her, but it was four months before I learned the truth, and then she never mentioned it again.

And Gene, who never missed anything, saw the pity and the love, and began coming to the apartment, where he pantomimed dismay at the rat droppings in the hall and uncurtained cracked windows in the front room. But it didn't stop him hanging about after meetings. "I can run Rhona home and come back to finish discussing business with you, Herman. Do you need a buck for the laundry? Those sheets are going to get up and walk off that bed on their own pretty soon."

Disgust didn't keep him from lying in those sheets. It was the day after I'd found her there with him, the day I beat her (long red fingers on the whipped cream skin, red fingers from her red lover, red fingers turning to blue, blue blood of the master class, it would rule her in the end) the day she left and didn't come back, the day I started to die.

The next twenty pages dealt with his dying: "Every man imagines he's Jesus, or at least Trotsky, important enough for execution. That's what I thought for the first five years I lay in the ground. Finally, I realized self-pity and booze were what really did me in." He compared himself to Lulu: ". . . she was in the same boat as me, unloved, unwanted, but she didn't turn her face to the wall. Instead she turned her back on all of us, went to Africa, painted her giant canvases whether anyone bought them or not."

If Pelletier's works were all—what had been Amy's phrase? A something of clay— Lulu definitely stood in for Kylie Ballantine. Kylie continued her work, she went to

Gabon, she refused to be bowed down by Taverner's spite in getting her fired.

And Gene stood for Calvin, the Boy Wonder. And Rhona . . . and Ken. Mac-Kenzie Graham. He'd been impotent, so Geraldine turned elsewhere for love? Was that what she meant, when she said she and MacKenzie had so little in common?

I drew circles on my notepaper. Edwards Bayard had overheard talk as an adolescent about someone who looked just like his mother, and so didn't seem to realize who his father was. Adolescent self-absorption, a fantasy yearning for the perfect father, made Edwards assume the neighbors were gossiping about him. And then his hurt and bitterness with Calvin kept him clinging to this adolescent version of events. Funny to see someone with so much education, and with the power of his personal wealth and his position in the Spadona Foundation, unable to let go of his adolescent view of the world.

I listed all the Bayards in one of the circles I'd drawn. In another, I put Darraugh's family, starting with Laura Taverner Drummond, then Geraldine and MacKenzie, whose father connived with Laura to marry the two wild children. Their daughter Laura, named after the formidable grandmother. Darraugh, born in 1943. Darraugh's son, young MacKenzie.

I slowly added a line joining the Grahams to the Bayards. Darraugh looked exactly like his mother. Everyone said Geraldine Graham had been a wild young woman. In his current illness, Calvin Bayard wandered to Larchmont in the dark. He had kept a key to the house. He had clutched me, crying, "Deenie." Geral-deenie. She had spilled coffee all over herself when I reported it. Whatever Pelletier had thought about Calvin, the Boy Wonder, Calvin had loved Geraldine Graham.

I again imagined Darraugh as a boy—not galloping around the fields on his horse, but kneeling in bed in the middle of the night, head cupped in his hands, watching Calvin Bayard appear through the woods and let himself into Larchmont after the servants had locked the place up. He had stood up fiercely for MacKenzie Graham; he had weathered his grandmother's fury by naming his son MacKenzie. Whether Calvin Bayard, MacKenzie Graham, or, for that matter, Armand Pelletier had been his birth father, MacKenzie was the man Darraugh loved. No wonder he hated Larchmont Hall.

The Ice Cube Man Cometh

I skimmed the rest of the manuscript. Armand's sense of personal grievance ran too deep for him to record a little thing like "Rhona's" pregnancy, so he didn't leave any hint about whether he or Calvin might have been Darraugh's father. On the other hand, he heaped a lot of scorn on Toffee Noble— an offensive name for anyone, even someone totally imaginary. If Noble was supposed to be Augustus Llewellyn—and it sounded like him, with his basement printing press—Pelletier must have really hated him.

Llewellyn was a prominent Republican donor these days, but in the forties he'd hung out with Calvin and Pelletier and Kylie

Ballantine at the bar where local leftists and labor organizers congregated.

Marc had read this manuscript. What if he'd gone to see Llewellyn after all: "I'm troubled, sir, by a manuscript Armand Pelletier wrote. It suggests you were some kind of fellow traveler in the forties." Maybe Llewellyn wouldn't want his Republican pals, or his sailing friends, to know this. If he'd asked Marc to meet him after hours— "Come with me to New Solway, I'll show you what that setup, what those people were really like"—Marc would have gone with him readily. Llewellyn did know all those New Solway people, after all. He was the one black member of the Anodyne Park Golf Course. Julius Arnoff was his registered agent as well as Geraldine Graham's and Calvin Bayard's—in his casual gossip with his clients, Arnoff had probably told Llewellyn about the nou-nous abandoning Larchmont Hall; what a shame it's standing empty—the ornamental pool is filling up with dead carp . . .

"V.I.! Wake up—you've gone catatonic on me." Amy was shaking my arm. "Didn't you say you had an appointment at four? It's three-forty, and you've been blanked out for the last ten minutes."

I blinked at her, trying to feel some urgency about my appointment. "Twenty to four? Yes, I guess I need to get going."

I started to put the manuscript into my briefcase, but remembered it was the library's a second before Amy squawked at me. "Sorry. Look, they'll be closing the reading room in an hour. Do you think you could read this by then? Or get a copy made? If it's a thingamajig, a clay something—"

"Roman à clef," Amy interrupted, spelling it for me. "A novel with a key. I can read it and tell you what I think, and get a copy made, but it's still a novel, even if it's a novel with a key, and I don't think you can rely on it for evidence."

The librarian came over to ask if we would carry on our conversation outside; other patrons were complaining about our noise. Amy walked out with me.

"Not as evidence," I said. "But come on: the article on Com-Thought you found said it started at an integrated bar on the West Side called Flora's, where left-leaning intellectuals and labor organizers met. Pelletier's manuscript talks about a West Side bar called Goldie's where artists and labor organizers met. This manuscript casts light on all these people. Even if Armand is distorting what happened for the sake of his story, or because he saw himself as a victim at Calvin's hands, or even at Augustus Llewellyn's, the manuscript suggests that Llewellyn and Ballantine and Geraldine all hung out together with Pelletier and Calvin Bayard back before the McCarthy hearings. They all dabbled in Communism. Which might be the secret Taverner sat on for fifty years. Although it doesn't explain why Taverner kept quiet until the night Marc came to see him.

I kicked a stone in irritation. "Damn it all! I'd better run. Look, just read the thing, will you—I'll call you tonight."

"Yeah, I'll read the blessed book, and I'll make you a copy of it. Now go, unless these are clients you want to blow off." Amy gave me a push between my shoulder blades.

I sprinted past the dorms stuffed behind the library to Fifty-fifth Street, where I'd left my car. My clients were in the west Loop, on Wacker Drive, which the city had completely dismembered; by the time I found parking and ran back to their building, I was over twenty minutes late. Not good for my professional image. Worse, I had forgotten to put a pen in my bag and had to borrow one from the client. Worse still, I had trouble keeping my mind on their problem, which wasn't fair, since they pay their bills on time. As I was looking at my notes in the elevator down to the ground floor, I saw to my embarrassment that I'd written "Toffee Noble" on my legal pad three or four times, like a schoolgirl with a crush.

The reports I'd read on Llewellyn said he still came to work every day—unless he was in Jamaica or Paris. I looked at my watch. It was five-thirty, and the lobby was thick with departing office workers. But I was only a ten minute walk across the river from Llewellyn's building, and it was possible that he stayed late. I stuffed my notes into my bag and started north.

When I got to Erie Street, my optimism was rewarded: a navy Bentley with a license reading "T-SQUARE" was parked in front of the building. A uniformed chauffeur sat inside with the *Sun-Times* propped open on the steering wheel. That meant the great man was still in his office.

As I'd trotted up Franklin Street, I tried to figure out how to get past the hostile receptionist in the lobby. It was one thing to crawl through a culvert to get into Anodyne Park, but more difficult to get into an office building where they don't want to see you. I still hadn't come up with a good idea when I saw Jason Tompkin about half a block away on Erie. I broke into a run again. When I caught up with him at the light on Wells, I tapped him on the arm and called his name.

He turned, brows raised, then gave his cocky grin. "The lady detective. Well, well. Have you come to arrest me for killing Marc?"

"Did you kill him? That would be a help. I could stop trying to ask people questions that they don't want to answer."

"I think a gal like you would develop a pretty thick skin by now. No one wants to answer a dick's questions. Not even me." The grin was still in place, but it pushed me back as effectively as a stiff-arm.

"Yeah, well, even a rhinoceros starts showing wear and tear if it's hit by enough big sticks. I don't imagine you killed Marc Whitby, but maybe I've been barking up the wrong tree all week; maybe you got tired of his ambition and his standoffishness, got him drunk, and drove him to a pond to drown him."

He stopped smiling. "I didn't kill the brother. I just didn't join in the choir of the blessed shouting 'Hallelujah' every time someone said his name."

"If you do me a favor, I won't ask you any more questions, or even expect you to shout 'Hallelujah' over Marc's name. I want to see Mr. Llewellyn. Without having to sweet-talk my way past your receptionist—she's one of the people who's whacked at my rhino hide recently."

"Ah, yes, the dulcet Shantel. I can't get you in to Mr. Llewellyn. He knows all his staff, of course, because he owns us, and, anyway, it's not like we're Time, Inc. At the Christmas party or in the elevator, when our paths cross, he greets me by name: he says, 'How are you today, Mr. Thompson. That was a nice piece you did for the last issue, a very fine piece of writing indeed.' One year he called me Mr. Pumpkin."

I laughed. "I'll take my chances once I'm in the building. If he hasn't left for the day."

"And in return?"

"If you lose your dog, I'll find it for you, no charge."

"Dang. You must've known I have a cat." He turned around and led me back to the Llewellyn building.

The chauffeur was still reading the *Sun-Times,* a good sign since it meant he didn't expect to see the boss for a bit. Inside the lobby, the hostile receptionist was gone, replaced by a uniformed guard, who asked for my ID but didn't make any objection to J.T. taking me up in the elevator. After all, the place published magazines. Writers are always bringing in people to interview.

On the sixth floor, I got J.T. to let me use his computer to type up a note for Llewellyn. "Do you know that Marcus Whitby tried to see you before he died? He had read Armand Pelletier's unpublished memoirs about the group that used to get together at Flora's on the West Side. He went to see Olin Taverner after he read the memoir. The forties must have been heady days for you. Can we discuss them?"

J.T. kept shifting from foot to foot as we waited for my note to come out of the community printer. He quickly deleted my file from his machine, told me Llewellyn's office was on the eighth floor and fled down the hall while I was stapling a business card to my note. By the time I reached the elevator bank, J.T. had disappeared.

When the elevator opened on the eighth floor, a woman about my own age was standing on the other side. Age was all that we had in common: the makeup on her cinammon skin was fresh but subtle, her hair was perfectly combed, her nails recently manicured. The wool in her rust-colored suit was that smooth soft weave that doesn't make it into the stores where people like me shop. She looked me up and down as if she could see the tear in the lining of my own jacket before asking if I needed help.

"I'm here to see Mr. Augustus Llewellyn."

"And you have an appointment?"

"I know you're not his secretary, and this is a confidential matter." The name of the daughter who ran Llewellyn's two women's magazines came to me. "I suppose you're Ms. Janice Llewellyn?"

She didn't smile back. "Mr. Llewellyn is leaving for the day. If you don't have an appointment and you want to talk to him, you can call his secretary in the morning."

Just at that minute, a door at the end of the hall opened, and Llewellyn came out in person, accompanied by a couple of young men and an older woman.

Janice called out, "Daddy, go back into your office for a minute, why don't you. I'm going to get this person out of the building."

In the second that everyone stood frozen, trying to absorb the situation at the elevator, I walked up the hall and handed Llewellyn my note. He took it reflexively, but the two young men formed a barrier between him and me and ushered him back into his executive offices, along with the older woman. As soon as they had the old man safely inside, one of the young men reappeared and joined Janice and me by the elevators.

He seized my arm and said to Janice, "You go in with Daddy and call down to Ricky in the lobby; I'll get her out of the building."

He had the stocky build of a middle linebacker. I knew I couldn't really fight him, but I never like being grabbed. And I was tired of being stiffed and pushed around by everyone I wanted to talk to. I moved into the circle of his arm and elbowed him sharply in the ribs. He cried out and dropped my arm.

"I'll leave if your daddy doesn't want to see me," I said, moving away from him. "But you don't need to help me."

Janice had her cell phone out. She was starting a firm conversation with the lobby guard, demanding to know how I had come to be in the building without permission, when the door to the executive offices opened again. The other brother appeared. In a voice overflowing with astonishment and indignation, he announced that "Daddy" wanted to talk to me.

Janice and her brother glared at me, but Daddy's wishes took precedence over their bruised egos, or rib cages, as the case might be. Janice's plucked brows met briefly over her nose, but she kept from wrinkling her forehead. It pays to work for a woman's magazine—you learn good tips on how to preserve your face. She put her cell phone into the side compartment of her briefcase and told me to follow her. Her brother stayed in step next to me.

When we got to the executive suite, the other brother took me into his father's of-fice. Augustus Llewellyn was sitting behind his desk, a leather-inlaid partners' specimen that might have been a couple of hundred years old. There were a number of interesting antiques in the room besides the desk, but the one that caught my eye was an old hand press standing on an octagonal table.

I walked over to look at it. "Good evening, sir. Is that what you used to print *T-Square* on?"

Llewellyn ignored me, turning to his children and telling them they could leave. When the son I'd elbowed protested that I might be violent, his father managed a small smile. "If she harms me, you'll know exactly who did it, and you can have her arrested. But for now I want to be alone with her. And that means you, too, Marjorie."

The last remark was addressed to the older woman, who I assumed was the secretary I'd spoken to the day before. When all four had left, I pulled up one of the two contemporary chairs in the room and faced Llewellyn across his desk. He folded his hands in his lap but didn't speak.

"I'm the detective whom the Whitby family—"

He cut me off. "I know that you and your underlings have been questioning my staff recently, young woman. Not much happens in this company that I don't know about."

"Then you know that Marcus Whitby wanted to see you shortly before he died. Did he talk to you about his meeting with Olin Taverner?"

"If he did, that would be of no concern to you."

"You agreed to see me, Mr. Llewellyn," I said gently. "I think if you knew what Taverner had told Whitby, you wouldn't need to talk to me. So I'm assuming you didn't see Marc Whitby before he died."

He nodded slightly, but didn't offer any comment.

"Olin Taverner held on to a secret, or maybe a series of secrets, about people in New Solway, and people involved in Com-Thought—the Committee for Social—"

"Yes, I know what Com-Thought is, or was." He cut me off again. "And I know Taverner was obsessed with it as a Communist front. I don't think they were ever the threat to America's safety that Olin claimed, but I had my fill of the left at Flora's all those years ago. They were a ramshackle lot who turned on each other like rats in a proverbial barrel. They had no real interest in the working man or woman, only in their stupid revolutionary rhetoric. America rewards self-determination. They could never see that."

"Pelletier says you sat in on the committee's beginnings at Flora's." I spoke flatly, as if what I were saying were undisputed truth, not my own unverifiable guesses

"You say this is an unpublished manuscript." Llewellyn tapped my note with his index finger. "How did you come to read it?"

"The same way Marc Whitby did—by going through Pelletier's papers at the University of Chicago. It sounds as though Flora's was an exciting place—meatpackers and novelists rubbing shoulders with dancers and journalists, a miniature Greenwich Village on the near West Side. Calvin Bayard dropped in from time to time, so you got to know him. And ultimately he guaranteed the loans that allowed you to abandon that hand press over there and move to real machines. What did you have to do in return, Mr. Llewellyn?"

"I fail to see how that concerns you, young woman."

"Did he ask you to make a contribution to Com-Thought's legal defense fund? And if so, why should that be a secret?"

"Again, this is no concern of yours. You come in here with tales of Armand Pelletier and Miss Ballantine, but you were hired, I believe, to find Marcus Whitby's killer, and, if I'm not mistaken, Mr. Whitby died last week, not in 1957."

I smiled evilly. "He died because of what he'd learned about 1957, about the relations among you and Calvin Bayard and Armand Pelletier. I'm tracking those down."

His pressed his lips together in a tight angry line, but said, "Armand Pelletier made Calvin's fortune. Not that book alone, that famous *Tale of Two Countries,* but he got Calvin the entree to the kind of authors Bayard Publishing needed if Calvin was going to turn a stodgy family firm into a success. If Pelletier was enthusiastic about something, Calvin was bound to be there, too. I never knew if Calvin was protecting his investment in Pelletier, or if he really was the eager puppy dog he acted around Pelletier. After all, Armand had been shot in Spain—that counted for a lot in the crowd they hung out with. I was a young and earnest journalist, Pelletier thought he could patronize me, Calvin tagged along. I paid back those loans. If you've dug enough dirt to find that Calvin secured them, you know that I repaid them."

"Yes, sir. But Mr. Bayard exacted a quid pro quo, which startled even some of the starchy old ladies in New Solway, who didn't share his enthusiasm for your enterprise."

"And if he did, you think I should tell you?" His voice was level, but a pulse throbbed in his temple.

"I'll find it out," I said. "Geraldine Graham—do you remember her from those days at Flora's?—may make up her mind to speak. Or I'll find out from Renee Bayard. Or—someone else. People like to talk, and when they get old, they get to be like Olin Taverner—they don't want their secrets to die with them."

A corner of his mouth lifted into a sneer. "Oh, I remember Geraldine Graham. She was like so many rich white girls of the forties. And the fifties. And the current age. Hot bored things who look for the secret thrill the black man can provide. In her case, it was the Red man, the Communist man, but the spice of feeling the sweat of black workers gave it an added zest for her. If she decides to talk to you about those days—I will be very surprised."

"Every generation likes to think it was the first to discover sex; Ms. Graham might enjoy reminding the rest of us that she got there ahead of us. If Pelletier can be believed, she was sleeping first with him, then with Calvin Bayard; meanwhile, you brought Kylie Ballantine to Flora's bar, where she met Pelletier and Bayard and all those other people." I was embroidering recklessly, both on Pelletier's manuscript and on the hints I'd picked up from Geraldine Graham. "So when they decided to hold a fund-raiser for Com-Thought's legal defense fund, you all went up to Eagle River together."

He said coldly, "It's not unusual for a journalist to write up a political fund-raiser, especially when it's an unusual political group."

"Pelletier wrote that you were a fellow traveler back in the forties. I'm sure that interested Bushnell's committee no end."

"Pelletier wrote a lot of crap in his later years. He was a drunk and bitter man. I didn't worry about it then and I won't lose sleep over it now."

"You wouldn't mind if the Republican National Committee found out you'd been

Communist, or at least a Communist sympathizer?"

He gave a derisive snort. "My fellow Republicans include many repentant former leftists. As a black man, I already command unusual attention in the party. If I confessed to Communism, it would only add to my luster."

"So it didn't bother you that Marc Whitby learned you'd been at the Com-Thought fund-raiser. Would you mind the world knowing it was you who sent Olin Taverner a photograph from that same event that cost Kylie Ballantine her job?"

"That's a damned lie!" In fury, his voice rose to a shout. "Whether Armand wrote that or not, I'll see anyone who spreads that rumor destroyed in the courts and damned in hell."

"Or pushed into Larchmont's pond to drown?"

He stood. "If that means what I think it does, my lawyers will talk to you about a slander suit, young woman."

"Slander is slippery in court," I said. "Marc's notes would be part of my defense. Which means the accusations would come into the public domain."

I was hoping he'd say, "What notes, I destroyed all his notes," but instead he said Marc couldn't have any notes about him sending Kylie's picture to Olin, because he hadn't done so.

"Taverner wrote a letter to Kylie Ballantine; she discussed it in a letter of her own to Pelletier." I took the photocopy from my bag and showed it to him. "See where she says Taverner told her not to blame him and Bushnell, but to talk to 'those of her own blood'? If he didn't mean you, who did he mean? The hotel workers?"

An ugly smile creased Llewellyn's face. "Even if I knew, you're not the person I'd tell. You will do well to inform the Whitby family that the tragedy of their son's death is one of those many murders of young black men that will never be resolved. Let them go home to Atlanta. Let them grieve decently and move forward with their lives. Get your stick out of that old pond you're stirring. The stench from the rot on the bottom could rise up and choke you."

The interview was clearly over.

Hamster on a Wheel

Llewellyn's children were waiting outside their father's office. When I emerged, the sons hustled me into an elevator which they'd kept waiting, then muscled me outside with more force than the situation really warranted. They watched until I turned the corner onto Franklin.

The sky was dark; the area restaurants and nightspots were just starting to fill up. I passed knots of eagerly chattering thirty-somethings on their way to jazz bars and dinner. Was there a Geraldine among them, escaping from an impotent husband and an overbearing mother into the city's nightlife? Or an Armand Pelletier, brilliant, impetuous, trying to organize them all to act?

I walked slowly, hunched over, my hands in my pockets. Llewellyn was yet another player from that old New Solway team with old secrets to keep. He said he didn't care if people thought he'd been a Communist, but that could be a sophisticated bluff: it's always the best strategy to scoff at threats, not to cower before them. What made him furious was the suggestion that he'd cost Kylie her career. If Marc thought he'd found evidence proving Llewellyn had betrayed her to Olin Taverner, maybe Llewellyn would have silenced his star reporter.

Those muscular sons of his were strong enough to carry someone from his car to a pond and hold him under until he drowned to death. And they would pretty much do whatever their daddy wanted.

The Merchandise Mart loomed in front of me, its mass ominous in the dark. I skirted it to Wells Street. When I reached the river, I didn't cross over, but walked east alongside it, picking my way through construction rubble, passing homeless men in makeshift shelters who froze at my passing. Rats skittered across my path.

The walkway narrowed and the concrete bank on my left grew steeper. Struts for the bridges loomed over me. Between the fathomless black of the water and the iron towering above me, I felt small and fragile. A chill wind cut down the river from the lake. I pulled my torn jacket tightly across my chest and plodded ahead.

I needed Benjamin Sadawi to reveal what he'd seen from the attic last Sunday night. He was afraid to tell me or Father Lou, but there was one person he would talk to: Catherine Bayard. It might be hard to persuade her to dig the information out of him, but I couldn't see any other road to pursue. She was supposed to come home from the hospital today. Maybe Renee would let me into the apartment to talk to her.

I took out my cell phone, but the ironwork around me blocked the signal. When I reached Michigan Avenue, I climbed the two flights of stairs to the street. I blinked as the lights of the night city hit me. Suddenly, instead of the solitary rustling of rats or homeless men and women, I was in the middle of crowds: tourists, students taking night classes at a nearby university, people shopping on their way home from work, swarmed around me. A mass of buses and cars crept up the avenue, honking irritably at each other. I picked my way along the street until I came to a hotel where the glass wall would block enough noise to let me use my phone.

I pulled open my PalmPilot to get the Bayard apartment number when I suddenly realized I hadn't called Mr. Contreras. When I reached him, my neighbor had already been on the phone to Freeman Carter to warn him that I'd disappeared. The old man's relief at hearing from me slid rapidly into a prolonged scolding. I cut him short so I could get to Freeman Carter before he spent billable hours trying to find me in a holding cell.

It was seven-thirty; Freeman was at home. "I'm glad you're still at large, Vic. Your neighbor has been anxious enough to phone me three times. For God's sake, if you're not in trouble, remember to check in with him on time—once he starts, he goes on for a year or two before he stops."

"Yeah, sorry: I was in a meeting with Augustus Llewellyn, trying to figure out what all these rich important people did fifty years ago that they don't want anyone to know about today. While I've got you on the phone, did Harriet Whitby talk to you about getting her brother's tox screen from the county?"

"The tox screen. Right. Callie told me it came in just as we were shutting down for the day. Neither of us have read it, but I'll have her messenger over a copy first thing in the morning. I'm going to dinner. Good night."

People kept hanging up on me abruptly, or shoving me out of their homes and offices, as if talking to me wasn't the pleasure it should be. Even Lotty . . . and Morrell, who should have been here to hold me close and tell me I was a good detective and a good person, where was he?

As if to underscore that I was a pariah these days, a concierge came over and asked if I was waiting for someone in the hotel; if not, could I go elsewhere to use my phone? Rage rose in me—useless, since I had no choice except to leave. On my way through the revolving door, I caught sight of myself in a lobby mirror: my face was haggard from lack of sleep, my hair wild from running across the Loop this afternoon. No wonder the concierge wanted me to leave. And no wonder Janice Llewellyn's first instinct had been to send for the guard—I looked more like the people in the shanties underneath the avenue than those passing me on top of it now.

I felt more like them, too, confused, tired, cold. My tired brain went round and round like a hamster on a wheel. At the top, yes, it was clear that Whitby had been killed. At the bottom, no, he'd gone into the pond on his own. How had Whitby . . . why wouldn't Benji . . . why had Llewellyn said . . . why had Darraugh . . . Renee Bayard . . . I was too tired to make decisions, too tired to do anything but doggedly plow in the direction I'd already started.

Under the dim bulb of a streetlight, I picked the Bayards' apartment number out of my PalmPilot and typed it into my cell phone. Yes, Elsbetta told me, Miss Catherine had come home today, but she was resting now and couldn't be disturbed. Could I call back later this evening? No, Mrs. Renee had given strict orders.

A request for Mrs. Renee brought the Wabash Cannonball to the phone. She wanted to know if I had located the missing Egyptian boy; if I hadn't, there wasn't much point in our talking. And, no, I couldn't see Catherine. I had caused enough disturbance in her granddaughter's life; she didn't want me bothering her again.

"I'm not the one who summoned Sheriff Salvi to Larchmont Hall Friday night," I said. "I was just a bystander, remember, caught in the crossfire you were generating."

"You're hardly a bystander, Ms. Warshawski. I'd call you more of an instigator. Thanks to you, I had an offensive call from Geraldine Graham, and I just got off the phone with Augustus Llewellyn, who says you all but accused him of orchestrating his own journalist's death."

Shivering under a streetlamp wasn't the best way to carry on this conversation. "Did he, now. That's quite telling, all the old crowd from Flora's rallying around. What I really wanted to know is why it was such a shameful thing to give money to Com-Thought's legal defense fund that neither Llewellyn nor Ms. Graham will discuss it. I gather your husband persuaded them to make their donations. Why should they be afraid to tell me?"

"Taverner and Bushnell's most despicable legacy was to make people afraid to acknowledge they had ever supported progressive causes. Even successful, rich people, or perhaps most especially successful, rich people. Augustus actually wanted to know what I had told you about Com-Thought. I had to remind him all that happened while I was still in high school."

The torn muscle in my shoulder began to ache from cold. "Did you know that Armand Pelletier left an unpublished manuscript in his papers describing where Com-Thought met, and who took part in the discussions? According to him, Mr. Bayard was prominently involved in those conversations at Flora's—I thought he might have told you about it, especially since you were helping him when he was facing down Bushnell's interrogation."

"Armand was a sad case, a gifted man who frittered away his talents on drink, and on blaming others for his problems. He never forgave Calvin for the poor sales of his book *Bleak Land,* and he never forgave me for suggesting to Calvin that we not publish it. Armand had served prison time for his beliefs and Calvin felt we owed it to him to help him out. My husband tried to help a number of the Com-Thought people in ways like that, to show Olin and Walker Bushnell he didn't care about their vulgar blacklist. That's quite different from being the driving force behind an avowedly Communist group, which Olin and Congressman Bushnell hoped to pin on Calvin. I wouldn't pay much attention to Armand's unpublished manuscripts; he was a bitter man with an ax to grind. All of that past is long dead. I think it's time for you to leave it to bury itself."

"Is that why Ms. Graham called you? To complain that I was resurrecting the past?"

Renee paused briefly. "I don't know which of the two of you is more intrusive. She wanted to inquire after Calvin's health, as if I didn't know how to care for him. An impertinence I wouldn't have received if you hadn't first invaded my privacy in New Solway, and then discussed Mr. Bayard with Geraldine. Unless you have something useful to contribute, Ms. Warshawski, don't bother my family further. You may not be an instigator, but you're certainly not a by-stander: you generate turmoil."

When she cut the connection, I had an impulse to run up to Banks Street and hurl a bazooka rocket through her window, something that would make an explosion big enough to match my impotent fury.

Instead I stomped over to Michigan and flagged a taxi to my car. Where I found yet another ticket. One more and I'd get booted. I kicked a piece of concrete savagely enough to hurt my toes. Damn it all, anyway.

At home, soaking in a hot bath, I tried to make sense of all the conversations I'd had today. Taverner's secret was about sex, the complicated relations among Calvin and Geraldine, MacKenzie Graham and Laura Drummond. But it was also about money. There was the money Geraldine had given Calvin's pet charity, presumably the Committee for Social Thought's legal fund. And the money Calvin had loaned Llewellyn. Sex and money. They led to murder in the heat of the moment, but the heat from these moments surely had cooled in the last fifty years.

Still, something about that past was upsetting people so much they kept menacing me. Darraugh called it quicksand, Llewellyn a pond filled with some kind of rot. Darraugh himself had threatened me when he realized what information I was starting to dig up, even though he was the one who brought me out to New Solway in the first place. He was strong, too, strong enough to overpower Marcus Whitby. But he was the person who'd brought me to New Solway to begin with. The hamster wheel began buzzing in my brain again.

I ran more hot water into the tub and sank deeper into it. My shoulder started to relax. My bones warmed up. I drifted away from Whitby and turmoil. My birthday last July, Lake Michigan warmer than this bathwater. Lying on an Indiana beach under the summer stars, the night air and Morrell's long fingers caressing me.

The shrill bell to my front door jerked me awake. I sat up, splashing water onto the floor. When the bell sounded a second time I climbed out of the tub and padded to the front room, wrapping a bath sheet around me. It wasn't cops, but a trio of boys on bikes doing wheelies on the walk. Pranksters. My lips tightened in annoyance. I walked back to my bedroom to dress, but, when they rang for the third time, I suddenly remembered that Father Lou had said he would send messages by his kids on bikes.

"Be right with you," I shouted through the intercom.

I dried off fast, pulled on jeans and a heavy sweater, tucked my damp hair into a baseball cap and skittered down the stairs. Mr. Contreras and the dogs were already in the lobby, arguing with the boys, who were backing away from Mitch—by far the most vociferous of the group.

"'S okay, I've got it." I pushed past them out the front door.

One of the boys came forward, striking a determinedly aggressive posture. "You the detective lady?"

"Yep. You the guy from St. Remigio?"

He nodded, eyes slits, detective on a mission. "Father Lou said to tell you you wasn't alone when you came to church this morning. Got it?"

"Is that all he said? Did he want me to call?" I demanded.

"Uh, yeah. Yeah, you should try to call him."

Mechanically, I thanked the boys. I gave them a five to share among themselves, and went back into the building.

"What was that about?" Mr. Contreras demanded. "You shouldn't give punks like that money, only encourages them to come around begging for more."

I shook my head. "They're from Father Lou. Someone followed me to church this morning. Somehow, some way. But—damn, I made sure I was clear. I have to call him, see whether the Feds got Benji."

I sprinted back up the stairs, the dogs racing ahead of me while the old man followed more ponderously in the rear. By the time he got to my door, I had on my running shoes and a coat. Mr. Contreras offered to let me use his phone, but I couldn't be sure that wasn't tapped—if they were listening to me they would know to listen in on him, too.

The nearest pay phone I could think of was in the Belmont Diner, a couple of blocks south of us us. I ran down there and called the rectory.

"No one was on my tail this morning; I triple-checked," I said when the priest finally answered his phone. "What happened?"

"Had a federal marshal and a Chicago cop here this afternoon. They asked after you—told them you're one of my parishioners, don't come often enough." He let out a rusty chuckle: I'm never sure whether he harbors secret fantasies of converting me. "They also thought I was hiding some runaway they want. Told them to be my guest, search the place, but it's a big church, took them the better part of two hours, got me behind in catechism and boxing classes both."

"Did they find anyone?" I asked.

"Boys playing hide-and-seek behind the altar was all, thinking it was a good joke to jump out on a cop. Gave them what for when I found them. But if you're bringing cops into the church, you'd better find someplace else to worship—too disruptive of education here."

Meaning, if I understood him right, that he'd put Benji in the crypt, which lies behind the altar, but that I'd better move him in case the Feds came again.

"Is this something I have to figure out tonight?" I asked. "You know I don't go to church very often—I don't have a second one right at my fingertips."

He grunted. "Can wait until tomorrow. Maybe the next day, not much longer."

The Feds might have gone to St. Remigio's because they'd done so much research on me that they knew Father Lou was a friend of mine and Morrell's. Or—they'd installed an electronic gadget on my car so they could follow me without putting manpower on the street. My stomach turned over. I tried to remember if I'd gone anywhere else incriminating the last few days. The hospital, the university library, back up to the Loop, then home. Maybe agents would next be down at the University of Chicago, demanding to know what I'd read today. Under the Patriot Act, they didn't need a warrant or probable cause to make the library tell them, but if the librarians told me the Feds had come around, the librarians would go to jail. So I'd never know—unless, of course, Pelletier's archives disappeared.

I'd been tired all day, but now I felt completely exhausted. It was what I'd tried to tell Lotty last night: I didn't know who frightened me more these days, radical Muslims, or radical Americans.

I hadn't eaten dinner and I certainly didn't have the energy to cook for myself. I went inside the diner and took a seat at the counter.

The diner is a gallant survivor from the days when Lakeview was a blue-collar neighborhood, from when Mr. Contreras and I had bought shares in our co-op. Now it's become a neighborhood we can barely afford. The diner has changed, too—I guess it had to in order to survive. The Formica tables are gone, and the chicken-fried steak, replaced by polyurethaned wood and grilled salmon. I didn't want modern trendy food tonight, but they still had some old diner standbys on the menu. I ordered a plate of macaroni and cheese. It wasn't anything like what my mother used to make, with her hand-rolled pasta and homemade white sauce, but it was comfort food nonetheless.

While I drank a cup of weak diner coffee, I tried to imagine where I could put Benji. I couldn't bring him home, either to me or Mr. Contreras. I certainly couldn't ask Lotty or Max to put him up. I hardly knew Amy Blount, and, anyway, she lived in a studio apartment. If I could get in to see Catherine Bayard in the morning, I'd see whether she had some fallback place. Maybe the family apartment in Hong Kong or London. No, that would mean getting him out of the country past a security screen. I gave up on it and went home to bed.

Tough on a Rhino Hide

When I woke, the sun was out for the first time in days. Perhaps that was an omen. I had slept for nine hours, deeply, hardly stirring, despite the anxieties I'd taken to bed with me. Another good sign.

I dressed for the day in jeans and running shoes. Since the cops had trailed me to St. Remigio's, I was going to leave my car at my office; I wanted to be able to move fast through the city. The dogs got the shortest of walks. I left them with Mr. Contreras, then drove to my office, where I went inside just long enough to check my messages. No tox report. No messages that couldn't wait. I put a fresh battery pack in my cell phone and took off.

On my way to the El, I turned abruptly into a bakery, then stuck my head out the door. No one had halted on the walk behind me. I bought a ginger scone and a bottle of orange juice, picked up the morning papers and hurried to the train.

The detective's life is harder on public transport. The train was so packed I had to stand. I couldn't eat or read and when I got out, I was still two miles from my destination, since the line to the Gold Coast is different from the one near my office. At Division, I flagged a cab to the corner of Banks and Astor. When I got out, a young woman swung into the backseat before I finished paying—it was eight-ten, the time when aggressive young lawyers and financiers race to their desks.

I crossed the street to where I could see the Bayard apartment. With the *Herald-Star* in front of my face, I called up and asked for Renee. She was still inside; I hung up just as she came to the phone. I made a little eyehole in the *Herald-Star;* while I ate my scone, I watched nannies and mothers hurry their children to school. I also got to see a ferocious competition for cabs among the work-bound—including a shoving match between two women. The one I was silently betting on lost.

Renee Bayard could probably have won a battle for a taxi, but she didn't have to fight: a dark sedan was waiting in front of the Banks Street apartment. At eight-forty-eight, the driver climbed out and stood by the rear door. At eight-fifty, Renee came through the front gate, a commanding figure in navy wool. Her son was with her. The driver tucked Renee into the backseat, but Edwards walked over to State Street and headed north.

He could be going anywhere, but the Vina Fields Academy lay in that direction. If he was going to pick up books or lesson plans for Catherine, Elsbetta would know about it, and I couldn't use that as my pretext for getting into the building. I bit my lip in indecision, but finally crossed the street and rang the lower apartments, starting with the first floor. No one answered there, the second floor hung up on me, but the third floor buzzed me in as soon as I said I was from the Vina Fields Academy. They buzzed me again through the inner door. Just to minimize suspicions in the building, I rode to the third floor, said I was there for

Catherine Bayard and was directed to five. So far, so good.

On the fifth floor, the entrance to the Bayard apartment stood open—they assumed the locks on the gate and lobby doors were enough protection. I shook my head disapprovingly: this is how ax murderers get into your home.

I slipped into the entry area, pausing to admire a Louise Nevelson bronze before passing through the arched doorway that led to the interior. I tried to remember how to find Catherine's room. The path to Renee's study lay to the left; I thought Catherine's bedroom was in the opposite direction.

As I walked down the hall, a vacuum cleaner roared into life. I jumped, but moved boldly forward. A furtive glance showed me a cleaning crew in action. Elsbetta stood with her back to me, barking orders in Polish. Excellent.

At the end of the hall, I came to Catherine's room. The door was shut. I gave a perfunctory knock and went in. The bedroom was empty, but an open door on the near wall led to a bathroom. When I peered around the door, I saw Catherine in front of a dressing table trying to button a man's shirt with one hand. Her dark hair fell unbraided down her back. She didn't look around at my entrance, but kept stubbornly trying to manage the buttons.

"It's easier if you don't watch in the mirror," I said.

She turned, startled. "Oh! It's you. I thought it was Elsbetta. Why are you here? Is Benji okay?"

I pulled up a chair to face her. "I saw him yesterday. He seemed fine, he asked after you, but there are a couple of problems."

Her eyes grew dark with dismay. "Like what?"

"Like the Chicago cops showed up late yesterday to look for him. Apparently, because I'd been there. So we need—"

"I thought you were a detective." Her voice was scornful. "Don't you know to watch for tails?"

"Check for tails! Now, you tell me. Gosh." I slapped my forehead. "Listen, you little mutt, I drove in circles at six in the morning. The streets were empty. No one was behind me. One of two things happened: they put a tracer on my car so they can watch me on a screen instead of wasting gas. Or they have been tracking down every person I know and checking up on them. Father Lou had time to get Benji into a safe place inside the church, but the kid can't stay there much longer. For obvious reasons, I can't take him to any of my friends. I was hoping you could talk to your grandmother and get her to agree to let him stay at your New Solway house. She's basically on the side—"

"No! She thinks I'm in love with Benji, or in love with Benji's adventure. She wants him out of the country. The only thing she and Daddy agree on is that Benji needs to go back to Egypt. If I tell her I know where he is, she'll call the Justice Department. But they won't deport him, they'll lock him up. You said I didn't read any news, but I've been reading on this and reading on this and reading on this. It happens all the time, people are caught with their visas expired, and they can't even go home. They get put in detention some place and held for months. I promised Benji, I won't let him down." She started to cry.

I patted her good hand. "It's okay, babe: we'll think of something else. You're recovering from a bullet wound. Try to calm down: you need to save your strength for healing. I'm on your side in this, really, truly. If I wasn't, I would have talked to your granny without consulting you, you know."

She blew her nose. "I can't even braid my own hair. I can't play lacrosse or ride for months until this stupid arm heals. Everything takes forever, or I have to get people to do stuff for me. I hate it."

"Speaking as one who's been through the wars, I agree: it's a pain. Want me to finish buttoning you? Just this once?"

She nodded, her eyes still tearing a bit. Judging by the size and the cut, the shirt must have been filched from her father's closet. It covered her casted right arm with room to spare.

"Your dad off getting your lesson plans?"

"Yeah. He's meeting with Ms. Milford to see what I can do online. It's only a few days, I keep telling him not to be so anal."

"And he says, 'Young lady, where did you pick up that kind of language?'" I suggested.

She gave a shaky laugh. "Something like that. And that it's a competitive world and I need to learn that losers are not strivers. Then he adds he's going to take me to Washington, to a school with my natural peers where I'll learn how to behave with proper respect. Like, learning how to totally trash the environment or something while I'm pretending to protect it, that's his idea of respect. Where can Benji go if he has to leave St. Remigio's?"

"I've only had one not very bright idea. I could put him up in a motel for a few days, while I try to find an immigration lawyer who can help him. It's not the best idea—I hate for him to have keep skulking around, not to mention for him to have to be by himself. It's not good for his spirits, and, anyway, as he himself says, there's no point in his staying here if he can't work. And he ought to be with kids his age—your age—and feel able to relax."

"But he can't do that as long as those racists are looking for him." She smacked the dressing table with her good hand. "I tried to get him to let me send his mom money, but he wouldn't take it. No matter what Daddy and Granny are saying, he isn't trying to exploit me."

"I have a tiny idea about that, too. Last Sunday night, when Marcus Whitby drowned in the Larchmont pond, Benji was standing at the attic window watching for you. I'm almost certain Benji saw what happened. If Marcus Whitby didn't go in on his own, Benji saw who pushed him in. Benji won't tell me or Father Lou, but if you could get him to talk about it, I might be able to work out a deal with the Chicago police. Captain Mallory, who's in charge of the city's antiterrorism squad, could—"

"No!" she shouted, her face very white. "You're not on my side or his, are you? You only want to use him for what you can get out of him about your stupid murder. I should have known better than to trust you. Get out of here! Don't come near me again. Don't go near Benji again!"

"Catherine. Something has to change if he's going to stay here without being arrested or deported. If he witnessed a murder—"

"Go away! If you don't leave now, I'll page Granny and she'll get our lawyers. I hate you, I hate you." She doubled over with sobs.

I stood up. "I'm leaving my card on your desk. If you change your mind, if you realize I'm on your side, you can call me on my cell phone at any hour. But I'm going to have to move Benji, whether he's willing to talk to me or not."

I waited another minute, but she only sobbed, "Oh, go, why aren't you gone yet?"

I left a card inside her laptop, away from her grandmother and father's prying eyes, but where she'd see it when she next went to log on. On my way out of the apartment, Elsbetta appeared from the other wing, the one that held Renee's office. She was taken aback, since she hadn't let me in, and demanded to know my business. I told her I'd been calling on Catherine, yes, I knew Mrs. Renee didn't want me here, but I had come anyway, and now I was leaving.

My visit was completed by running into Edwards Bayard just as I opened the gate to the street. He also wanted to know what I was doing there.

"I peddle Tupperware door-to-door; it augments my agency income. I hit Schiller Street yesterday, but this neighborhood is a tough sell."

He reacted as predictably as Peppy to a squirrel: he was a presidential adviser, he was a Bayard, no one talked to him like that.

"Yeah, you're a Bayard when you want to call up some privileges. The rest of the time, you slink away from your parents."

I stomped west, away from the island of wealth and privilege, back toward my own world. I felt exhausted, the morning's good omens dissipated by Catherine's outburst. Her wound and the anesthesia that lingered in her system were knocking her off balance. And then, she was sixteen, it wasn't like her judgment was the steadiest to begin with.

I knew these things, but her tantrum left me feeling as though I had been beaten by sticks. I kept replaying the conversation, wondering what I should have said differently. I should have described Bobby first, explained that he was at odds with the Feds, I should have spent more time talking to her on neutral topics first, I should have this, I shouldn't have that, over and over. You'd think a detective like me would be thick-skinned by now, as J.T. had said last night, but lately every whack against my rhino hide was making me more prey to self-doubt.

Seizures

I walked up to North Avenue, where I caught a crosstown bus to my office. The street is an important conduit between the city and the expressway, which is why I suppose the big national chains have stuffed it full of outlets. The traffic is so heavy on North these days that it took half an hour for the bus to trundle the three miles across town. Delays like that usually leave me gnawing my nails in annoyance. Today I welcomed the chance to rest.

When I finally got off at Western, I didn't bother to check for tails. I was tired, I didn't care and, anyway, it didn't matter if people followed me to my office—if they were tapping me, they'd know I was in there.

It was close to lunch time. I walked down to La Llorona for a fish taco. The lunchtime crowd was heavy, so I didn't chat with Mrs. Aguilar but ate my taco at one of the high tables in the corner while I finished glancing through the papers.

The taco was so good, and I was feeling so sorry for myself, that I took a second one back with me to eat at my desk. At Division Street, where Milwaukee changed abruptly from a neighborhood street to an extension of Yuppie Town, I stopped in one of the coffee bars for a cappuccino. Either protein or caffeine would revive me, or at least that was my theory.

While I was out, Freeman's secretary had messengered over the toxicology report. Tessa had signed for it and taped it to my office door. I took it in with me and laid it on my desk. I almost couldn't bear to read it: I'd moved heaven and earth, or at least medical examiners in two counties, to get this document. If it told me nothing, I might lie down and never get up again.

I finally took the report from the envelope and began reading. Callie had sent a photo-copy of a ten-page fax, so it was blurry in places. The text bristled with "epithelial cells of the distal part of the renal tubules" and "immunocytochemical electron microscopy of the hepatocytes." Fascinating, if you knew what it meant.

I slowly went through the whole ten pages. The analysis of Marc's last meal (skinless chicken, broccoli, baked potato and a lettuce-tomato salad, consumed three hours before death, with a statistical variation of so much based on digestive whatever) was so detailed that I abruptly tossed the second taco into the trash.

The lab had found no trace of cocaine, diazepam, nordiazepam, hydrocodone, cocaethylene, benzoy-lecgonine, heroin hydrochloride or marijuana metabolites in Marc's urine. He had alcohol in the vitreous humor and phenobarbital in the blood plasma, discovered with "high-performance liquid chromatography." The report gave the drugs in milligrams per liter, with the information that Marc had weighed eighty kilos, so I couldn't tell how much Marc had drunk on top of the drug, but Vishnikov had provided a summary at the end: ". . . a six hundred milligram dose of phenobarbital taken with approximately two shots of bourbon would have depressed respiration and most likely killed him if he hadn't first died of drowning."

I leaned back in the desk chair. It wobbled badly; I needed to get a screwdriver out to tighten the castors.

All I knew about phenobarbital was that it was used to treat epilepsy. If Marc had epilepsy, he should have known better than to mix alcohol with his medication. He would have known better: by all reports he was a careful man; he wouldn't have taken a drug without knowing its side effects. But maybe after years with the disease, he knew he could drink a modest amount without getting into distress with his medication.

The sinking feeling returned to my diaphragm; he had gone into that pond alone. Unless—a couple of shots of whisky wasn't much for a man who weighed—eighty kilos—I scratched arithmetic on a scrap of paper—a hundred seventy-five pounds. But I didn't know how to evaluate the amount of phenobarb he'd taken.

Since I couldn't ask Vishnikov to explain, I phoned Lotty, who was in her clinic today. Mrs. Coltrain, her longtime administrator, said Dr. Herschel was with patients and couldn't be disturbed.

"All I want to know is how much of a dose six hundred milligrams of phenobarbital is.

Can you ask her, or Lucy Choi?" Lucy was the advanced practice nurse who did a lot of the routine patient care at the clinic.

After a minute on hold, Lotty came to the phone herself. "Six hundred milligrams is a huge dose, Victoria. Did someone prescribe that for you? It could kill you if you took it all at once."

"How long would it take?"

"This isn't a game, is it? I don't know. It moves fast into the system, depresses respiration. You might have an hour for someone to try to revive you, possibly only half an hour."

"What if I weighed thirty pounds more than I do?"

"Still far too much. If someone prescribed that for you, don't ever see her again."

She hung up. I looked again at the report. If Marc had epilepsy, he wouldn't have taken such a lethal dose on purpose. Not unless he wanted to die. But then, why go into the Larchmont Pond? Why not stay in the comfort of his bed? Maybe he didn't know he would die from it—maybe he thought it would just make him unconscious enough not to mind drowning. But why go all the way out to that foul pond at

Larchmont instead of the welcome expanse of Lake Michigan? And then, his car—I shook my head, trying to stop the incessant buzzing: hamster on its wheel again.

My hand hesitated over my phone. Harriet Whitby had planned to move in with Amy after her parents left for Atlanta yesterday. If I phoned Amy's apartment, would that get the law to monitor her calls, too? I shook my head angrily: I couldn't live like this, second-guessing whether anyone was listening to me and my friends, or following me. And I wasn't going to spend an hour on public transport just to make sure I talked to her unsupervised.

Amy answered, sounding relaxed: she and Harriet were enjoying a comfortable day alone together, she explained, without having to worry about Harriet's folks. As she called her friend to the phone, I felt like a vulture, intruding on their light mood.

"Dr. Vishnikov sent me your brother's autopsy report," I told Harriet. "Would you like me to come to Amy's so we can discuss it in person?"

"Are you trying to prepare me for something awful?" she demanded. "Something I don't want to know? Tell me now. This has been the hardest week of my life—I don't want even a half hour of agony imagining things while I wait to see you."

"Marc had a lot of phenobarbital in his system, but only one largish bourbon. Did he suffer from epilepsy, or have any history of seizures where he would have been taking this drug?"

"No," she said blankly. "No, he's always been—always was—really healthy. What does this mean?"

"I'm afraid it means what we've been saying all along: he really was murdered. Someone gave him a drug that knocked him out, and then put him in that pond to die."

Saying it out loud brought me a sense of relief. The wheel stopped turning, the buzzing in my head ended. Murder. Not suicide. Not accident. I didn't have to make a plaster cast of the wheel marks in the culvert: Mark's killer had driven him to the pond in a golf cart.

Harriet became so quiet I thought perhaps she'd gone away, but at last she said in a dull, dead voice that sounded like her mother's, "We've known this, anyway, all week. Not about the drug, but that someone killed him. It's just hard to hear it finally said out loud. Marc wasn't really healthy after all, was he? It didn't matter that he attended the University of Michigan or was a prizewinning writer, or kept a healthy diet, did it? He still died from the black man's disease."

"I'm sorry?" I was confused—all I could think of was sickle-cell anemia.

"Murder," she hiccupped. "It doesn't matter if you're educated and live a decent life, it's still going to get you."

"I'm sorry," I repeated, helplessly. "I'll come to Amy's right now if you want."

"No, thank you. I know you've been working hard on my behalf—on my family's behalf. I know you're only doing what I asked you to do. But I need to be alone with a sister for now."

When she hung up, I felt embarrassed: the news that elated me had brought her distress. I got up and walked around the room. We'd found Marc's bottle of Maker's Mark when we searched his house last week. Bourbon and branch: his drink, Amy had told me. If there were fingerprints on his bottle— if the whisky had been doctored—I wanted to collect that Maker's Mark and get it tested, even if I had to pay for the job myself.

After Amy and I had finished inspecting Marc's house on Friday, what had I done with his keys? I dumped the contents of my briefcase onto my desk. The set I'd borrowed from Marc's housekeeper tumbled out in the jumble of papers, tampons and my PalmPilot. So did the key Luke Edwards's locksmith had created for me to get into the Saturn.

I picked up the car key and turned it over in my palm, studying it as though it were a text in an unknown language. I could take the train down to Marc's house, collect his bourbon and borrow his car. As long as I didn't park it near my office or home, I should be able to drive freely around town for a few days. I might even be able to pick up Benji. And instead of taking him to a motel, I could leave him at Marc Whitby's house. Tell the neighbors Benji was my cousin, needing a job and a place to stay—we were letting him look after the house so it didn't stand vacant until the family sold it. Gosh, you're good, V.I.!

I stuffed the toxicology report back into its envelope and put it in my bag. Picklocks—you never know. A loaded clip for my gun—because, again, you never know. Latex gloves, a gallon-sized plastic bag for the bourbon, pulled clean from the box and inserted into a second clean bag to make sure there was no contamination of the specimen.

"Far from this something bosom haste, ye doubts, ye fears that laid it waste," I sang, dancing to the door.

It was a long El trip to the South Side, since I had to ride into the Loop to change trains. I danced impatiently on the platform while I waited, and found myself leaning forward in my seat, as if that would move the train faster. At Thirty-fifth Street, I jumped down the stairs two at a time and ran over to Giles.

When I jogged down the walk to Marc's house, a half-dozen girls were jumping double Dutch out front. They watched me go up the stoop and unlock Marc's front door. Maybe this wasn't such a good place to bring Benji: nothing happened unobserved in this neighborhood. Except for someone coming here to steal all Marc's papers.

The house had taken on the forlorn, musty aspect of any abandoned building. After a week, dust was visible even to my unhousekeeperly eye. I took a quick look around. I didn't think anyone had been here, robbers or cops, despite Bobby Mallory's assertion that the police would reopen the investigation into Marc's death.

In the kitchen, I pulled on the latex gloves, picked up the Maker's Mark at the base with my thumb and forefinger and slipped it into the clean plastic bags. The whole package went into my briefcase.

On my way out, I stopped to look up at the poster of Kylie Ballantine in the stairwell. "What could you tell me?" I demanded. "Were you Calvin Bayard's lover? Were you Augustus Llewellyn's? What secret do those New Solway people care about so much that they killed your young champion to protect it?"

The vital silhouette floated above me— above all the petty concerns of the people she had known. Kylie Ballantine had moved on, had not let her life be mired in the bitterness the McCarthy era had generated. She had struggled financially, but unlike that crew of wealthy people, she had shrugged off the wounds of those turbulent times. Even if she'd known hardship, Ballantine had been fortunate to die with her powers intact, her spirit strong. Unlike Calvin Bayard, whose mind once overmatched Olin Taverner's, and now was happy to watch the cook boil milk.

My fingers clenched on the handle of my case. I started toward the front door, trying to make myself think about the best way to deliver the Maker's Mark to Cheviot Labs, but the image persisted: urine masked by talcum, Calvin's nurse shepherding him toward the kitchen.

My hand was on the front doorknob when I stopped. The house around me was quiet as death. The nurse, Theresa Jakes. Who had seizures, Catherine Bayard told me; Granny mustn't know about them.

I hadn't wondered where the phenobarb had come from. But there it was, right out in New Solway where Theresa took it to control her own seizures. Where Ruth Lantner, the housekeeper, threatened to tell Renee about them if Theresa slept through Calvin's wanderings again.

I turned around and walked back to stare again at the poster. Nothing happened at New Solway that Renee didn't know about. Even if Ruth Lantner hadn't told her about Theresa's seizures, Renee would have found out somehow. Renee exulted in her organizational skills: during the day she juggled details of a mammoth commercial enterprise; at night she stayed effortlessly on top of a major domestic one.

If she had killed Marc, it would have been to protect Calvin's reputation. But Calvin didn't need protecting. He was the man who had stood up when few people would, who had confronted Taverner and Bushnell and walked away.

Fragments of conversations passed through my head. They turned on each other like rats in a proverbial barrel, Augustus Llewellyn said last night. Pelletier's Boy Wonder, skimming the cream from Pelletier's work, from Pelletier's love life.

Who had sent Taverner that picture of Kylie and told him where it had been taken? Who wanted people to give money to Com-Thought's legal defense fund without coming forward himself? What had Llewellyn done to get that money from Bayard? Taverner had kept a dastardly secret about Calvin Bayard, only because Bayard knew one just as bad about Taverner. That truth had been staring me in the face for days. I just hadn't wanted to see it.

Not about the hero of my youth. Not Calvin. Not, not. My knees buckled. I collapsed on the stairs.

Terrorist on the Run—
or in an SUV

I sat under Kylie's picture a long time. Someone else might have access to pheno-barbital—it was a common drug, it didn't have to have come from the Bayards. It didn't have to be Renee who used it to dope Marc's whisky—it could have been Theresa Jakes herself, or Ruth Lantner. Ruth Lantner could have had the necessary strength to push Marc into that pond if he was close to death already. But she had no reason to do so.

What about Edwards Bayard, determined to protect Olin Taverner's memory? After all, it was Edwards who had broken into Olin's apartment last week, Edwards who held a grudge against his parents, who was desperate to establish some kind of ascendancy over those two strong personalities.

The cold in the hallway was getting into my bones and making my sore shoulder ache. I wanted it to be Llewellyn or Edwards, rather than Renee—I liked her, I didn't like her son. But the truth, oh the truth, was—if Calvin Bayard had done—had done things I didn't want to say, even in the silent space of my own mind—I couldn't bear it. He had done much that was good. Didn't that count?

If Renee had killed Marcus Whitby, she'd done it to keep the world from knowing her husband had betrayed Kylie Ballantine. Couldn't I let it go, to keep Calvin's reputation intact? In these times, any whiff of wrongdoing by a prominent progressive would only give right-wing radicals more cause for triumphalism. I couldn't bear to contribute to their jubilant trampling on human rights. I couldn't pursue this investigation further.

I looked again at Kylie Ballantine's silhouette. She had lost her career because someone had betrayed her to Olin Taverner. Marc had lost his life for the simple crime of trying to revive her memory. No amount of good that Calvin had done, through his foundation, or the books he'd published, could outweigh the crime of killing Marcus Whitby. If it was Renee who'd killed him. And look at the probabilities: she was the one who relished organizing great enterprises. I could imagine Edwards ordering a subordinate to "take care of this problem for me"; I couldn't imagine him doing it himself.

I shouldn't discount Augustus Llewellyn. He could have given Marc doped whisky more easily than a stranger. And he, too, had secrets he was determined to hide.

I tried to imagine a confrontation that would make Renee or Llewellyn show their hand. Nothing came to me. Let the police figure it out. Bobby Mallory had been telling me for years that murder was police work. I'd give him all my tangled ideas, the nurse with seizures, every little thing I'd learned from Geraldine Graham and from the archives. He could turn the police machinery on and if it led to Renee then that's where it would go.

I pushed myself to my feet, my joints stiff from sitting so long in the cold. The weight in my bag reminded me of my own brief jubilation. Marc's bottle of bourbon—I'd turn that over to Bobby, too. In exchange, I'd ask Bobby to protect Benji, tell him that Benji was his material witness to whoever put Marc in that Larchmont pond. Bobby was at odds with the federal attorney, he'd work out something.

I thrust away a nagging voice that said Bobby would brush off my ideas as insubstantial, or unsubstantiable. Or that he'd be so angry with me for hiding Benji he wouldn't listen to me. I didn't have evidence, the nagger said, only the connections that came from reading archives and listening to people; I didn't have hard evidence. I fought the notion that Bobby would flat out refuse to investigate that New Solway crowd.

Anyway, I shouldn't go to Bobby without talking it over with Benji and Father Lou. I'd explain to Benji that things had changed since yesterday morning: now I knew the murderer was one of two, maybe three, people, all I needed from him was a shortcut to the person's identity. Bobby and Benji would both do my bidding. They had to.

I went slowly down the stairs to the front walk and climbed into Marc's Saturn. To my astonishment, it was only four o'clock: I felt as though the day had been going on for thirty or forty hours by now.

The girls were still jumping double Dutch in the road. Among them was the one who'd pointed out Marc's car to me last week. She nudged someone waiting a turn at the ropes. They all stopped jumping to stare at me. I waved as I climbed into the driver's seat.

"You with the police, miss? The police want that car or are you stealing it?" my informant asked, hands on hips.

"Stealing," I said, rolling down the window so they could hear me.

That made them laugh and draw closer. "What the police want with Mr. Whitby's car, miss?"

"Clues. He was killed, you know. We're hoping the car will hold some clues about who killed him. None of you saw the person who drove this car back here last Sunday night, did you?"

That was too strong. They pulled away, huddling together, quiet. A killer coming right onto the block, no, they didn't need that fear over their young heads.

I said cheerfully, "Don't worry if you see lights on in the house tonight. We're bringing in a caretaker, someone to live here until the family decides to sell. Okay? And don't worry about this killer—they're not going to come back here."

"How do you know?" one of them demanded. "No one been arrested, no one been suspected."

"Three people are suspected. They live far away. You're safe here in your neighborhood."

When I drove up the street, I could see them in my rearview mirror, jump ropes dangling from their hands. While I waited at the light on Thirty-fifth, they finally started turning the ropes again, but the energy had gone out of their play. Good work, V.I., sucking the enthusiasm out of little girls.

I took a look at the traffic stalled on the Dan Ryan Expressway and stayed on the side streets, driving slowly but quietly up to St. Remigio's. Marc's green Saturn was just the car for these streets, not flashy, not the kind that people stare at and remember. I parked two blocks west of the church and made a great circle around it on foot so that I came up to the school entrance from the south.

I walked briskly through the gates to the playground, not looking around, although the back of my head prickled as I wondered if any lawmen had me in their sights. Inside, a hall guard still sat on duty. Although it was four-thirty now, afterschool activities were going full spate. No one could come into the school without an ID or a legitimate reason to be there.

The guard made a phone call: Father Lou was in the gym; I could talk to him there. The priest was standing in front of one of his punching bags, dressed in sweats, showing a group of ten-year-olds how to move their arms. Curious glances from the boys made him turn to look at me. Barking a few hasty instructions to them, he came over to my side.

"I got a clean car," I said. "And I think I have a safe house where Benji can stay for a couple of days. But—I want to turn the murder investigation over to the police. It's too big for me. I really need Benji to cooperate. I think I can get Captain Mallory to protect Benji if he'll only say what he saw last Sunday night. Can you help me persuade him?"

He nodded. "Should be in here now, but maybe this is one of his prayer times. I'll find him. Wait here."

He trotted out of the room, light on his feet as a dancer. After a couple of minutes, I put my briefcase down in a corner and picked up a basketball. My first shot caromed off the backboard at a crazy angle, but after that I sank five in a row before the priest returned, jerking his head at me to follow him back to the hall.

"He's gone. Girl came for him thirty, forty minutes ago. Had to be *the* girl—one arm bound up inside her clothes. She asked the guard for Benji bold as brass—said he was her cousin from Morocco. Guard sent her to the principal, principal called Benji in, says kid was thrilled to see the girl, walked off with her. Idiots all, principal, guard, the lot. None of them sent for me."

His Popeye cheeks swelled larger with anger, but I felt only cold. If Catherine had taken Benji back to her grandmother—as I'd counseled this morning—if Renee had put Marc Whitby in the Larchmont Pond, he was as good as dead.

Dully, I followed Father Lou to the principal's office. I went through the motions with the guard and the principal: Had either of them seen how the kids left? Taxi? Bus? They didn't know—the school was an old building, put up when windows were built high off the ground to keep you from looking at the street.

Father Lou ordered the principal to summon any teachers or staff still in the building to her office. One of the janitors, moving cartons in from a supply truck, had seen a girl with one arm bound up inside her jacket leave with an older student. He was pretty sure they'd gotten into a white SUV, but he hadn't been paying close attention.

The old priest was furious. After having the FBI in yesterday looking for Benji, he couldn't believe the principal would let the youth leave without even trying to discuss the matter with Father Lou.

"We're trying to make a safe place here. If anyone can come in this school, ask for any kid without you blinking an eye, what's to stop gangbangers, kidnappers, the whole lot from destroying our peace?"

The principal turned red, angry in her turn: Was she supposed to know that a girl Benji was thrilled to see constituted a menace? If Father Lou wanted to run the school, he should take over—she'd be glad to re-sign on the spot.

The principal's red face broke into wavy lines, her mouth moving up and down, as if she was a puppet. The cabinets behind her began moving, too, in the same unsteady waves. It seemed so funny that I started to laugh. The floor began moving, which seemed funny, too, and I was still laughing when I fell over.

My head was wet. Father Lou was wiping water from my neck and face with a rough gym towel.

"No fainting from you, my girl. Need one working brain around here besides mine. Sit up and pull yourself together."

I sat up. The priest hoisted me to my feet with only a mild grunt. Hundred-and-forty-pound women are nothing to an old boxer. He held a cup to my mouth and I swallowed hot tea, choked, then drank down the rest. I put my head between my knees and willed the gray cloudy pieces of my mind into some kind of order.

"Where would the girl go?" He spoke to me roughly to make me concentrate.

"It depends partly on why she ran away." My voice wobbled. I steadied it and continued. "She turned hysterical this morning when I asked her to talk to Benji. I also suggested she confide in her grandmother. I just hope she didn't follow that piece of advice."

I pulled out my cell phone and called the Bayard apartment. Elsbetta answered.

"Why are you making trouble here?" she demanded. "Mr. Edwards, he wants to fire me because you came this morning. Now Miss Catherine has run away, all because of you."

"Is Renee or Edwards there?" I ignored her outburst. "I want to talk to them about Catherine."

"You cannot be bothering them. They have ordered no phone calls."

"Tell them I'm reporting Catherine's disappearance to the Chicago police," I said coldly. "If they want to speak to me, they can call me on my cell phone: I'll give you the number."

At that, she put me on hold. Within a minute, both Renee and Edwards were on the phone, each trying to order the other to leave the conversation to them.

"Do you have Catherine?" Renee demanded.

"Isn't she with you?" I said.

"She's run away," Edwards said. "Without leaving a note."

"You acted like a Victorian father, Eds, ordering her to pack for Washington and no argument allowed. Elsbetta phoned me at my office, but—"

Edwards shouted over her voice. "If you'd thought she deserved half as much attention as Calvin and your goddamned publishing empire—"

"If you listened to anyone but your—"

"Knock it off, both of you," I said savagely. "When did she leave and what was she driving?"

"You cannot call the police," they said in chorus.

"I can damn well do what I want. Someone reported seeing her in a white SUV. Do you seriously imagine she's safe driving a three-ton vehicle with one arm?"

That briefly united them: they wanted to know who had seen her. I grew angrier, pushing on them until they admitted Catherine had taken Renee's white Range Rover, that they knew she hadn't shown up at the New Solway house, that she'd left around three-thirty, after her fight with her father.

"Have you called Julius Arnoff to see if she's gone back to Larchmont?" I asked. It didn't seem likely to me, because she and Benji had been flushed from the mansion once already, but neither teenager was probably thinking much right now.

"My first thought," Edwards said. "While Renee was still cursing you for taking Trina to her Arab boyfriend, I had a guard stake out the house. She isn't there."

"When you came uninvited to the apartment this morning, did you or did you not arrange an assignation for Trina?" Renee demanded.

"Grow up," I snapped. "I don't know where Benji is, nor Catherine. Stop casting around for who to blame for her disappearance and tell me what you're doing to find her."

"Edwards is using his private security connections," his mother said bitingly. "They're likely to shoot her if they see her. If you were looking for her, where would you start?"

"Nowhere I'd tell either of you," I said nastily, and closed my phone.

"They have a private security force out looking for her," I turned to Father Lou. "That really scares me."

"Girl adored her grandfather, isn't that what you told me the other day? Maybe they had some special place. Everyone goes to ground where they feel secure; place connected to her grandfather would feel secure to her."

"He's got advanced Alzheimer's. He won't be able to tell me—never mind. I know who can. I'll call you from the car."

I ran from the school.

Loves' Labors Lost

North of Madison, Wisconsin, a freezing rain began to fall. The interstate turned glassy on the overpasses; I had to keep my speed down to stay in control. Except for the occasional giant rig charging through the slush at eighty, we had the road pretty much to ourselves.

Geraldine Graham was snoring lightly in the seat next to me. She had insisted on coming: she still had keys to the cottage— she had found them easily, in a drawer in her bedroom, and put them into a black Hermès bag that rested now at her feet. I tried to force her to stay home, but she said she knew the route, which I didn't, and more important, at least to her, she needed to make sure Benji and Catherine were all right. "If I'd told you these things last week, they might not be in danger now."

When I'd reached Anodyne Park, Lisa had answered the bell—bustling, officious: you can't come in, Madam is resting. I pushed her aside and strode down the hall, opening doors. I found Geraldine dozing on her bed with a reading light on and a book open beneath her fingers.

Lisa darted in under my arm. "Oh, madam, this detective is here, breaking in. Shall I call Mr. Darraugh or Mr. Julius?"

Geraldine sat up with a start. "Lisa! Stop dithering. The detective? Mr. Darraugh's detective is here? Oh, there you are, young woman. Wait while I collect myself."

I knelt next to her. "Something urgent has come up. I need your help; I don't need you to put your clothes on."

"Grant me the foibles of my upbringing, young woman. I think better while dressed than naked. I will be with you directly."

I walked impatiently up and down the hall outside her room, but she was, in fact, remarkably quick, despite her age and Lisa's interference, and in a few minutes was talking to me in her alcove in the sitting room. I told her I was going to tell her things that were utterly confidential and that Lisa could not be a party to them. After a look at my face, Geraldine summarily dismissed her maid. Lisa gave me the kind of expression that makes you glad a handgun isn't backing it up, but she retreated.

When I heard the door close—and made sure Lisa was on the far side of it—I told Geraldine about Catherine and Benji.

"I know you and Calvin were lovers all those years ago. It was you he meant when he called for Deenie last week, wasn't it?"

Her fingers clenched on the arms of her chair, but she nodded. "How did you know? Was it the key to Larchmont that he had kept?"

"That, and some other things. Armand Pelletier left an unfinished manuscript among his papers that pretty well spelled it out."

"Ah, Armand. I wondered if he would come back to haunt me. He was so passionate about workers' rights, and for a time I reflected that passion—because I was passionate and needed some object for my ardor. He was bitter when I left him for Calvin; he accused me of being too fastidious, of needing the fleshpots of Egypt. I told him clean sheets would suffice. But it had more to do with—Calvin was a generous lover, and Armand . . . took more than he gave. His passions ultimately were for himself alone. With Calvin, too, it was only a way of getting what he himself desired, but I didn't see that until much later."

"There was never a question that you would leave your husband?" Involuntarily, I let myself be sidetracked.

"I thought—I had the notion that if I divorced MacKenzie, Calvin and I might marry. But however much Mother hated MacKenzie, she couldn't stand the scandal a divorce would cause, and before I'd nerved myself to stand up to her—Calvin had married Renee." She twisted the great diamond on her right hand. "I had gone to Washington when he was called before the committee. I was in the hearing room. I was one of the spectators. I had gone with the idea that I would surprise him. I loved him; I thought he loved me and that if I declared myself it would be a help to his spirit during those difficult days."

"And he turned you down?"

She turned her head so I couldn't see her face. "I never made the offer. He left the room surrounded by lawyers and reporters. I looked for him in his club at the end of the day and they told me where he was dining. When I got to the restaurant, I saw him sitting with Renee—as he had often sat with me—so close the clothes themselves might melt from our bodies. I walked away, walked blindly, walked through the night, thinking only that I must never let anyone know how humiliated I had been. I walked for hours, until I ended up weary in some district I didn't know. I went into a bar, thinking I would have a brandy and get them to call me a cab."

She stopped, her fingers still working on her ring. "And saw my husband. With Olin Taverner. As close as Renee had been to Calvin. It was that kind of bar. MacKenzie looked up and recognized me."

"Your husband was gay? Not impotent? Was that the night you found out?"

"'Gay'? What a strange word for a man whose homosexuality weighed on him like a Druid's stone. No, I had known for years. My only surprise was seeing him with Olin. When we married, MacKenzie was often in

New York, it was an open secret between him and his parents that he went there to visit homosexual bars. Marriage was supposed to cure him of that as it was supposed to cure me of—lovers and unwanted pregnancies. I suppose I took lovers in the hopes of shocking my mother away from me, but she was far more tenacious than I; she would take me to Europe, to those Swiss sanitoria. After she and Blair Graham married MacKenzie to me, he and I tried for a few years; my daughter Laura was his child. But MacKenzie was miserable in my arms, in any woman's arms, so we arrived at a tacit understanding: we would present a bland united front to the world and seek our pleasures privately. We were both discreet, and we came to be good friends for a time."

After another pause, when I thought she would slice her finger to the bone with her diamonds, she said, "And then I met Armand, at a party Calvin gave for him, a triumphant party, when Armand's *Tale of Two Countries* had been on the *Times* best-seller list for twenty weeks. I started going to organizing meetings with him—but you know that part."

"Yes," I said gently. "I know that part. Was Calvin Darraugh's father?"

"I've never been sure." She turned bitter eyes back to me. "It might have been Armand, but I think it was Calvin. It doesn't matter. Darraugh and MacKenzie loved one another, oh, I think better than most fathers and sons do, even though MacKenzie knew the boy couldn't possibly be his, and Mother suspected as much. And when MacKenzie died—when I killed him—"

"No!" the exclamation came out, involuntary.

"Oh, I didn't pull the noose tight. But I let Calvin know what I saw in that Washington bar. My last gift to him as a lover. I thought—it would give him leverage with Olin. And it did."

My eye was on the clock. I tried to hurry her, to get to the point where she'd tell me a place Calvin might have taken his granddaughter. Geraldine wouldn't be rushed. She was telling me a tale she had rehearsed so many times in her mind it had worn a groove there. Now, her first chance to say it all out loud after all those years of silence, she could only tell me the story as she'd memorized it.

"It was all on account of the Committee for Social Thought and Justice's legal defense fund. Olin had learned that Calvin supported it, and he was on Calvin like a dog to a rabbit. They'd despised each other for so many years, you see."

"You gave the fund money so Calvin's name didn't appear?" I prompted her, trying to curb my impatience.

She smiled sadly. "Yes. Those were the days when I would do very nearly anything Calvin demanded. He told me that if he gave to the fund directly, Bayard Publishing couldn't operate freely during those bleak blacklist days.

"Since then, I've come to see—Calvin was generous, and handsome, and spoiled, and cowardly. He couldn't face hardship—but I only realized that later. What mattered at the time to me was that my mother found I had written checks for him to the legal defense fund." Once again she turned to look at the portrait.

"When I told Calvin that she was going to give her shares in the press to Olin if I donated more money to the fund, Calvin turned to Augustus Llewellyn. Llewellyn was a fellow traveler back then, I knew that from my months with Armand. When I withdrew, Calvin got Llewellyn to donate a great deal of money into the fund. But it was money Calvin actually contributed himself by creating loans for Llewellyn to start his business. Calvin was quite pleased with his own cleverness. We lay in my great bed at Larchmont one night while he laughed and told me about it."

She shut her eyes, holding her breath for a long moment. "I've never known exactly what happened between Olin and Calvin after that first committee hearing. No one ever talked. We live by secrets in New Solway, they are our meat and breath. I assumed that Olin went to Llewellyn because his name was on the checks, you see, the checks written to the legal defense fund. And I supposed that Llewellyn told Olin he would give him the name of the ringleader, if he didn't have to go to prison himself, and if his name never appeared. But Augustus Llewellyn must have reported Calvin's involvement to Olin. Who else could have known?

"When Olin confronted him, Calvin in turn revealed Kylie's and Armand's names—they were prominent in the Committee for Social

Thought and Justice, back when we met so often at Flora's bar. Calvin would have turned them in, perhaps he would have turned even me in, to avoid public disgrace himself. A part of me knew that. The part that wasn't still painfully in love."

"Did Renee know this about Calvin when they married?" I ventured.

"I think Renee suggested that Calvin trade Kylie and Armand for his own safety," she said with surprising calm. "She would never have seen it as a betrayal of principle, you see, but as an organizational necessity. I think that now; at the time, I only saw that she was twenty and I was forty-five, and I made one last effort to bind Calvin to me. I told him about—Olin and MacKenzie. I left a note in his club on my way to the train station.

"I went up to New York City so that I could be alone for a time, away from Mother's eyes. And also so I wouldn't have to face MacKenzie. He was a good man, MacKenzie, and I knew I had done a terrible thing in betraying him to Calvin." Her mouth worked.

"The committee halted their investigation into Calvin that afternoon, while I was sleeping in my suite at the Plaza. I assumed Calvin and Olin came to a 'gentleman's agreement.'" She gave the phrase a savage inflection.

"Olin would cease and desist, Armand would go to prison, Kylie would lose her job and Calvin would keep Olin's affair with MacKenzie to himself—that would have ruined Olin in the fifties, you see. I made all of these assumptions because MacKenzie returned to Larchmont and hanged himself. Neither of us knew that Darraugh was sent home unexpectedly from Exeter."

She looked at me bleakly. "Of course—Renee knew everything. About me and Calvin, about Olin and MacKenzie. And she flaunted her knowledge to me, in those subtle ways one can in a closed community. I was never more thankful for anything than when she and Calvin bought that apartment in town."

I went to the kitchen and brought her a glass of water. "Ma'am, I didn't mean for you to tell me so much, or to have it be so upsetting for you. But you see, I think Olin told this story to Marcus Whitby. And I think Marc went to Renee for her version. Marc was working on a long project on Kylie

Ballantine, and he was a careful journalist; he wouldn't print such a story without hearing the Bayards' side. Renee killed him, in an efficient way. She gave him bourbon dosed with phenobarbital, and when he fell into a coma, she drove here to Anodyne Park, where she borrowed a golf cart, and drove him to your old pond. Now—I'm afraid she'll kill the Egyptian boy if she gets to him before I do."

Geraldine drank the water. "And you think I can stop her? I showed no capacity for that when I was younger and more vital."

"I'm wondering if Catherine ran away to some place that was important to her and her grandfather. I desperately need to know—it may be too late already now—but—was there some private special place that you and Calvin cherished?"

Her mouth twisted in a sardonic smile. "Many special places, all by necessity private. But—I suppose—his family used to own a hunting lodge near Eagle River, up in northern Wisconsin. When the North Woods became a national forest in the thirties, the family had to give up their land, but Calvin's father worked out an agreement where the family could keep the lodge for private use for twenty-five years. The agreement must have expired about the time Calvin married Renee.

"The lodge is where we held the committee benefit that caused so much questioning in Congress. And it's where Calvin and I used to go sometimes in the fall. Besides the great lodge, which would sleep thirty people, there was a cottage in the woods behind it. We were happy there, in a place where we could—be intimate without wondering who was outside the bedroom door. I think Calvin took the girl up there when she was younger."

It was a long shot, but it was my only shot. I got to my feet and braced myself for the long drive north.

The Dead Speak

In Portage, fifty miles north of Madison, the rain changed to snow. I pulled over for gas and hamburgers. Geraldine woke, used the gas station toilet without comment, although it hadn't seen soap for a few decades, and ate one of the cardboard burgers.

"I drove up here through the snow with Calvin one December," she said. "I told Mother I was going to St. Augustine to ride; I often did that in the winter, to get away from New Solway. Even in daylight it was a difficult passage. It was still a two-lane road then, with stop signs every so often. Of course the war was on, with gas rationing and rubber rationing; only the wealthy, like

Calvin and me, could afford to be driving such distances. We didn't pass many other vehicles."

I wondered if she would remember the route to the lodge, but I would worry about that when we got to Eagle River: right now, keeping the car on the road was taking all my energy. That, and staying awake.

"I dredged the pond out at Larchmont on Friday," I said. "I found a ring—I forgot to tell you when I saw you on Sunday. Something that looked like a beehive of diamonds with ruby and emerald chips along the base."

She made a sound that might have been a laugh. "So it was in the pond all those years. It belonged to Mother. She actually fired one of the maids for stealing it, although I always thought Darraugh must have taken it. It was a terribly ugly thing, that ring, but Mother prized it because her father gave it to her at her coming-out party. It disappeared soon after MacKenzie died, when Mother was in her element, holding the press at bay, publicly flaunting herself in black crêpe, privately gloating. Darraugh turned on her in an almost violent way.

"He turned on me, too, but I felt I had earned it and did nothing to try to deflect his rage. Everything was gray for me then, losing Calvin, losing MacKenzie, losing Darraugh, all in one short spring. My daughter, Laura, was away at Vassar. And anyway, she shared my mother's attitude toward— me, toward her father. She held herself disapprovingly aloof from all of us and our turmoil. She's a wonderful matron now; her grandmother would be proud of her for upholding the ancien régime."

"Does Darraugh know that your husband wasn't his father?" I asked.

"I never told him. Mother hinted at it, but she couldn't have known with certainty. Although of course she made burrowing into my private life her major business, bribing servants, searching my room." Geraldine's flutey voice wavered. I turned my eyes briefly from the slippery road to look at her: she was staring straight ahead, her hands knotted in her lap.

"Darraugh and Mother fought in an interminable, intolerable way after MacKenzie's death. She called MacKenzie ugly names, cruel names, to my son and suggested MacKenzie could never have fathered a child. Darraugh came to me. I said of course he was MacKenzie's son. But Darraugh didn't believe me, and he felt Mother's words bitterly, felt them as my betrayal of himself and of MacKenzie. He ran away from home. We hired detectives such as yourself, but couldn't find him.

"I finally fled to France, where I stayed for almost a year, until I learned that Darraugh had suddenly reappeared at Exeter. One of the masters inspired his confidence, it seemed. It was still years before he talked to me again, but when he married, his wife acted as a peacemaker. Elise was a lovely girl. She softened all of us—well, she softened Darraugh and me. Certainly not Mother, who kept trying to make us despise her for having been a typist when Darraugh met her. When we lost Elise, to leukemia, Darraugh froze over again."

I pulled over to the side of the road to clean off the headlights and the buildup of snow at the bottom of the windshield. When I got back into the car, Geraldine asked if I'd found anything else in the pond.

"Bits of Crown Derby. One of Kylie Ballantine's masks."

"That was my doing," she said. "How strange it is to talk about all of this so calmly, when I held it fast inside me for five decades. We all bought masks to support Kylie after she lost her teaching position at the University of Chicago. And then, after Calvin brought Renee home, Renee made it clear to me that I had only been one of Calvin's loves. Only one of the women who traveled this road to Eagle River with him all those years ago. I threw the mask in the pond in the middle of a night much like this one."

She was quiet for a bit; I thought she'd gone back to sleep, but it was the past she'd journeyed to. "I don't believe Calvin ever took Renee to the cottage. The family's agreement with the government had expired, as I said, and Calvin wouldn't come here if it wasn't his private home anymore. Besides, he was busy establishing himself in political and social circles with his new wife: after the hearings, he became a public darling. I couldn't help noticing him, you know. Even when I returned from France and found my wits again, I couldn't help noticing his comings and goings. It was a small balm to the spirit to know that even if Kylie Ballantine and a dozen others had lain with him on the bearskin rug before the cottage fire, Renee herself never did so."

"So Catherine doesn't know about this cottage?" I cried out. "Have we come all this way for nothing?"

"I would much prefer it if you didn't shout at me, young woman. Calvin didn't have much interest in children. He didn't care that Darraugh might be his son, and he paid little heed to his and Renee's boy. But when Catherine was left to Renee's care and to his, he became as proud as if he had just invented children and she was the first example ever created. He was growing old, but Renee was still young. Renee had always worked for his firm; he let her take over more responsibility. She was in her element, hiring and firing, buying and selling. Calvin devoted himself to the girl. He used to take Catherine to Wisconsin to fish and ride, until he stopped driving some four years back."

"He told you these things?"

She gave a brittle laugh. "Good heavens, no. I kept in touch with him through servants' gossip: it's how the wealthy have always kept track of each other. One's servants know everything that one does, and their friends are the servants in the other great houses. Until Renee built a thick wall of silence around his illness, I would know whatever Calvin did; Lisa could tell me. If she wanted to punish me, it was with tales of great events Renee and Calvin had taken part in, with him glowing proudly over Renee. If Lisa wanted to comfort me, she told me of their quarrels."

I thought of my mother's words on the worries of grand ladies. I was glad of the poverty I'd grown up in, glad of having to earn every dime I'd ever spent. You pay a high price for money, too high a price.

We fell silent while I concentrated on the road, stopping every thirty or forty miles to clean the headlights. By the time we reached Wassau, it was midnight, but the snowplows were out and the road became easier to negotiate. I pulled over at a truck stop for a cup of bitter coffee and a detail map of the north woods. Back in the car, I handed the map to Geraldine and asked her to see whether she could piece together the route to the lodge. She couldn't read the map, she said: the print was too small, even with her glasses.

She dozed off again. I had started the journey exhausted; the cones of snow swirling into the headlights hypnotized me into drowsiness. I turned on the radio, but only picked up all-night revivals of religion. I pushed the tape player in case Marc had been listening to something.

An old man's scratchy voice came through the speakers. "Oh, no, young man, no tape recorders. You may take some notes, but no one puts my words on tape."

A younger, deeper voice responded, "Very well, sir."

Several loud clicks followed, and then the young man spoke again, his voice muffled. "I'm writing a book about Kylie Ballantine. I found a letter from her to Armand Pelletier in which she mentions a meeting with you."

The Saturn fishtailed madly. I fought for control, spinning the steering wheel in the direction of the skid. By some miracle, we ended up in the middle of the road, facing south, but we weren't in the ditch.

"That's Olin," Geraldine sat up in surprise, ignoring the car's gyrations.

"And Marc Whitby," I agreed.

I pulled over as close to the edge of the road as I could without going into the ditch and rewound the tape to the beginning. Marc apparently had put his tape recorder in his pocket or a briefcase, but hadn't turned it off; he'd recorded the whole conversation.

Olin laughed thinly. "The Negro dancer—what was her name? Ballantine, yes, that's right. She was very exercised. But I told her she had made a gross error in judgment if she thought weeping and shouting would change my mind: emotional women have always disgusted me. And an emotional Negress is a terrible parody of feeling."

"Is that why you sent the letter to the university demanding that they fire her?" Marc asked. "Because her emotions disgusted you?"

The muffled mike didn't pick up everything Olin said, so the first part of his response was missing. "The University of Chicago deserved better than the Red faculty that infested the campus in those days. She was one I could prove to have an association with a Communist front. If I could have proved it about any of the others, I would have seen that they lost their jobs, too, young man. Don't imagine this was about race or about sex. It was about the safety of America."

"I've seen the photograph—it's in the university archives. How did you know it was

Ms. Ballantine? And how did you know where it was taken? I guessed it was her troupe because the masks were like those she'd brought back from French Equatorial Africa, but you couldn't have known that."

"I haven't talked about this for forty-plus years, young man. Why should I tell you?"

"Because I'm going to write about it. If you don't tell me your story, I'll make assumptions about what you did and why you did it, and that will be the version that the whole world will know."

The tape was muffled here, but then Olin called out to Domingo Rivas to help him get to his desk. I hadn't seen Marc's tape recorder anywhere, but he must have owned a good one, because it picked up the sound of Olin's walker tapping across the floor. Marc apparently followed him, because I could hear Rivas's soothing murmur, "Yessir, here we go, sir, a few more steps," and then the noises of the lock in the drawer scraping open and Olin muttering what Rivas had reported when we spoke last week: "I am old and the time for holding on to secrets is past. Even the secrets that I've kept from myself."

Papers rustled. It was maddening to sit in Marc's car and not know what he'd been reading.

After a moment, Olin said, "I signed one copy, Calvin the other. Julius Arnoff witnessed the documents and put a third copy in Lebold, Arnoff's vaults."

Marc exclaimed, "But why did you sign it?"

"Calvin signed one copy of what?" I screeched.

"Mr. Bayard sent you the photograph?" Marc said.

"He gave it to me. After Llewellyn sent me to him."

"Mr. Llewellyn?" Marc echoed. "Who owns *T-Square*?"

"Oh, you work in his organization, don't you, young man? I had forgotten *T-Square* was his precious magazine. Yes, he'd signed all those checks and we had him dead to rights. Bushnell wanted to lock him up: he hated Negro agitators even more than he hated Reds, and he figured Llewellyn as a Red-and-Black agitator. But I knew what kind of slippery bastard Calvin could be, so I believed Llewellyn. We called Calvin before the committee. He sat there smiling as though he owned the world. My God, I hated that smile more than anything else about him. I let him smirk his way through his testimony, and then I made a mistake."

Marc was too experienced a reporter to push; he waited until Olin picked up the story himself. "I confronted him after the meeting and told him we had Llewellyn's testimony. That I was going to put it into the record the next day, that he'd bullied Llewellyn into writing those checks. Unless Calvin began naming names. And if he didn't, he could go to prison. He said he'd have to think about it, but I knew Calvin would never go to prison. He loved himself too much—he wouldn't make the grand gestures of people like Pelletier or Dashiell Hammett. Calvin came back to me two days later with the dancer's photograph. And Pelletier's name. Of course, we already had Pelletier in our sights, and we didn't care much about the dancer."

"Only enough to destroy her career." Marc spoke hotly, forgetting his reporter's façade.

"She destroyed it herself, young man, by taking part in those Communist activities.

But we couldn't prove she'd ever given them money, or been a party member, so we let her go. I told Calvin he had another day to give me some real names, and he came back in the morning—with that letter."

"That was enough? Why did you let Mr. Bayard off the hook?" Marc sounded bewildered, as bewildered as I felt.

"It's there in the document, young man. I don't want to discuss it."

The tape ended soon after that, with Marc thanking Olin, and the apartment door shutting behind him. I ran the tape to the end, but there wasn't anything else on it.

Geraldine and I stared at each other in the dark car.

"Your young man went to Renee after that, didn't he?" Geraldine said.

"Marc was careful; he wouldn't publish anything without checking the whole story," I agreed sadly. "If he hadn't been such a good journalist, he wouldn't have died."

Someone's Packing

At one-thirty in the morning, we finally reached Eagle River. Nothing was open, not a gas station, not even a hamburger stand. I wished I'd bought food back at the truck stop instead of the thin coffee, which had burned a hole in my stomach—and now was making me desperate for a bathroom.

Eagle River is a little resort town. It comes to life in the summer when Chicagoans by the thousands move up to their summer homes. Some return in the winter for snow-mobiling, but in mid-March everything was shut up tightly as the locals rested between waves of outsiders. If we couldn't find the lodge on our own, we'd have to wait until morning. We might even have to sleep in the car—none of the motels we passed showed any lights.

Geraldine was dismayed by the strip malls lining the highway. "All of this is so new! When I came here with Calvin, none of these monstrous sterile stores existed."

"Do you think you can find the lodge with the landmarks so changed?" I was testy. "If you can't, we're in trouble."

"Not so impatient, young woman. I only need to get my bearings. Look at that map. There should be a forest northeast of town."

"The Nicolet National Forest, yes."

"Is that what they call 'the North Woods' these days? You need to find a road into the forest that goes past Elk Horn Lake."

I studied the map. The lake was about three miles northeast of the forest's edge. I drove north through the town, found a county road east, and made my way under the canopy of giant sycamores and pines.

In the dark, with the snow, the forest felt cold and menacing, the wild woods of fairy tales, where writhing trees held demons. The little Saturn skittered on the unplowed surface. I got out to check the road, to make sure we hadn't slipped off it—and to crouch shivering in a ditch to relieve myself.

No tire tracks lay ahead of us. Catherine, if she had come this way, had a four-hour start; the snow would have covered her tracks. But what about Renee? How long would it take the master organizer to work out where her granddaughter would flee for refuge?

After half an hour of hard driving, I spied a sign covered in snow. I climbed out again. It pointed to Elk Horn Lake. When I told Geraldine, she shut her eyes, rebuilding landmarks in her mind. I was to take the second turning north.

Grimly hoping that more roads hadn't been added since she was last here, I took the second turn to the north. The snow had stopped, but the wind kept whipping the tree branches in their tormented dance. My arms ached; I could hardly bear to keep them on the steering wheel, and the muscle in my left shoulder began to throb, just below the level of unmanageable pain.

After two miles, when I thought I couldn't drive another yard, I saw the sign. Grand Nicolet Lodge, one-quarter mile. When I told Geraldine, she smiled in triumph. She'd been right—I couldn't have found it without her.

A heavy chain slung between two posts blocked the entrance to the turnoff. The lodge was open from May 1 through November 30, a sign on the chain explained, giving a phone number to call for reservations. If Catherine and Benji were here, they could have taken the Range Rover around the pillars. In fact, they probably had—a bush on the left looked recently mangled—but the Saturn wasn't built for that kind of driving.

Under its headlights, my fingers thick with cold, I worked my picks into the padlock. Geraldine came out to watch: she had never seen a professional lock breaker at work and wanted the experience, even though she slid in the snow and was saved from falling only by crashing against one of the pillars.

The padlock wasn't a sophisticated one, fortunately, or I could never have undone it in the cold. When I'd driven the car through the entrance, I pulled the chain across the road again. If Renee was behind me, that might slow her down—for thirty seconds.

I cut my lights and crept forward, driving with my left hand while I warmed my right fingers under the heating vent. We slipped and slid a quarter mile, until the lodge loomed suddenly in front of us, a giant timbered shape blotting out trees and sky. Geraldine directed me to its left, where the drive led to outbuildings and the cottage. The Saturn stuck briefly in the snow, then bucked forward.

At the rear of the lodge, Geraldine pointed out where the rear walls could be unhinged and opened: they had done that to create an impromptu stage for the famous 1948 benefit. The audience had sat on chairs and blankets in the yard.

We crept onward to a barn which served now as a garage and equipment shed. Beyond the barn lay Elk Horn Lake, black showing through white as the wind whipped the snow cover away from it. In a clearing on the shore stood a stone house. Compared to Larchmont Hall and the lodge behind us, I suppose you could call it a cottage, but it was about twice the size of the bungalow I'd grown up in.

Geraldine handed me the keys she'd brought with her. "The big one used to open this barn. If not, you'll find your way in, I daresay."

To my amazement—and relief—the lock hadn't been changed in fifty years. I slid the doors open, glad now of the wind: it blew snow into my eyes and mouth, but its moan through the trees blocked the noise I was making.

I let out a small woof of relief: inside the barn stood a white Range Rover. It had a fresh deep scrape on its right side where Catherine had misjudged the clearance around the pillar, but she was here.

I drove Geraldine as close to the cottage as I could. She climbed out, absurd for the setting in her nylons and heels and Hermès handbag, but still possessing a touching dignity. Before she left the car, she told me what she remembered of the cottage's layout: the main rooms faced the lake. We would be entering through the kitchen. To the right was the dining room, and beyond it a living room that ran the length of the house. A staircase rose from the living room to the bedrooms above.

I backed the Saturn into the barn, shutting the door but leaving it unlocked in case we needed to get away in a hurry. When I rejoined her, I told Geraldine to stay behind me on the way in.

"I need both hands free to deal with whatever lies on the far side of this door. And I'm going to have my gun out, so don't run into my back."

She handed me the key. Like the barn door, the lock here hadn't been changed, either. It was an old dead bolt, which slid back with a snap. Taking my gun in my right hand, I went into a crouch, turned the knob and slid inside.

A high young voice cried, "If you come one step closer, I will shoot a hole through you."

Death for the Undeserving

It was Catherine, sounding wobbly with fear. I couldn't see her. I couldn't tell how far away she was or what kind of angle she had. Or what kind of weapon.

"Don't be ridiculous," I said irritably. "Geraldine Graham is with me. Even if you could shoot a hole in me in the dark, Ms. Graham will tell your grandparents and your father, and you'll have a hell of a time avoiding juvie court, let alone a Washington school. Is Benji here?"

"It's *you!*" Her voice quivered with—what, disappointment? rage? "I ordered you to stay away from me!"

"Put a sock in it, Catherine." I crawled forward, feeling for a chair or something to use as a shield. "I'm not interested in your temper tantrums. Do you imagine yourself as some kind of heroine, living in the north woods on the muskrats you'll trap? What happens when the crew comes around to get the lodge ready to open—you'll shoot them, too?"

I bumped into a stool. Behind me, I could hear Geraldine's slow clumsy step.

"We'll think of something before then. We have a month. Go away, unless you've already told Daddy and Granny where I am."

As my senses adjusted to the space, I could tell she was above me, probably on a back staircase, a servants' staircase, that hadn't registered in Geraldine's mind when she was recalling the layout.

"Darlin', there are no secrets in New Solway. Ms. Graham told me you'd likely be here, where you spent all those golden childhood days with your grandfather. For that same reason, your grandmother has probably guessed you're here, and I daresay your father may have also. So put away your rifle and come along with me before your folks show up. You don't want your granny to find you like this, do you? Not with Benji. Let me get you home to your bed, and let me take Benji to Chicago where I can negotiate his safety."

She began to cry, racking sobs of frustration, exhaustion, adolescence. I heard Benji murmur to her, words too soft for me to make out over her sobs.

I moved toward her sobs as fast as I could in the dark. The stairwell opened in front of me suddenly, a blacker black in the dark room. I climbed up, left hand feeling the steep risers in front, right hand keeping hold of my gun, just in case. Fifteen stairs and I touched the metal of the rifle barrel. I grabbed it and pushed it aside. Catherine pulled the trigger.

The noise was overwhelming in that narrow space. The shock from the barrel knocked me off balance. I jammed my spine against the bannister. Below me, Geraldine Graham cried out. Above the whining in my ears, I heard the thud as her body hit the floor and then Benji's appeal of "Catterine, Catterine, why you are doing this shooting?"

"Turn on the light, one of you." I snapped.

After a moment, the lights came on in the upper landing. I could see Geraldine lying at the bottom of the stairs. I yanked the rifle out of Catherine's hand and stomped down the stairs with it. Blood covered Geraldine's foot and leg and pooled under her.

I slid the safety onto my Smith & Wesson and stuck it in my jacket pocket. In the light coming from the stairwell, I found the kitchen switch. I needed towels, water, soap—a miracle. I rummaged in the drawers, found a stack of dish towels and ran back to the old woman.

As nearly as I could tell, the bullet had grazed the side of her left foot. She might have a broken bone in the instep, but as I probed her leg she didn't seem to have any other injuries.

I turned the taps in the sink. Water came out; a boiler hissed to life. Catherine said something, but the whining in my ears was still too loud; I couldn't hear her. As I wrung towels out, she appeared at my side.

"Is she—did I kill her?"

"No. You hit her foot."

"I'm sorry," she said in a small voice. "I'm so sorry. She—she isn't moving. You're sure she isn't—isn't dead?"

"She's unconscious—I hope just from shock, not from hitting her head. I'm wrapping up her foot; you find some ammonia.

Look under the sink. If you don't find any there, hunt for a supply closet. Benji!" I yelled up the stairs. "Bring down blankets."

I lifted Geraldine's skirt. She wore old-fashioned nylons attached to a garter belt. I pulled down her stocking and cleaned her leg. I tore a towel in strips and wrapped her foot. Now we had a crippled old woman, a disabled teenager, an Egyptian fugitive. And a detective whose skin was itching from fatigue. I had to stay awake, I had to stay alert enough to get us all out of here and into a place of greater safety. And I had to do it fast.

Benji appeared with two blankets before Catherine found ammonia. I got him to help me wrap Geraldine and to carry her to the living room, where I fumbled one-handed for a light. When I got a lamp switched on, I saw the long wide room was filled with furniture and useless knickknacks. A couch was set against the far wall under a line of windows that overlooked the lake. We lay Geraldine there. As I straightened her legs, I saw one of Kylie Ballantine's masks hanging by the fireplace.

I ran back to the kitchen, where Catherine was looking ineffectually in drawers. I pulled open a corner door and found a shelf of cleaning supplies. Bleach, furniture polish, bingo—household ammonia! I dashed back to the living room, poured some onto a towel, held it under Geraldine's nose. She sneezed and twisted her head away from the smell. Her eyes fluttered open.

"Lisa? Lisa—what is going—oh. It's you, young woman."

"Yep." I shut my own eyes briefly, sick with relief that she recognized me. "Do you remember where we are?"

"The cottage. Calvin's granddaughter. What happened?"

"I fired a twenty-two, Mrs. Graham. I shot you. I never meant to—I'm so sorry." Catherine appeared under my left shoulder.

"Sweet words don't make ice cream," Geraldine snapped. "You've caused us all—"

"Yes. A lot of trouble," I interrupted. "We need to get out of here, Catherine. Really fast. Geraldine—excuse me, ma'am—Ms. Graham, I'm going to leave you here for a minute while I bring Catherine's Range Rover up to the door. I don't like to make you travel with this wound, but I think we can lay you flat in the Rover. Benji!"

The youth materialized at the entrance to the living room. "Go upstairs and pull together whatever you brought with you. Catherine, sit down and don't do anything for two minutes. Don't cry, don't run away, don't shoot anyone."

She stuck out her lower jaw for a second, then smiled weakly and collapsed obediently in an armchair that faced the lake, nursing her casted arm on her lap. "Benji and I turned on the propane feed and the water. He knows where the taps are."

"We won't bother with those. Just give me your car keys."

She fished them out of her back jeans pocket. I took them to the kitchen with the used towels. The floor looked as though we'd fought the Battle of the Bulge in here. I wiped up enough of the blood that I wouldn't be slipping in it when I carried Geraldine out and dumped all the towels in the sink: the caretakers could deal with those when they opened the lodge in May.

I had dropped my briefcase by the back door when I came in—twenty days ago, was it, or only twenty minutes? I put Geraldine's shoe and nylon in the case and called up the stairs to Benji to hurry up. "I'm going to get the car. You bring everything of yours and Catherine's downstairs. And then I'll need you to help me carry Ms. Graham to the car."

The whining in my ears was dying down. When I went outside, I could hear the wind again, whipping the tree branches around. I slid the barn doors back and started the Range Rover. I'd have to figure out some way, some other time, to come back for Marc's Saturn.

The Rover's engine turned over with a roar that made me jump, but, as soon as it caught, it ran so quietly I couldn't hear it at all. It felt queer to be perched so high above the ground, and it was hard to judge the sides. I inched forward cautiously, not wanting to scrape Marc's car, nor ram into the barn door.

When I jumped down from the Rover to slide the doors shut behind me, the whining in my ears returned. I shook my head impatiently, trying to clear my ears. The whining got louder. It wasn't my ears; it was a snowmobile roaring past the lodge and skimming to a halt in front of the cottage door. A compact figure with dark hair in a dark parka jumped off.

"Renee!" I shouted above the wind.

She whirled around at my voice. "The detective! I should have expected to find you with my granddaughter. I knew you were lying about the Egyptian boy. You used him to lure my granddaughter from her home, didn't you?"

"A good story, but don't run the presses with it just yet," I yelled.

I was about ten feet from her when she fired. I hit the ground, struggling to get my gun out of my jacket. Before I could shoot, she had opened the cottage door and gone inside.

When I had made it back into the kitchen, I could see Catherine at the bottom of the stairs, Renee above her on the second step.

Catherine was clutching at her grandmother with her sound arm. "No, Granny, nobody forced me to come; it was my idea, not V.I.'s, not Benji's. I kidnapped him, he didn't force me to do anything."

"Catherine, they call this the Stockholm syndrome; I'm all too familiar with its effect on people. I'm not surprised, after the week you've had, with your injury, and the anesthesia still in your system. Go outside now and wait in the Rover; I'll be with you directly."

Catherine turned to me, tears streaming down her face. "Oh, tell her, tell Granny. Benji came with me, he didn't force me, you didn't force me! Granny, Granny, it's all right!" she screamed.

"Catherine, go out to the Rover. You're in the way in here." Renee stepped down to point her gun at me. "You! Drop your gun! Now! Kick it under the table!"

I couldn't risk a shot at her without hitting Catherine. I dropped my gun and kicked it under the kitchen table.

Catherine's eyes were black holes in her white face. "Granny. You don't understand. V.I. came here to help me. She's a friend."

"And you don't understand, Catherine. You've gotten involved in something too big for you right now."

Catherine ducked under Renee's arm and ran up the stairs. Her grandmother fired at me, a reckless shot that made me hit the floor. She ran after her granddaughter. By the time I had crawled under the table for my own gun and gotten back on my feet, Renee and Catherine were both at the top of the stairs.

I heard Benji scream, "No, I doing nothing, nothing to Catterine, not touching, you not shoot," and Catherine shouting, "You mustn't, you mustn't shoot him, he's my friend. Granny, no!" and then the gun sounded again.

I pelted up the stairs, but before I reached the top, Renee appeared in the stairwell head and shot down at me. Plaster fell on me, blinding me, and I flattened myself against the side of the stairwell. Squinting through the plaster dust, I could just make out Renee's legs and the motion of her hand. I tried a shot. Her legs moved back, but she fired again. Crouching down, hugging the wall, I ran up the stairs, shooting twice to back her away.

Renee's legs suddenly crumpled. Her gun clattered past me on the stairs. I climbed the last three steps uncertainly. On the upper landing, Geraldine Graham was standing over Renee, the Gabonese mask clutched in her arthritic hands. She was trembling, and blood oozed through the towel on her left foot, but she was smiling grimly.

"Look to the children," she said.

Benji and Catherine lay in a heap of coats and blood. Flowers of blood spread petals around them. I didn't know at first which one was wounded, so closely were they entwined, but when I knelt to feel them, Catherine was warm and Benji's fingers were ice, his pulse a thread. He opened his eyes, said something in Arabic, and then, in English, added, "I seeing Granny before one week. She driving thing like tonight, thing not car, like tonight I seeing from window, she putting man in water."

"Hush. I know you did. You hush now. Catherine, let go of him, I'm going to carry him downstairs and take him to the hospital."

I pried her fingers from his cold side. "You bring the coats so we can keep him warm."

I picked him up, a slight youth, a feather in my arms. "Hold on. You hold on to me, Benji."

Catherine followed me, leaning against me so she could keep her good hand on Benji's body. In the kitchen, I kicked Renee's gun in front of me, tipping it into the snow on my way out. Before we reached the Rover, Benji was dead in my arms.

54

Unnatural Sleep

I longed for sleep more than I had wanted anything my whole life. I wanted a bath and a bed and oblivion, but instead I had the Eagle River cops and the Vilas County sheriff, as they tried to make sense of the senseless.

When Catherine and I returned to the house with Benji's body, I laid him on the dining room table, a catafalque of sorts, a laying out in state. Catherine refused to leave him, even though she was shivering so violently that her hand couldn't stay in place on Benji's head.

I went to the living room for the blankets we'd wrapped Geraldine in earlier. When I brought them back to the dining room,

Catherine had climbed up on the table beside Benji. She was cradling his head in her lap. I swathed her in blankets, but her shivering wouldn't stop.

I took my cell phone from my bag and looped the mike around my neck. While I tracked down the local emergency services, I folded my arms around Catherine, trying to rub some warmth into her. By the time I was finally connected to the county dispatcher, the worst of her shaking had eased, but the room was filled with the sickly sweet scent of her fear, and her urine.

A shadow in the living room made me let go of her and run to the arched doorway. It was Geraldine, not Renee, drawing on her own formidable will to hobble down the stairs on her wounded foot. She looked from me to Catherine shivering in her blankets, then limped over and draped her sable coat across the girl's shoulders. I tucked it around Catherine as best I could. She wouldn't move or look at me, but stared straight ahead, Benji's head in her lap.

I'd seen a set of wicker chairs in one corner of the living room. I brought two of them over to the arch connecting living and dining rooms, so we could sit but still keep an eye on Catherine. I pulled over a coffee table for Geraldine to prop her foot on. She'd lost the towels I'd tied around her wound; blood oozed onto the glass table-top.

"That was a terrible deed, shooting the boy in front of her own granddaughter," Geraldine said, adding in a conversational tone, "I wasn't able to kill Renee. What are we going to do with her when she revives?"

"Try to get our story in first," I said grimly. "The law will be here soon, and she's going to be spinning her line about Benji as a ter-rorist kidnapper."

"Was he a terrorist?" Geraldine asked.

"I think he was an orphan boy far from home who got caught in a war he didn't know was going on. All he wanted to do was make money to help his mother and his sisters." Tears pricked the back of my lids. I shook them off angrily—I needed my wits, not my emotions, for whatever lay ahead.

Geraldine and I sat silent, both of us ex-hausted. At one point, she said, "How odd Darraugh and Edwards will find it, to know their mothers have been fighting."

I grunted, but didn't move or speak until I heard Renee stirring on the upper landing. I got up, gun out, as she staggered down the front stairs, disheveled but haughty.

She looked past me to Geraldine. "You have a knack for hovering around my family when you are least wanted, Geraldine. You may leave my granddaughter to me now."

I felt my temper rising. "Renee, I don't know if you're insane or just giving a good impersonation, but a high-handed act isn't going to work tonight. Catherine is in shock because she saw you murder Benjamin Sadawi in cold blood. We will not leave you alone with her."

Renee looked at me loftily. "I thought you and that terrorist had kidnapped her; I shot him in the belief I was protecting her."

"I should have hit you harder, Renee," Geraldine said in her flutey voice. "It brought me such satisfaction, I should have hit you forty years ago. Perhaps I could have beaten some sense into you. I understand what you're doing; I understand you believe you can persuade a policeman and a judge of what you are saying, because you have the power and position of the Bayard name behind you. You think Victoria is a servant of no account who can be belittled and discounted the way my mother treated detectives forty years ago. But times have changed; detectives are sophisticated nowadays, and Victoria stands high in my son's and my estimation. Very high. We are prepared to support her version of tonight's events."

"You can't forgive me for marrying Calvin, can you?" Renee said, amused contempt in her voice. "After all this time, you still don't understand that he was weary of your posturing and your neediness—and your aging body; he turned to me for relief from all those things."

Geraldine smiled. "I'm the one he calls for when he's frightened, Renee. Not you nor Kylie nor any of the others. Your staff may think he means you when he cries 'Deenie,' but I was always Deenie to him, from the time we first tried swimming together in the Larchmont pool when we were four."

"I'm the one who protected his reputation," Renee snapped, her composure cracking. "I'm the one who saved him from prison, who helped build up the Bayard Foundation and the press. I'm the one who turned him into an international figure, while you sat withering, turning grayer and grayer in that mausoleum, buried alive by your mother."

"Until Calvin's reputation became so important to you that you killed three people to protect it," I put in. "I'm not going to pretend to weep over Olin Taverner, but Marcus Whitby was a fine young journalist, a fine young man, while Benji Sadawi was a helpless bystander. Do you think your granddaughter will ever want to live with you again, now that she knows you killed these people? You sacrificed their lives, you sacrificed her well-being—"

"Catherine knows me. She knows I love her as deeply as I do Calvin," Renee said.

"So she'll stay with you because she knows you'll kill anyone who threatens your idea of her? I don't think so. I think nature made something finer than you or Calvin in your granddaughter. She'll recoil from you the way she would from sewage."

Renee smiled contemptuously. "You have no children, no home life. I doubt very much you are a judge of family relationships."

I thought of my mother's fierce love for me, and my father's more level affection; the price they demanded in return was not adoration, nor achievement, but integrity. I could not lie or cheat to avoid trouble. I didn't try to tell Renee that.

"The sad thing is that I liked you, Renee. I admired your husband to the point of hero worship, but I genuinely liked you. You have the kind of energy and competence I've always admired."

She flushed and left us to go into the dining room. Catherine sat motionless on the table, like a small furry Buddha, but when Renee took her good arm and tried to move her, she jerked away and lay down next to Benji, kissing him on the lips.

I could hear the sirens from the emergency crew keening their way up the drive. A moment later, the cars poured into the yard, their strobes staining the night sky red.

Shoot-Out at the Eagle River Corral

A cold sun hung well over Elk Horn Lake before I got into a bed. It took hours to sort things out with the local authorities. I didn't blame them—the carnage in the house was shocking. Nor did I blame them for first wanting to haul me away—a youth lay dead in the dining room, a teenager and an old woman both had gunshot wounds and I was the one with a gun.

The officer in charge, a raw-faced man named Blodel, ordered a couple of deputies to hold on to me and my gun. When she realized what they were doing, Geraldine put on her grandest dame manner. She commanded Blodel to listen to her before he did anything he might afterwards feel "had been regrettable." Despite her pain and her loss of blood, she gave a short, fluent account of Renee's role in the evening's wreckage. She stayed in the wicker chair, but her air of command was such that Blodel stopped what he was doing to attend to her.

"She shot the boy, she tried to kill Victoria. Victoria, where is Renee's gun?"

I told Blodel he would find the gun in the snow outside the kitchen door. "It will have Ms. Bayard's fingerprints on it. And you'll find its bullets will match the one that killed the youth in the dining room."

Blodel sent a woman out to look for Renee's gun, but his other officer kept a grip on me. Renee saw this as her opportunity to seize control of the situation. She left Catherine's side, wearing an air of command like a second jacket, to tell Blodel that Benjamin Sadawi was a terrorist, wanted by the FBI, and that she had shot him to protect her granddaughter. She would appreciate Blodel's help in getting her granddaughter to an airplane; the child was in shock, was recovering from an injury, and needed to be flown back to Chicago for medical care.

Geraldine and I listened to this with mounting indignation, but we couldn't edge in a word to contradict her: Blodel kept silencing us when we tried to speak.

Geraldine's wrath finally pushed her to her feet. "Oh, these lies, Renee, these lies; they fit you like the glove to hand. And you should know, Renee, that Marcus Whitby saw the agreement Calvin and Olin signed together. Whatever was in that agreement, Julius Arnoff has a copy of it."

Before she could go further, her bad foot gave way and she collapsed, scrabbling at Blodel's arms on her way down. My deputy let go of me to help get Geraldine back into a chair, and to make sure she hadn't suffered further hurt. While their attention was on Geraldine—and on Renee, who was saying, "Oh, Geraldine, must you always play the victim to garner attention?"—I retreated to a corner of the living room with my cell phone.

My first call was to Freeman Carter. My lawyer wasn't happy to hear from me at four in the morning, but he took in a summary of what had happened. He said he knew a lawyer in Rhinelander, the nearest big town, and put me on hold while he looked up the number. When he'd given it to me, he told me to wait half an hour before phoning so he could put the local guy in the picture.

I called Bobby Mallory next. Years of midnight emergencies brought him to the phone grouchy but coherent.

"I'm in Eagle River, Bobby. Renee Bayard just shot Benjamin Sadawi."

"Give it to me fast, Victoria. And straight, no frills."

I gave it to him straight. Mostly straight. Not too many frills. I told him how Catherine ran away with Benji yesterday afternoon, at which he interrupted: How did I know? It wasn't because I had known where Benji was and helped him escape?

I sidestepped that issue and told Bobby about the phenobarb, about Calvin Bayard's nurse with her seizures. I even told him about Calvin's secret deal with Olin Taverner, although I choked over the words, hardly able to utter them.

"Renee helped broker that deal forty-five years ago, Bobby. Marc Whitby stumbled on it and went to ask her about it. She wasn't going to let Calvin's secret see the light of day. She'd built her life around making him into the great man; she wasn't going to let the world see him as lesser. She probably killed Olin, too."

"Your say-so?" Bobby was sarcastic.

"The family lawyer has a copy of an agreement Calvin Bayard and Olin Taverner both signed. I don't know its details, but the firm is Lebold, Arnoff. If he'll let you read it, it may make everything clearer."

Bobby grunted in my ear. "So what got the kid involved in this?"

"He saw Renee Bayard put Marcus Whitby into that pond last week. Right before he died, Benji said he saw Renee drive up in some kind of vehicle that wasn't a car; he watched her put Marc's body into the pond. Remember that golf cart I told you about on Sunday? It would have been so easy for her."

I had been picturing how she'd worked it. She would have invited Marc to meet her—privately: "Keep it to yourself so there isn't a possibility of Llewellyn hearing about it," she would have said. "You don't want to ruin your career by having him know you talked to me." Marc played his cards close to his chest—everyone agreed to that—so Renee could have counted on his silence.

Catherine was spending that Sunday night in New Solway; Elsbetta had the night off. Renee invited Marc to Banks Street, gave him his favorite bourbon doctored with Theresa's phenobarb. As soon as he started feeling ill, before he lost consciousness and couldn't walk, she would have hustled him to his car—"I'd better get you to the hospital," I could imagine her saying, the organizational genius at work.

When Renee reached Coverdale Lane, Marc would have been barely conscious. She could safely leave him in the car, go under the culvert, get a golf cart, push his body from car to cart and drive him to the pond.

Bobby listened to me all the way through, but he was skeptical when I finished. "Picturesque, but no proof."

I almost stamped my foot in frustration. "If I'm right, that cart in the equipment shed will have evidence for your forensic techs to find. It would be great if they got to it before the golf course repaints it or trashes it."

He paused. "All right. I'll move that up the priority list, but what does your fairy tale have to do with the mess you're in now?"

"Renee hightailed it up here to silence Benji, so he couldn't identify her. But Geraldine Graham and I both heard him say he'd seen her put Marcus Whitby into the pond when he was up in the Larchmont attic."

"Yeah, hearsay testimony of a dead terrorist. I'm not even going to try to take that into court."

"Well, try some real evidence, then, with some real police work." My temper was fraying. "Before Renee returns to Chicago as a triumphant heroine who killed a terrorist, it would be great to nail down Calvin Bayard's nurse and the housekeeper, and find out how much of the nurse's phenobarb is missing. Whether Renee's prints are on the bottle. Whether they saw Renee last Monday night when she claimed to be in Chicago. Also, someone might have seen Renee go into Taverner's place the night Taverner died. Also, someone might have seen Whitby go to Renee's apartment last Sunday."

"That's a lot of mights," Bobby objected, adding with heavy humor, "and a hundred 'mites' don't add up even to a flea."

"The golf cart is pretty damned concrete." I tried not to shout.

"Don't swear, Vicki, it's ugly in a woman. I told you we'll look at the cart. We'll do it today, but for the rest of it, you know I don't like playing with your theories, especially not when they cross jurisdictions like this. And even more especially not with a wanted man like Sadawi involved."

"And especially not with a family like the Bayards. But the Grahams will back me up on this. And I'm going to sic Murray Ryerson on it; if the police don't find evidence, he will. It's even possible one of the DuPage deputies will have the guts to go to the Bayard house if I tell her what I just told you."

"I don't stand for your threats any more than I do your insinuations, Vicki." Bobby's temper was also wearing thin. "You know *damn* well that my work is always by the books, regardless of who or what a suspect is. And you know, too, I'm going to have to talk to Jack Zeelander in the federal attorney's office about what happened to Sadawi, and I'm not going to feed him your line about the helpless orphan boy. You hear?"

"Oh, Bobby, if you were here now, if you could see Catherine Bayard, lying like Juliet in the tomb, you wouldn't—"

"Okay, Vicki, calm down. You've had a long day, you've seen too much blood, you need to go to bed. I'll tell Zeelander Sadawi's dead and we'll leave the rest until we've got some ballistics. Okay?"

"Thank you, Bobby." His sudden switch to kindness made me want to cry again, which I couldn't afford right now. "Will you talk to the officer in charge here, see if you can move him along? Ms. Graham's lying down with this wound in her foot, and she's ninety-one. She needs a doctor. I need a bed."

Bobby talked to Officer Blodel. To my face he might pooh-pooh my detecting, but he would support me—support Tony and Gabriella's daughter—to an outsider.

After talking first to Bobby, and then to the lawyer Freeman had recommended, the tenor of Blodel's questions began to change. He stopped addressing me as cop to perpetrator, and began speaking as one law professional to another.

Finally, around six in the morning, someone collected Benji's body to deliver to the county morgue. It took two officers to move

Catherine away from him. When they finally lifted her from the table, she started to follow them to the hearse. One of the deputies picked her up and carried her back into the kitchen. She stumbled over to me, clutching me as an infant would. I put my arms around her and murmured those senseless coos one gives to aching children.

An ambulance came to take Geraldine to the local hospital. The EMS techs wanted to take Catherine with them as well, to treat her for shock and check on her wound, but she burrowed deeper into my arms, her cast digging into my breast.

Renee bustled forward, the Cannonball in full throttle. "Come along, darling. Let's get you checked over by a doctor and then we'll charter a plane for home."

Catherine clung to me. "Go away! Don't come near me. You shot Benji, you shot him like he was a horse with a broken leg. I don't want to see you again. Go away, go away, go away!"

I didn't know if the law would ever catch up with Renee Bayard, but Catherine's outburst shocked her as nothing else had all evening. For a brief moment, her face collapsed; she looked like a stricken old woman, not the brigadier in charge. This wasn't retribution that I could offer to Harriet Whitby or Benji's mother, but it was a small offering on the scales of justice.

Renee tried to argue with Catherine, but her granddaughter began to scream. Two officers hustled Renee away. They weren't charging her with anything, they said, but they wanted to question her more about her gun.

Blodel saw that he couldn't possibly take me to the station for a formal statement, unless he was prepared to deal with more hysteria from Catherine. In the end, he talked to me in the living room at the cottage while a deputy took notes. I finally had a chance to recount everything—well, almost everything—that had happened since Geraldine and I left Chicago. I left out the tape we'd found in the Saturn, because I wanted to take that home to Chicago with me.

While Blodel and I finished talking, a woman officer fetched clean clothes for Catherine from her own teenage daughter's closet. She also roused a local motel owner to get us a bedroom.

In the motel, the woman officer helped me bathe and undress Catherine and get her into a nightshirt. I spent a long time under the shower myself, trying to stop my skin from feeling as though it were turning inside out. When I got into bed, I collapsed into sleep so fast I couldn't even remember lying down. I woke once around noon, because Catherine's cast was digging into my back, but was asleep again as soon as I turned over.

When I finally came to at three that afternoon, she was still sleeping, her narrow face gray and puffy. I stumbled to my feet and into my well-worn clothes, wishing the woman officer had brought something clean in my size last night.

I roused Catherine to tell her I was leaving to find food, but would be back within an hour. She blinked at me dopily and went back to sleep.

When I returned with a bag of groceries and a hot pizza, I was stunned to find Darraugh Graham waiting for me. He had hired a small plane to collect his mother, he said, and he planned to fly Catherine and me down to Chicago with him. I explained that I already had two cars at the cottage, but he told me he'd send up a team later in the week to drive them back.

"Mother told me what you did the last twenty-four hours. For her, for the boy, for

Catherine. It's enough for one week. I'm going to collect Mother at the hospital now; I'll swing back for you and Catherine. My pilot is instrument rated, but it's a small plane, it's better to fly while we still have light."

I said I needed to check with the local lawyer to make sure everything was settled with the local police, but Darraugh had taken care of that, too. I think I was twelve the last time anyone took care of things for me. I thanked him shakily and went down the hall to rouse Catherine.

On the flight south, we sat in a stupor for most of the journey. At the little airport on the lakefront where we landed, Darraugh had a car waiting. He sent his driver out to New Solway with his mother and escorted Catherine and me into the city in a cab. When he directed the cab to the Banks Street apartment, Catherine started sobbing again: she couldn't see her grandmother, she wouldn't see her father, not now, not after seeing Benji die and listening to everyone call him a terrorist. Finally, not knowing what else to do, I said she could come home with me.

56

Death Notices

At my apartment, Darraugh paid off the taxi and walked us to the door, saying he wanted to talk to me.

"That's good, because I want to talk to you, too," I said. "I have to explain to my neighbor what I've been doing and get Catherine settled in. Do you want to meet tomorrow?"

"Tonight. I need to go to Washington tomorrow. I'll use your phone while you do what you have to do."

Mr. Contreras and the dogs boiled out of his apartment just then. Darraugh withstood the onslaught remarkably well. He and Mr. Contreras had met once or twice, but they had about as much in common as a fish and a giraffe—they were both animals, but that was as far as it went. Catherine, on the other hand, took to Mr. Contreras at once. Peppy helped, but Mr. Contreras's direct, unpretentious personality reassured her as little else had these last few days.

My neighbor came upstairs with me to help set up a portable bed in my dining room for Catherine—and to hear the blow-by-blow details of our adventure. I had called him from Eagle River, but he wanted to know everything, from the moment Geraldine and I left Chicago, until we got on the plane to return this afternoon.

Darraugh sat in my living room with the phone while I showed Catherine how to work the locks and where things like toilets and tea were. I wondered how long she'd be comfortable staying in four rooms, with no housekeeper to get the dust out of the corners or make sure she had the Bulgarian yogurt and particular tofu she required.

While I showed her around, Mr. Contreras had been poking in my refrigerator and cupboards. "You don't have no food in here, doll. You been living on the fly, like I keep telling you is bad for your health. You going out with Mr. Graham? I'll make spaghetti for this young lady."

"No meatballs; she's a vegetarian," I said.

"Tomato sauce. I make my own tomato sauce and your own ma couldn't do a better job, that's a fact," Mr. Contreras assured Catherine.

She smiled shyly, apparently not bothered by the reference to the mother who'd died when she was one. The old man took Catherine and the dogs downstairs. I changed out of my rank clothes and washed, putting on wool crêpe trousers and a rose silk shirt. Whatever Darraugh had to say to me, I wanted to feel alert and attractive.

When I joined Darraugh in the living room, he wrapped up a complicated conversation with Caroline, his personal assistant. I offered him a drink, but he wanted to go out; he didn't want Mr. Contreras or Catherine coming in on us midconversation.

We picked up a cab on Belmont and rode down to the Trefoil Hotel on the Gold Coast. Darraugh got us one of the little tables in the corner that overlooks Lake Michigan, ordered a dry martini for himself, Black Label for me, sent the waiter about his business.

He made a job out of his lemon peel, rubbing it around the rim of his glass, twisting it until it broke apart. I wasn't about to try to help him.

"Larchmont is a terrible house—sucks the life out of everyone who comes near it," he said, tearing the peel into smaller pieces. "I should have known when Mother told me she was seeing lights—should have known disaster would follow. You did well. Under the circumstances, very well. No one else could have been as effective with my mother."

"She's a remarkable woman. It's a pity she let your grandmother dominate her life."

A muscle twitched in his jaw. "Laura Taverner Drummond was a dreadful person. She did terrible damage to everyone around her. When my father died—she made my life hell. I didn't talk to her for ten years, until I married and my wife insisted we make some kind of effort at reconciliation. And then my grandmother tried to belittle Elise in the eyes of everyone out in that wasps' nest of a village. Elise was the gentlest person who ever lived, and Laura—but that's neither here nor there."

He swallowed half the martini, then spoke rapidly, not looking at me. "I found my father's body. I know Mother told you that. She doesn't know I found his suicide note."

I put my glass down so fast that whisky slopped over the rim.

"It was meant for her, for Mother. If he'd known I was going to find his body, he would never have killed himself as he did, or where he did. Exeter sent us home in a hurry because three of the boys came down with polio. I didn't bother to telegraph them. I was used to coming home alone and I knew Mother was in Washington. With Calvin.

"There's a study on the first floor, where my father would read, watch television. I went to look for him when I arrived, hoping he was in. And found him hanging over the desk. It was—" He covered his face with his hands. The image was vivid in his head even forty-five years later.

"I cut him down, I tried to give him artificial respiration—they taught us that at summer camp or someplace. All I could think was that Grandmother must not know. She hated my father using the study: it was a man's room, she said, built by her husband for doing man's work, so she would never enter it, once my father took it over. I covered his face with my coat. And then I saw the note." He took his wallet from his breast pocket and removed a much-creased sheet of paper. A schoolboy's round hand covered the page.

Did you begrudge me a little love, Geraldine? I never held your loves against you, but you've used mine to help your own lover. I know Olin and Calvin have always been at odds. I know Olin believes things that no right-minded person can support, but love's a malady without a cure, and I loved Olin. Now that you've seen us together, and told Calvin, Olin plans to tell the world that I tried to seduce him, that I shocked him with my homosexual declarations.

The truth is—no one knows the truth. Olin and I recognized each other the first time we met. We fell in love. We snatched odd meetings in New York or Washington. And now he plans to betray me to the world to save his own skin—no, not even that, to gain advantage over Calvin.

I am sick in heart and body and mind and there is no cure, no way to continue on this planet, watching you helplessly in love with Calvin while he abandons you, watching Olin betray me, watching your mother watch us all with her malevolent glare. Only Darraugh ties me to the earth and he will soon be in the wider world, leaving me behind. Do as you will when you find me.

When I handed it back, Darraugh continued harshly, "We didn't talk about homosexuality when I was a teenager, not the way they do now. I was shocked. Everything that afternoon was a shock. I was like young Catherine, reeling from watching my universe disintegrate. Sitting there with my father's body, my one thought was to protect him. From my grandmother, my mother, Olin. I didn't know anyone to talk to. In my panic I chose Renee. I thought she was an outsider, a newcomer, she could keep Olin from doing what he threatened. I showed her the letter and she said she could manage things to protect my father's secret."

"I see," I said. "Renee must have used the letter to force Olin to end his interrogation of

Calvin. I haven't been able to understand why Olin kept Calvin's sins to himself, even after homosexuality in public life ceased to be so shocking. But all these years Renee must have used the note as an enforcer: if Olin betrayed Calvin, she would show the world the kind of man he was—not his being queer, but his willingness to betray your father to save his skin. And he kept quiet, until Marcus Whitby came along."

Darraugh finished his martini and ordered a second.

"Did you tell her she could always get the letter from you if she needed it?" I asked.

"This is a copy. I wrote it out for myself and carried it with me, not knowing what I'd do with it. I lived on the streets of New York for a year. I lived—as a prostitute, I guess you could call it that. Yes, I tried to live my father's life, but I finally knew it wasn't mine and went back to Exeter." He gave his wintry smile. "I was fortunate it was before AIDS. As it was, I experienced other nasty diseases and maladventures."

I reached across the table to clasp his hand. He squeezed his eyes shut, but not before I'd seen the glint of candlelight on the tears in them.

After a moment, I pulled my hand away. "Why were you so angry last week over where my investigation was heading? You were threatening me, in a way that left me wondering whether I would or could ever work for you again."

"Renee called me. She told me you were trying to dig up all that old dirt on my father, on Calvin, on my mother." He bit his lips and turned his head away for a moment, then looked back at me. "I loved him. MacKenzie Graham was a good man, he was a good father. His death, his life, that's a scar on a wound that still hurts. I thought you were trying to slice it open. I should have known you better."

57

Lovers Lost — and Found

During the next week, I had dinner with Darraugh several times. One evening, I almost went to bed with him in his East Lake Shore Drive condo. At the last minute, I realized I couldn't do it—not as Penelope, faithful to the absent Ulysses, but as a detective: it was only loneliness, mine as well as his, that was drawing us together. That would pass, and when it did, I'd find it hard to work for him again. I think he understood. I think we parted on good terms.

Catherine stayed with me for over a week. Wisconsin officials held Renee briefly, but released her without filing charges. Those might come later, if the police machinery ground through all the forensic evidence around Marc Whitby's death, but for now, Renee was home. In fact, she was back at work, running Bayard Publishing. She even appeared on *Good Morning America* to spin her version of what happened that night in Eagle River.

When Catherine wouldn't take her phone calls, Renee wrote a letter to her granddaughter. The letter was in the spirit of the times, not acknowledging guilt or shame, but begging Catherine to understand that if Renee had done anything that distressed Catherine, it was done out of love for Calvin and the ideals they shared. The letter upset Catherine so much that we had to stay up until three the next morning discussing it. I'd forgotten how much emotional energy adolescents absorb.

Geraldine and I both put such muscle as we had into trying to convince both Illinois and Wisconsin authorities that Renee had shot Benji only to protect herself from his testimony, but we were no match for the government's itch to shed Islamic blood. And Catherine, while bitter with her grandmother over Benji's death, wasn't going to try to send Renee to prison: she refused to testify.

Marc's death was also a sticky matter. Despite his frosty words to me, Bobby had dispatched his right-hand detective, Terry Finchley, to work with the DuPage sheriff on looking for evidence. The tape I'd found in the Saturn of Marc's interview with Olin helped piece some of the story together— the part I'd learned from MacKenzie Graham's suicide note I kept to myself.

I was hopeful when Terry found a cab-driver who'd picked Renee up at Thirty-fifth and King the night Marc died, but I still knew we were facing an uphill struggle, as I tried explaining to Amy Blount and Harriet. The three of us got together for frequent strategy sessions, and to try to make sense of why or how Marc had died.

"Why did Renee take Marc out to Larchmont?" Amy asked.

I shrugged. "My guess is, she figured he'd be there for months before anyone found him. The house was empty, and in this economy no one was looking to buy it. The agents aren't doing a lot of mainte-nance on the grounds, so it was a good bet that Marc's body would disintegrate to where it would be hard to identify him, or get a real cause of death. It was just one of those pieces of luck that Renee's granddaughter was also using the deserted mansion."

"I hate it when you talk like this, like it was a game," Harriet said.

"Sorry. But it was a game to Renee—her wits against the world. She drove Marc's car back to his house in the middle of the night, let herself in and destroyed all his notes and computer files. She killed Olin with the phenobarb in his nightcap and destroyed the papers in his secret drawer and showed up at her office the next morning as bright as a new lightbulb. Her son says Renee has always prided herself on her organizational gifts. The last couple of weeks, she was in her element. Trouble was, she was trying to organize too much, and it started oozing out around the edges."

One afternoon I took Catherine to see Father Lou, who left her in a chastened frame of mind: she had been irresponsible in racing off to the North Woods with Benji. Renee had shot him, but Catherine had put him in the line of fire. The priest was still angry—no one who had come to his church for sanctuary had ever died while under his care; he wasn't softened by Catherine's pale face and quivering upper lip.

The next day, Catherine and I went to Benji's funeral at his mosque. We stood outside with a handful of other women while the men conducted the service. A couple of women hissed at us—the two Westerners who had led Benji to his death—but several commiserated with Catherine, imagining her in love with him. As perhaps she had been. Romeo and Juliet. When you're sixteen, everything seems as though it will be forever, the bad as well as the good.

It was Mr. Contreras who brought Catherine the consolation she needed. He was delighted to have a beautiful young waif to fuss over. In the daytime, while I was working, he brought Catherine down to his place, where she convalesced on his couch and watched horse races on television with him and the dogs. As someone who rode and groomed horses, she even gave him tips on animals that might run well; on her advice, Mr. Contreras won a hundred dollars at the offtrack place he frequents and bought us all steaks. Catherine, vegetarian that she was, wasn't proof against his ingenuous good will: she ate a bite to please him.

Catherine knew that I was trying to build a case against Renee for Marcus Whitby's murder, but Whitby had never existed for her. One evening, after I'd been on the phone with Stephanie Protheroe in the DuPage sheriff's office, going over Theresa Jakes's statements about how much of her medication had disappeared, Catherine asked if I couldn't just let it go.

"I know Granny behaved terribly, but I don't want her to go to prison."

"You want two things that can't both happen," I started to say, then told her instead to come for a ride with me.

"Not home," she said suspiciously.

"Not home. I want you to meet someone."

We drove to the South Side, where I introduced her to Harriet Whitby. "This is Catherine Bayard. Her arm's in a cast because some excitable deputies shot her a couple of weeks back. Tell Catherine about Marc; I want her to know what kind of man your brother was."

Harriet thought for a minute. "He was a writer. He was a careful man, quiet and private, really quite shy, but when he'd made up his mind to stand up for someone, he could be fierce, and always loyal. When I was six and he was twelve, I had a bad infection on my face, some kind of out-of-control acne.

"Some kids used to wait for me and taunt me on my way to school, until it got to the point where I would leave home in the morning, then hide in the park all day. When Marc found out I was skipping school, he told me I *would* go, that no bully could keep me from my right to an education, and he walked me to school, holding my hand. When we got to the waiting children, he stopped and said, 'This is my sister, who is a beautiful black girl child. I expect you to recognize her beauty and respect her.' He said it as calmly as if he were reading the weather report. He walked me to school every morning for three months, and fought five of them, two of them more than once, and I will never know a better man if I live to be a hundred and twenty."

Catherine didn't say anything on the ride home, but the next afternoon when I got in from work, she tried to sort out her complicated feelings.

"I loved Granny. I thought she and Grample were the most wonderful people on earth. I thought of them the way Harriet thinks of her brother. So how could they give Kylie Ballantine's name to that creep Olin and then set themselves up as the biggest free speech defenders in the universe?" She was sitting on my living room floor with her good arm around Peppy.

I shifted in my chair: these same questions had been churning in my own mind. "Everyone has a different breaking point. And a different fear point. The things you can't bear to face, I mean. The McCarthy and HUAC blacklists shattered lives. People never worked again, or never worked well. They were ostracized, they lived in terrible poverty. Some committed suicide. Many went to prison, only for their beliefs, not for anything they'd done—not in China or Iraq, but right here in America.

"You don't race to embrace that kind of martyrdom. At the same time, your grandfather feared for the future of Bayard Publishing. Geraldine Graham's mother was constantly threatening to give her shares in the company to Olin Taverner. If Laura Drummond had known your grandfather supported a group that she thought was a Communist front, she'd certainly have given Olin her shares. And that would have turned Bayard into a right-wing organization. They wouldn't publish the great magazines they do today, such as *Margent,* or writers like Armand Pelletier and the guy you worked with last summer, Haile Talbot."

"So you think Grample was right to betray Kylie Ballantine and Pelletier and—whoever else he did betray? To save the press?" Her eyes blazed.

"No. I don't think it was right. I don't believe that considering the greater good—the integrity of Bayard Publishing, in this case— justifies betraying friends."

"And now, with his mind gone, I can never ask him what he was thinking, why he did it!" she cried. "I can't stand any of this. Seeing him sick when I loved him so much—I used to feel so smug, knowing Granny and Grample were my family, compared to the kind of people my friends have, the kind who only think about money all the time! And now—my family is thinking, maybe not about money, but they don't think about people and how to live a principled life, like they always claimed they did."

"You and I are judging this in the calm and safety of my living room," I said. "We're not facing a congressional inquiry that would use our beliefs to turn us into criminals. If that ever happens to us, then we'll know what we're made of. I spent a month in prison once. It was a terrible experience, one that very nearly destroyed me. If I knew I had to go to prison again, I don't know how strong I would be in standing up for my values. I hope strong to the end, but even more, I hope I never have to find out. I'm only trying to say that what your grandfather did makes me—oh, incredibly sad, heartbroken, really. But I can't judge him, because I haven't been on that battlefield, looking into the mouths of those cannons. But your grandmother crossed a different river when she resorted to murder. And I want to see her pay the price she earned by killing Marcus Whitby. Which is why you should move out, instead of staying here to watch me do it."

"But how can I ever live with them again?"

"You could go to Washington with your father," I suggested.

"Yeah. You know he calls me every hour on the hour."

It wasn't quite that often, but he did call from Washington once or twice a day, alternatively cajoling and ordering Catherine to follow him east.

"Daddy can't believe I'm not ready to embrace the right. He thinks seeing that Grample was a fraud means I should abandon all his and Granny's ideals. Daddy's fed up with me trying to defend them."

"So I gathered. You can't stay here forever, you know. After a while, the romance of living on a trundle bed would pall; you'd start wanting your private bath, your widescreen television and all the other simple pleasures of home. Anyway, aside from your grandmother, you need to be in school."

"Back to Vina Fields, with everyone staring at me and talking about me?"

I grinned. "A chance to show what you're made of. But you're a rich girl, and a smart one: you have choices. You can go to Washington, but insist on a school with more progressive values than the one your father picked out. You could go to boarding school—doesn't your family have a tradition with Exeter? But you only have one more year after this one; transferring for your senior year might not be in your best interest. Isn't there a friend you could stay with?"

She muffled her face in Peppy's fur. "I've been through too much this winter. None of my friends is close enough to understand. And anyway, school seems totally pointless. Lacrosse, who's dating who, it's like—after seeing Benji die, none of it means anything."

"You could take a year off to work with Habitat for Humanity or a similar group that tries to help people as poor as Benji's mother. My lover—if Morrell—when Morrell comes home, he can help you find a good program."

That suggestion appealed to her at once. We spent the next several days discussing hows and whens. Catherine finally decided to finish out her year at Vina Fields, since she couldn't do much until her arm recovered, then try to start in a program like Habitat during the summer.

I hadn't heard from Darraugh since the night I'd abandoned him in his bedroom, but he surprised me again after Catherine had decided to go back to school: he called to offer her a home for the balance of the school year. To my relief, Catherine accepted: I was more than ready for someone else to have care of an ardent adolescent.

She decided to spend a weekend in New Solway with her grandfather. She would collect her things and move in with Darraugh on Monday morning. She talked to Renee, making her promise to stay in town, and on the last weekend in March, when daylight savings time began, climbed with me into the Mustang for the drive west.

I brought the dogs with me. After I'd seen Catherine into the Bayard mansion, where Ruth Lantner refused to say a word to me, I drove over to Larchmont and let the dogs out. I took Mitch and Peppy with me through the woods, retracing the route that Catherine followed as she slipped home after bringing Benji supplies. The dogs loved it: they found deer and chased them through the woods.

I wasn't really thinking about Catherine and Benji as I walked back to Larchmont, but about Calvin Bayard and all the nights he walked this path to lie with Geraldine. To lie with Geraldine, to lie to her.

The Boy Wonder, had he been a golden calf, an idol too false for worship? Or just a flawed human being? Calvin shone, that was his problem. When I heard him speak all those years ago, he seemed literally to shine like gold itself. I was dazzled to the point of enchantment. If you had that gift, the gift of enchanting those around you, what would ever make you want to temper it?

The dogs caught up with me as I passed the Larchmont outbuildings. Mitch dove into the pool and pulled out one of the rotting carp. He rolled in it before I could grab him. I got Peppy into the car before she could join him, then went back to leash him up. "One thing's certain in this life, my friend," I told him. "You need a whole lot more dazzle than you've got to make me overlook that stench."

When I'd shoved him into the back of the Mustang, I drove the short distance around Coverdale Lane to Anodyne Park. Geraldine Graham was home, the guard at the gate told me; I could go right up.

Geraldine answered the door herself, as she had when I first came to visit her. Her left foot was still in a cast, she was using a walker, but she was managing on her own. She did ask me to get down her Coalport mugs for tea, but she handled the boiling water and the tea bags without my assistance.

I carried the cups to her alcove, burning my fingers on the thin china as I had on my first visit. The space looked bigger and lighter. At first I couldn't figure out what was different, and put it down to the greater light in the room from the coming of spring. When Geraldine clumped in behind me on her walker and sat, though, I realized she had taken down her mother's portrait. The small mountainscape hung there instead.

She saw me looking at the wall and smiled in satisfaction. "When I hit Renee with Kylie's mask, it brought me a sense of pleasure I don't believe I ever experienced before, not even in Calvin's arms. Certainly not in Armand's, or any of the others."

She paused, then added, "I loved Calvin, you know. I knew his weaknesses, but I loved him nonetheless. I didn't think I could forgive Renee, for sweeping in and taking him over, for queening it over me or for setting him up on a pedestal and indulging his weaknesses. But when I brought that mask down on her head—I felt an extraordinary lightness. I am ninety-one now; I have not now the strength to move heaven and earth, but I am grateful for a freer spirit for whatever remains in life to me. I decided you were right: I didn't need Mother up there reminding me of past humiliations."

I stayed with Geraldine for an hour, rehashing the case, her life, Darraugh's life. She had finally told him this week that Calvin was (probably) his father. That explained why Darraugh had invited Catherine to live with him, I supposed—the startling realization that she was his niece. How did it feel to know Edwards Bayard was his brother, I wondered.

"It upset Darraugh, of course," Geraldine was saying in her high, tremulous voice. "He loved MacKenzie. I told Darraugh it didn't matter, that he did right to love MacKenzie as a father: MacKenzie was the man who stood beside Darraugh's nursery bed when he had chicken pox. MacKenzie, not the nurse, certainly not I, bathed his face to keep him from scratching the pustules. MacKenzie read Darraugh nursery rhymes and put him up on his first pony. MacKenzie did all those things a father does. And some that a mother who wasn't fleeing the torments of her home might have done."

"Darraugh should tell his son, his own MacKenzie," I said. "You guys live such an incestuous life out here—it would never do for young MacKenzie to fall in love with Catherine Bayard."

She looked at me with a momentary return of hauteur, then relaxed and said she would suggest it to him. "What is happening with Renee? They have not yet arrested her."

I grimaced. "I don't know if they ever will. The evidence is there, but it's all circumstantial, in a way. So what that her prints are on Theresa Jakes's phenobarb bottle—why shouldn't Renee have picked it up, wondering what medication her husband's nurse was taking? And the rest of it—the cab she took from the corner near Marcus Whitby's house, the valet at the golf club who saw her climb into a golf cart and ride off, she's taking a firm hand with that and claiming they must be mistaken. The police tread warily when it comes to arresting people from places like New Solway."

She caught the bitterness in my tone. "Don't make that the only way you think of us, Victoria. We do some good as well. Without us, there wouldn't be money for symphonies and theaters, after all."

I rubbed my fingers wearily through my hair. "I don't think there's a ledger of good and evil, this much good offsets that much evil. It's just, oh, you know, there was that popular book a few years back, when bad things happen to good people, or whatever it was? That's pie-in-the-sky stuff, to keep all us working stiffs from rising up in fury at the inequities in the world. No one ever writes about all the good things that happen to bad people, how the rich and powerful walk away from the messes they make, and people like me, like my neighbor, like my parents, pay for the clean up.

"I get tired of it. I've been pampering a confused rich girl all week. I like Catherine, but she put Benji at risk when she ran off with him. She can take time off from school to focus her life, while Benji's mother and sisters can't even come to America to mourn at his grave, and who knows what they'll live on."

"Yes, that's very wrong," Geraldine said. "To leave them wanting. I will talk to Catherine when she's with Darraugh and remind her that she must look after Benji's family."

She pushed herself upright with her walker to escort me to the door. "I hope you will visit me again, despite your misgivings about our New Solway morality."

I walked slowly along the winding paths, trying to shake a sense of melancholy the conversation had given me. The rich are different than you and me: they have more money and they have more power.

I finally dragged myself back to my car. The stink of rotting carp filled the Mustang. I indulged in a moment of melodrama and imagined it as the stink of New Solway riding with me to Chicago. But it was just Mitch, after all, doing what dogs love to do. I opened all the windows and drove along the tollway at a fast clip.

When I got home, I dragged Mitch up the back stairs and chained him to the porch rail. I fetched a bucket and a scrub brush from the kitchen. He was covered in lather when the phone rang; I almost let it go, but just before it kicked over to my answering service, I sprinted in to pick up the kitchen extension.

A man with an Italian accent answered. He was looking for Victoria Warshawski. That was me? He was Giulio Carrera with Humane Medicine.

My heart stood still. The scrub brush clattered to the floor.

"Morrell?"

"Yes. We have Morrell. He was shot, out in the Afghan countryside. We don't quite know what happened yet, but local women found him and took care of him. We traced him through rumors and airlifted him to Zurich early this morning."

"He's alive?"

"He's alive. The women saved his life. He is weak, but he gave us your telephone number and told us to ring you. He said to tell you it was not the Khyber Pass where he was shot. Do you understand that?"

I laughed shakily: my worry about his being shot and left to die in the Khyber Pass—he was alert, he could remember that, he remembered my phone number. He remembered me. "Where is he?"

Carrera gave me the name of the hospital. I sent messages to Morrell, I babbled in Italian and English. Long after Carrera hung up, I still clutched the phone to my chest, my face wet. Once in a blue moon, in the midst of pain and helplessness, life hands us a reprieve.